THE CALIFORNIA RUN

THE CALIFORNIA RUN

by

MARK A. RIMMER

The California Run by Mark A. Rimmer
Copyright © 2018 Mark A. Rimmer

ISBN-13: 978-1-946409-54-6(Paperback)
ISBN :13: 978-1-946409-55-3(e-book)
BISAC Subject Headings:

FIC014000FICTION / Historical
FIC002000 FICTION / Action & Adventure
FIC047000FICTION / Sea Stories

Edited by Terri Carter
Cover Illustration by Christine Horner

Address all correspondence to:
Penmore Press LLC
920 N Javelina Pl
Tucson, AZ 85748

Dedication

Tony Rimmer (1927—2001)

Chapter One
New York

If there was one thing in particular that Harry Jenkins prided himself on being especially good at, it was attracting women.

Indeed, Harry was not beyond adopting a hefty deal of smug self-satisfaction regarding this fortuitous fact. Notwithstanding his own lack of effort in creating for himself the type of innocent boyish looks that most women fawned over, as well a fairly decent aspect by way of the male physique, the overall package his Creator had afforded Harry could by no means be considered wanting. And yet he was quite willing to take full credit for this himself, employing the argument that, although the tools may have been given him for free, it is the manner in which they are utilized that distinguishes the true craftsman from the occasional handyman.

And if there were two things in particular that Harry Jenkins prided himself on being especially good at, then surely the second would be separating the aforementioned women from their most valued possessions.

Because Harry was a scoundrel.

He held no qualms about this. He never had. This innate

quality had been with him from such an early age and had come so naturally that he had never once questioned its propriety, nor really known himself to be anything different. At the delicate age of twelve he had casually cheated his way into Eton without giving it a second thought; proceeded to bluff and lie his way through Cambridge with scarce the batting of an eyelid; positively wheedled and, let us be frank, outright blackmailed his way into a commission with Her Majesty's Royal 8th Irish Hussars, and from there had steadily bamboozled his way up through the ranks to the dizzying heights of captain. Until, that is, he had gone on to perpetrate the most serious and unforgivable of all sins, the type of which had brought down better men than Harry could ever aspire to be. He had, in short, committed the most grievous error of shagging the wrong Irish gentleman's daughter.

But in all fairness, Harry had argued at the time, how was one actually supposed to know which were the right ones? He had never quite gotten the hang of the Anglo-Irish gentry. They were either an exceedingly noble race or a remarkably dull-witted one. After more than six months living in Cork, Harry still remained none the wiser on that issue. Ireland, he had finally been obliged to concede, was clearly not the country for a man of his unique skills and talents and consequently he had been glad to be shot of the place.

Nonetheless, and with all notions of injustice set aside, Harry was still paying the price for his diverse indiscretions. As was evident by the fact that here he stood on a South Manhattan dockside carrying a carpet bag containing his one remaining dress suit and with a crumpled wad of banknotes stuffed into the pocket of his old winter coat. And damned lucky to still be alive, if truth be told. For by all accounts he had 'stolen' the young lady's honor. As if Harry had actually cared a fig about her honor, let alone the stealing of it. Besides, it had been something altogether more tangible that Harry had been after stealing and if he had realized then how much trouble it would lead him into he would never have bothered in the first place. Resigning his commission in the regiment had been the easier part. Escaping Ireland and the irrepressible wrath of the young lady's father while at the same time retaining the integrity of his essential bodily parts had been the trickier maneuver by far.

Women, Harry had finally concluded in light of these most recent exploits, were becoming hazardous to his health. They were his collective nemesis; he was beginning to realize this now. The inescapable agent of his own eventual downfall. They would surely prove his ruination one day and he realized this full well, yet at the same time also realized that, by virtue of simply being the man he was, there was not a thing he could do about it.

Which brings us now to Lady Margaret Thompson, Harry's fellow first class passenger these five weeks past and a young woman who had remained fixed in his sights as the source of a little spending money, or 'flash cash', for his upcoming trip to San Francisco. Yet sadly, thus far, very little had come of it. Despite all his best efforts: the nightly strolls up on deck, the numerous muted conversations whispered under the soft lamplight of the passenger saloon, none of it had created any effect whatsoever. Or at least not in the way he had expected.

And herein lay Harry's ambivalence. For while he had so ardently aspired to persuade the young and, incidentally, remarkably attractive, Lady Margaret to at least develop some modicum of desire, if not genuine affection, for himself, Harry had been rather alarmed to discover that over the course of the transatlantic voyage the very opposite had occurred! It was now he who desired her, and in such a way as he had seldom heretofore experienced. Indeed, it was becoming near to obsessive, something akin to an opium habit in his desire to merely be in her presence and, as he stood there on the dockside waiting for Lady Margaret to appear, he finally decided that there was only one way to deal with this unforeseen predicament.

He needed to grab this woman's valuables and run like hell.

"Harry!"

Harry visibly jumped, then quickly recovered his composure. He had been busily calculating his worth and he reached up again to pat the reassuring bulge in his coat pocket. At least the voyage from Liverpool had not been a complete waste of time. He still had his cards. His poker. And if there were three things in particular that Harry Jenkins prided himself on being especially good at...but no, unfortunately there is neither the time nor the space here to list them all so best we leave it at that and move on. Suffice to say that Harry was now the proud possessor of seven hundred and twenty-two dollars; enough to purchase a first class passage on the next departing clipper ship (as he dared not tarry a moment longer than necessary in New York, not with that mad Irish bastard so close on his tail, possibly even on the next inbound packet ship), yet with scarcely enough left over to last even a week in San Francisco. He needed more. He needed to get his hands on Lady Margaret's jewelry if he ever hoped to make the most of those opportunities he knew awaited a man of his talents out in California. Not from digging stupid holes in the ground, of course, but from playing cards with those who did. With a decent amount of stake money to start out with, Harry was sure to be a wealthy man after only a couple of months.

"Harry Jenkins! Look at you."

Harry looked up to see Lady Margaret descending the gangplank. Or perhaps gliding down it might be the truer description, as it appeared to Harry's admiring eye that neither she nor the dress she wore wavered in the slightest as she faultlessly drifted down the steep incline with perfect poise. Now there's breeding for you, thought Harry. You can't just learn stuff like that. You have to be born into it. And such a beauty! Seeing her now in all her finery; the bright green of her dress matching those lovely eyes and the dark locks of hair cascading freely about her shoulders, Harry found himself experiencing a condition that could only best be described as something akin to besotted. He was, indeed, rendered near to speechless. Which, considering Harry, was quite the unwitting feat on Lady Margaret's part.

"Why, Harry, you already look every inch the prospector! All you require now is a bucket and a spade and I am certain your fortune will be assured."

Margaret beamed at him in that mildly taunting way of hers and this made Harry's heart skip a couple of beats and he brusquely ordered the pesky organ to stop all that nonsense this instant. Then he went on to silently berate certain other bodily parts and remind them that this was business, so bloody well behave. Adopting his flashiest of smiles he grinned up at the approaching vision, hoping against his rising misgivings now that he would actually be able to pull this off. Because he was beginning to seriously doubt his own resolve here.

"I should hope so," he replied, twirling his mustache and in just such a manner as he knew women found to be most endearing. "Looking the part is half the job, don't you know?"

As she reached the foot of the gangplank Margaret smiled

brightly up at Harry and she replied, somewhat mysteriously, "I could not agree more." Then she turned to the nearby sailors who were wrestling with her several trunks of luggage and she spoke to them in subdued tones; giving them directions to some hotel or other, Harry supposed.

Again Harry wondered at the fact that Lady Margaret had no maid accompanying her. It was rather unusual, if not unwise, for any woman of substance to be traveling alone across the Atlantic. But then, Harry reminded himself, here stood no ordinary woman. Lady Margaret, in spite of a clearly privileged background, was just as clearly the type who was more than capable of getting by on her own wits. In fact, she seemed much akin to Harry himself in that respect and it was one of the many qualities about her that he was finding so appealing.

Then he caught himself gazing at her again with all the blank soppiness of a love-struck schoolboy and he silently reminded himself again to snap out of it.

Margaret then turned to Harry, smiling pleasantly.

"Now then. Where shall we take lunch?"

"Well," replied Harry, reaching out casually and in a most gentlemanly fashion for the lady's purse before offering her his other arm. She relinquished the small bag readily and with an inner smugness Harry tested its weight and knew that he had been right. For of course no lady traveling alone would ever allow her valuables to leave her sight for even an instant. She would certainly not think to leave them sitting on a Manhattan dockside unattended. Harry even fancied that he could actually hear the dull clanking of certain precious metallic items within, but this was probably only his eager imagination.

"I hear that Delmonico's is a fairly safe bet. Not too far from here, either."

The California Run

"Then Delmonico's it is." Margaret gazed up into the clear blue October sky. As she did so her eyes sparkled in a most attractive fashion and once again Harry was obliged to reiterate his earlier admonitions to those rebellious organs of his. "And such a beautiful day! But Harry, you must be anxious to arrange your passage to San Francisco! We should do that now, to get it over with."

This caused Harry to pause, as it did not quite correspond with his own designs. In fact, it rather threw a spanner into them. He silently cursed himself again for having been overly forthright with this woman, for having actually told her of his plans to book a passage to San Francisco. What had he been thinking? He never divulged such details to someone he was planning to deceive. Yet somehow she had managed to draw it out of him.

"I took the liberty of inquiring," Lady Margaret was saying, "and it appears that the clipper booking offices are on the other side of Battery Park. It does sound like a pleasant stroll, Harry, and the perfect way to build up an appetite. And from there we can take a carriage to Delmonico's."

This being decided, apparently, Lady Margaret awaited no response as she promptly grabbed Harry's arm and began leading him through the throng of humanity that was busying itself about the docks. And this was done in such a commanding fashion that it immediately caused Harry to feel that he was five years old again, being guided by Nanny through the streets of London and he was momentarily thrown off balance. Indeed, he was finding it difficult to think as Margaret, with an ongoing barrage of oohs and aahs, animatedly pointed out all the visible wonders of South Manhattan.

Then they were inside Battery Park and it was too late and Harry silently swore to himself. For how could he possibly hope to make a clean getaway in this wide-open space? He needed busy streets, narrow alleyways, plenty of handy corners, that kind of thing. Here on the open grassland there was scarce a tree worth ducking behind. But perhaps an opportunity might present itself later. Until then, Harry consoled himself, he could think of worse ways to spend a sunny morning. So why not just relax and enjoy it, as well the fair Margaret's company, while he thought up an alternate plan?

As they continued strolling through the park Margaret's hand gradually worked its way down Harry's forearm and into his. This both surprised and delighted Harry all at once. But before he could even think of anything to say she murmured, now in a discernibly coy fashion,

"You know, I am not sure that I am all that hungry, after all."

Margaret's gaze was fixed downwards at the gravel path they were walking as her fingers slowly intertwined with his.

"Not for lunch, at least." She glanced briefly up at Harry, her fingers now tightening their grip.

"Oh?" Harry had to cough to clear his throat. "I'm not sure what you mean."

Then, on seeing his comically bemused expression, Margaret laughed out loud.

"Oh, come now, Harry! Has this not been your scheme all along?"

"Scheme? I say, now look here—"

"For goodness sakes, let us at least be honest with one another. You desire me, that much is plainly obvious. And now here we are, the two of us alone together in a strange city for only a day. I am traveling on to Boston tomorrow to join my family and you are off to California to seek your fortune. So where is the harm in us having a little fun?"

Harry almost spluttered out loud. Ye Gods, he was thinking. This was coming on a bit strong!

"The harm?" Well, for one thing…. But Harry could not even come up with one thing, try as he might. What harm indeed? Aside from an absolute forfeiture of any and all respect he had thus far gained for this woman, then none whatsoever really.

Harry could feel his cheeks turning unexpectedly red as Margaret gazed up at him now with a candid expression.

"Perhaps we might skip lunch altogether, and instead find somewhere more private?"

"Of course," agreed Harry, clearing his throat once again. "Well, yes… um, actually…."

But before he could even begin to reassemble his scattered wits Margaret abruptly announced,

"Oh look! Here we are! The clipper ship offices."

Indeed they were, directly across the road from the edge of the park. So much for the old grab-and-run plan, mourned Harry. So now what? Well, for once Harry Jenkins was at a loss. For words as well as for ideas.

Inside the small booking office a solitary man stood behind a counter. A rather emaciated-looking article, in Harry's opinion; one with such pale and narrow features as might befit any bookish type, even down to the sunken boniness of his cheeks and the receding head of wispy hair that seemed altogether at risk from any stiff ocean breeze. At the first indication of the door being opened the man visibly jumped, then with all the alacrity of a startled cockroach he scurried around his counter and somehow made it to the door just in time to be of some belated assistance in opening it the remaining two and one half inches. He then stood there with hands clasped together and with a kindly smile directed at this seemingly affluent couple as he announced,

"Welcome sir, welcome madam! A passage to Frisco, is it? Why, bless my soul, you have arrived just in time. Only two staterooms remaining for tomorrow's departure and not another to be had for love nor money for at least another week."

The man simpered ingratiatingly and rubbed his hands together like a mantis preparing to feast as he scurried back to his position behind the counter. A sheaf of papers magically appeared in front of him and, donning his spectacles, he began busily rifling through these as he continued to croon with all the blandness that was apparently his to muster.

"Yes, indeed. Only two staterooms available for tomorrow's sailing. One aboard *Achilles* and the other aboard *Sapphire*. Both vessels are due to depart tomorrow morning."

Then, addressing Harry, the man explained, "Both clippers are of the 'extreme' design, sir, and all but guaranteed to reach Frisco within one hundred days, or close thereabouts. And, as I am sure the good madam will appreciate, all clipper staterooms are first class and considerably more comfortable and dare I say less populated with your common riff-raff than those terrible Nicaraguan steamships. Oh, the tales I have heard about those poor souls who have been obliged to take that mule train across the isthmus! The hardships, the disease, the delays on the Pacific side. Why, only last month...."

"I do like the sound of *Achilles*," announced Margaret. At the same time she gave Harry's arm an affectionate squeeze and this was done in such a way as to be clearly noticed by the booking agent, who immediately piped in,

"*Achilles* it is then, sir?" The thin man paused with quill held aloft, peering expectantly at Harry. "A stateroom for two?"

"For one," corrected Margaret, then turned to Harry with such a mournful expression that for a moment he was quite taken aback. "Unfortunately my husband and I must part for the duration. But not for long, is that not so, my darling?"

Then she surprised Harry further by way of a casual and familiar peck on his cheek before turning back to the booking agent.

"The name is Jenkins. Harry Jenkins," she informed him, and much to Harry's dismay, as his intention had been to use one of his many pseudonyms when booking this passage, not only to ensure giving Lady Margaret the slip but so too the mad Irishman. But it was too late now and, as the booking agent returned to his diligent scribbling, Margaret drew Harry aside and whispered, with a smile, "Oh, don't look so put out, Harry. I'm merely practicing for when we register together at the hotel."

Before Harry could even begin to respond to this their business was concluded, his five hundred dollars paid out in cash, the clipper ticket deposited safely into his coat pocket and they were back out onto the street again.

Margaret then gripped Harry's arm and smiled up at him with such warmth and unconcealed desire that it actually made his legs go wobbly.

"Now, for goodness sakes Harry, take off that silly coat and let me hold it for you while you hail us a carriage. You must be sweltering in that thing!"

The truth was Harry did feel a little warm under the collar. But not, he suspected, from the coat's fur lining. Nevertheless he took it off and handed it over, his mind now searching desperately for a contingency plan. He was sorely disappointed, and more so than he would ever have thought possible. This surprised him. But it was not right. He wanted to woo this woman, not merely shag her. Now that she was offering herself up to him on a silver platter he found himself strangely lacking in appetite.

"Let me hold your bag as well," urged Margaret. "You'll never hail a carriage with both hands full."

The street they now stood on was a busy one, exceedingly noisy and bustling with both pedestrian and carriage traffic. It would have been the perfect spot for Harry to make a run for it. But now he realized that this was no longer an option, so he handed his carpet bag reluctantly to Margaret, still retaining a tight grip on her purse and again feeling the weight of all those precious treasures he now realized he would never get his hands on.

Well, Harry consoled himself, at least he would get his hands on other treasures this afternoon. Which, he supposed, was better than nothing, wasn't it? And with this comforting reassurance he managed to reaffix the boyish grin to his face as he turned to where Margaret was standing only a few paces behind him and....

She was gone.

So was his carpet bag.

And his coat, with all his money in it.

And his ticket to San Francisco.

It was one of those moments in which realization broaches like a wave upon the senses and clarifies all the otherwise inconsequential moments that have preceded it. And in that instant Harry Jenkins knew that he had been duped. Well and truly.

He looked up the street. Then down it. Then repeated the process, twice. But there was no sign whatsoever of Lady Margaret. Harry did not even need to look inside the purse. He did so anyway, and found it stuffed with rags and useless trinkets; washers, shackles, even a few old rusty ship's nails.

He swore. Loudly.

Then his instincts took over and he began rapidly scanning for possible escape routes. And he saw it almost immediately; the entrance to an alley that stood only a few yards to his right and he took a couple of strides towards it. And sure enough, as he peered around the corner there she was, not fifty yards away and nearing the far end! She was walking briskly and, as she approached the end of the alleyway, she glanced back and, on seeing Harry, promptly doubled her pace and rounded the corner and out of sight.

Harry swore again, dropping the useless purse and breaking into a full run. How dare she even *think* that she could get away with something like this? Oh, he was going to teach this 'lady' a thing or two and no mistake. She would positively rue the day she ever considered crossing swords with Harry Jenkins. Why, for starters he was going to....

As he continued sprinting down the narrow alleyway the expanding patch of daylight that signified its far end became oddly diminished and it took a few seconds for Harry to perceive why this was, and by that time it was too late. For the cause of this inexplicable reduction in daylight came in the form of a trio of rather large and brutish-looking individuals who now stood blocking the far end, and by the time Harry had managed to bring himself to a full stop he was as near to on top of them as not. Indeed, he might yet have backtracked and sprinted away again if not for the sudden cry of alarm from beyond these tough-looking articles, arising from Lady Margaret herself.

"That's him! That's the man who tried to steal my bag! Somebody please stop him!"

Harry's mind barely had time to register the cleverness of it. Damn, she's good, he admitted. But then the more pressing business of having to deal with these three large gentlemen loomed unavoidably. But perhaps the term 'gentlemen', Harry now realized, would be affording these individuals a kindness unbefitting. For in his mind the term 'gorilla' was one that leapt forth more readily, alongside a fuzzy image of some long-ago memory involving a circus, a large ape and most oddly a near-identical style of hat which, being two sizes too small and perched at the selfsame angle atop the larger fellow's head, was indeed the most alarming aspect of all.

And as this towering mass of rippling muscle with a bowler perched upon it set about launching a ham-sized fist in Harry's direction there was time enough remaining for only one final, fleeting thought.

Bloody hell, thought Harry. Look at the size of that fist. This is going to hurt like a...

Gideon was not a hired killer.

As this account opens with the blade of his knife held close against the exposed throat of a scantily-clad and utterly terrified seventeen-year-old girl, it seems prudent at this early juncture to clarify this one point if no other, as there exists too much leeway here into which one might all too easily drift of one's own accord and thus strand upon the wrong conclusion altogether.

Gideon was simply a loyal servant who did whatever was required of him.

The incidental fact that he took a most singular pleasure in the act of killing for its own sake is, in this context, neither here nor there.

Indeed, the true focus of his present undertaking shares very little in common with this poor terrified slip of a girl, except in name only. For what might she know of finance, banking or mercantilism? Or indeed of those more refined qualities which invariably accompany them; namely of greed, treachery and deceit? Not too much, one might suppose. Had Gideon been of a more agreeable temperament he may have gone on to reassure the girl of these things; to explain to her that none of this was personal, nor should it be taken as such. It was merely the way things were done here in New York. Or at least the way his employer did things.

But Gideon had never been the most agreeable of men, even at the best of times. Therefore he did not.

No, it is the other person present who remains the focus of Gideon's attention. The father. The one who now stands in the doorway of his daughter's bedroom peering in with rising disbelief and with dawning terror now evident in his eyes at this so very un-domestic scene laid out before him. The fireside poker hangs slackly from his right hand, already forgotten, as the fingers of the other rub fervently at his sleep-bleary eyes, no doubt hoping against hope to wipe away this present dream in favor of another, more agreeable one.

But unfortunately for him, he was very much awake.

With only the glint of his eyes visible between neckerchief mask and cloth cap, Gideon reached out with his free hand to extend the wick of the bedside lamp. This seemed to break whatever spell the old man was gripped under, along with any residual uncertainty for now, with the full illumination of his predicament, Gideon could see the wind spilling from the old fellow's canvas as he stood there with mouth agape, absorbing the full seriousness of the situation. This was good. Now it was time to talk.

"William Sloane?" Gideon's voice remained soft, almost inaudible and not only because of the servants sleeping upstairs. He had always found a quieter tone to be the more effective in situations such as this.

The old fellow nodded, carefully.

"And this must be Eve," said Gideon in the same soft tone. With his free hand he gently brushed the girl's blonde locks away from her dampened brow. She appeared even more terrified than her father, her wide blue eyes darting back and forth between the knife's blade and the old man. But it was, in all fairness, a preposterously large knife: of the hunting variety with a single-edged blade and a full twelve inches of glistening, razor-sharp steel. Chosen for its visual impact rather than for any utilitarian purposes.

"What...what is it that you want?" the old fellow finally stammered.

"A cargo of chinaware was landed yesterevening from the *Fortune*," Gideon announced. "Nearly twenty tons."

"Yes, yes," confirmed Sloane and Gideon could see the old man's mind working swiftly towards comprehension. "Which I purchased wholesale in Shanghai and is now stored in my warehouse on pier twenty. There is no secret about it."

"A loading team will arrive at the warehouse at sunrise. A man by the name of Walters will have all the necessary paperwork."

Young Eve was now visibly trembling, her back pressed hard up against Gideon's chest as the two of them sat on the girl's bed. Through the thinness of her nightdress he could feel the warmth of her body and, with his arm being positioned fully across her chest, he could feel the rise and fall of her young bosom and he suddenly realized that he was beginning to respond to it! He needed to get this business concluded, and quickly.

"It would be in your best interest to sign those documents. It would also be in your family's best interest."

"Oglesby!" spat the old man. "Why, you are one of Thaddeus Oglesby's men! The devil take him!"

The old man's eyes now blazed furiously. "This is about the loan, is it not? The five thousand dollar loan!"

"Repayment was due in full by midnight," confirmed Gideon. "Two hours ago."

"Which I have every intention of repaying!" the old man protested. "First thing in the morning, at the start of the business day! That is the time-honored custom, my friend! It will scarcely be one day overdue!"

"A day nonetheless."

"So is this how your master does his business, is it? He cannot wait like any civilized, reasonable man, so he sends one of his hired thugs in the dead of night to bully and to intimidate!"

"I am not a hired thug!"

This was an unfortunate choice of phrase for the old man to settle on, for if nothing else it was guaranteed to propel Gideon into the most unpleasant of humors. With an audible snarl he raised the knife and pressed its blade against the throat of the girl who immediately squealed and squirmed backwards even further until she was all but sitting squarely in Gideon's lap. He was certain now that she could feel his own unwilling excitement and in his rising humiliation he tensed his arm in readiness; for what did one more dead merchant's daughter matter to the world? It would teach this man a valuable lesson. It would teach him respect. And no law could touch either himself or Old Man Thaddeus for it. Thaddeus Oglesby *was* the law in this city.

But perhaps there could be no greater testament to the true measure of Gideon's devotion and loyalty to his mentor and guardian, Old Man Thaddeus, than the fact that he did, at that moment, desist. For through his mind now echoed the words of his life-long protector, loudly and clearly. *"Impulsive actions, my boy, have proven the downfall of princes and paupers alike. Count to ten, then think again."*

Gideon closed his eyes, retaining a tight grip on the girl, and he began counting silently to himself. Taking deep breaths as he tried to clear his thoughts, keeping his ears tuned for any sound from the old man, whom he knew without even needing to look would be staring at him in both bewilderment and uncertainty, but with his knife still pressed up against his daughter's throat he was confident that he would never be so foolish as to attempt anything.

But yet, as his mind did begin to clear itself of such violent tendencies, in their stead came other thoughts, and ones that were in no way conducive to the settlement of his tormented mind. For he was unable to shake off the suspicion that this young girl, despite her apparent fear, was yet deliberately seeking to entice him. The little bitch was doing it on purpose; he was certain of it now. He was beginning to lose control of the situation. This was unacceptable.

Impulsiveness be damned, Gideon decided there and then. Tensing his arm again, he readied his knife for the upward thrust and was only a split-second short of doing so when, to his surprise, he felt a sudden spread of warm dampness across his lap and, glancing down, saw that the girl had gone and wet herself!

Gideon almost laughed out loud, but instead this turned into a disgusted snort as he promptly rose to his feet and tossed the girl, who by this involuntary action alone had just saved her own life, onto the bed and he turned to the old man with the knife now pointed in his direction.

"My employer does not tolerate disrespect," he snarled. "You would do well to remember that. The chinaware covers one day of interest payment. Tomorrow, the price goes up."

"To what?"

Gideon motioned towards the girl.

"To whatever you think your daughter is worth to you."

Then, with a final glare at the girl on the bed and wondering how on Earth he could have been aroused by such a wretched creature, he took his leave and promptly departed through the front door.

The furious cries of the old man followed him all the way down the garden path to the front gate, and beyond into the street.

"You tell that son of a bitch Oglesby that his greed will get the better of him one of these days! Mark you my words, it shall be his ruination, damn him!"

But Gideon was no longer listening. His work was done here. He needed to get home and change his clothes and pack a sea-bag. Because he had a ship to board this morning. A clipper bound for San Francisco.

Chapter Two
The Contenders

There are very few sights quite as attractive to the eye of the landsman, nor yet by the same token quite as unsettling to any true man of the sea, as a newly built vessel fresh off the blocks.

It was the morning of October 4, 1850 and the clipper ship *Achilles* lay calmly at anchor on the East River, awaiting the turn of the tide. Beneath a pale blue autumnal sky that was broken only by the occasional fair-weather cumulus scudding northeastwards and high above towards the open ocean, down here in the sheltered confines of the river came only the sporadic breaths of an uncertain wind; one that carried with it all the warmth and sounds of nearby land as well the manifold smells of teas and exotic spices that emanated from the warehouses lining the bustling strand of South Manhattan directly to windward.

Her overall aspect, decided Nate Cooper as he continued to peer aloft with a keen and critical eye, was one of unnatural cleanliness. Freshly daubed Stockholm tar coated every shroud and backstay, glistening darkly in the forenoon sunlight, as did her lanyards, both alow and aloft, shimmer likewise under their fresh coatings of grease. Atop each of her fifteen yards the harbor-stowed canvas projected a snowy whiteness against the black-stained pinewood that each sail was bent to, as yet unblemished by either tarred finger or chafing stay. As too did her running rigging, which in itself measured a full five miles and more of hemp and manila cordage, illumine forth with an unnatural brightness between all three towering masts in a lofty and surreal web of tan and pearly hues.

And yet, despite all her newness, concluded Nate, she nonetheless displayed every outward assurance of proving herself a damned fine ship.

Achilles' newly appointed second mate strode the full width of her open quarterdeck, five and thirty feet from starboard to larboard, to peer upwards again into this dense assemblage of masts, yards and rigging and for the first time he felt a combined thrill of excitement and fear at the very prospect of serving as watch-keeping officer aboard this, a newly built East River clipper on her maiden voyage.

In his broad and calloused hand was gripped a solitary sheet of parchment, one that had been alternately crumpled and opened again several times over. Penned in a female's hurried scrawl, it remained familiar though somewhat wanting now in consideration as much as for style as wordage and Nate was presently finding it difficult to believe that he had until this very morning regarded this selfsame scrawl as something altogether special; as a source of such precious warmth stowed close against his heart throughout the coldest of climes and of unfailing comfort each time to unfurl and behold. Yet now it appeared more the work of some grogged and malevolent spider; one that had scurried out of its inkwell and staggered blind drunk across the page, yawing like a rudderless sloop as it spewed forth its pitch-black venom before finally tumbling overboard in the wake of that wide and flamboyant signature; once adored but now utterly scorned and with such newfound contempt by Nate that he could scarce even glance at the note now without another involuntary contraction of his fist.

She had been married these past eight months, the letter stated, and rather bluntly at that. Brutally, even, in its apparent determination to get directly and unerringly to the point.

And so that, it would appear, was the end of that.

But in all truth Nate could not find it within himself to condemn her for it. When he had departed on his sabbatical from Harvard and set out on his 'adventure' as deckhand aboard a brig bound for the East Indies, it had been on the understanding that he would return within six months. But when six months turns unavoidably into three years, how reasonable would it be to expect any young lady to merely sit around waiting for her betrothed's return?

Now here Nate Cooper stood, contemplating this sudden and unexpected turnaround in his life. He had just spent three years at sea and there was little remaining, if anything at all, that he did not know about the duties of an able hand. And so when, on his return to New York this morning, he had received both this letter along with another from *Achilles'* owner, Mister Harding, offering this promotion, the decision had been made all the easier, considering that Harvard, being in no ways such a fickle entity as was the female of his species, would still be there waiting for him in another six months. And what man in his right mind would even think to turn down such a rare opportunity, of sailing a newly built clipper to San Francisco and witnessing the California Gold Rush for himself?

He bunched the letter up again and tossed it overboard. A

large gull, mistaking it for an easy morsel, descended on it greedily and gulped down the entire wet mass before promptly spitting it up again, as if such caustic wordage proved too bitter for even the most indiscriminate of scavengers and this caused Nate to smile, despite the increased apprehension he was beginning to feel.

He was twenty-six years of age and this was to be his very first trip as a watch-keeping officer. And such a position was, at best, a tenuous one, because it was common enough practice for any second mate, at the whim of either his captain or by the consensus of his own shipmates, to be returned promptly to the forecastle again for his lack of ability and another taken up in his stead. The second mate's role was a transitory position, one that occupied that narrow and edgeless strand which divided officer from seaman; the aft cabin from the forecastle and it afforded a man the privilege of berthing and dining aft alongside the captain and his passengers, as well the more dubious honor of being the first aloft in all kinds of weather. For no sailor ever rescued his hands from the tar bucket by becoming second mate; to the contrary, it was expected of him to continually prove himself the ablest hand on board.

He would, in effect, be standing the captain's watch, under the direct supervision of the captain himself who, although not obliged to stand alongside his second mate day and night up on the quarterdeck, would nonetheless be keeping a close eye on him and remain awake and within easy reach at all times throughout the watch.

Aboard any ship this would prove challenging enough. But *Achilles*? As a newly constructed Yankee Clipper she represented all that was modern in American shipbuilding design and technology. She was a three-skysail-yarder; two hundred and twenty feet in overall length and fifteen hundred registered tons of cargo carrying space and surely those men who sailed her would be just as tough as her new-laid keel of solid white oak; each one as able as Nate himself and doubtless many who were even more experienced.

Yet thus far Nate had scarcely encountered more than a handful of *Achilles'* crew, which he considered strange to say the very least, as they were due to set sail within the hour, just as soon as the tide turned to the ebb. Already several nearby ships in the anchorage were beginning to turn to stem the light offshore breeze, no longer kept in line by the fast-moving flood. Nate rested a hand atop the braided amidships spoke of the huge wheel that stood connected to its steering box in the center of *Achilles'* raised quarterdeck and he squinted out into the low October sunlight, lost in his own thoughts. Until a voice suddenly called out,

"Mister Cooper! Now where the hell did he get to?"

Nate recognized the voice as belonging to *Achilles'* chief mate. It came from somewhere forward but he was unable to see beyond the raised trunk cabin that was set into the forward section of the quarterdeck. From here he could only see the distant foredeck and very little of the one hundred and twenty feet of lower main deck that divided the two. His first impressions upon briefly meeting *Achilles'* chief mate earlier had been in no ways encouraging and so he now sought to make his way forward promptly, following the narrow walkway of deck that skirted the trunk cabin, thence down the ladder and onto the main deck.

"With a will, mister!"

He could now see Robert Biggs standing by the deckhouse that dominated *Achilles'* main deck between her fore and main masts. The tall and solidly framed Block Islander was eyeing his second mate in such a manner that in no way assuaged the already severest expression of disapproval affixed to his pockmarked features. He stood there with one bared foot resting on the washboard of the galley entrance, talking with the cook and with the few other men who were gathered close about. As Nate approached, Biggs turned to face him, now with legs astride and with clenched fists resting casually on his hips. He was dressed in a pair of loose, tar-stained canvas trousers that were turned up just above the ankles and a bright red jacket with tarnished brass buttons which lay halfway undone to expose the golden hairs of his upper chest. Robert Biggs did indeed cut an imposing figure; at nearly six feet in height and with a habitual mocking grin that displayed a missing upper front tooth, one that he now turned toward the men who stood around him.

"Well now, boys. What do you make of this one?"

Nearby stood the carpenter, a pale and dark-haired fellow with square features and a long mustache, along with the sailmaker, an older salt with a full dress of white whiskers concealing the type of weathered countenance that only decades of exposure to the elements can create; both men remaining silent and watchful, their expressions neutral. The other man present, a dark-complexioned individual, sat perched atop some spare timbers stowed close under the waterway, sifting through a sack of potatoes and discarding the rotten ones overboard. He was clad in a leather apron which covered much of his tattoo-laden chest but did little to conceal the remarkably detailed seascapes of ships, whales, mermaids and the like that extended the full lengths of both arms to the very tips of his fingers. Hoops of gold adorned each of his ears and he too was watching Nate with an expression that remained steadfastly indifferent.

Meanwhile *Achilles'* cook, a Greek by the name of Nikos, was giving Nate the eye, and quite literally, for the other one, his starboard, was covered by a patch of tanned leather. He studied Nate closely, at the same time scratching absently with a set of long, dirt-laden fingernails at the rough carpet of gray stubble that covered his frowning face. The short man's soiled apron strained to bursting against the frayed spun yarn that cinched it tightly against his paunch and upon this, as well as being splattered here and about within his untidy galley space, were already the dried remnants of only a few day's worth of cooking. How much more squalid was this space likely to appear, Nate wondered, after a couple of months at sea?

Finally the cook, as if having arrived at a judgment, tilted his head back, snorted loudly and wetly from the farthest reaches of his throat then stepped over the galley's washboard, taking three long strides to the bulwark before spitting up and over the high monkey rail.

"We'll see 'bout dis'n, maite," he said, wiping his chin as he continued eyeing Nate closely. "By an' by."

Nate was already foreseeing himself several pounds lighter by the time this voyage was over, but then all further prospects of continuing this inspirational conversation were suddenly dispelled by a loud cry from without.

"Ahoy Achilles! On deck!"

The carpenter, finding himself standing closest, walked over to the break in the bulwark from which the accommodation ladder was rigged and he peered down towards the water. He turned directly to his chief mate with a frown, one that perfectly complemented the downward turn of his mustache and which appeared to sit fairly comfortably, as if properly belonging to and very much at home there, upon his pale and disagreeable features.

"Crimper."

"Rig the ladder," responded Robert Biggs, and both he

and Nate went to the break in the bulwark. On the river below, approaching along *Achilles'* starboard side, was an open boat manned by four oarsmen and a coxswain. Perched upon the thwarts and wedged in between the oarsmen wherever they could be fit, as well as crammed together in the boat's bows, were several wretched-looking individuals, about a dozen in all, as well as three or four others who were laying prone on the boat's floor, apparently unconscious. At the coxswain's command the oarsmen tossed their oars to the vertical and the boat drifted in alongside the small square platform at the foot of the sloping accommodation ladder. Nate now noticed that several of these men, even some of the unconscious ones, had their wrists and ankles securely bound in irons.

Biggs reached for the nearest pair of unused belaying pins; hefty sticks of eighteen-inch locust wood that were set into the rack rail that lined the inner planking of the solid outer bulwark and he handed one of these to his second mate.

"Let's get these bastards aboard. Stow 'em in the fo'c'sle and we'll sort through 'em later!"

Nate, now bewildered, finally spoke out.

"Crimps? We need to use crimps for an East River clipper?"

This caused the chief mate to grin broadly and toothlessly but without very much humor being evident. He looked around for someone to share a quip with, but with *Achilles'* steward now assisting the carpenter with securing the accommodation ladder and with the sailmaker and the cook both returned to their duties, he merely huffed aloud and the grin disappeared.

"How long have you been away? No ship leaves New York these days without crimps, mister. And you'd better be damned thankful for 'em!"

Then he led his second mate aft, gripping his belaying pin by its narrower end and, with each step, banging the heavier part loudly against the monkey rail that was on a level with his shoulder.

"With me now, mister! Let's you and I say hello to our crew!"

"Crimp boat approaching Achilles, *captain!"*
The shrill cry from aloft pierced the morning calm as well as Jonas Blunt's left eardrum, or so it felt to him in his tender and bleary state and it caused him to wince in pain. And needlessly too, as from where he was standing on *Sapphire's* quarterdeck he could see clearly enough across the river to where *Achilles* lay at anchor.

Sapphire's captain raised his spyglass to study the vessel against which he was now obliged to compete. *Achilles* was the latest in an ongoing series of new-builds that continued to roll out of the local shipyards at an impressive rate. It was Jonas Blunt's misfortune that the timing of *Achilles'* maiden voyage coincided precisely with *Sapphire's* second run to California. Consequently it would now be a race between the two ships; the first to pass through the Golden Gate receiving the lion's share of profit from an isolated town that remained in perpetual need of both freight and produce, and a town which also had the money to pay top-dollar for it.

In the twelvemonth leading up to April 1848 only 13 ships from the East Coast had arrived in the sleepy settlement of Yerba Buena, soon to be re-named San Francisco and which had then boasted a population of less than one thousand. But during the year of 1849 a total of 775 ships had entered the Golden Gate from ports all along the East Coast and, combined with those hardier folk who had stampeded westwards overland, helped to swell this ill-prepared town's population by the end of that year to more than 20,000.

These Forty-niners, as they would later call themselves, had stopped at nothing in their quest for easy riches and had willingly paid the price to get themselves there; as much as $1,000 for the 15,000 mile, 200-day voyage around Cape Horn. From the very outset speed had been the dominant factor and whenever any particular ship, whether by mere good fortune or by the superior skills of her captain, managed to trim a few days from this average voyage time, then her rates would immediately soar and she would attract more passengers and freight than she could ever hope to accommodate.

In 1849 a new class of ship had still been in the early stages of development. Modeled on the sleeker lines and narrower beam of the famous Baltimore Clipper of 1812, these ships were also designed with the concept of speed taking precedence over tonnage capacity and were built specifically for the China to New York tea trade, where prices for the first of each season's crop attracted premium rates from those who considered freshness of paramount importance. With their concave-shaped bows and steeply raked masts dressed high with canvas, less than a dozen of these Yankee Clippers were yet in existence, as many considered them, in view of the ongoing development of steam power, to be already obsolete. But the unrefined paddle wheeler, with its natural clumsiness on the open ocean, was further confined by its own vast appetite for coal which could only be found in a couple of ports south of Central America. So scarcely a handful of these vessels were able to cover the lengthy passage around Cape Horn in anything approaching a respectable clip.

Then, on August 28, 1849, the tea clipper *Memnon* had

arrived off the Golden Gate from New York after an astonishing voyage lasting only 122 days, almost half the time of any other ship, sail or steam, and with this another rush had gotten underway.

Suddenly shipyards all along New York's East River, down east in Boston and to the uppermost reaches of Maine found themselves hard pressed to keep up with a growing backlog of orders. An entire fleet of new Yankee Clippers, especially strengthened now for the Cape Horn run and further refined with broader dimensions and wall-sided, flatter-bottomed hulls to allow the maximum cargo carrying capacity without any compromise in speed, began descending the slipways, many of which on their maiden voyages alone would earn enough in profit to pay for their own construction costs. No longer filled with passengers, for already a quicker and cheaper route had been established; for only $300 and a five-week journey via Nicaraguan mule portage across the Panama isthmus, but instead laden with much-needed freight. A $5 barrel of flour purchased in New York would sell on arrival in San Francisco four months later for ten times as much, or during the famine of early 1850 for thirty times as much. A $20 keg of nails would sell for an average of $80 or, if landed close in the wake of one of the countless fires suffered by this growing city of tents and wooden shacks, could fetch as much as $200. A one cent New York newspaper, four months old, would easily sell for a dollar and cheese, butter, tea, coffee, spices and all manner of other perishables could demand prices depending on its freshness and, in the most recent record-breaking run in July of this year, *Sea Witch* had made the passage in only 97 days, to sell her cargo for a profit of nearly $200,000; four times her own construction costs.

Now with such clear proof that steam power did not, by a

long shot, yet hold dominance over sail, there was no stopping the growth of the clipper industry any more than there had been those Forty-niners who had started it all.

Jonas Blunt watched as the first of the crimp boats arrived alongside *Achilles* and he lowered his spyglass with a somewhat contemptuous smile. For there was no need for the crimp to visit *Sapphire*. Her complement were loyal crewmembers to a man, most of them having served aboard her since her launching twelve months ago. Men such as Jonas Blunt himself and his chief mate, Fergis.

Although in truth the term 'loyal' did not have very much, if anything whatsoever, to do with it. 'Beholden' would, Blunt supposed, be the more apt term. For were they not all, in one way or another, beholden to the same man? It was a lucky fellow indeed who was able to have any dealings whatsoever with Thaddeus Oglesby and walk away from it without some residual stench of it remaining on him. That was the true genius of Old Man Thaddeus. As well the very devil of him.

It was not by chance that every sailor who resided inside *Sapphire's* forecastle was a family man. They all had wives and many had children, some of whom also worked aboard *Sapphire* as ship's boys alongside their fathers. And they all lived here in Manhattan. Old Man Thaddeus had insisted on it. He had also provided their housing, retaining the deeds for himself and deducting monthly payments from each of their salaries. Consequently there was not a single man among *Sapphire's* crew who would even think to jump ship in Frisco, let alone show himself to be disloyal in any way whatsoever.

Beholden. Yes, indeed.

Jonas Blunt squinted briefly up at the sun then back down to where the tendering barge lay alongside unloading its cargo of chinaware. It was tedious work, as they were obliged to use the foresail yard as a lifting boom; its clew, sheet and tack line as halyards and guys respectively as each crate was hauled inboard and down into *Sapphire's* hold. He looked to where his duty helmsman stood by the wheel but made no move in that direction. He had no desire to be seen checking the hourglass again. But surely time must be getting on.

Already the tide had turned to slack and it occurred to him that, for the sake of this extra twenty tons of freight, they might yet miss the ebb. And that would place *Sapphire* a full twelve hours behind *Achilles* before they even made sail. Was Old Man Thaddeus so confident in *Sapphire's* superiority that he would risk arriving in Frisco in her wake, to have their cargo worth only a fraction of what it would if they arrived first? For the sake of twenty tons of chinaware? What the hell was the old man thinking?

Finally his helmsman turned the hourglass and strode forward to ring four bells. Ten of the forenoon; a respectable enough time for a drop of refreshment. Blunt idled his way forward with all the nonchalance that his heavy frame could muster and he casually squeezed his way down the narrow companionway ladder into the trunk cabin and thence to his own stateroom.

And, to crown it all, he had the man's brat on board for this voyage. Young Thomas Oglesby, five and twenty years of age and still as wet behind the ears as any damned greenhorn, and infinitely more threatening, considering his stock. His father's son, was young Thomas. Near-identical to the old man in so many an aspect, except of course for the wisdom and experience that only time itself can teach and thus all the more dangerous for his lack thereof.

Blunt located the brandy flask and rationed himself out a

decent brimmer, then sat down at his desk to savor it. At least, he consoled himself, the boy did possess a modicum of common sense in certain quarters. At least, unlike his temperate father, young Thomas enjoyed his share of liquor along with the next man, and 'dry ship' be damned. Blunt finished off the cup, feeling a little more awake now. Then he tossed down another for good measure, suspecting that he might need it on this morning, before making his way back up again to the quarterdeck.

His chief mate, Fergis, was waiting there for him, wearing his usual deadpan expression. This, as always it did, irritated Jonas Blunt to an unreasonable degree. Despite their many months of working together in such close confines and despite this tough, no-nonsense Bostonian being the best chief mate Blunt had ever sailed with, it frustrated this captain to no end that he had never been able to read from the expression on the man's face what to expect next. It could be anything. And the damnable part of it was that the miserable beggar would never simply come out with it. He always needed to be asked!

"Well, Mister Fergis?" Blunt inquired in his usual wearied manner. "Have you managed to locate my second mate yet?"

"Nowhere to be found, cap'n. We've searched everywhere. He's not on board."

Blunt swore irritably. It was not like the man to simply disappear like this. At this rate they would be sailing without him and that would prove a detriment to the voyage because he was one of the best seaman Blunt had aboard *Sapphire*. But still he was not irreplaceable; there were others able enough to take his place, if needs be.

"Well we can't be waiting around for him. How long before we finish loading?"

"Only a dozen more crates to go, cap'n. Mayhap another

three bells and we'll be ready to start sealing hatches."

"Well enough. Then we ought to catch this ebb, after all. Let's loose some gaskets and rig the ground tackle for heaving. We'll make sail just as soon as the barge is away."

Jonas Blunt immediately regretted the impulsiveness of these words, as Fergis promptly reached for the chain around his neck and, on raising the boatswain's whistle to his lips, set about sounding a series of high-pitched notes which had the immediate effect of all but blasting his captain's eardrum, this time the right one, clear out the other side. Blunt scarcely had time enough to reach up with a curse to protect himself from its painful shrillness.

But it also had the coincidental effect of creating an immediate and satisfying scurrying of activity throughout the entire ship, as all spare hands and idlers rapidly emerged from all quarters to either sprint to the foredeck ladder or begin laying themselves nimbly aloft. Nor was a solitary voice was to be heard; only the thundering stampede of several score of bare feet which caused the deck underfoot to tremble and, from somewhere far below, the muffled sound of a dog's excited barking.

Sapphire's chief mate paused with the whistle at his mouth for precisely five seconds. Then he let forth a very distinct signal, consisting of three individual blasts of varying tones and immediately from the trunk cabin below emerged a small white blur of a creature, one that dashed pell-mell along the main deck in a frantic, uncontrollable frenzy of yapping and snarling, its bared fangs desperately seeking any ankle with which to affix themselves to.

"Go get 'em, Snapper me boy," chuckled Blunt, enjoying as always the sport of seeing if any of his men would pay the price for being either too slow up the foredeck ladder or into the ratlines before the terrier managed to draw blood. It happened occasionally, but not this time. Much to the captain's disappointment.

Now with things finally beginning to stir Jonas Blunt felt a renewed sense of optimism about this upcoming voyage. *Sapphire* was as fine a ship as any captain could wish to command: a true workhorse of the ocean and she had been thoroughly tested against the elements and had proven herself worthy. Despite her weathered appearance she was neither worn nor beaten from having sailed twice around Cape Horn and she had achieved a very respectable maiden run earlier this year: 104 days from Sandy Hook to the Golden Gate, which was already a reputation to be proud of.

All things being equal, it ought to be a close race with *Achilles*. But then, Jonas Blunt reminded himself, wherever Old Man Thaddeus was involved there was no such thing as equality, let alone fairness. Surely that crafty old devil had something up his sleeve. Yes, that must be it, he decided. That was why these few hours of delay were of such little consequence. Surely there was some scheme or other in motion that would give *Sapphire* the edge, although for the life of him he could not imagine what it might be...

It was at this moment that young Thomas Oglesby himself chose to make an unwelcome appearance on the quarterdeck and this had the immediate effect of souring the captain's mood all over again.

"What's going on?" demanded the youngster brusquely as he emerged from the trunk cabin's companionway. "Have you not finished loading yet?"

Young Oglesby Junior, still dressed in his best shoreside suit, pushed rudely past *Sapphire's* captain as he strode forward to peer over the railing and down to where the cargo hatch remained open.

"What's the delay here?" he demanded, his expression

now as dark as the slick mat of greased-back hair atop his privileged head. "Doesn't anybody here realize we have a tide to catch?"

Jonas Blunt sighed.

"Everything is well in hand, Master Thomas. Pray do not concern yourself with such matters. We shall make sail in good time."

Then, on the off chance, Blunt inquired, "I do not suppose you might have any idea as to where my second mate has gotten himself to?"

Thomas Oglesby merely grunted and his features twisted into an unattractive frown. It was common knowledge to all on board that there was something bordering outright malice between young Master Thomas and *Sapphire's* second mate, although despite the numerous rumors and speculations that abounded nobody could say exactly why this was.

"He won't be sailing with us. He has been assigned other duties."

"Oh, is that so?" Blunt huffed, becoming quickly angered now. "And on whose authority, might I ask, young sir, was that decision made? On your own, perchance? If so, then I must..."

"Not mine." Thomas Oglesby interrupted the captain. "My father's. He has better use for him than you do."

Jonas Blunt stood there for a moment staring at the youngster in puzzlement. Then, with slow-dawning suspicion, he glanced across to where *Achilles* lay at anchor, then back to Thomas Oglesby. What he saw in the young man's expression confirmed his guess and he suddenly laughed out loud.

"By God, he's over there, isn't he? The old man has put Gideon aboard *Achilles*!"

Blunt raised his spyglass again and peered through it

toward the other ship. He could see a procession of men making their way up *Achilles'* accommodation ladder, one of whom he now realized was his former second mate. He decided then that, despite the loss of one of his best hands, it was well worth the sacrifice and, with a shake of his head and a chuckle to himself he muttered,

"Oh, you poor sons of bitches."

Now considerably cheered, *Sapphire's* captain left Fergis to deal with the owner's son and he cut a direct wake back down to his stateroom again for another reinforcing drop of refreshment.

Chapter Three
Welcome Aboard

Achilles was down to her marks, sitting low in the water with a full cargo consisting of tools, clothing, shoes, boots, wood stoves, spare machinery parts and an abundance of luxury goods and perishables. Now her hatches were sealed and all she required was a crew to sail her.

It was now almost two years since President Polk had publicly announced the discovery of gold in California, and by now any New Yorkers who had been of a mind to venture forth to find a nugget or two for themselves had long-since departed, leaving a thriving seaport even the size of this one with something of a problem. For this newly coined term 'gold fever' was one that respected neither class nor occupation; it freely traversed all such boundaries. From the richest to the poorest, the professional to the unemployable, it cared nothing for any such distinction and was just as liable to infect any one individual as another. Yet how much more so for those fortunate few who found themselves entering the Golden Gate as working seamen on a fixed salary of $12 a month, to find themselves within a lead line's cast of these abundant gold fields and in a town where they could easily earn upwards of $50 a week by working as saloon bouncers or by laboring on some lucky miner's strike?

Entire ships were abandoned on arrival as an exodus of experienced sailors disappeared into the foothills, leaving their vessels adrift by the score in the cove of Yerba Buena. And back in New York, with the addition of so many clippers being built and with a fast-dwindling supply of professional seamen, it was a proud captain indeed who could boast the presence of more than a handful of able bodies inside his forecastle.

With this demand for sailors there inevitably came, from those who sought to profit by it, a ready supply. Crimps appeared all along New York's waterfront; roving gangs of thugs armed with pistols and clubs and they began rounding up any and all men, young and old, who appeared able enough to crew a ship; that is, any who could stand themselves upright. Tavern owners along Water Street and Cherry Street earned commissions by slipping opium derivatives into the drinks of the unwary, many of these being immigrants newly arrived on the packet ships from Europe. Boardinghouse owners, in collaboration with these crimps, lured boarders in with promises of cheap drink and women aplenty, and by so doing placed these unfortunates so heavily in debt that there was but one way to escape it; by having them willingly sign themselves aboard a departing ship for an advance note of up to two months' wages so as to pay off the merciless crimp. Even experienced sailors would, for the sake of idle convenience, willingly enter into such an arrangement, only to find themselves more often than not shortchanged and waking up inside the forecastle of an outward bound vessel well before their allotment of two months' wages were expended.

And so it was that boatloads of dazed and stupefied men

daily found themselves bound and adrift on the East River, being sold as cattle to any ship that required a crew. And so it was that, when *Achilles* lowered her ladder to take on this particular load of wretches, it was not with a welcoming hail but with a harsh command and the raising of a belaying pin.

Robert Biggs stood at the break of the bulwark at the head of the accommodation ladder and greeted them each one in turn. It was here that Nate Cooper witnessed the true nature of his chief officer. For no sooner had the first man, an older gray-bearded fellow who was visibly trembling and mumbling to himself in apparent confusion, set foot upon *Achilles'* main deck than he was struck violently about the head; the belaying pin connecting solidly with a sound alike to that of a half-empty barrel and the man, his hands still bound, cried out in pain and collapsed headlong to the deck, more unconscious now than awake and he was promptly grabbed by his collar and hauled forward by the frowning steward towards the forecastle.

"I will have silence!" the chief mate bellowed, his face now twisting into an ugly sneer as he turned back towards the ladder. As the next man approached and likewise began to beg and plead in some language that nobody could comprehend Robert Biggs repeated this savage procedure, then once again, until finally those coming up the ladder understood and lapsed into a terrified silence.

In this manner a dozen men were brought on board. Then came the unconscious ones; four of them carried over the shoulders of the burly crimps who helped stow them forward with the other unfortunates while their coxswain, a weasel of a man with a greasy aspect and restless demeanor, stood by the head of the ladder and negotiated his price with the chief mate. The standard crimping deal was to turn over each man's advance note of two months' wages to these crimps, in return for which each would be supplied with a sea-bag containing boots, oilskins, a belt, a knife and one pound of tobacco. Biggs took a moment to check on some of this provided gear, its quality being minimal at best, as he spoke with the coxswain, pausing only once to turn irritably to his second mate and to bark out impatiently,

"Shake a leg, damn it, mister! They won't stow 'emselves! And here's more on the way!"

And so there was. Another boatload was approaching from abaft and Nate, already sickened by such an unnecessary display of savagery, turned reluctantly to help the steward lead these men forward. He felt that he had no choice but to shove them along also, these silent, miserable wretches, using the rounded end of his own belaying pin to herd them toward the fore scuttle, the only access to the forecastle space below. The forecastle occupied the foremost section of *Achilles'* upper 'tween deck and was partitioned by a transverse watertight bulkhead that separated this small triangular space from the cargo stowage directly aft. The scuttle itself was little more than a square opening in the deck directly between the foremast and windlass, skirted by a raised mahogany coaming inside of which a sturdy flight of steps led down into the darkness. Nate and the steward directed these men one by one into the scuttle, the steward with a measure of roughness not quite equal to the chief mate's nor yet was it as constrained as Nate's and, as he pulled the sliding cover that protected the scuttle from the weather firmly closed over the opening, Nate turned to him and asked,

"Is all our crew to be gotten this way?"

Achilles' dark steward, Pepin, having already made it pretty clear that he was not the bandying type when it came to idle converse, merely snorted derisively, shook his head and did not even look in Nate's direction. Then, as if thinking better of it, he condescended to reply, his voice tinged with a French accent.

"Not all of 'em," he said. "Some're out for the gold fields. Dregs, every last one of 'em."

Then he slid home the sturdy bolt that secured the scuttle's lid and looked up at Nate, his frown remaining in place.

"Best keep 'em stowed safe 'til we start heavin' up."

The second boatload was already alongside and this one, Nate noticed, was clearly different as the men who occupied it were neither bound nor anywhere near to as wretched-looking. Some were even laughing and kidding with one another and each man carried his own dunnage; the standard crimp supplies stowed in either a sea chest or a canvas duffel. These were the men who had crimped themselves willingly and, as they began to make their way noisily and for the most part drunkenly up the accommodation ladder, there came no harsh commands from above for silence, nor was there any sign now of the belaying pin which until only moments ago had been gripped firmly in the chief mate's right hand. The pin was now returned to its hole in the rack rail, its rounded end glistening darkly and to Nate's astonishment there was now something vaguely resembling a smile upon Robert Biggs' face as he greeted each one with a civility thus far unseen. As each man arrived on board the chief mate instructed him to stow his gear below and be ready to make sail.

This was not at all what Nate had expected. A ship crewed by landsmen, by God! And to sail around the Horn with such a rabble!

He then realized the full extent of the challenge he must

now face. He realized also that there were indeed worse things than being put in charge of a crew of hardened, experienced seafarers. It was certain to be tough going for the first few weeks, if not indeed the entire voyage. But these men would eventually have the soil washed out from between their toes and they would become useful seamen, whatever that took. For as Nate himself knew all too well from his own experience, there was no room aboard any ship of the sea for a no-hoper son of a bitch.

A third boat was now approaching *Achilles'* starboard side and this one was as different again from the two that had preceded it. Laden this time not to the gunwales with slovenly-dressed wretches or drunken revelers but, quite contrarily, with what appeared to Nate to be the type of personages more befitting a leisurely scull across a boating pond than out here on the busy East River. It was a Whitehall boat, one of the many water taxis that plied this river, except that this one had been rigged and painted in such a way as to suggest that this particular vessel was reserved for a more discerning class of passenger. Indeed, those who sat on its spacious thwarts were dressed most neatly and there was now a general stirring at the head of the ladder as Robert Biggs, now buttoning up his jacket to conceal the hairiness of his chest, summoned his second mate to stand by.

The steward was also now dressed more formally, his leather apron having been hurriedly replaced by a rig of tidy white duck canvas trousers and a monkey jacket to match and he stood at the break in the bulwark alongside the chief mate, reaching up occasionally to fiddle with his collar as he welcomed each passenger with a polite and somber nod, his expression remaining steadfastly indifferent. As each one arrived he directed them aft, toward the door of the trunk cabin wherein the passengers' as well the captain's and officers' staterooms were located.

Achilles' passenger complement consisted in its totality of five ladies, four of whom were traveling together as a group which in itself was cause enough for the raising of an eyebrow, considering the ship's destination. One of these ladies, an older woman somewhere in the vicinity of her fortieth year, was obviously the group's mistress, as she walked a pace or two ahead of her three companions and, unlike them, labored under no luggage of her own. On greeting Pepin she seemed both surprised and relieved that he was able to speak her language, which Nate recognized as French and Pepin, for his part, became almost deferent as he escorted the ladies aft, leaving Robert Biggs to peer skeptically at each of these cloaked figures in turn, his thoughts clearly echoing Nate's in that San Francisco was surely not the choicest of destinations for any group of females traveling together unescorted.

The remaining female passenger, a young lady with fair features and a noticeable abundance of dark hair which protruded from beneath an emerald green hat, remained down in the Whitehall boat for a few minutes longer, conversing with a thin and bookish-looking man and in such a way as to suggest that between them they were clearing up some manner of misunderstanding. Indeed, the few words that drifted up to Nate's ear seemed only to confirm this.

"Once again I do apologize, Missus Jenkins," the thin man was crooning, and in a rather toadying manner, in Nate's opinion, "but I naturally presumed that it was your husband...."

But the lady appeared understanding enough about it. In fact she even went as far as to place a comforting hand on the man's forearm, which promptly shut him up and caused him to become all the more flustered for it and turn a few shades redder as a result. Then he hurriedly scribbled some notation or other on what appeared to Nate to be a boarding ticket before handing this, along with a formal bow and the doffing of his hat, to the lady, who in turn accepted it in the most gracious manner Nate supposed was possible.

Nate found himself smiling as he turned away to attend his duties. Now there, he reflected with a degree of admiration for this unknown passenger, was a lady who clearly had what you might call 'good breeding'.

Had Nate Cooper but realized the truth of it, it would scarcely have made any difference to his own lot, but it certainly would have surprised him considerably that his judgment could have been so flawed. For no sooner had Mrs. Harry Jenkins, formerly Lady Margaret Thompson, formerly yet Miss Sarah Doyle, lady's maid to the genuine Lady Margaret Thompson, closed the door to her stateroom, bolted it securely behind her and looked around at the lushness of its interior, than she laughed out loud, clapped her hands together in pure delight and, with a girlish squeal, launched herself into the spacious lower bunk and began drumming her feet happily up and down upon it.

Yes indeed, good breeding can be mimicked, and very convincingly too.

Especially when one had been made to endure such lengthy service as had young Sarah Doyle, in both waiting upon and pandering to each and every ridiculous whim of that hateful old cow Lady Margaret Thompson for eight long and tortuous bloody years. Even now she could not even find it in herself to regret her actions in the slightest, any more than she had back in Liverpool six weeks earlier.

Standing there on the Merseyside dock surrounded by trunks filled with Her Ladyship's luggage and with both tickets in hand, it had been the unexpected arrival of the messenger boy that had initiated it all.

"Unforeseen delay," the message had read. *"Make arrangements for next week's departure then return to hotel with luggage."*

Sarah had stood there pondering this message for a very, very long time. Long enough to reflect upon the fact that here she stood, a young woman of four and twenty years of age and in the very prime of her life with no family, friends nor any obligations whatsoever beyond a life of servitude that could only be described as nothing short of outright slavery. What in the world did she have to look forward to? Even this proposed trip to New York would allow her little time to enjoy any of it, if she knew Her Ladyship, which unfortunately she did and all too well. She would be lucky to get even a moment to herself. It would, she had realized, be absolutely torturous, being in America for the first and perhaps the only time in her life and yet to be so utterly constrained.

Indeed, she had stood there pondering all this for such a long time that it was finally the sound of her mistress' name being called out that had broken her trance.

"Lady Thompson! Lady Margaret Thompson?"

The worried-looking purser holding the passenger manifest had already inspected the labels on the nearby luggage which, for Sarah, had only made it all the easier.

"Last call for boarding, Your Ladyship," the purser had urged, and with a measure of deference that Sarah could see was already fast beginning to wane as the man surreptitiously regarded her dowdy style of dress, which was clearly not befitting any person of nobility. But Sarah understood all too well the ways of the upper classes and eccentricity itself was an integral part of belonging to this elite club. Because when it came down to it, it was all about attitude and thus, with a casual raising of her chin and a lazy drooping of her eyelids, she had responded coolly,

"Then for heaven's sakes, my good man, why do you stand there dithering? Have my luggage taken aboard this instant, then escort me to my stateroom."

Even Lady Margaret herself could not have done better.

Now, as Sarah reclined upon *Achilles'* spacious first class bunk, she eyed the luggage that had been brought on board ahead of her. Only two of Lady Margaret's trunks remained, filled with some of the more useful items, including several dresses that needed only some minor alterations plus a few decent-looking hats but sadly no jewelry. The tight old bitch had never trusted Sarah with her valuables. And with good reason, apparently. Sarah smiled, then her eyes alighted upon Harry Jenkins' carpet bag and her expression turned instead to a frown.

There had been nothing inside the carpet bag of any real value; just a bunch of man's things including the dress suit that Harry had worn to impress his fellow first class passengers on the voyage over from Liverpool. She had seen Harry Jenkins coming from a mile away, of course. At first it had amused her to play the part of Her Ladyship and to watch the dashing Mister Jenkins attempt to woo and to win her favor from all possible directions. He had a good many tricks up his sleeve, did Harry, and she had rather enjoyed thwarting each and every one in turn. But then, as she had found herself unexpectedly beginning to enjoy Harry's attentions, as well his amusing conversation and his company in general, this had quickly turned into resentment for she had known all along that for Harry it was all just a game. He was only pretending. Nothing about Harry had been genuine at all.

There had not been as much cash in Harry's coat pockets as she had hoped. Scarcely two hundred dollars, which was better than nothing but she would certainly be needing more, especially considering her destination. Which, incidentally, she was still berating herself over. Just because she had obtained a ticket to San Francisco did not necessarily mean that she had to use it! This was becoming a bad habit. It was the impulsiveness of Sarah's nature; it would be the ruination of her one of these days, she was certain of it, perhaps now sooner rather than later. For how in the world was she ever going to survive alone in a town like San Francisco? She would either require a lot more money or some manner of guardian, ideally a gentleman to look out for her. She had been rather hoping that there would be one or two potential candidates here amongst her fellow passengers aboard *Achilles*. But now it appeared that there were to be no male passengers on board at all! It was the most rotten luck.

Sarah sighed. For now she realized that Harry Jenkins himself would have made the perfect traveling companion. He was clever, witty, resourceful; oh yes, she had seen how resourceful Harry could be, if only by the way in which he had so shamelessly swindled his fellow passengers out of their money during those nightly card games. How they had failed to spot his clumsy sleight of hand, even under the dimness of the saloon's lantern light, she would never understand. It takes one to know one, Sarah supposed. Now as she lay there gazing at Harry's carpet bag (she had discarded that tatty old coat just as soon as she had emptied its pockets), she wondered why she had not thrown the bag away as well. She supposed that she had kept it as a keepsake. A memento, of sorts. For in all honesty she was unable to deny even to herself that she did rather miss Harry, despite everything.

Sarah sighed again. Yes indeed, Harry would have made the perfect traveling companion. If only he had been a little more honest. At least with her.

Reclining into the comfort of her bunk and readying herself for a short nap, Sarah found herself wondering again what poor coatless, penniless Harry Jenkins was doing right now. She had no doubt that he would survive, whatever came his way, and probably come out of it landing squarely on his feet and smelling of roses. Because, much like Sarah herself, that was simply the kind of person Harry Jenkins was.

And with this reassuring thought Sarah drifted off into a peaceful slumber.

Harry Jenkins was back in London again, inside the small bedroom above his father's factory.

It was raining; he could hear the water trickling down the gutters outside, as well as the sound of a multitude of voices drifting up from the street below, those of the factory workers as they busied themselves about their daily activities. In fact it sounded uncommonly busy out there this morning, Harry noted, as the volume did seem rather excessive. How the hell was a chap supposed to get his beauty sleep with all this hullabaloo going on?

Then Harry smiled, for the very fact that he was here in his own bedroom must surely mean that this was a school holiday, although for the life of him he was unable to recall precisely which one, nor for that matter what month of the year it presently was. But then, judging by this persistently painful throbbing that threatened to burst his cranium wide open with every pulse, he must surely have gone to town with a rare vengeance last night. This was not such an unusual condition for Harry. He had woken up in far worse states than this before. All he needed here was a moment or two to gather his wits, along with his memory.

He finally decided to open his eyes. Yes indeed, here he was in his own bed, looking up at the old adz-scarred ceiling beams and the yellowed plasterwork that filled the spaces between. He stretched lazily and was about to turn over and snooze some more, hopefully to rid himself of this damnable headache when he realized with some irritation that now that he was awake he had the sudden urge to relieve himself.

He grumbled as he detached himself from his comfy sheets and blankets and staggered bleary-eyed across to the washbasin under which the night pot stood. Then, as he was busily fishing around inside his nightshirt in search of his tackle an odd realization entered his addled mind and caused him to pause, now in some uncertainty.

Because he now recalled that his father had sold the factory to old Mister Watkins back in '38, when Harry was only nineteen.

Harry opened his eyes. He was in a small, dark space. Slush lanterns hung suspended from the overhead beams to either side and supplemented what little daylight entered through the four small glass ports set high in the walls. Through the gloom he could see several tiers of bunks, each about five and a half feet long by thirty inches wide and stacked two high, between which stood a large table and a couple of benches which all appeared to be bolted securely to the floor. There were enough bunks here for perhaps thirty men and now he noticed that at least half that number were presently here in the space with him; a noisy, chattering bunch of unsavory-looking types who were apparently busying themselves with unpacking their gear. Several other men, some with chains binding their wrists, were either looking on, as Harry was now, with expressions of combined confusion and dread, or tossing about and moaning fitfully as if in the throes of some drug-induced slumber. On the bunk directly to Harry's right lay one individual who was merely gazing at him with wide-open eyes. And rather rudely at that, in Harry's opinion, and he was about to offer some sarcastic remark to the impertinent fellow when he realized with a sudden start that he was staring directly into the eyes of a corpse!

"What the...!" exclaimed Harry, now fully awake as he bolted upright. But unfortunately for Harry, having failed to notice the rather limited headroom available to him here in his new quarters, his already severely-bruised forehead came into direct contact with the bunk situated only eighteen inches above him and with a grunt of agony he slumped back down again, out cold once more and, we can only hope for poor Harry's sake, back to the safe warm comfort of his childhood bed in London, or at least for the time being.

The Whitehall boat pulled up alongside Pier 15 to find a rather irate-looking gentleman awaiting its arrival. Irate, impatient and somewhat Irish-sounding, if the booking agent was any judge of a foreign accent, which coincidentally he was, and rather proud of it too. From the southern region, he surmised; Cork, or thereabouts. With a benign smile he was about to inquire for the sake of his own curiosity when, most rudely, the Irish-sounding gentleman called, rather yelled, down to himself and the four oarsmen who tended the boat as if they stood a full league's distance out to sea rather than directly below and not even ten feet away.

"Achilles!" repeated the Irish-sounding gentleman, whom the booking agent had heard perfectly clearly the first time and was rather put out now at being so obviously regarded as

either deaf or stupid, neither affliction thankfully he was in sufferance of.

"You have just returned from Achilles!" shouted the Irish-sounding gentleman, as if by way of clarification. Yet still it remained unclear to the booking agent as to whether this was in the form of a statement or a question. So he merely smiled pleasantly up at the irate gentleman and nodded in a most agreeable fashion.

"I want Jenkins! Is there a passenger on board by the name of Jenkins? I'm looking for Harry Jenkins!"

It rather struck the booking agent, who also prided himself on being something of a particular creature when it came to the correctness of grammatical composition, that to sandwich an interrogative between a pair of redundant pronouncements was nothing short of shoddy syntax and as a result this man's respect dropped a notch and consequentially along with said notch so too did the term 'gentle' in reference to this increasingly rude Irishman who now stood above him.

"There is indeed a passenger aboard *Achilles* by that name," responded the booking agent, and rather stiffly at that. It had not escaped his attention that the term 'Missus' had been noticeably absent from the Irishman's rant and he wondered briefly whether he ought to clarify this, in much the same manner as it had recently been clarified to himself. But then he decided, and with a rather delicious twinge of mischief, not to.

"Then you must take me there at once!"

"I *must?*" retorted the booking agent, becoming himself a little irritated now. "I regret to say, sir, that all staterooms are now fully booked aboard *Achilles*. Besides, she will have heaved anchor well before we could reach her."

The Irishman swore, loudly and most immodestly.

"There *is* still a stateroom available aboard *Sapphire*," the agent informed him, seeing no reason to forego another commission for himself. "She is due to set sail in an hour or so, also bound for Frisco. She is a well-proven vessel, and this will be her second voyage around the Horn, so there is every chance that she will overhaul *Achilles* en route and arrive there first."

The Irishman was already inside the boat. Delving deeply into his pockets he retrieved a wad of banknotes, more than sufficient to purchase his passage thrice over and he shoved these into the startled booking agent's face.

"Then I must get aboard *Sapphire*! Take me there immediately!"

Chapter Four
Making Sail

The last to arrive aboard *Achilles* was her captain; one Samuel Jacobs, staunch Quaker and former whaling man from New Bedford, reclining in comparative luxury in the spacious stern sheets of his own thirty-foot gig as a crew of four men labored at the oars. Seated directly opposite were Messrs. Harding and Ives, *Achilles'* two principal owners and alongside him sat his niece, Emma, a quiet and inconspicuous young woman who, but for such drabness in her style of dress and hair that was bunched severely into a tightened knot at the rear, might yet have been regarded as passingly attractive by anyone who took the time to notice. Yet so few did, for such was her manner of quiet humility and stoic reservation that more often than not she was entirely overlooked, as indeed she was presently being as the three men continued in the conversation they had begun ashore.

"*Sapphire,*" repeated Henry Harding, now for the third time. He was a large and for the most part a cheerful man, with a ruddy countenance and long curled waxed mustache that spanned the full width of his beaming face. He was dressed up for the occasion, as was his partner, in his Sunday best with new silk topper and ivory-capped cane; very much in keeping with the prosperous South Street merchant and more especially with the clipper ship owner he now was. He was alternately glancing at his new captain, whom he barely knew for they had only secured Samuel Jacobs a week ago, then up towards the vessel in question. *Sapphire* could now be glimpsed less than a cables' distance from where their gig was presently weaving its way through the crowded anchorage.

"There stands your quarry, sir! There stands the vessel that you shall beat into Frisco!"

Indeed, Harding was an optimistic man, for a ship owner. Unlike his partner Edward Ives, who as always stood ready to counter any such naïve giddiness with his own ample supply of cold, hard reason.

"With an untried ship and a reluctant crew," Ives grumbled, shifting again uncomfortably on the hard wooden thwart. His bony behind was not used to such abuse, nor was he enjoying being out on the water half as much as was his partner. But it was customary on a maiden voyage for the owners themselves to see their vessel safely out of port and thus Edward Ives was obliged to endure such hardship, if only for the sake of appearance.

"*Sapphire* is manned by professionals," added Ives, as much to Captain Jacobs as to his partner. "And she has already proven herself a most able vessel."

"She has proven nothing!" countered Henry Harding readily, as though they had repeated this conversation countless times over. "Except that she enjoyed the good fortune of catching the right winds on her maiden run. And if that old rogue Thaddeus Oglesby has the gall to imply that we ourselves lack confidence in *Achilles'* ability, then he can dashed-well put his money where his mouth is!"

He paused for effect before looking away again, this time towards his own vessel that was now approaching up ahead. *Achilles'* lines were true to any clipper; her bulwarks flush in height from stem to stern and with her main deck monkey rail on a level with both her foredeck and quarterdeck. This gave her hull a solid, continuous aspect which, combined with all three towering masts that reached as high as one hundred and ninety feet, each one raked aft at one and a quarter inches to every foot of height, gave the entire vessel a streamlined, swift appearance.

"Fifty thousand dollars!" Harding announced. "That is what *Achilles* cost to build, and that is the precise sum that Thaddeus Oglesby will pay forth when she arrives in Frisco ahead of *Sapphire.*"

"A fool and his money are fast parted," grumbled Ives.

"Oh, for heaven's sakes, man! Why, just look at her! She has the sharpest lines of any clipper afloat and I'll defy any man who tells me otherwise! A fool and his money, my eye!"

Harding glared reproachfully at his partner and received the same wearied look in return. But Henry Harding had never been the type to allow another to sour his mood, least of all Ives, the mean-spirited beggar, so he returned instead to gazing up at his ship.

Only three years ago *Achilles* would have been the largest American vessel afloat. Today, with nearly a dozen new clippers bettering her in size and already a dozen more perched on the blocks soon to be launched, she was comparatively average. But she had been designed, at Harding's express encouragement, along the more 'extreme' lines, making her comparatively longer and narrower and with every expectation of not only being able to endure the strongest winds but also take unusual advantage of the lightest, and this would always give her the edge over any ship of her class, especially when hauling to windward. What she sacrificed in tonnage she would more than make up for in weatherliness, being able to reach into the wind where others could not and pinching so close to the eye that she would rival a pilot schooner in such abilities. In light airs few ships would be able to match her on any aspect. In heavier winds she ought to perform well enough, or at least such were her builder's expectations. These had, of course, yet to be proven.

"Who is *Sapphire's* captain?" asked Samuel Jacobs, disrupting Harding's train of thought. The captain's weathered features, shaded beneath his wide-brimmed and salt-encrusted hat, were peering up into *Achilles'* rigging with a somewhat doubtful expression. He was combing absently at the gray whiskers that extended as far south as his lower jaw, his face now contorted into a web of creases and wrinkles; the result of decades of exposure to salt air and no doubt from squinting to sunwards in relentless search of his quarry. He reached into his side pocket to retrieve his pipe and began chewing on its stem.

"Fellow by the name of...John Blunt?" Harding looked to Ives for confirmation but instead, and to everyone's surprise, it was the captain's niece who corrected him.

"Jonas," she stated quietly, shifting her eyes only momentarily from *Achilles*. Emma Jacobs was also finding herself gripped under a spell of awe-inspired fascination. Indeed, through her busy mind swirled a continual series of comparisons, between the average New Bedford whaler, upon which her own experiences had been thus far solely confined, and this, a newly built East River clipper. Such comparisons left the poor whaler, with its perpetually scabby paintwork and its loose, un-tarred and sun-bleached rigging on every count falling well short of this veritable queen of the oceans. *Achilles* was indeed a magnificent vessel and Emma could now feel the first stirrings of anticipation at the prospect of applying all she had learned thus far into achieving the best possible maiden run for her. Finally, she had a real ship to work with; a ship designed for speed and with this the opportunity to stretch both *Achilles'* and her own muscles and to see just how well they might perform together. And yet her voice displayed only the mildest trace of interest as she continued looking up at the ship.

"Jonas Blunt," she added, appearing quite nonchalant about it. "This will be his fourth trip to California, his second with *Sapphire*. She made one hundred and four days on her maiden run back in May."

Henry Harding stared at her for a moment before nodding.

"Indeed. Anyway, she also departs on this morning's ebb and she is as good a match as ever might be found for *Achilles* to test herself against. Both ships are near identical in sail area and tonnage, but with *Achilles'* design she will surely enjoy the advantage and it is bound to be the most exciting of races. Would that I were able to join you, sir!"

Edward Ives looked at his partner but opted to say nothing. Unlike Harding, who was so easily taken with such foolhardy notions as making private wagers with the likes of Thaddeus Oglesby over lunch at Delmonico's, Edward Ives' priority, as always, lay squarely on the bottom line. He turned to Captain Jacobs and said,

"The thing to remember, captain, is that no clipper has departed New York or Boston for almost three weeks now, so the demand for goods in Frisco will be exceptionally high and huge profits will be had by the first ship to arrive. And you must also bear in mind that *Achilles* is no whaling ship.

A clipper is designed for speed, sir, so you must crack on, come what may! *Achilles'* performance on her maiden run will determine her future freight rates, so you *must* press her hard if you ever hope to gain port in a respectable time. And of course..." he glanced at Henry Harding, "there is a substantial captain's bonus to be earned, should you arrive in Frisco ahead of *Sapphire.*"

"As you shall, sir, I have no doubt of it!" declared Harding. "And we shall yet see that scoundrel Oglesby eat his hat at Delmonico's, to the delight of all and sundry!"

Emma Jacobs, still gazing up in quiet wonderment at her uncle's new command, nodded her head absently in agreement. Yes, it can be done, she was certain of this now, on seeing *Achilles* close-up for the first time. With a modicum of luck and a good measure of persistence they ought to be able to beat *Sapphire* into Frisco. The northeast Trade Winds would be the critical factor. Being so close following the summer months the airs surrounding the northern tropical belt had been dulled by days upon end of tedious calm, and this must surely hinder both ships in the seas north of the equator. But, with Lieutenant Maury's help, *Achilles* ought to fare well enough. Emma now felt a positive thrill at the very prospect of this upcoming voyage; a sense of optimism at the full scope of possibilities that were now laid out before her. The faintest trace of a smile played itself across Emma's young face, transforming her erstwhile unremarkable features for an instant into something quite blissful as she realized that here, finally, was a challenge that she could properly sink her teeth into.

They were nearing the small platform at the foot of *Achilles'* accommodation ladder and Henry Harding, his eyes now glistening with pride, gazed aloft with an expression of almost child-like wonderment at his new ship as he declared happily,

"Now then, gentlemen, let us put her to work! And I daresay we shall soon see what she is capable of!"

Standing at the break in the bulwark, Nate Cooper watched as *Achilles'* captain stepped onto the platform with both his chronometer and sextant boxes held carefully out in front of him as if fearful that the slightest knock might affect their delicate mechanisms. Then came Messrs. Harding and Ives, followed closely by a shabbily-dressed young woman who struggled with carrying an identical sextant box as well as several rolled-up charts under the same arm while gripping the rope handrail with the other. The gig's coxswain tried to offer his assistance but she would have none of it; both the instrument and the charts she carried were too precious, it would appear, to be entrusted to any other.

Brief introductions were made at the head of the ladder and Captain Jacobs, a broad-shouldered man albeit considerably shorter, peered up at his new second mate briefly before nodding in a vague, noncommittal manner. He then cast a sharp and critical eye about the immediate deck area, thence aloft to see that all was shipshape. Varnished mahogany and gleaming brass work from *Achilles'* capstans, skylights and deck fixtures greeted his eye from every lower quarter whilst aloft could be found no ready cause for fault either and he nodded in a curt fashion, as if this were no more nor less than was expected, although in truth as a whaling man he must surely have been equally as struck in wonderment that any ship could possibly be made so tidy.

Then, seemingly satisfied with his surroundings, Captain Jacobs drew in a deep breath and, between one sentence and the next, he figuratively cast aside his shoreside ways; tossed them by the board and in their place donned his captain's hat.

"Now signal me a pilot, Mister Cooper, and let us make ready for sea!"

His voice, now attuned to the open deck, boomed forth loudly and with all the deep resonance of a nearby foghorn on a weather shore.

"Heave her up short, Mister Biggs, and ready me a jib and a brace of tops'ls if thee'd be so kind!"

Then, as he was turning away, he noticed those more recent stains on the otherwise spotless deck, of fresh-spilled blood and he frowned, pausing for a moment in consideration before finally nodding, resigned, it would appear, to what he might so readily condemn as a Quaker yet as ship's captain so clearly understood. He turned to his chief mate and, with a brief glance to his niece and the two owners who were now walking away aft, he lowered his voice accordingly.

"Thee'll find me not an inch forward of the quarterdeck this trip, Mister Biggs," he said. "And what happens beyond my eye is thine own business. But a shrewd workman breaks not his own tools, I say, and I'd advise 'e to remember it."

Then he turned away and strode briskly aft, motioning to the sailor who had coxed the gig to stand ready by the ship's helm, and with this *Achilles* was stirred into action. Nate Cooper, knowing well the duties of a second mate, went directly to the mizzen to hoist the pennant requesting a pilot while his chief mate cut a direct wake to the fore scuttle, where he pounded his fist several times on the hatch cover before sliding it open with a loud bang.

"All hands ahoooy! Ready to make sail! Tumble up now, with a will!"

As each man emerged Biggs propelled him either forward to the windlass that stood under the break of the foredeck or aft to wherever a spare hand might be required. And all the while he continued to bark out orders.

"Hands to the windlass! Make ready to heave short! Loose gaskets on courses and tops'ls! Ready the outer jib!"

In the midst of the stream of humanity that subsequently spewed forth from the fore scuttle came a very dazed and utterly confused Harry Jenkins who, having barely seconds earlier been shaken violently from his slumber and thrown bodily into the midst of this upward stampede, now squinted about him with numb incomprehension.

"You there! Lend a hand to the windlass!"

Harry stared dumbly at this large and brutish-looking article, who for some odd reason was dressed in a bright red military tunic and speaking absolute gibberish to him. He was also glaring at Harry with such unfounded malice that he fast arrived at the conclusion that he must still be dreaming, and with this reassurance he relaxed a little.

"Who in the hell is the Wind Lass?" Harry mumbled. "And why can't she do it herself, the lazy cow?"

He promptly received a slap in the face for his efforts. And no girly slap, either. In fact it bloody well hurt!

"What the devil? Now look here!" Harry protested. Dreaming or not, by God, that demanded satisfaction.

Harry was about to call this ugly ruffian out on the spot when he felt a strong hand grip his upper arm and he barely had time to glimpse its owner, a muscular, tattooed and rather irritated-looking black individual dressed in a steward's uniform, before being propelled bodily towards the item of machinery in question. And it was around about this point, as he fetched hard up against the windlass and for the first time managed to get a proper look around him, that he realized where he was. On board some bloody huge ship that was getting ready to set sail!

It was also around this point that Harry began fervently praying; hoping against his own fast-rising doubts now that he really was still sound asleep, even if this did entail having to wake up face down and penniless in some dingy and rat-infested New York alleyway. For surely, he decided, *anything* was preferable to this!

The chief mate now stood up on the foredeck, this being the most advantageous position for him to monitor all quarters of the ship at once. Standing between the knight-heads where *Achilles'* bowsprit emerged close underfoot, he directed those men who were now clambering aloft in the rigging. Yet not a one of them belonged to *Achilles'* crew; these were the longshoremen and riggers, until now busily applying the finishing touches to their pride of work and who were enjoying this rare opportunity to be sailors for the day.

"Yardarm and bunt gaskets away! One man to remain on each yard!"

Biggs watched closely as each sail was freed of its lashing, leaving only a single jigger line securing it to its yard and with one man remaining there waiting to let it go.

In the meantime the steward supervised the manning of the windlass. Four men were stationed two aside at the pump-action lever and they began working it up and down to begin the laborious process of raising the anchor chain, one link at a time. The chain led directly from the windlass through the topgallant forecastle space beneath the foredeck, from where it passed out through the starboard hawsehole and down to the water. The topgallant forecastle, having only four and a half feet of headroom and no aft bulkhead, housed the paint locker and the rigger's store, as well as the two enclosed heads, or toilets, which were merely openings in the outer bulwark surrounded by timber partitions. It was also home to the ship's livestock: an assortment of pigs and chickens that would supplement *Achilles'* supply of eggs and fresh meat for both passengers and crew.

"Main and mizzen, brace up sharp for the starboard tack! Headyards abox! Bear a hand there!"

The heavy yards aloft began to slowly rotate, all five in unison on each mast; main and mizzen set to catch the light offshore breeze and foremast yards braced aback to turn *Achilles'* head away from the wind.

"Set the outer jib! Let her fly!"

As the jib ascended the forestay, Robert Biggs glanced over the side to check on the anchor's progress. Seeing the chain rising sporadically in jerks and starts he swore and strode aft to the windlass. Those men working it were either drunk, clueless or both and, glancing aft to where his captain, the pilot and *Achilles'* owners all stood looking in his direction, Biggs' fingers twitched of their own accord around the belaying pin in his hand. He strode forward again, angrily batting the loose jib sheets aside as he returned to monitoring the anchor's painful progress, until finally the chain led vertically down from the hawsehole to the water.

"'Vast on your windlass! Ready to trip anchor!"

Biggs raised his arm high, to signal that the anchor was now hove short and he received a brief nod in response from his captain who stood almost two hundred feet away.

"Up anchor ahoooy! Jib sheet, haul to weather! Fore and main tops'ls, let fall! Halyards haul! Tend to lifts and braces! Sheets home and look lively about it!"

From aloft the bunched canvas of *Achilles'* topsails were let go, showering those below with an accumulation of dew and rainwater and, as each yard began to ascend its topmast, its sheets were hauled down promptly and secured to the fife rails below.

"Weather sheets haul! Now your lee! Well enough, the

main! Well the fore, belay! Sweat those halyards, damn you!"

Near the foot of the mainmast a group of particularly noisome-looking individuals, consisting of several of those who had arrived drunk on the second boat, were busying themselves with wrapping the main topsail halyard around the drum of the capstan and they were doing this in such an unexpectedly knowledgeable fashion that Nate Cooper found himself pausing and wondering whether he need interfere here at all. For they appeared to know well enough what they were doing as one of them, a lanky Irishman, took a step apart from his fellows who stood ready around the capstan and, hooking his thumbs into a pair of tattered rope suspenders, began singing forth at the top of his voice.

Whereupon his companions, in unison, promptly rejoined as they each one leaned into their handspikes, the long wooden bars inserted into the pigeonholes around the capstan's upper drum, and the capstan began to rotate, its ratcheted pawl clicking into place and the main topsail halyard, now drawn tight, began to haul the heavy yard aloft. And in such a fashion they continued to pace slowly around the capstan, the clicking of the pawl in time with the chanteyman's rhythm.

Nate Cooper, being half reassured that these men were experienced seamen, yet at the same time half dismayed that these men could possibly be experienced seamen, stood by in uncertainty as the capstan continued to rotate and those men gathered around it fell into a steady rhythm which, and this being the signature of any true sailor, gave every outward appearances of supreme effort yet concealed within the utmost economy. The result created by this shared rhythm made a striking contrast between those men who worked at the windlass, in that by coordinating all their efforts they were making good and easy work of it.

But were these really seamen, Nate wondered, for if so they were unlike any he had encountered before. But surely they must be, for without even needing to be prompted one of the men detached himself from his handspike and, with a silent nod to his chum who was tailing the halyard, used the grubby heel of a bared foot to drive down the turns of rope that had begun riding up the drum, and this coincided so precisely with the tailing man's brief slackening of the line that together they must have performed this task countless times over.

When finally his presence was noticed, one of them, on sizing Nate up with an unsteady and lopsided grin, piped up,

"'Allo! Who's this fuckin' joker? An' how come 'e ain't pitchin' in wiv 'is shipmates?"

"Dunno, Jacko. Prolly an officer. Wot you reckon, Spuds?"

"Looks loike a greaser to me, Scraggsy."

"Second mate, eh? Well that's no excuse. If he ain't helpin' he should keep outa the way. That's how no-good idle buggers get 'emselves hurt."

Before Nate could even begin to respond to this barrage of disrespect the unruly gang had already secured the main topsail halyard and, with another bout of enthusiastic chanteying, were employing themselves likewise with the fore topsail. All of which left Nate standing there wondering how, exactly, he was supposed to gain any semblance of control over such men as these. He realized then that it would be easier by far if this were indeed a ship crewed entirely by landsmen.

Now *Achilles* sat motionless on the river as, with a final heave that required half a dozen strong hands at the windlass, her half-ton anchor was tripped and freed itself from the suction of the riverbed. Now supporting the entire weight of the anchor, the chain rose steadily until the light gray mud that clung to its flukes could be sighted through the murky water.

"Anchor aweigh! Chain stoppers on! Hands to the capstan and hook the cat! Headyards, brace full about! Sheet in that God-damned jib!"

All foremast yards were promptly braced around in unison until both fore topsail and outer jib filled out with a satisfying luff and a shake and now *Achilles*, underway and free to run, began to slowly draw herself ahead.

"Achilles is getting underway, captain!"

Jonas Blunt visibly started, swore aloud then lowered the spyglass through which he had been watching *Achilles* closely. He glanced irritably aloft before turning to his chief mate.

"What the devil, Mister Fergis, is that boy's problem?"

Fergis gazed aloft thoughtfully for a while before replying.

"Stone deafness would be my surmise, cap'n."

Blunt stared at his chief mate, trying to discern whether or not Fergis was joking. As usual he could not even hazard a guess and with a huff he raised the spyglass again. But before he was even able to focus through it his chief mate added,

"Water taxi approaching. Starboard side."

Blunt glanced aloft again, to where the boy stationed at the main top was still peering ahead at *Achilles* and he shook his head and muttered, "stone blind to boot," then ambled over to the quarterdeck's starboard taffrail. He recognized the booking agent immediately, but not the solitary and rather agitated-looking individual who stood upright alongside him in the boat; a man dressed in such plain and travel-worn attire that it was difficult to ascertain from sight alone either his station or occupation.

As the boat approached the rather agitated-looking man finally appeared to notice Blunt and, apparently finding it a fairly easy task (for, as may have been alluded to earlier, Jonas Blunt was a particularly well-upholstered individual and clearly unlikely to squeeze even a fraction of his ampleness into any fore scuttle, let alone to lay aloft with his shipmates with any measure of alacrity) to discern that he was speaking to *Sapphire's* captain, he promptly called forth in a somewhat Irish-sounding tone,

"I need you to take me to San Francisco!"

Jonas Blunt smiled and responded, pleasantly,

"I pay fifteen dollars a month, with free grub and lodging! Take it or leave it!"

There were a few chuckles from those sailors nearby as the man below gaped up at him, not understanding at first.

"What?" responded the man finally. "No, no, you misunderstand me!"

"Well, my friend," declared Jonas Blunt, rather enjoying himself now, "There are only two means by which you might reach Frisco aboard my ship! One will cost you five hundred dollars for a first class stateroom ticket, while the other will cost you nothing at all! Perhaps you might care to express a preference. Before I make sail, that is."

"Why, as a passenger, of course!" the Irishman returned, clearly doing his utmost to remain civil despite the furious expression now evident on his face.

"Well, as luck would have it I do have a stateroom available," replied Blunt, noticing that the booking agent, who was now holding aloft a boarding ticket, was himself finding it something of a chore to maintain a neutral expression. Blunt turned to Fergis.

"How much longer?"

"Another hour at least, cap'n."

"Very well. Rig the ladder. Bring him aboard."

Sapphire now had a full complement of seven passengers in her four staterooms. It was enough, in Jonas Blunt's view, to be hauling fifteen hundred tons of freight around Cape Horn without the addition of a cargo that continually moved around of its own accord and needed to be pampered to and socialized with on a daily basis.

After gazing down at the rude Irishman a while longer, Blunt added, "There's a whiff of devilry about this one, Mister Fergis." He was no longer smiling. "Best keep a weather eye on him. And try to keep him out of my face while you're at it."

Chapter Five
The Watches Are Set

As *Achilles* proceeded downriver on the increasing ebb she continued to pile on sail, beginning with topsails then progressing to spanker, courses, topgallants, royals and skysails. Then came the four headsails that were affixed to the forestays and five staysails between masts, each one setting well in this light breeze and without any of the customary snags and hitches so common to a first trial at sea. As the shoresiders bent-to willingly with the hauling of lines and the inexperienced and mostly drunken crew struggled to raise and cat the anchor, those gathered on the quarterdeck exchanged nods of approval at the agreeable manner in which she was thus far behaving.

Drifting past Battery Point, *Achilles* did indeed cut a handsome figure to those watching from the shoreline and she elicited a chorus of spontaneous cheers from those New Yorkers who habitually gathered at the promenade to see the clippers come and go. Raising their hats high in salute, they bid her farewell and Godspeed as she continued onwards through the Narrows and into Lower Bay, setting and trimming canvas as she went.

By the time she passed Governor's Island she was under full plain sail and, making her numbers to the semaphore station by way of a series of coded pennants hoisted to her mizzen top, she proceeded out into the open waters of the bay, now harnessing a steady ten knots of southwesterly breeze and beginning to pitch gently under her tall press of canvas.

"Capital!" declared Henry Harding with unrestrained delight. From where he stood on her quarterdeck, *Achilles* truly was a sight to behold. With her full dress of spotless white canvas towering high above and her gleaming brass work and varnish all around, she was just as tidy as an oil painting. Even his partner, Edward Ives, seemed for the moment to have set aside his own misgivings as he too peered aloft with what, for him, was about as near to a smile as could reasonably be got.

But for Robert Biggs and Nate Cooper there was scant time for any such romanticism. They now had a ship to sail and a crew to train and they had to somehow combine the one with the other before either sea or weather got the better of them. The first order of the day was to select their watches and, as the longshoremen continued to work aloft, all hands, including those who had until now been confined inside the forecastle (apart, that is, from the dead man who had been generously excused all duties until further notice), were assembled on the main deck just abaft the deckhouse.

And a sorrier sight had seldom before been Nate Cooper's misfortune to behold. A scurvy-looking bunch; ranging from the old and apparently infirm to those so frightful in appearance alone that no honest citizen would think twice about crossing the street to avoid them. When all were gathered together the chief mate stood before them and, after closely scanning each face in its turn, announced,

"Now, let's see our experienced hands! To the fore with you!"

There was an uneasy shuffling of feet in response to this command, in particular from that group of ten or so individuals Nate had witnessed earlier at the capstan and who all now turned to the man who was clearly their spokesman. He was a burly type, almost a match to the chief mate in bulk although slightly less in height and his bearded features, under the mop of dark hair that was clumped into unruly strands atop his head, were bronzed by the sun and stained even darker in places where tar had worked its way indelibly into the creases of his skin. As he raised a knuckle to his forehead it could be seen that the man's fingernails, or as much as remained of them, were black crescents of inlaid pitch, and his tattoo-laden forearms and hands also bore the additional yellowed hues of linseed oil that had ingrained itself so deeply into the hardened calluses as to be all but a permanent feature of the underlying flesh.

"By yer leave, Mister Mate," the man nodded, his keen blue eyes remaining fixed on Robert Biggs. "Scragg's the name, sir. Willum Scragg, bosun's mate. The boys an' me, we's off the Black Ball."

"The devil you say! Packet-rats, eh?"

Biggs stared closely at this man now, then to his diverse companions, each of whom was also studying the chief mate just as closely as he now eyed them. The chief mate's humorless grin then reappeared, for he knew well the measure of these men. They were from the Black Ball Line, the transatlantic packet ships that kept a regular schedule between New York and Liverpool; their crews driven hard with a ready fist and a belaying pin and those men who worked them were of the most unruly, dishonest and ungrateful type as might ever be encountered aboard any ship at sea. They were a tough, independent breed and it was said of them that they only endured such brutality under the Black Ball's crimson pennant so as to voyage between the dance halls of Cherry Street and the grog shops of Liverpool's Ratcliffe Highway.

With a prolonged glare at each one of these packet-rats in turn the chief mate finally declared,

"You'll find no favors here! If it's the gold fields you're out for, then you'll damned-well earn your passage!"

He then turned to the remainder of the assembled crew.

"Are there any more experienced seamen?"

It was at this juncture that Harry Jenkins deemed it appropriate to speak up.

"Pardon me, but I think there's been a misunderstanding," Harry ventured, adopting his most winning of smiles. "You see, I really shouldn't be here."

A few muted whispers and suppressed giggles came from the direction of the packet-rats, then died away again just as quickly as the chief mate raised his belaying pin in a casual yet clearly threatening manner.

"You'll be wherever the hell I tell you to be," Biggs responded, and not very kindly at that. "You're aboard *Achilles* now, and your ass is mine to do with as I see fit!"

"*Achilles?*" declared Harry. "Well, thank heavens for that! You see I actually have a...." But, as Harry reached unwittingly for the missing ticket in the absent pocket of his nonexistent coat, the full realization as well as the full awfulness of his situation finally dawned upon him and, looking around and seeing nary a familiar face nor anyone who might even confirm his predicament, his voice faded away into a quiet, despairing groan.

"What you *have*, my friend," responded Biggs, "is one last

chance to shut up before I give you a drubbing you'll never forget!" Then he turned back to his assembled crew and repeated, "Are there any more experienced hands?"

One man, of sizable build with dark eyes and a beetle-browed countenance, raised his hand. He was dressed in a mariner's pea-coat similar to Nate's and it had not gone unnoticed by the latter that this man had been eyeing him particularly closely, and far from cordially, all the while they had been standing there.

"Frederick Weeks, Mister Mate, sir," announced the man with alacrity. "From the *Osprey*, out of Boston. If you have need of an *experienced* second mate, sir, I can be of service...."

Biggs' grin reappeared to expose the missing upper front tooth.

"I already have a second mate, *Mister* Weeks. You'll be in the fo'c'sle. Larbowline!"

The chief mate motioned with his belaying pin toward the larboard, or port, bulwark and, to the accompaniment of another muted chorus of chuckling, the man calling himself Weeks was directed to stand there.

Nate, it now being his choice, could scarce see any other hopeful among this bunch whatsoever. Except, he now recalled, for the able-looking sailor he had seen coxing the captain's gig earlier and who was presently stationed at *Achilles'* helm.

"I'll take the helmsman," he said, pointing aft and Biggs scowled, clearly irritated but he could do nothing about it, because this was the way things were done.

In such a manner each mate took his turn in selecting his watch. The first drawn were the more experienced men, those whose extensive skills allowed them to proclaim themselves Able Hands and who numbered only four in total, these being Frederick Weeks, the sailor at the helm whose name was George Evans, a tough and surly-looking article by the name of Silas Rigsby and a Portuguese fisherman who called himself Bacas.

Then came the lesser-experienced men, who toiled for a lower wage but with far fewer expectations. These packet-rats, as Robert Biggs knew all too well, were seamen of the most dubious type yet seamen nonetheless, in that they could each hand, reef and steer with at least some modicum of proficiency when propelled to it with a shove and a curse. Thus they were ranked as Ordinary Seamen.

Lastly came the boys, traditionally the younger lads who lacked the physical strength to perform even these basic duties and with them were also included the old and infirm who suffered a likewise disadvantage, as well as any other inexperienced hand of whatever age. There were fourteen such 'boys' aboard *Achilles*, twelve of whom were grown men, including Harry Jenkins and nine Swedes who could scarcely, it seemed, knock together a single coherent sentence of English between the lot of them.

When finally their watches were selected, the chief mate's Larbowlines and the second mate's Starbowlines, Biggs commanded all hands to remain where they were under the watchful eye of *Achilles'* steward, then turned to his second mate.

"With me, mister," he grunted, then led the way to the fore scuttle. They descended the steep ladder into the forecastle space and there, under the filtered daylight and yellow gloom of the slush lanterns, they began to systematically empty out and sift through each man's possessions.

They emerged with quite a haul: knives, pistols, billy clubs, knuckle-dusters and several bottles of varying ullage, the former items being tossed immediately overboard and the latter, being taken promptly into the chief mate's care, mysteriously disappearing somewhere between forecastle and bulwark. Then they returned to where the crew was still gathered aft and the chief mate ordered each man to turn out his pockets.

One knife for each man was the allowance and, amidst much quiet grumbling and many a sullen glare, Nate took each of their knives to the carpenter's shop located adjacent to the galley inside the deckhouse, to have the tip of each one broken off.

"A knife to cut with is the only tool a sailor needs!" reiterated the chief mate. "If I ever catch sight of a sharpened point, there'll be a flogging for it!"

"I thought flogging was outlawed on American ships," piped up a voice from the crowd and Robert Biggs, with the uncanny instincts of a cobra, homed directly onto it.

Harry Jenkins, finding himself once again the sole focus of the chief mate's attention, realized somewhat belatedly that he had no desire whatsoever to be this. So he tried stepping back a pace to re-merge himself into the obscurity of his fellow misfits but suddenly encountered solid resistance against the ranks that had promptly closed in behind him and he was left standing there, all alone. He smiled at Robert Biggs, and in a manner that he sincerely hoped would come across as disarming.

"Just thought I'd mention it," he added lamely.

"A sea lawyer, eh?" snarled Biggs, eyeing the Englishman now with all the warm-hearted fondness of the aforementioned reptile. "Never mind. We'll soon beat that out of you."

Then he turned to his second mate.

"All hands aloft, Mister Cooper! Ready weather stuns'ls!"

Now Nate took over, and with a distinct lack of enthusiasm, for although he too found himself despising this mixed group of landsmen and packet-rats, he yet had serious misgivings about Biggs' excessive methods. Surely there must be a better way to lead a crew than this. But to look around him now and to be met by so many a hostile glare, it was all Nate could do to square his shoulders to the task and give it his best shot.

"Climb the weather shrouds! Always keep the wind to your back! Hold onto the shrouds, not the ratlines! Silence aloft!"

For the most part the packet-rats complied willingly enough, but not without first a glance to their leader, William Scragg, who merely nodded. But for the remainder, which sadly encompassed the majority of *Achilles'* crew, it took a fair amount of coaxing by way of Robert Biggs' fist as well as the belaying pin that he already seemed so fondly attached to, to convince them that climbing aloft was, despite their own better judgments, by far the safer option. So they too began reluctantly making their way aloft.

Nate then noticed the man calling himself Frederick Weeks holding back, as if in obstinate defiance. He was standing there glaring at *Achilles'* second mate with such unconcealed malice that Nate, in accordance with what he believed to be his duty, sought to bring this to the attention of his chief mate.

"Mister Biggs," Nate called out. "This man is refusing to..."

Robert Biggs immediately turned with his belaying pin raised high and before Weeks even had time to protect himself he was struck violently about the head with it. Weeks, uttering a loud curse and with another hateful glare towards Nate, stepped up onto the rack rail and began making his way rapidly aloft, overhauling several anxious-looking Swedes as well as an extremely nervous Harry Jenkins who barely noticed as he continued to silently will himself to *not* look down, damn it, as he forced his reluctant feet to keep moving towards the main top.

Biggs then turned to his second mate.

"Did you have something to say?"

Nate, now feeling quite inadequate and hopelessly out of his depth here, simply shook his head.

"Then get 'em aloft," snarled Biggs, "And stop wasting my fucking time."

Achilles hove-to briefly off Sandy Hook by bracing her main yards full about and, using her backed sails as a brake, she slowed to a crawl as the pilot, the two owners and a score of riggers and longshoremen, two of them carrying the excused dead man with them, descended the accommodation ladder and piled into the cutter that drifted alongside.

Then, with ahoys and cheers from those who were not otherwise distracted by the absolute terror by being aloft for the very first time, *Achilles'* main yards were braced about once more and she got properly underway.

Emma Jacobs, to all intents and purposes, was a fairly typical example of a whaling captain's wife, and this despite the most obvious fact that she was in actuality Samuel Jacobs' niece. But, with he being a widower and she an orphan, and with neither having anyone else in their lives from whom to draw companionship, theirs had evolved into a comparable type of relationship and one whereby he, as captain, maintained overall authority by way of his regular presence up on the quarterdeck while she, being a woman and thus less suited, not to say less expected, to project any such lordly presence, kept herself mostly below decks and out of sight, occupying herself with those more mundane duties such as existed aboard any ship at sea.

A limited degree of housekeeping, including looking after provisions, mending the crew's clothing and administering medicines to any who required them, would keep most whaling ladies busy and generally distracted, particularly during the latter stages of any voyage when the crew's garments would begin to wear as thin as their health. It was by no means an easy life for any woman but it was, to many, the preferred option to remaining ashore with all the other ladies of New Bedford with one eye permanently affixed to the horizon and the other on the road along which the messenger boy from the semaphore station in Providence would always be the first to arrive with the most grievous of news.

Indeed, very few women found themselves able to endure more than a solitary voyage, which oftentimes lasted upwards of three years, aboard a whaling ship. By now Emma Jacobs had completed three such voyages and still was showing no signs whatsoever of tiring from it. She had, however, long since tired of any and all housekeeping chores and, although faithful to these and performing them to the best of her ability, she had over time and with a steadfastness of determination gradually infiltrated her way into the more masculine world of charts and compasses, minutes, degrees, hour angles and declinations and she was now just as capable an ocean navigator as her uncle; if not more so.

Since Samuel Jacob's brother and fellow whaling captain had slipped his hawser homeward bound off the Falklands, leaving behind little of value save an ancient pocket watch and a sixteen-year-old daughter, he had willingly accepted responsibility for Emma and had done so with eyes open and with the full knowledge that to take this young woman out to sea was to deprive her of such opportunities as she might otherwise enjoy ashore. But, with the absence of any other surviving relatives to any quarter, there really had been no choice in the matter, for either of them. And when it had quickly become apparent that Emma's scholastic abilities, particularly her navigational skills, were fast coming to equal, if not better, his own, Samuel Jacobs had himself encouraged his niece wholeheartedly, realizing that this young woman with neither husband nor home was alike to a vessel adrift without a compass, and that subsequently an alternate means of fulfillment, if only for the mere sake of distraction, was hereby called for.

Being herself only five and twenty years of age and her uncle forty-nine, this might give some indication as to how naturally attuned Emma was to this complex science, as Samuel Jacobs himself was no dunce. He had successfully rounded the Horn and returned home again on eight separate occasions, voyaging to the Sandwich Islands and beyond, as far west as Okinawa and north to Point Barrow. Yet nowadays he always conferred with his niece and allowed her a generally free hand in all matters navigational, just as he did on this day as he remained up on the quarterdeck while she toiled below in the small chartroom inside the trunk cabin and plotted out *Achilles'* passage to San Francisco.

Using parallel rulers, Emma drew the initial track line in soft pencil; a direct line running the full three and a half thousand miles between Sandy Hook and a point on the equator midway between the meridians of thirty and thirty-five degrees west. It was not expected that *Achilles* would remain precisely on this line, nor would it be advantageous for her to do so, for although the wind lay fair enough now from the southwest and afforded her a favorable aspect on a direct southeasterly course, as they approached the tropical latitudes it would steadily shift towards the northeast to become the Trade Winds. If they drifted too close against the lee shore as they approached South America they would be obliged to pinch her up close, perhaps even to change tack and in either event lose valuable time in working her back out to weather. The line Emma drew now was one that *Achilles* must remain to the east of, yet not too far, as a similar peril existed if the Trades were met too far out in the Atlantic, whereupon in order to cross the equator between these two vital meridians they would need to come about again and work back in towards Brazil, and at such an acute angle that they would lose just as much valuable time in doing so.

It was called 'running down her eastings', and it was an inconvenience shared by all captains en route to the Horn. For the first week and more they must work themselves more to the east than to the south, almost halving their longitude between New York and London, yet at the same time this did afford the opportunity for a wise captain, especially one who was embarking upon a maiden voyage, to begin testing his ship in southwesterly winds that remained generally fair and constant; laying either square on the beam or large on the quarter.

With these considerations in mind Emma reached into her dress pocket and withdrew a small object that she placed gently, almost reverently, atop the chart. It was bound in a strip of decorated Japanese silk; a bolt of which she had purchased during a stopover in Lahaina to replenish drinking water on her first whaling voyage. Together with its contents, her father's gold pocket watch which still kept better time than any ship's chronometer she had yet to encounter, these two items made up the totality of Emma's valued possessions.

The appearance of the watch, heralding as it did the commencement of another voyage, caused her to smile and once again, as if her long-maintained neutral expression had become unaccustomed to any such maneuver toward the upturn, as a ray of sunshine glimpsed briefly through a wintery overcast it transformed her features immediately into a state of rare attractiveness. For in truth she was a striking young woman when she did not go about, as always she did, sporting that habitually somber and uninviting frown of hers. But then, having spent a full seven years at sea in the company of so many a homesick and lonely sailor, said frown had long since become so intuitively established as to have rendered the present wearer quite oblivious of its continued existence.

She picked up the watch and it fit snugly into the palm of her hand as if it had been made to measure, and she compared its reading to the bulky chronometer that her uncle had purchased only this morning from the clockmakers on Water Street. The discreet lettering stenciled onto the chronometer's lacquered face read, J. Eldridge & Son, New York. Emma, with only a cursory glance, dismissed the chronometer's worth altogether and instead began winding the watch, turning its ornate golden screw with practiced care and keeping to her late father's prescribed eight full turns and one small increment, until a slight click was felt and not a whit farther so as to not risk over-winding it. As she did this she continued to study the chart and she decided that, for ten thousand dollars, this being the proffered captain's bonus for beating *Sapphire* into Frisco, there would certainly need to be a continued sense of urgency throughout this voyage.

Her uncle would be obliged to press both his ship and his crew hard if he ever hoped to remain equal to such a challenge. Samuel Jacobs, a whaling man for whom speed had never heretofore been such an overriding factor outside of the occasional sighting of a nearby pod, had to now adjust himself to his new command.

And, as Emma would soon come to discover, he was to do so with such a degree of enthusiasm and seemingly boundless energy that it would not only surprise her but considerably alarm her, too.

Harry Jenkins could not believe it.

Not the fact that he had actually managed to climb all the way aloft and perform all those tasks demanded of him without having once spewed his guts out or tumbled to his certain death, although this in itself might have been considered by many to be worthy of at least a self-congratulatory pat on the back. It might even have been considered by some to be a confidence inspiring, even life-altering, achievement. But not Harry.

No, Harry's disbelief stemmed from the fact that here he was on board the very ship for which he himself had purchased a first class stateroom ticket, along with all the rich trimmings and idle comforts that went along with it, and had instead somehow ended up on the same ship working as a common bloody deckhand!

Were the Fates having a laugh, he wondered. Surely they must be.

Having returned to the safety of *Achilles'* main deck he now found that his legs were trembling so much from his exertions aloft that he could barely stand himself upright, so he slumped to the deck instead and sat there with his back propped against the aft trunk cabin bulwark, close to the stairs leading up to *Achilles'* quarterdeck. It was a fairly concealed spot here and, for the moment at least, he could not see anyone else around. But he knew that this would not last and, for as long as it did, he racked his brains in an attempt to find some way out of his predicament.

He had no money, no luggage and no means whatsoever of proving who he was. Nor did he know anyone on board who could verify his identity. So what possible good would it do him to even try explaining his situation to anyone? More harm than good, he supposed, as nobody was going to believe him anyway. He was, in effect, pretty well buggered.

In his despair Harry's head slumped backward and it struck against the cabin's bulwark with a loud, solid thud, yet he barely felt it, being generally numb all over by this point. He needed a catnap. Forty winks, that was all. Just to reassemble his wits. Yet he realized full well that there would be scant chance of his being left alone in peace here for even another minute, let alone to enjoy the luxury of a full and proper sleep, not for a long while yet.

And it so happened that he was right.

For, on the very subject of naps, it was by pure chance that the thudding of Harry's head against the wall directly adjacent to her soft feather pillow awoke Sarah Doyle from one of the most refreshing ones she had enjoyed for a very long time.

Opening her eyes and immediately sensing the movement of the ship, Sarah realized that *Achilles* was underway and she wasted little time in detaching herself from the comfort of her cotton sheets, briefly adjusting herself in the stateroom's mirror, then heading out into the main passenger saloon and forward through the trunk cabin alleyway that led out onto *Achilles'* main deck.

Where, turning sharply left and taking two steps towards

the outer bulwark, she all but tripped over the outstretched legs of a very tired and miserable-looking Harry Jenkins.

To Sarah's credit she recovered remarkably quickly. In fact, her response was just as cool as her former mistress' might have been upon unexpectedly encountering a long-unseen and not-particularly-favored acquaintance.

"Why, Harry Jenkins," Sarah blurted, glancing swiftly around her but seeing nobody else in sight. "Look at you." Then she actually smiled. Yes, indeed she did.

To Harry's credit he did not immediately leap to his feet and begin choking the life out of this thieving bitch with his bare, blistered hands. Instead he simply groaned aloud and banged his head, even harder this time, against the trunk cabin's bulwark. But no, sadly this was no longer a dream. He was, much to his dismay, wide-awake and consequently stuck with it.

"How in the hell...?" Harry began, but even as he spoke he realized how. Of course, she had managed to use his ticket on the pretense of being his wife. Which would explain her odd performance in the booking office back in New York. She must have planned this all along. Damn, she *was* good.

"*Missus* Jenkins, I presume?" Harry sighed.

"Oh, please, call me Sarah."

She was still smiling, yet now with a discernible caginess underlying her expression as she continued glancing around, still seeing nobody.

"So it's not Margaret then?"

"God, no." She snorted as if this was amusing, then glanced around again.

Harry noticed that her accent had changed, too. No longer was she speaking in that plum-in-mouth manner of the English aristocracy. Now she sounded more like a scullery maid than any titled heiress. Damn it, thought Harry again. She really is good.

"So not only do you steal my ticket, but my name too. Some bloody nerve!"

This seemed to dispel Sarah's uneasiness and she immediately retorted,

"And what would *you* have stolen from *me*, Harry Jenkins, if given half a chance?"

Well, she did have a point there, Harry had to admit. His wearied mind turned to the last female who had caused him such inconvenience; the one whose father had chased him clear across Ireland and quite possibly to New York in his thirst for vengeance and he could not help but smile. For he had actually thought himself to be in trouble with that one. But now?

"Well obviously not your honor," Harry quipped. Then, on seeing how clearly unrepentant she was about any of this, he barked, "Damn it, I'm going to expose you and your little scam right here and now! I'm going to have you arrested on the spot!"

Sarah merely gaped at him as if he had altogether lost his wits. And, most infuriatingly of all, she smiled again.

"Did you actually happen to notice where we are, Harry?" She motioned outwards, beyond *Achilles'* bulwarks. "Do you really think that this captain is going to turn his ship around on your say-so and return us to New York? On the ramblings of some common and, might I add, rather tatty-looking deckhand? I must say Harry, a decent wash and a shave would do you no harm whatsoever. Have you seen yourself in a mirror lately?"

This was too much for Harry. She was having a go at his personal hygiene now, by God. Were there no limits to this woman's vindictiveness? He began to haul himself to his feet, now fully prepared to follow through on his former urge to choke the living breath out of her but already it was too late. In fact, his timing could not possibly have been worse, for at that very moment *Achilles'* chief mate happened to round the corner and the sight that greeted Robert Biggs' eye could not have been more damning for Harry. For here stood one of his crimped sailors, fists clenched and glaring daggers at one of *Achilles'* passenger ladies who in turn was backed up against the outer rack rail with a look of genuine alarm now on her face.

"You again!" snarled Biggs, raising his belaying pin threateningly as he advanced. "What's your name?"

Harry froze, his fists still half-raised towards the startled passenger. This, he realized, probably did not look very good. He immediately lowered his arms, knowing how futile it would be to even try offering up any explanation. Then he sighed. For he was also now beginning to realize the full extent of how truly buggered he really was. He glared at Sarah as he replied, testily,

"Well it *used* to be Harry-bloody-Jenkins! "

He did not even see the belaying pin heading his way and it struck his temple with a very loud and incredibly painful thud and the next thing he knew he was looking up into Robert Biggs' scowling and far-from-genial face.

The Fates, decided Harry, as *Achilles'* chief mate began hauling him bodily away by his shirt collar, must now be rolling around helplessly on the ground, clutching themselves tightly so as to prevent their sides from splitting wide open.

Chapter Six

Belaying Pin Soup and Handspike Hash

For the first few days *Achilles* was put through her paces, and so too was her inexperienced crew. Now with studdingsails set alow and aloft on her weather side she ran freely for Bermuda under a steady twelve knots of southwesterly breeze. It gave Captain Jacobs the opportunity to test her rigging; the suppleness of her masts and spars as well the opportunity to stretch out her new hempen shrouds so that each could be hardened down again properly. It also gave his two mates the opportunity to determine the caliber of crew they had working under them.

The men were driven hard and driven continually. Not only with the usual work-a-day routine, which in itself is a full-time occupation aboard any ship at sea, but so too with the stowage of all remaining loose items below decks and the fitting of chafing gear aloft so as to prevent the wearing of canvas against stay. And, most importantly, that one task from which no man or boy was exempt: that of learning the location of every running line, of which there numbered more than two hundred.

Each line had its own designated belaying pin or cleat and these had to be memorized, for it was of vital importance that any sailor be able to go directly to the correct line, even in the blind darkness of a moonless night, without mistaking it for any other. Casting off or hauling in on the wrong line altogether could quickly prove disastrous in any situation, and so from the very outset each man was bullied relentlessly into learning. At any given time, day or night, the captain or his chief mate might raise the speaking trumpet and call forth, "Double-reef tops'ls!" or, "Ready weather stuns'ls!" upon which all hands were required to go immediately to their stations and the last man to reach the rack rail or fife rail to take hold of his line would feel the chief mate's ready fist and God help the man who was holding onto the wrong line altogether, for then his knuckles, after encountering the business end of the chief mate's belaying pin, would be sore as hell for a good long week.

An even more extreme method of encouragement existed, one that was reserved especially for the dullest of wit amongst *Achilles'* crew. The long wooden bars, or handspikes, which were inserted into the pigeonholes of the capstans, served also as a most effective learning tool for those who persisted in failing to memorize their lines. One of these three-foot long by four-inch square bars of oak, when wielded by an irate Robert Biggs in the wake of any given command, could deliver remarkable results after only a single application.

Even the packet-rats, Nate was beginning to notice, appeared to expect no more or less from their chief mate. And perhaps, he was also beginning to suspect, from himself, too. Because it seemed that the raising of the belaying pin itself was to these men as much an element of their recognized vocabulary as was any spoken command. And whereas the chief mate would oftentimes feel obliged to follow through on his threats with one of the greener hands by connecting said pin solidly against either skull or shoulder, and this being dependent solely upon the quickness of the intended victim's reactions, he rarely needed to do so with these packet-rats. Indeed, Nate was beginning to suspect that if Biggs did actually strike one of these men without good and proper justification, the result would likely prove contrary, in that he would be promptly challenged and openly resisted for it, his ranking as chief mate notwithstanding.

All of which, to this increasingly bewildered second mate, was creating no end of doubts as to whether he himself was even up to the task in hand. It might, Nate supposed, require the dispensing a bloodied nose or two from himself before any semblance of control could be gained over these men. A prospect that, as an experienced hand who had been bullied himself enough times into proving his own toughness, he did not particularly dread but, as a generally fair-minded individual and a first-tripper second mate, felt that he could quite happily live without.

The daily routine itself was the very foundation of life aboard any ship at sea and it remained for the most part independent of either climate or latitude, as both were in a continual state of change throughout any voyage. Each day was carved into watches that were stood alternately by the Starbowlines and Larbowlines and were set as follows:

First watch: 8 p.m. to midnight
Middle watch: Midnight to 4 a.m.
Morning watch: 4 a.m. to 8 a.m.
Forenoon watch: 8 a.m. to noon
Afternoon watch: Noon to 4 p.m.

The California Run

First dog watch: 4 p.m. to 6 p.m.

Second dog watch: 6 p.m. to 8 p.m.

The ship's two bells, situated aft by the helm and forward above the windlass, signaled the passage of time; each full hour by a double-ring and with a solitary ring added at the half hour. Eight bells signified the changing of the watch and was also sounded after the second hour of the dog watch, which was divided into two shorter segments of four bells apiece so as to allow for a two-day rotation rather than a daily one. Only the more experienced seafarer, one who had spent time enough stood motionless by the helm or perched high aloft on lookout duty in the face of ice-laden blizzards or the squally temperaments of the higher latitudes during winter, could fully appreciate that wide gulf of difference between turning-to at midnight with only one watch being his to endure that night, or turning-to at four in the morning after only a few hours of fitful sleep and, with the galley fire being doused for the night, having to dress himself again in the sodden and oftentimes frozen clothing he had been wearing at midnight.

And so it was that, even on a ship of temperance as most clippers were these days, as it afforded a ten percent reduction in their insurance rates, a small measure of grog, or watered-down spirits, was the accepted allowance after most night watches. As too after reefing, or at any time at the captain's or chief mate's discretion, a small 'warmer' might be allotted the crew whenever it was considered deserving.

At five-thirty each morning, at the sounding of three bells, the duty watch gathered on the main deck to begin the morning wash-down while the cook and the steward unlocked the galley and rekindled the stove. The carpenter rigged the head pump to ship seawater directly onto deck for the wash-down and also pumped the daily ration of one gallon of fresh water for each man from the ship's five thousand gallon tank into the scuttlebutt on deck. Then he took soundings of all spaces below decks and the flywheel bilge pump near the mainmast was manned for the ten minutes or so that it took for the day's accumulated bilge water to be expelled overboard. The wash-down of the decks continued until seven bells, whereupon a breakfast of salt-pork or beef with hardtack flour biscuits and tea was had by the upcoming forenoon watch, who then took over at eight and the morning watch, after breakfasting, was stood down until noon. The forenoon watch then worked on various tasks, ready to be called away to tend sails or to relieve the helmsman or lookout, usually in 'tricks' lasting two hours. At seven bells the watch below was called up to lunch and the afternoons were spent with all hands working on deck until either sunset or 6 p.m., whichever came earliest.

Sundays afforded at least some break in this routine, with a day of lighter duties that did not involve working aloft except as needed to tend sails. After the usual morning wash-down and the tidying of lines, the morning's work was generally of a less demanding nature, though still under the strict rule of absolute silence as on any other day of the week. Shortly after lunch a prayer service and bible reading was held by the captain himself, who stood over his assembled crew and read from his own leather-bound volume, then the remainder of the afternoon was spent by the crew in airing out and mending their clothing and bedding up on deck, if weather permitted, or lounging below inside the forecastle and smoking and talking if it did not. There was also a welcome addition to the normal blandness of the galley's menu by way of a duff: a flour and saltwater pudding boiled inside a bag and, if it should also happen to contain plums or dried apples, then so much the better. It was a good, solid meal that clung firmly to the ribs and, as with any such trivial favors found at sea, these being so few and far between, it was looked forward to with such keen and boyish enthusiasm by even the toughest of salts as might understandably bemuse any landsman.

In addition to all this they were continually being trained, day and night, to steer and to reef, to brace yards and to set and hand each sail in its turn, so that when the time did come for a quick and ready response to any unexpected shift in the weather they could perform without hesitation those duties required of them. And throughout all this the chief mate was there to help drive them on, with belaying pin or handspike held at the ready for any signs of slackening, or even a glance in his direction that was not to his particular liking.

He was fast proving himself to be a 'bucko' mate: one who recognized no limits and would drive his crew relentlessly to keep the ship running. And already there were several men and boys who displayed the cuts and bruises to show for Biggs' impatience. The very sight of the chief mate's bright red jacket with its double ranking of brass buttons had already become as much a warning signal here aboard *Achilles* as would any likewise-dressed creature be in a tropical forest; one whose attention one instinctively sought to avoid, at all possible costs.

The third morning at sea proved beyond all remaining doubt, if indeed any doubt remained whatsoever, that Robert Biggs was not a mate to be dallied with.

At the sounding of seven bells, shortly after the morning watch had finished the wash-down and were stowing away their tools, and as the forenoon watch was emerging from the fore scuttle with jackets buttoned to their necks against the chill dawn, to gather themselves about the windlass to enjoy their breakfast of tea, salt-pork and hardtack, all hands were summoned aft to witness punishment.

It was true, as Harry Jenkins himself had so unwisely stated out loud, that flogging had been prohibited aboard American ships, since Congress had voted on it earlier that year. But, alike to any law pertaining to the sea, since man had first set himself adrift upon it, there also existed an unspoken understanding by those who dictated such laws that, what may very well work for the shoresider with his eight-to-six working day and his opportunity to return home every evening, did not necessarily hold true for those who found themselves bound together day and night out here on the wide and lonely ocean.

The added phrase, 'if without justifiable cause,' was one that was left entirely to the discretion of the captain. And, when it came to maintaining shipboard discipline, it was customary for the captain to freely pass on any and all such discretion to his chief mate.

The justifiable cause in this instance was the accosting of one of *Achilles'* passenger ladies by this common sailor. It was enough, apparently, to earn the man who called himself Harry Smith half a dozen strokes of the lash and all hands were summoned to the area immediately abaft the deckhouse, where the main deck's forty-foot width was unobstructed by either mast or hatchway, to witness the chief mate's justice being dispensed.

Harry Jenkins stood amongst his shipmates in a state of nervous anticipation. But this was nothing new to Harry; it was in fact the very same feeling as had beset him each and every time he had been obliged to wait outside the headmaster's study at Eton. Too many times to count, if truth be told, for young Harry had not exactly been a model pupil. And in turn old Headmaster Bartleby had not exactly been the most benevolent of headmasters, and his own intolerance for Harry's continual misbehavior had been inversely proportional to Harry's increased enjoyment of it. Thus for five long years it had remained something of a ritual between the two of them; an unspoken understanding, if you will, with Harry remaining intent on continuing his delinquency for the mere sake of proving himself unbreakable and in turn old headmaster Bartleby continuing to exercise his caning arm on a weekly basis for that very same reason.

The point being, that not only was Harry accustomed to this kind of thing, but he also prided himself that throughout that entire five years he had never once allowed the old bastard to see him suffer for it. Despite the raw, fiery agony that only someone who has themselves experienced a yard's length of bamboo cane striking their bared arse at close to the speed of sound six times in succession could fully appreciate, Harry had never once allowed even a solitary tear to emerge, let alone a single sound to escape his compressed lips and this, he had quickly learned, was the very trick to it. For by not allowing old Bartleby the satisfaction of witnessing the true effect his repeated canings were having, it seemed only to anger and frustrate the old bugger even more and thus, to Harry's logic, he had gained an absolute victory over the headmaster. Having a perpetually sore arse throughout most of his time at Eton was, in Harry's view, a relatively small price to pay for such overall satisfaction.

Now, surreptitiously glancing at *Achilles'* chief mate as he awaited his punishment, Harry saw that very same look there in Robert Biggs' eye as he had in old Bartleby's, and he inwardly steeled himself with this very same determination. For he was not about to show this tyrant any more than he had the former. Harry now prepared himself to adopt that method he had learned so long ago; to relax, breathe deeply and to focus the entirety of his mind solely upon one image and one image alone: the intoxicating vision of 'Pinky' Carter's eldest sister's tits.

It was customary aboard most ships for the boatswain's mate to be the one to deliver the lash. But with *Achilles'* crew being newcomers all there had not yet been time for Biggs to select a boatswain, let alone a boatswain's mate. Which meant that the honor now fell upon the only remaining person who was deemed even remotely qualified for the job, and that person was the second mate.

Nate Cooper was feeling quite nauseated as he stood by the main shrouds with the cat-o-nine-tail's wooden handle gripped in one hand. With the other he was absently combing through all nine separated strands, each one dipped in tar and with a knot at its end that lent weight to the tip and directed its force into small, hardened pellets. He was watching his chief mate closely, as too were each one of *Achilles'* crew.

Harry was detached from the group and drawn to the fore by Biggs himself. The Englishman's expression, even in the face of what was about to happen, was one of apparent indifference as he stood there gazing idly around him with a relaxed smile as if without a solitary care in the world. And this seemed to have the desired effect of immediately irritating the chief mate.

"All hands to witness punishment!" Biggs announced. This was not so much a statement as a command, which was made perfectly clear by a few taps of the chief mate's belaying pin against the sides of those heads that were not turned in his direction.

"Half a dozen strokes! Carry on, Mister Cooper!"

Nate began by removing Harry's shirt. Then he lifted both of Harry's arms and lashed each thumb tightly with spun yarn to the shrouds directly overhead. Biggs, watching closely and still seeing nothing beyond casual nonchalance from the man about to be punished, became all the more irritated by it.

"What are you waiting for?" he barked at his second mate.

Yet still Nate hesitated, causing his chief mate to frown even more darkly at him. He realized that he was rapidly losing favor with Biggs, if only for his inability to share in the man's appetite for such relentless hazing. Biggs clearly wanted a second mate who echoed his own sentiments to the letter but just as clearly was not getting one. But before Biggs was able to say anything more Nate stepped forward and readied himself, intent now on getting this distasteful business over and done with.

Standing with legs braced apart, he measured his distance carefully, aiming for the very center of Harry's pale back. The first stroke landed across Harry's spine in a hail of dull slaps and several welts immediately appeared. The second stroke raised small droplets of blood which began to trickle down and soak into the waistband of his trousers and the third, in addition to creating several more welts, also smeared and picked up the blood already there and by the fourth stroke it appeared that Harry's back was already beaten raw.

Uttering no sound whatsoever, inside Harry's head his own screams were deafening. Ye Gods, the agony of it! This was like no headmaster's caning he had ever experienced! But damned if he was going to show it and, with renewed fortitude, Harry bit down even harder and somehow managed to keep his lips pressed together.

Biggs was now keeping a sharper eye on *Achilles'* crew than he was on the man being punished. He was making sure that each and every one of them was watching, even the ship's carpenter and the aging sailmaker. None were exempt from witnessing the chief mate's punishment, except the duty helmsman and the ship's cook. And of course the captain himself, along with *Achilles'* passenger compliment, all of who, conveniently, were still breakfasting inside the trunk cabin.

All, that is, except one.

Sarah Doyle had been standing at the forward railing of the quarterdeck admiring the sunrise when she had first noticed the sailors beginning to gather aft on the main deck. And, with her curiosity aroused all the more by the sight of a strangely nonchalant-looking Harry Jenkins among them, she had remained behind when the other passengers had gone below at the sounding of the breakfast bell.

Now Sarah looked on in both astonishment and...well, to be honest she was not quite sure what this other feeling was, except that it was considerably disturbing and it was not going away, no matter how forcefully she tried to quell it. It was a feeling that she was wholly unaccustomed to, nor could she recall having ever felt it before as she stood there affixed to the spot and looking on as poor Harry had the flesh systematically flogged from his back and all, it would appear, on her account.

Then she suddenly realized what it was, and it gave her quite a start.

It was guilt.

From the main deck below came no sounds from either the man being flogged or from those who stood watching as the cat continued to hum through the air, following a slightly different arc each time, as Nate was trying his best to distribute his strokes widely and at the same time not appear too obvious about it. But by the fourth stroke Harry's back was already a mess of gore and, most sickeningly of all, a small flap of loose yellow skin now hung off it. But there were still two more strokes to go and the expression on the chief mate's face yielded no mercy whatsoever as he nodded stiffly for his second mate to continue. Nate did so, using the same wide swinging arc and not daring to slacken his effort, much as he wanted to. The knots continued to rain across Harry's back and the blood continued to fly and now it festooned several of those men who stood in the front rank; their faces and shirts now bespeckled as from a red paintbrush shaken out to windward.

Yet throughout all this Harry had somehow managed to remain silent and, apart from the rhythmic tapping of the reef-points against the taut canvas high aloft and the rasping of the second mate's breath as he worked the lash, all else was quiet too.

For poor Sarah, who continued looking on from the quarterdeck, her own sensibilities, she was quite certain, were causing her as much agony as the lash was Harry. For now another, more powerful emotion was rising within her and one that made guilt itself seem quite insignificant in comparison. It took her a few moments to recognize exactly what it was, because this too was a sentiment that until now had remained all but foreign to her.

Suddenly, and with an irritable huff, Sarah turned away, now seeking to return below and to a breakfast that she no longer had any appetite for.

I do not believe I care very much for this 'compassion' thing, she decided, there and then. Not one little bit.

Now semi-conscious and burbling incoherently, Harry was unceremoniously cut loose and carried forward, but not before the final insult of a bucket of cleansing seawater which finally elicited a solitary groan. From the ranks of the assembled crew now arose a muttering, much of it coming from the packet-rats, but this was promptly silenced by the raising of the chief mate's belaying pin. Yet the atmosphere on deck had now thickened considerably, and the mutterings continued, now with more indignation than fear being evident as each man envisioned himself being equally at Biggs' mercy, for there was no justifiable cause in their minds for any of this.

When finally the chief mate dismissed his assembled crew he instructed one of his able hands, Frederick Weeks, to oversee the mopping of the nearby deck. He then turned to Nate Cooper.

"How's your stomach, mister? Not to your taste, eh? Well, you'd better start getting used to it!"

"He was right, you know," responded Nate, now determined to have his say. "Indiscriminate flogging has been outlawed. Why, even the lady herself said that it was nothing but a misunderstanding."

It was Frederick Weeks who piped up readily at this, but only after making certain that the rest of his crew-mates were out of earshot.

"I'd say he got off pretty lightly, did he not, Mister Mate? A full dozen would have been more deserving."

Biggs glanced at Weeks and nodded, in much the same way as one might to any dutiful underling. Then to Nate he said,

"At least somebody here seems to understand the importance of discipline. Perhaps also the *proper* duties of a second mate."

Weeks, shooting a malicious grin in Nate's direction, turned away to make a good show of supervising the green hands in mopping the deck as Robert Biggs turned back to his second mate. He suddenly grabbed Nate's arm roughly and pulled him aside.

"And if you *ever* go easy on the lash again," he added with a venomous hiss, "I'll see your cowardly spine too, by God, and you'll be back down in the fo'c'sle with the rest of 'em!"

Chapter Seven
The Bully of the Forecastle

As within the forecastle space aboard any ship at sea, wherein the common sailor finds himself closely confined day and night alongside his peers, without respite nor any opportunity to exercise his own qualities as an individual, a pecking order will invariably become established by means that are determined not so much by a person's own ranking and experience as by one's sheer obstinacy in projecting his own baser qualities to his fellows. As with any despotic system that arises from an assemblage of the generally unlearned, it is always the toughest dog that ends up ruling the pack.

William Scragg, ordinary seaman, was just such a dog. And, having already been commonly acknowledged as bully of *Achilles'* forecastle space, within this territory, as well as up on deck beyond the immediate view of the captain and his mates, his word was as good as law. It did promote his cause in no small way, of course, that he had all nine of his packet-rat chums to reinforce his position, yet even without their help he would have gained the rank of bully anyway, only it might have taken a little more time and a few extra bashings to achieve this. Another week, perhaps; a fortnight at most.

Scragg was of that troublesome breed of rough and ready Londoner; born against his will into abject poverty and hauled kicking and screaming through a childhood of relentless torment and misery, and as a result he was as hard as they came. So hard, indeed, that even his threats did not need to be squandered on the trivial, as he had nothing left to prove to himself on that score. Nor did he have much left to fear from any man's fist, having survived so many a childhood beating himself that he had gained all the confidence he would ever need to reassure himself that even the worst face-drubbing or nose-bashing was a moderately tolerable event. Scragg was tough, and he knew it. And this, combined with an innate craftiness and a sharpness of wit that even the deprivation of any semblance of an education had thus far been unable to dull, lent him all the prospects of being a particularly dangerous individual.

It was presently the second dog watch and, with the weather outside remaining pretty foul, the majority of *Achilles'* crew were sheltering here inside the forecastle. One of these, a first-tripper of eighteen years of age named Jerome Stiles, was a lad whose silver-spooned and delicate ways had already induced the hazing of the packet-rats into affording him the title 'Jimmy Ducks', whose task it was to daily muck out the pigpens and chicken coops inside the topgallant forecastle. Jerome was presently kneeling by his sea chest searching in vain for the shirt he had purchased only a week ago from Brooks Brothers. He could not find it and, as he wearily rose to look further, his eyes alighted on William Scragg's own soiled jersey, beneath which the collar of said shirt was now protruding. Jerome, in his youthful naivety, immediately made the mistake of stepping up to where Scragg sat atop his upper bunk and challenging him.

"Why, that's mine!" Jerome declared, all affront and for the moment not caring. But it was a very brief moment indeed and it ended rather abruptly with Scragg's arm suddenly appearing out of nowhere and wrapping itself tightly around the youngster's neck in a chokehold that cut off his air supply altogether.

"Ain't nothin' here yourn, young feller-me-lad," Scragg reminded him, in all good reason, at the same time rapping the knuckles of his other hand playfully atop Jerome's head as though it were a bongo, "exceptin' wot I apportions yer." Then, with a deft twist and a savage kick he sent the boy hurtling headlong into the opposite tier of bunks.

"Now, go an' fetch the grub."

Indeed, and in all fairness to these packet-rats, this thin, greasy-complexioned example of American youth, with his acne-erupted features and his infuriatingly idle and daydreaming manner, might have provoked challenge enough for even the most saintliest of men to not cast some form of ridicule at. He had, furthermore, been crimped by his very own father, a wealthy New York insurance underwriter, under some vague pretense of it being beneficial to the boy's health, as well as making a more rounded fellow of him. But even the most gullible of onlookers might have been tempted to declare poppycock to that. The truth of it was evident: that young Jerome was just another blue-blooded castoff sent away to sea, dispatched beyond sight and mind for his being an ongoing embarrassment to those who had born him and a veritable boil on the backside of his own family's elevated social status.

Now in a full-blown huff and making a show of nursing his head, Jerome set off on his task, of collecting the mess kid, the wooden tub containing the crew's salt-pork and beef rations, more commonly referred to as salt-junk, from the galley space and bringing it to the forecastle.

William Scragg, now sporting a happy grin, relaxed into his bunk and gazed idly about the forecastle space as if Lord of all he surveyed, until his roving eye finally stranded itself upon Harry Jenkins who was laying in a lower bunk nearby. Harry had done well thus far to avoid any excessive hazing beyond the norm for any first-tripper. Unlike Jerome Stiles, Harry had not in fact been born into a life of 'uppercrustyness', as Scragg would have termed it. He was, in fact, fairly lowborn by comparison, being the son of a factory owner and as a result had associated with as many common types throughout his childhood as he had so-called 'genteel' ones later in life. He was thus able to pick and choose freely which role to play at any given time and consequently adopt whichever style of accent best suited the occasion at hand. It was, in fact, one of those things in particular that Harry prided himself on being especially good at.

Right now, however, Harry was feeling downright wretched as he lay prone on his stomach with his chest wrapped tightly in strips of old sailcloth. Even the slightest movement made his entire back feel as if molten pitch were being poured over it. He was also bewailing his misfortune at being stuck in both the chief mate's as well as William Scragg's Larbowline watch, because he was still unsure, despite his recent flogging, as to whom he ought to be more wary of. He also remained uncertain as to who exactly was leading this watch, for seldom was any order given by the chief mate, he had noticed, that was not subject to the silent verification of Scragg himself, by way of a sly wink or a nod just as soon as the mate's back was turned.

Thus he was immediately put on his guard when Scragg

unexpectedly and for the very first time spoke directly to him.

"How're you faring, shipmate?"

This rather surprised Harry, as Scragg's tone actually sounded benevolent.

"I've 'ad worse," quipped Harry, adopting his best London accent. "Tickled a bit, but. Had ter hold back the giggles."

Scragg laughed aloud at this and by doing so seemed to signify his approval and thus give license for his packet-rat chums to talk to Harry also. It was Scragg's fellow Londoner, Jacko Jackson, who chimed in first.

"Now wot kind o' name is 'Arry Smith, anyways? Sounds like a proper dodgy one to me."

"Aye," responded the chanteyman, Tyrone Pete. "Dat's the truth. On the lamb, are we, *Mister* Smith?"

"Wouldn't surprise me," added Taffy Owens in his lilting Welsh accent. "Why, not even one day at sea, look you, and he's already trying to get 'is end away with one o' them passenger ladies. Can't keep it in yer trousers, that's your problem, boyo."

"Now, now." Scragg held a large palm aloft to quiet his chums down. "Man has a right to keep 'is business to 'imself. All wot matters is that 'e knows how to take 'is punishment like a man. An' I don't give a fig wot else he done, that alone gets my respect."

There were grunts of acknowledgement from several of the packet-rats to this statement and Scragg added,

"Aye, we've all had our share o' the lash, at some time or 'nother, ain't we, boys? An' you appear to know the very trick on it, Harry me lad. Don't ever let them fuckers know what yer thinkin'. Ain't that right boys?"

Amidst the ensuing mumbles of agreement Harry could

not help but smile to himself, despite his ongoing agony. For it appeared that he had inadvertently raised his status considerably in the eyes of these packet-rats. And, despite all the eloquence that his own extensive education had placed at Harry's disposal, he realized also that he could not have worded Scragg's statement any better himself.

Achilles' deckhouse measured thirty-three feet by fifteen and was located directly amidships on the main deck between the foremast and the main cargo hatch, with a stretch of open deck between it and the ship's outer bulwarks of two fathoms to either side. Atop its flat roof, between the iron smoke stack from the galley's coal stove and the long skylight that opened onto several of the compartments within, were stowed the captain's gig and the studdingsail booms. The deckhouse enjoyed a full seven feet of headroom within and in the fore part were situated, athwartships and with a door to either side, the galley, the sailmaker's locker and the carpenter's shop, all of which were locked up securely every night. In the house's aft section, accessed by a single doorway from the main deck that led into a narrow corridor within, were located several independent spaces. These included the crew's pantry, wherein nightly snackings of various leftovers were put out for the night watches, and the cook's storage locker immediately adjacent to it which was kept locked even tighter than the galley space itself. Also located aft were five cabins, four of which measured only a fathom square and which housed two bunks apiece, one stacked close atop the other. The carpenter, sailmaker and cook enjoyed the use of one of these cabins each. The larger compartment took up most of the aft starboard section of the deckhouse and it contained six bunks, again stacked two high with very little space between. This was the boy's cabin, which berthed *Achilles'* two genuine boys, aged twelve and fifteen respectively.

Jerome Stiles, making his way carefully aft against the erratic movements of the deck underfoot, finally arrived at the galley's leeward doorway without incident and, on poking his head into the space, was greeted immediately by a blood-curdling scream from within; one that raised every hackle on his neck and caused him to promptly withdraw it again. When finally he summoned the courage to peer into the space again he saw, standing inside the galley, two of the Swedes from the Starbowline watch, as well as the grouchy cook and the sour-faced carpenter, only on this occasion both men were grinning broadly and with genuine, uncharacteristic merriment. The two Swedes, contrarily, were frowning and clutching their hands tightly under their armpits and, with much affronted hubbub and offensive-sounding foreign gibberish, they pushed rudely past Jerome and back out onto deck, whereby one of the Swedes, wearing a particularly pallid and gray aspect, hove-to promptly at the bulwark and began retching voluminously, much to the ongoing amusement of both cook and carpenter who looked on happily from the galley's doorway.

Had poor Jerome but one inkling as to what this was all about he would never have squandered a single moment in requesting of the cook the mess kid, which had already been loaded with meat and now sat on the galley's counter ready to be collected. Instead, he would have simply grabbed it and run like hell. But when the cook motioned for him to step inside his galley and requested in the most benevolent of fashions to have a look-see at poor Jerome's blistered, rope-burned hands, he complied with all the naive expectation that a kindly dose of sympathy, if not the beneficial application of some home-brewed balm, was soon to be coming his way.

And, in a manner of speaking, if one were to discount the sympathy aspect and perhaps also take the beneficial part with a hefty pinch of salt, this was indeed the case. With the most disarming of collective smiles, both the cook and carpenter promptly took ahold of one of Jerome's wrists apiece and, with their grips suddenly becoming vice-like as it finally dawned upon the youngster what they were about to do, they plunged his raw blistered hands, which until now had been sore yet tolerable, or at least for as long as nobody expected him to go pulling too hard on any ropes or anything, into the saucepan of hot beef pickle standing atop the stove and Jerome's agonized screams, which consequently resounded throughout the entire ship, brought howls of merriment from both cook and carpenter alike as they held his hands up to his wrists in the pickle until finally the pain, along with the screaming, had subsided.

Then, with their cheerful reassurances that it was the chief mate's orders and that it was, tried and proven, the best thing by far to heal such ailments, they let him go and the cook, apparently deeming this a fair enough price to pay for such rich amusement, tossed Jerome a couple of old rags of cloth to wrap up his pickle-burned hands.

With head reeling and his hands still afire, Jerome cursed all the way back to the fore scuttle. It was difficult enough to maintain his balance against the rolling deck underfoot with the heavy mess kid held in one bandaged hand and a flask of piping-hot tea in the other, but the very notion of spilling anything and thus depriving the men below of their dinner was incentive enough for him to take particularly good care. When finally he did make it down the scuttle's ladder he found his shipmates waiting impatiently for their grub.

William Scragg, still perched atop his bunk, received the

kid with a grunt and he dismissed Jerome with a casual wave of his hand. Rather than wait around to collect his share, Jerome instead chose to make his escape and he promptly retreated back up to deck, perchance for a moment's peace and to bewail his fate once again at having to endure possibly another six months of this.

Scragg and his gang set about selecting for themselves the most prime cuts and as they did so Harry Jenkins could make out through the dimness of lantern light that the tips of each of these men's knives had already been re-sharpened into points.

"Is not right!" came a voice from somewhere in the far corner. It was the Portuguese fisherman, Bacas. "Able hands is ones should get first draw of kid!"

Scragg chuckled with amusement as he continued picking through the contents of the kid, which now sat in his lap.

"Bless 'is foreign ignorance," he stated, kindly, to his fellows. Then, to Bacas, he called out, "Able is as able does, ol' chap! An' if yer able enough to come over here an' fetch it for yerself, then bully for you, I say!"

Bacas scowled and spat forth something in his own language that was almost certainly not very polite.

William Scragg, now sporting a broad grin, was sitting with the kid all but forgotten between his knees and was staring thoughtfully into the farthest corner of the forecastle. He appeared to be recalling some past pleasantry or other and this was soon made evident as he turned his head and called,

"'Ere, Spuds! 'Member ol' cock-billed Lil? The melancholy widder from Southport?"

From the darkest reaches of the forecastle space came a shuffling noise and the other Irish packet-rat, a short and solidly framed man in his mid-twenties with a prematurely ebbing hairline, stood upright and grinned. He was holding a thick woolen sweater, one drawn from the sea chest next to his feet, which by all rights belonged to one of the several Swedes who were sitting around looking on in reproachful silence, and he was holding it up against his chest to measure its size.

"Jaysus! Loike Oi'm after fergettin' dat miserable slapper! Wot of it?"

Scragg jerked his head in the direction of the Portuguese fisherman, who now sat with the most indignant expression bent to his dark features, still glaring daggers at Scragg and his company.

"Unnat'ral likeness, ain't it?"

Spuds turned to look at the morose Bacas and he snorted loudly.

"Feck me! It's herself, so it is! Now dat's uncanny!"

Spuds tossed the jumper aside with an expression of disgust, it being too large by far, and he scowled dangerously at the nearest Swede as if this were entirely his fault.

"Come'n now Scraggsy! Hows about summit Oi can actually swaller this toime?"

Scragg cheerfully obliged by tossing his chum a hefty chunk of meat and Spuds set to with relish, caring naught further for either Bacas, the nearby Swedes or their oversized clothing.

Scragg selected a piece of salt-junk for each of his fellows in turn, then surprised Harry by tossing a piece to him also, along with a wink and a grin. Then finally the kid was passed on to the able hands, which included Bacas as well as the three others, Frederick Weeks, Silas Rigsby and George Evans, none of whom spoke: for, unlike Bacas, they each one realized the futility of even attempting to oppose such numbers as these packet-rats enjoyed.

When finally the kid arrived in the hands of the Swedes and the remaining inexperienced men there was little remaining save a few gristly remnants and a couple of splintered bones. Scragg, chewing happily on his lion's share, lapsed into a reflective silence for a while, gazing idly out from his bunk in a state of regal contentment.

"One thing wot puzzles me, but," he announced finally, his gaze now settled again on Harry Jenkins. "Is that when you first come on board, Harry," and his features suddenly narrowed into a suspicious aspect, "you was talkin' like you was a gentleman. All upppity, wiv all them what-hos an' jolly-goods an' suchlike."

Several grunts from his fellow packet-rats resounded through the forecastle at this announcement and the largest amongst them, Jimmy the Bruiser, hauled his not insubstantial bulk out of its nearby bunk and now stood there, glaring down at Harry and alternately glancing to Scragg as if waiting for some manner of clarification. Scragg, still peering closely down at Harry, was now pointing his knife, from which the remnants of a tiny piece of pork still dangled from its end, directly at him.

"But now," he declared, "you're talkin' jus' like you was one of us. A common sort, I meantersay."

Bloody hell, Harry was thinking. As if I don't already have enough on my plate.

But to Harry's relief Scragg, with mouth still full and knife still held aloft, motioned for his chums, who were now beginning to mutter amongst themselves as they eyed Harry with newfound suspicion, to settle down, then added,

"I seen you, Harry. Aye, that's right. I seen you when you was talking with that passenger lady. Or arguing with her, more like. And it 'peared to me as you was both talking like you was equals. Like you both belonged ter the same social class, as it were."

"So wot is he then? A toff?" inquired Jimmy the Bruiser, who had steadily worked his way even closer and whose huge muscular frame now loomed threateningly over Harry. Jimmy's brow was now creased. Indeed, the entirety of Jimmy's huge shaven head was now creased.

"Steady on, Jimmy! Hold yer horses!" warned Scragg. Then, to Harry,

"Yer see, Harry, I 'appen to be one o' them people what enjoys a good mystery. An' a good mystery is wot I'm seeing here. Now, after pondering the issue some, here's my surmise."

Scragg finally swallowed and placed the empty mess kid aside. He leaned forward to peer closely down at Harry, his knife still pointed in that direction.

"See, in *my* experience, the only time, an' I mean the *only* time, I ever seen two people from different social classes communicatin' that way wiv each other is when they're involved in some manner o' romantic fling."

Harry could not prevent himself from snorting derisively at this and Scragg, with a nod and a brief wag of his knife, appeared to agree.

"Aye, that was a long shot, I shall admit. 'Cos from wot I seen I wouldn't say there's too much love lost between the two of yers. In fact, from wot I seen I would guess, and it's only a guess, mind, that it was the lady herself wot had you crimped! Only she wasn't expectin' you to end up here on the same ship with her, was she?"

Harry, realizing that he had seriously underestimated this man's cleverness, could not think of any ready response to this whatsoever.

"Aye, and it's the truth, ain't it Harry? Cos I can see it written all over yer face!"

Scragg suddenly laughed out loud and with genuine merriment.

"Oh, that's bloody priceless! Ain't it boys?"

They all appeared to agree and a chorus of laughter and taunts erupted from the surrounding packet-rats. All, that is, apart from one.

"So... he *is* a bloody toff?" deduced Jimmy, his fists now clenched tightly and ready to do some proper damage. But once again Scragg, with hand raised, stalled his chum.

"Now, see, that there is the very question wot we needs ter ponder," he declared. "But at the same time there ain't no simple answer on it."

"Wot you talkin' about Scraggsy?" Jimmy's entire head was now furrowed like a plowed field ready for sowing. Indeed, it appeared to be causing him some pain, which in turn was making him even more peevish. "Let's jus' do 'im now and have done!"

"I'm talking," said Scragg, "about one of only two possibilities here. Either Harry here is, in actual fact, a gentleman wot's down on his luck, or..." Scragg paused for effect, enjoying himself now. "Or that there *lady*," he pointed his knife aft, "is naught but a common wench wiv airs above her station."

Scragg was watching Harry closely now, gauging his expression.

"So, what's the answer on it, Harry?" Scragg glanced towards Jimmy who remained looming threateningly, in his increasingly uncertain and irritated state, over Harry's bunk. "Take yer time. Think on it. Not too long, mind, 'cos Jimmy here's not exactly famous for 'is patience."

Harry sighed, realizing that the only thing he had left to rely on here was the truth. Or at least his version of it.

"You're right," he said. "She ain't no lady. But she puts on a bloody good show."

"Is that so?"

"Talk to 'er yerself if you don't believe me." Harry sincerely hoped that this dare would go unchallenged. But no such luck.

"Well now, I reckon I might just do that, Harry." Scragg reclined on his bunk, eyeing Harry now with renewed interest.

"I reckon I might. Then we'll see wot's really wot, won't we?"

Throughout this discourse Gideon had remained silent and watchful. He was keeping himself concealed in the darker shadows of the forecastle, laying atop his own bunk and looking on with a sense of growing contempt for *Achilles'* crew. It had been a while since he had berthed inside any ship's forecastle, though not so long to have forgotten the ways of the lower decks. And, if to judge by what he had so far witnessed, he was indeed aboard a ship of fools.

He did not belong here. He was *Sapphire's* second mate, and had been for more than a year now, since her launching. He was proud of this fact, and it still grated on his pride considerably that he had been obliged to sign himself onto *Achilles* as a common hand, and under an assumed name, with the sole purpose of laying low and at the same time keeping a close and watchful eye on this rabble.

Achilles had little prospect, he realized this now, of beating *Sapphire* into Frisco. Not with this green and undisciplined mob. Her chief mate was the only man on board with any balls, and perhaps therefore the only man Gideon had to watch out for, and take care of, if necessary. Why, even her second mate was a bumbling newcomer to the task and it positively angered Gideon to watch Nate Copper go about his duties, for just about everything the man did was wrong. He was too soft; too considerate of others' sensibilities and altogether not of the mettle that was required to handle a crew such as this one. It was ironic that Nate Cooper would have been better suited aboard *Sapphire*, with her experienced and well-drilled crew whereas, by the same token, Gideon himself would have found himself much more at home here aboard *Achilles'* as second mate, where perchance he might enjoy sharing in Robert Biggs' penchant for cracking skulls, which is what this rabble was so sorely in need of.

But this was all irrelevant, because Gideon was here on Old Man Thaddeus' account, not his own and therefore he needed to contain his patience, sorely tested though it was already becoming. He was here as a safeguard; to ensure that *Achilles* did not, by some freak intervention of chance, actually achieve a good enough run to beat *Sapphire*. To Gideon's mind this already seemed most unlikely, but it was the very least he could do. For he was beholden to Thaddeus Oglesby in more ways than he could count and there was very little, if anything at all, that he would not do for him.

Even if that did mean sending *Achilles* to the bottom of the ocean rather than allowing her to overhaul *Sapphire*.

Chapter Eight
Breaking Her In

On the eighth day out from New York, now having crossed the thirtieth parallel and being well east of Bermuda, *Achilles* began to experience the first shifting of the wind and a steady rising of the barometer which signaled her approach to the Horse Latitudes and the northeast Trade Winds that lay beyond.

It was not entirely unexpected for the Trades to extend this far north, particularly in the early fall, and they were welcomed heartily by Captain Jacobs who was determined to put *Achilles* further to the test in some heavier airs and perhaps with a little hauling to weather for good measure. So far she had been enjoying a steady breeze from her quarter and still he had found no reason to even consider taking in her skysails, except for the practice.

The transition lasted two nights and a day, throughout which Captain Jacobs himself remained on the quarterdeck and his niece, Emma, spent much of it alongside him, seeming to match her uncle's keen interest in examining the various attributes of their ship. They stood together by the weather taffrail, fully exposed to wind and spray but appearing so accustomed to it that neither seemed to even notice. They occasionally conferred with one another, to share an observation, but otherwise remained for the most part silent and watchful as *Achilles* pressed on southwards as best she could, sometimes steering full and large on a quartering wind, other times straining against a taut bowline as the winds began to shift and haul now in an erratic confusion of alternating lulls and squalls. All hands also remained on deck throughout this period, to tend braces and to lay aloft to reef or to set royals and skysails, as many as half a dozen times each watch, for now every slight variation in the wind was viewed by Captain Jacobs as a test, of either his ship or his crew and more oftentimes of both.

This was also the first opportunity to practice maneuvering *Achilles* onto the opposing tack, a procedure that required every man to attend his appointed station, and to this end a 'Tacking and Wearing Bill' was drawn up by the chief mate and posted inside the forecastle space and by the aft doorway of the deckhouse. During such maneuvering it was customary for the chief mate to stand on the foredeck to tend the foremast, the second mate to oversee the mainmast and the captain himself, being already on the quarterdeck, the mizzen. The cook and steward worked the mainsail sheets while the carpenter, with one man to assist him, sweated down the main tack line. The remainder of the crew was divided between the yard braces, with the stronger ones hauling on the heavier lower yards while those of slighter frame, in particular the boys, dealt with the higher royals and skysails.

During these maneuvers a timely response to each command was critical. To have *Achilles* miss stays and get caught head to wind with an entire mast of square sails blown aback could not only prove disastrous but also provided a great deal more work for all involved. Inducement to learn came not only by way of the chief mate's belaying pin but so too through the discovery that, if one hesitated only a moment too long before bracing this yard up or hauling that jib sheet down, the wind would fill the sail so rapidly as *Achilles* turned that it could make such a task near to impossible without the help of several additional men. Each man was assigned his own designated station and so there was little need for any individual to properly understand all the theoretical principals involved, nor the mechanics of this sail or that; all he needed to know was when to haul in on and when to let go any particular line upon any given command, and even the dullest of wit amongst them eventually had it squared away by the time the second night descended upon them.

When finally the wind did settle in from the northeast and continued to gain in strength, all sails were set again and *Achilles* was steered 'by and large' on a course of south-southeast, one that would afford her the best aspect on a broad larboard reach and would, at Emma Jacob's insistence, place her at the equator between those most favored longitudes of thirty and thirty-five degrees west.

Up on the foredeck *Achilles'* crew loitered over their lunch and looked idly on in combined amusement and growing interest as their steward, Pepin, made preparations to separate tonight's dinner from its more preferred habitat.

With his best Temple Toggle harpoon held at the ready, its cruel double-barb honed to a razor sharpness, Pepin carefully positioned himself astride the starboard jib boom guy with his lean, muscular frame hanging half in and half out of the bow netting that was rigged to it. Whereas any other man might content himself with sitting astride the jib boom farther forward and trolling a line with a rag-baited hook close under the ship's cutwater, Pepin, being a whaleman and a harpooner besides, naturally considered this his preferred tool of trade.

Now, as he sighted along its shaft down towards *Achilles'* churning bow wake directly beneath, he sought to single out his quarry from among the dozen and more porpoises that darted and weaved about below.

With what appeared to be little more than a brief tensing of his arm and a flicking of his wrist, the harpoon magically relocated itself with a blur unseen by any keenly-watching eye into one of the smaller of the animals below and with such force that fully a quarter of its length penetrated, all the way up to its wooden haft. Pepin immediately began hauling back in on the line that was attached to the harpoon, the other end looped around his own wrist, and he began retrieving the writhing porpoise, which measured, to the astonishment of many an onlooker, almost four feet in length and must surely weigh upwards of a hundred pounds. With his feet braced firmly against the rope netting and his arms draped over the jib boom guy, Pepin steadily hauled in on both porpoise and harpoon as if he were reefing canvas aloft and, as the shaft reached his hands, he gave it an almighty heave and cast both harpoon and skewered animal safely into the netting alongside him.

By now most of the crew had gathered themselves on the foredeck and were vocalizing their most ardent admiration for this unexpectedly impressive feat and calling loudly for an encore performance, to which Pepin, his erstwhile stoic countenance now faltering into something approaching a smile, readily obliged. Detaching the harpoon from the porpoise, which caused it to promptly cease its gulping and writing, he positioned himself again above the cutwater with harpoon held at the ready as before.

This time a loud cheer went up as another small porpoise was skewered and the commotion drew the chief mate, Robert Biggs to the foredeck, where he strode immediately forward to stand between the knight-heads. Yet, rather than silence his crew as he might have done on any other occasion for creating such an unholy ruckus, he too was drawn into the spirit of it, even so far as to lend a shout of his own in encouragement, particularly when this second catch, on slipping back down the length of the harpoon, began to weigh alarmingly against the barbs which sliced deeply into its flesh just as Pepin was heaving it inboard. He landed it safely, however, and to the delight of all, before deciding to call it a day.

Pepin clambered back up onto the foredeck, staggering under the weight of each of his catches and with such evident pride that he might have just returned from the slaying of a full-grown sperm whale. With head held proudly aloft he set aside the largest of the pair for the aft cabin, then hauled the smaller one, that was to be shared amongst *Achilles'* crew, to the galley space where he unceremoniously tossed it to the deck. This was regarded with some skepticism by the cook who, in his discomfort and with the eyes of his shipmates now upon him, could do little other than force a weak smile and get on with the business of seeking a volunteer, hopefully one who would not demand too much of his dwindling whiskey supplies in payment, to gut and to clean it for him.

Now with studdingsails rigged to their extended booms on both foremast and mainmast and with her yards audibly groaning with the added strain, *Achilles* bore away under fifteen knots of a rising northeasterly breeze. Her canvas drew taut as the wind quickly increased to almost twenty knots and her untested sheets and braces were stretched even farther, to the point of having to be hardened down again. Both Captain Jacobs and his niece, bone-weary and red-eyed but affixed to the spot near the weather taffrail, remained together on the quarterdeck as night fell again, each keeping one eye aloft and one on the nearby helmsman, who was beginning to struggle now with a following sea that was driving hard against her rudder and surging upwards precipitously beneath her stern with the imminent threat of breaking over her quarterdeck. Yet with her rounded champagne-glass stern there was none of that heavy pounding associated with a more hollow-shaped counter and she rode it well, even at this increased speed which caused her bows to raise slightly and her stern to drop even lower and, whereas a lesser ship might have been roughly shaken and begin to take water over her quarterdeck, *Achilles* merely nudged each rising crest harmlessly aside with every downward plunge of her stern.

With the wind freshening beyond even the normal strength of the Trades, Captain Jacobs finally allowed the studdingsails to be brought in, as they were not made for such abuse and their lower booms were starting to dip perilously close to the wave crests on the weather roll. But all remaining canvas was kept sheeted home and finally it fell to the officer of the watch to remind his captain, who held command of the deck for as long as he stood upon it, of the perils that might result from this. It was Nate Cooper who first approached, doffing his cap respectfully to Emma as he stood aslant on the quarterdeck to maintain his balance against its steep incline. He pointed aloft, to where a solitary shaft of moonlight had pierced the overcast sky and now illuminated the entire spread of canvas above.

"Skysails are looking seriously strained, captain!"

"They'll hold, Mister Cooper!" boomed the response above the rising weather. "Leave 'em as they are!"

Two bells later it was the change of the watch and Robert Biggs, with only a cursory glance aloft, likewise approached the weather quarterdeck.

"Those skys'ls are getting mightily pressed, cap'n!"

"Leave 'em be, Mister Biggs!"

Another five knots of wind came on with the dawn and still Captain Jacobs kept all skysails and royals sheeted home, even as their tortured leeches could now be seen in the growing twilight to shiver and strain forcefully against their bolt ropes and the topgallant poles, taking the full combined force of all three upper sails, began to bend alarmingly. Until at last, with a sudden lurching of the deck underfoot and with the sound of splintering woodwork and tearing canvas from high aloft, the entire main royal and skysail hamper, consisting of a broken topgallant mast and now several pieces of tattered sail and bolt rope, collapsed into a loose, tangled heap atop the main topgallant yard and topmast stay.

Captain Jacobs, having watched all this closely from the quarterdeck, turned aft and gripped the taffrail as he leaned into the quartering wind, facing squarely into it so as to accurately gauge its relative strength and he nodded, satisfied now with the limitations of his ship.

"All hands ahoy, Mister Biggs!" he finally announced. "Hand all skies and royals! Let's tidy up that mess, quick as can be!"

Then, with his niece trailing closely in his wake, *Achilles'* captain finally headed below to his stateroom, to treat himself to a couple of hours of much-needed rest.

In the meantime *Sapphire*, with the northeast Trades now filling her lower canvas and with little cause on Captain Jonas Blunt's part to spend any more than the occasional spell pacing her weather quarterdeck, and this for appearance's sake only, was cracking on southwards at an impressive rate under the direction of her chief mate, Fergis.

With her well-drilled and experienced crew she was making easy work of it. Having already successfully completed one return voyage to Frisco, even *Sapphire's* boys knew her limitations when it came to wind against canvas, and it was a rare occurrence indeed upon which the chief mate's whistle would even reach his lips before the majority of *Sapphire's* crew stood ready beneath her ratlines or up on her foredeck awaiting the signal. This was proving rather frustrating for Snapper, the terrier, who had yet to enjoy his taste of human blood this trip, but in this he remained alone in his disappointment.

Thomas Oglesby was standing by the forward railing of *Sapphire's* quarterdeck alongside Fergis and they were discussing one of their passengers: the mysterious Irish gentleman who had boarded *Sapphire* at the last moment back in New York. Neither of them had yet managed to glean much information from this man, who remained politely formal yet doggedly tight-lipped when it came to anything pertaining to his own background. All they did know was that he was steadfastly intent upon reaching Frisco before *Achilles* did. Which, naturally, lay the field wide open for any and all speculation and it was becoming something of a ritual between Thomas and *Sapphire's* chief mate to exchange theories on a daily basis as to what this passenger's true story might be. Thomas' money lay on his suspicion that the Irishman was on the run from the law, while Fergis, having a sharper eye for the ways of his fellow man, was more inclined toward the contrary, in that the man appeared to be running *towards* something rather than away from it. As if he were chasing something. Or someone.

But sadly their conversation on this day was rudely interrupted by the sudden appearance of *Sapphire's* captain on the quarterdeck directly behind them. With the wind coming from abaft they both caught the whiff of whisky on the captain's breath as Blunt exclaimed, loudly,

"All is well, I see, Mister Fergis! Any sign of *Achilles* this morning?"

As his captain raised his spyglass to squint ahead at the distant horizon, and rather futilely since high aloft there was a lookout posted for just this purpose and who could also see at least four times the distance, Fergis allowed himself a rare smile and he glanced at Thomas Oglesby before replying,

"I fancy that'd be the wrong direction to be looking for *Achilles*, cap'n. Mayhap if you pointed that thing astern you might yet catch sight of her main truck before it disappears."

Jonas Blunt lowered his spyglass and frowned.

"A little early to start counting chickens, Mister Fergis."

His chief mate smirked at Thomas Oglesby and added,

"Why, with Gideon aboard her, I doubt she'll even reach Frisco, cap'n. Not in a month of Sundays!"

Both men then returned to their conversation and Blunt, being in no ways encouraged by the suddenly alarming notion of these two actually becoming the best of chums, announced,

"Nor shall we at this rate, mister! We must crack on! Weather stuns'ls, if you please!"

This caught his chief mate entirely off guard, as well as *Sapphire's* crew. Because now their captain was in the mood for some sport and, with the shrill tone of the boatswain's whistle, his unprepared crew was roused along with the ever-hungry Snapper who, anxiously waiting below for the command to begin chomping, did indeed get his taste of blood that morning.

It took two days to fully repair the damage aboard *Achilles*, during which time scarce a wink of sleep was enjoyed by anyone other than her captain. Her main topgallant mast, measuring twenty-seven feet in length and supporting its own yard as well as the royal and skysail poles, had to be replaced with one of the extra spars that were stowed along the waterways of the main deck and new sails had to be hoisted aloft and bent to their respective yards. In fair weather and with an experienced crew this would have provided challenge enough; with *Achilles'* mostly green hands and with the continued pitching and yawing created by a steady twenty knots of breeze from abaft filling her remaining canvas, it oftentimes seemed impossible. But somehow it was achieved, in small increments, one task at a time, and when finally the topgallant mast fid was hammered home and all three upper main yards, with new sails bent to each, were trussed in securely and their halyards re-rigged, all hands were rewarded with a proper Cape Horn measure of whiskey; the first such allowance thus far that exceeded each man's small nightly ration of grog.

It was, in its own small way, cause for celebration and when the time came to allot each man his portion at the end of the first dog watch they sought to make the very most of it. The second dog watch was the only time of day during which the entire crew was able to gather together on deck. It was also the only time of day during which they were allowed to talk freely and within earshot of the mates without being promptly reprimanded into silence, and so they oftentimes grew quite noisy about it and on this day in particular, having their tongues well lubricated by the extra ration, they were more cheerful and animated than they had thus far been on this voyage.

On the quarterdeck Nate Cooper, who traditionally stood the first bell of the second dog watch and was only afterwards allowed to pick through the captain's and chief mate's leftovers, was enjoying the rare freedom of having the deck all to himself. Apart, that is, from his helmsman, who was presently the able hand Silas Rigsby. Nate had already come to regret his decision to select Rigsby to join George Evans as the other able hand for his Starbowline watch. He should have chosen Bacas instead; he realized this now, but all too late. Rigsby was too akin to Frederick Weeks; a surly, uncommunicative individual who, like Weeks, clearly coveted Nate's position and who would if given half a chance take it any way he could, by fair means or foul. Even now Nate could feel Rigsby's eyes burning into his back but, determined not to have his mood soured by it, he strolled away from the helm, to stand by the break of the quarterdeck to gain a better view of what was going on up forward.

The various groups and individuals that made up *Achilles'* forecastle crew were as diverse a lot as could ever be found. There were, for example, only six American citizens among the entire twenty-eight of them, the remainder being a mixture of all nationalities with the predominant ones being English and Swedish. But it was by good fortune that a full fourteen of them, including the four able hands and all ten packet-rats, had ever been to sea before.

These packet-rats were fairly typical of those who habitually worked the transatlantic packet ships, where short voyages, inflexible deadlines and brutal treatment lent proof to the old axiom that to work hard was to play hard.

Voyaging solely between the grog shops and dance halls of Liverpool and New York, it was rightly said of them that they worked like horses at sea and spent their money like asses ashore. In addition to William Scragg, Jacko Jackson and Jimmy the Bruiser, all hailing from London along with the seventeen-year-old Albert Tucker, there were Freddie Dobbs and Billy Grimes, both from Liverpool, Tyrone Pete, Danny Devlin and Spuds Monahan, all from Ireland and one Welshman, Taffy Owens, from nobody quite knew where, Welsh towns being for the most part wholly unpronounceable to all but the Welsh themselves. Between any one of these men on any given dark night it was anybody's guess as to who was who, for so identical in appearance and character had the Black Ball Line molded them. Many of them had spent more than five years at sea, but with such short and intensive voyages as the packet ships undertook none had yet had the opportunity to learn those more advanced marlinespike skills that were necessary to becoming an able hand. Nor had they even the first notion of what it meant to spend a full three months and more aboard a clipper that was set to pass around Cape Horn.

Mixed in with this assemblage were the four able hands: the self-proclaimed second mate Frederick Weeks, the Portuguese fisherman Bacas, the ever-contrary Silas Rigsby and the quiet and somewhat mysterious George Evans, who in Nate's opinion was possibly the most skilled seaman of them all.

Of the remaining forecastle residents, none having ever worked aboard a ship before and none of them having volunteered on this occasion, nine were Swedish immigrants newly landed in New York and crimped within hours of stepping ashore, one was a Moroccan and the final two were Jerome Stiles and Harry Jenkins.

The California Run

Residing in the more privileged domain of the aft trunk cabin alongside the chief mate and second mate was a man who had shared many a past voyage with Captain Jacobs and his niece, and as a consequence was considered by both to be as close to family as could ever be got. This was the steward, Pepin, who also happened to be one of the best harpooners in the entire New Bedford fleet and could, in his captain's shrewd judgment, also steer a whaleboat without equal.

Along with an ill-tempered Greek cook who, with the crew's stomachs at his mercy, wielded almost as much power as did the chief mate himself, a carpenter from Albania who shared a likewise cranky disposition and an aging sailmaker, Caleb Clarke, who was in contrast perhaps the most cheerful man on board, this made up the diverse complement that was *Achilles'* crew.

And, as with any combination of men and boys thrown together at random into an enclosed environment for an extended period of time, it was also anybody's guess as to what might evolve from it. As could be seen now, with this first display of celebratory behavior on the forward main deck.

They were gathered around the area of the fore scuttle, some perched on the windlass drum just inside the topgallant forecastle space, others leaning against the rack rail of the tall outer bulwarks, and they were experiencing Tyrone Pete at his musical best. The Irishman was a true master at the fiddle and even more so, his shipmates were fast coming to learn, with a few tots of whiskey inside to fuel him on. He was well primed now and, in the failing daylight, his face glowed a bright orange as the lively strains of *Oh! Susanna* drifted as far aft as the captain's table by way of the opened skylight of the trunk cabin, to where the captain, his niece, the passengers and even Robert Biggs himself paused for a moment to listen as the steward served them their evening meal.

They had been at sea for only ten days now; too early by far for those who had been brought on board against their wills to either fully accept or to properly adjust to it. There were still several unhappy faces to be seen, although some of the younger Swedes were presently tapping their feet in time with the music and a couple were even chattering happily together. The old sailmaker, Caleb, was sharing a joke with William Scragg and the two younger boys were attempting a complicated jig while the Portuguese sailor, Bacas, was merrily prancing about trying to teach them his own curious version of what appeared to be a hornpipe.

All in all, Nate decided, it was too early to predict which direction the mood of this crew was going to take. It appeared equally divided so far, between the willing hands and the surly ones. Between a smooth voyage and a potentially hellish one. And it was most unfortunate that, in such a situation, the deciding vote would always fall to the one man who held the greatest influence over the mood of any ship's crew.

And that man was *Achilles'* chief mate.

Harry Jenkins had gotten into the habit, during the darker hours of his watch and when little else was going on, of loitering near the aft main deck bulwark with a half-coiled line in his hand, ready to make a show of acting busy should anyone pass by. He liked to make the most of these rare opportunities to be alone and to immerse himself in his own thoughts while he gazed out into the blackness. It was difficult enough to find even a moment's peace aboard this ship and Harry had still not had time to fully assess his situation, let alone to begin the process of deciding how he was going to deal with it.

He was once again weighing his options and sadly they numbered few. Unless he somehow managed to retrieve the money that Lady Margaret, or Sarah, or whoever the hell she really was, had stolen from him, he would be arriving in San Francisco all but penniless and dressed only in the rags he was presently wearing, the ones provided to him by the New York crimps. Digging his way out of this particular pile of shite was going to be something of a challenge.

"Penny for your thoughts, Harry."

Harry visibly jumped at the sound and he spun around quickly. And speak of the devil, there she stood! He winced, not only from the very sight of her standing by the foot of the quarterdeck ladder but so too from the sudden wrenching on his still-tender back muscles. In the dim light being cast from the trunk cabin's windows he could see Sarah frowning in uncertainty as she took a cautious step backwards.

"What are *you* doing here?" he asked testily. "Haven't you tormented me enough already?"

"I just wanted to see how you were faring, Harry." Her voice was all but a whisper and in response Harry lowered his own tone, despite the strong urge to yell.

"I'd be doing a lot bloody better if I'd never met you in the first place," he hissed. "And where's my money? You can at least give me my money back!"

"Your money is quite safe, Harry. All two hundred dollars of it. But don't you think I ought to hold on to it for you? Or do you trust your shipmates down there in the fo'c'sle?"

She did have a point there, Harry conceded. Not that he was prepared to admit it. But before he could continue rebuking her she added,

"I also have your bag, with all your things. I'll have the steward clean and press your suit for you before we get to

Frisco."

"What is it that you want from me?" asked Harry, suspicious now at all this unexpected generosity.

"A truce," Sarah replied. "That's all. I'd just like us to not be enemies anymore."

Harry pondered this for a while in silence. He could not deny, even to himself, the attractiveness of this proposition, despite everything. And besides, galling as it was, he still needed this woman's help.

"That depends," he stated finally. "If you truly want to make amends, there's something you can do for me."

"Oh?"

"That Scragg chap, down in the fo'c'sle. He thinks I'm one of the upper class. A gentleman."

Sarah could not help smiling.

"I cannot imagine what gave him that impression."

"Well actually, *you* did. He saw us arguing the other day, so he knows that we're acquainted. He suspects that we're both genteel types. So I need you to help me convince him otherwise."

" And how do you propose I do that?"

"By telling him who you really are. Whoever that might be."

"Well I don't think that's going to happen, Harry. What kind of idiot do you take me for?"

"Then make something up! Just convince him that you're one of his sort. Lowborn, that is. Just pretend to be, oh, I don't know, a lady's maid or something, traveling to Frisco to join your mistress."

Sarah pursed her lips.

"A lady's maid?" she replied, sounding rather dubious. "Hmmm. Well, that might be a bit of a stretch. But I suppose

I could give it a try. Just for you, Harry."

Harry stared closely at her through the darkness. He still did not trust this woman. Not one bloody inch. And, as if reading these very thoughts, Sarah added,

"Don't worry about your money, Harry. I'll keep it safe, along with your other things. You have my word."

"Your word?" Harry scoffed. But he knew that he had little choice but to accept it, for now, at least. There would be plenty of time before they reached Frisco for him to decide how he was going to retrieve not only his money but also everything else of value this woman had on her.

So Harry finally shook Sarah's proffered hand and he walked away forward, leaving her to ponder on the fact that there would be plenty of time before they reached Frisco for her to decide how she was going to give Harry the slip, while at the same time keeping hold of all his money.

Chapter Nine
A Stowaway Discovered

Before a fresh northeasterly breeze that remained so constant that it rarely hauled or veered as much as half a point astray by the compass, *Achilles* ran southwards, now engaged proper in the business she was intended for; clipping along at such a rate as to impress even the hardened Black Ballers, whose own scope of experience did not extend beyond those sufferings imposed by the ever-temperamental Atlantic southwesterlies. The Trade Winds of both the northern and southern hemispheres blew steadily from their respective tropical high pressure belts toward the equator and once gained might be comfortably ridden for days, or even weeks without any significant variation in either force or direction. They now propelled *Achilles* swiftly towards the equator, making up for much of the time that would inevitably be lost with the arrival of the doldrums and the opposing Trades that lay beyond.

With all plain sail set to her skysails, *Achilles* was also able to carry studdingsails on both her fore and main topmast and topgallant yards to each side, but not on her lower courses due to the continued choppiness of the surrounding ocean and the ongoing danger of her lower booms dipping down too far and being carried away. When running before the wind there was a reduction in pressure against her canvas that was equal to her speed over the ground and this enabled her to 'carry on' in the way that a clipper was designed to. She began to exhibit her finer qualities: those of stability under speed, in that her hull was so streamlined that to look aft from her quarterdeck was to assume that she was making very little headway at all, as there was no churning of water under her counter and only the faintest of narrowing wakes that extended aft and all the way to the northern horizon.

There had been, for several days now, an ongoing situation whereby suspicions were fast arising that *Achilles* had a thief on board.

It had begun with the cook arriving on the quarterdeck in a state of some agitation, vociferating mightily about the nightly pilfering of foodstuffs from his galley space. From eight in the evening until the morning wash-down the galley was routinely locked up for the night and the only possible entrance was through the narrow skylight above, which was far too small for anyone to squeeze themselves through, yet the cook, in his own caustic fashion, continued to insist that this was the case. One night it was half a pound of salt-pork missing, the next a large chunk had been removed from his leftover sea pie and, this being the final straw for this cook, on opening his galley this morning he had found one of his whiskey flasks half-consumed and the entire space in absolute disarray, with pots and pans scattered all around and with a coating of flour like an overnight drift of snow covering everything inside his galley.

"Somebody gotta catch dis sonnbich, maite!" the cook pressed Robert Biggs, who himself remained only halfway interested as he knew that the cook habitually incremented the ullages of his own private whiskey supplies on a nightly basis. "Den we'll string 'im up good 'n tight, an' I gotta me bes' knife sharped up 'n ready fer slicing 'is bastard bollocks off! Sonnbich!"

It was only on returning below at four in the morning to the officer's pantry inside the trunk cabin to discover a similar state of disarray and, most alarmingly of all, a conspicuous absence of his own nightly snacking of plum duff and small warmer of grog to wash it down with, that Biggs finally did pay attention. After testily confronting his second mate, who shared the pantry and whose own protestations of innocence he was finally obliged to accept, albeit reluctantly, he decided to get to the very bottom of this. Because now the culprit had stepped across the line; they had stolen directly from the chief mate himself and it had now become a personal matter.

Such it was on this morning, as the duty watch were setting up for the day's work under the second mate's supervision and the chief mate stood in the galley's doorway alongside the scowling cook, peering up at the small skylight and shaking his head for the dozenth time.

"Nobody can get in through there. Not even one of the boys. Are you sure the door locks itself properly?"

At which the cook rolled his eyes heavenwards and hawked loudly, took an extended stride to the bulwark and spat messily up and over it before returning to the doorway.

"Course I'm bluddy sure! You callin' me crazy? You t'ink I been tottin' too much Cape Horn rainwater?" at which he mimicked the raising of a bottle to his mouth. "I'm a tellin' you, maite, we gotta catch dis bastard an' learn 'im a lesson!"

Biggs was frowning, and all the more deeply now, not so much at the cook's outburst as at the reminder that there was indeed somebody on board this ship who needed to be taught a lesson. Whoever it was, crewman or passenger, it made no difference to him. He was now determined to get to the bottom of it.

And serendipitous it was that at that very moment there came the sounds of a commotion from forward: of raised voices and alarmed shouts which immediately prompted Biggs to march purposefully in that direction. He arrived at the windlass just in time to see his second mate emerging from the topgallant forecastle space under the foredeck, somewhat shaken-looking and gripping his forearm, upon which his shirtsleeve was soaked bright red.

"There's somebody in there!" declared Nate, turning back to peer into the gloom under the foredeck but seeing nothing of his assailant. Whoever it was, they had taken him completely by surprise; striking suddenly out of the darkness and dealing his forearm a heavy blow with what had felt like the business end of a marlinespike. His arm, sticky with warm blood, was still numb and he could not tell exactly where he was injured so he began rolling up his sleeve to inspect it while the chief mate took over as the crew now milled around uncertainly, themselves trying to peer into the dark space.

"Now he's killin' the porkers!" somebody shouted, and sure enough it could be seen that several of the pigs inside the pen were bleeding, some of them profusely as they struggled to make their way aft and away from their unseen assailant, piling up in a squealing panic against the rope netting which contained them under the foredeck.

"You men!" Biggs shouted to the nearest ones around him. "What are you waiting for? Arm yourselves! Get in there and haul the son of a bitch out!"

But no sooner had they began shuffling their feet reluctantly than Nate called out,

"It's only paint!"

He was holding his arm aloft to show them. It was daubed with patches of sticky red and he was still inspecting his forearm and seeing no signs whatsoever of any injury.

"It's red paint!"

"What the devil?" Biggs, deciding that this was enough, by God, raised his belaying pin and promptly ducked himself into the topgallant forecastle but no sooner had he disappeared into the darkness than he re-emerged just as quickly, now with a bright splash of red coating both the belaying pin and the hand that gripped it.

"What...?" was as much as he had time to utter, as at that moment his assailant chose to reveal himself, stepping out from the topgallant forecastle into the bright sunlight to stand himself upright and to square boldly up to Biggs with teeth bared and with paintbrush gripped in one hand and an open pot in the other.

He was mostly gray, apart from a white dress of side-whiskers, and he stood nearly two feet tall when upright, with a snake-like tail that extended as much again. Red paint covered both his arms and several other areas where it had spilled and, to some of the crewmen who were gathered around, his appearance seemed not so much a surprise as something of a disappointment, in that he had finally been discovered.

"Why, it's one o' them Monas, ain't it?" mused old Caleb Clarke who stood there looking on with about as much idle disinterest as one might lend a passing seagull.

"Africa species, if'n I recall. Prankish li'l critters, though, ain't they?"

And the old sailmaker chuckled as the monkey began daubing paint onto the nearby windlass in broad clumsy strokes that splashed everything within a yard's radius. As he dipped the paintbrush fully into the pot each time, it spilled over in big messy globs onto the otherwise spotless deck.

"Got 'im proper trained then, Jacko," came a voice from the assembled crew.

"Stow it Billy, fer fuck's sake," came another, but too late as Biggs turned directly to the packet-rat.

"This yours?" he demanded and Jacko, with a cheerful grin, responded readily,

"Well, aye, I s'pose in a manner o' speaking you might say he is, sir. But only, which is I meantersay, insofar as any one chap might be so presum'chus as to lay 'is claim over another."

Jacko rubbed at his tar-stained nose, turning his head slightly away from the chief mate as he did so and tipping his chums a wink on the sly. His blue eyes sparkled with a mischievous humor and a daring that, given his present circumstance under Robert Biggs' stony glare, might have been considered by some to be downright insane if not close to heroic.

"See, I thought that bein' as we was short on skilled hands," explained Jacko, "young Smudger here might do well to start working 'is passage, for the good and well-bein' of all concerned, natcherally. He's a quick learner, see, and 'e takes to the English a sight quicker than these bloody Souwegians. So this afternoon we're goin' to teach 'im his compass points, an' then we'll tackle the lead line. So don't you fret none, Mister Mate, sir, 'cos we'll make an able hand out of him afore you can say..."

Biggs had heard enough. In a single stride he descended upon the monkey and grasped it roughly by its scruff and the monkey screeched in alarm, dropping both the brush and the paint pot to the deck where it spilled into an expanding pool and the chief mate swore loudly. Still gripping the writhing animal, he began using it to mop up the spillage, employing its fur to absorb much of the sticky mess, then in two strides he was at the bulwark and, with all his strength, he cast the monkey over the ship's side.

Robert Biggs was clearly inexperienced in the matter of monkeys. Because when this particular specimen found itself traveling freely through the air it did what was most natural for any monkey to do; it sought to grab onto anything within reach that might possibly save its bacon and in this instance it was the mainsail tack line that hung slackly just beyond the lee bulwark. With all the dexterity of an acrobat it affixed itself securely to this line with all four hands and a tail and then began scurrying quickly upwards, still screeching until it reached the clew of the mainsail, then upwards farther, gripping onto the sail's leech bolt rope and climbing nimbly along the edge of the square sail until it reached the yard, leaving a trail of small red handprints on either side of the otherwise spotless canvas in its wake.

"That'll be a bitch to clean," muttered the old sailmaker, shaking his head.

Biggs, with a furious curse, turned immediately on Jacko and began striking him about the head with his belaying pin, but already the sailor's arms had risen to protect himself and the blows were mostly ineffectual, which only made Biggs all the more angry.

Tossing the belaying pin aside the chief mate instead selected one of the capstan handspikes and, raising it aloft with both hands, he made ready to swing the heavy wooden bar against Jacko's torso, which surely would have broken several ribs in the process. Biggs was now clearly intent on violence but at the same time William Scragg was going to have none of it and, with an urgent nod to Jimmy the Bruiser, the two packet-rats immediately lunged at Biggs and drove both him and the handspike hard up against the lee bulwark.

Scragg's face was now within inches of the chief mate's and he was looking him directly in the eye, his own expression now one of deadly seriousness.

"That'll be enough now, Mister Mate," Scragg panted, "if you know wot's good for you. Sir."

Scragg's expression left little doubt that he himself did not give a damn one way or the other as to whether Biggs actually knew what was good for him or not. This was not a debatable issue. Now, with all ten packet-rats gathered close around and looking on in stony-faced seriousness, Biggs finally appeared to come to the realization that perhaps he had gone too far.

The chief mate immediately changed tack. He backed off a pace, angrily shrugging the hands of the packet-rats from his shoulders and stood there with handspike raised, looking around, and perhaps in some desperation now, for something else to focus his anger on. Because to stand there looking ineffectual was simply not an option, and everyone present knew this.

Everyone, that is, apart from two of the younger Swedes, who could not resist looking up at the painted monkey aloft and grinning to each other.

"You think this is funny, do you? Just one big fucking joke?"

And Biggs laid into both of them with a vengeance, wielding the handspike freely now and driving both men aft with cries of protestation and pain as the wooden bar connected with a satisfying degree of resistance against both men's torsos before they finally managed to escape and run from it.

Biggs then pointed the handspike aloft.

"No-one stands down until that mess is properly cleaned! And from now on you keep that fucking animal out of my sight!"

Jacko watched as the chief mate departed. He was scowling deeply now.

"I'll take 'im, Scraggsy. I'll take that bastard down, so I will."

Scragg shook his head. He was closely studying the expressions upon the faces of those sailors gathered nearby and he drew Jacko aside, beyond earshot, and he whispered,

"You'll do no such thing, Jacko. You'll bide yer time, d'you hear me?"

"But you saw what 'e did, Scraggsy! We can't let that..."

"Patience, Jacko! Patience. The way things are going," Scragg added, glancing towards *Achilles'* assembled crew, and at the Swedes in particular, "it won't be too long afore someone does that job for us."

Achilles' trunk cabin measured forty-one feet by twenty-three and in its foremost section were situated both the mate's quarters and the officer's pantry, while aft, surrounding the main saloon itself, were the more luxurious staterooms belonging to the captain and the passengers.

Each of these four passenger staterooms was only seven feet by six, containing a small bunk measuring five and a half feet by thirty inches wide and with another suspended directly above it. But the limited space afforded by these staterooms was compensated for in no small measure by the very plushness of their interiors. Thickly-piled carpeting covered every available inch of deck space and ornately carved mahogany paneling and gilded moldings of floral work dressed every wall and door frame, as well as the bordering of the wide mirror that was mounted to the bulkhead close above the wash basin. All of which was diffusely illuminated by oil lanterns at night and, during the day, through small glass prisms set into the quarterdeck directly overhead, as well as by a pane of stained glass set above the doorframe through which the filtered sunlight entering the spacious saloon beyond by way of its opened skylight was lit up during the day in a veritable rainbow of colors.

Inside her own stateroom Emma Jacobs checked her pocket watch and noted that it was now seven o'clock, Greenwich Mean Time, an instant before the ship's bell sounded from directly overhead in four sets of muted double rings. This signaled the turning-to of the first dog watch; four in the afternoon and time for tea.

It had always been part of Samuel Jacobs' routine to spend an hour or two every afternoon with his niece, so that they might catch up on that day's events and chat about various issues concerning the general running of the ship. But not so this past fortnight. Not once during this time had Emma and her uncle enjoyed a moment's conversation together inside the captain's stateroom. Her uncle had taken to his new charge with an uncharacteristic enthusiasm, and was now displaying an aspect of his personality that Emma had only briefly glimpsed before, and only then at the direct sighting of a nearby pod. There had existed from the very outset of this voyage a likewise sense of urgency, but one that had yet to show any signs whatsoever of easing off. She was becoming concerned that it might prove too much for the poor man.

Poor man indeed, she scoffed. Poor man, who now

enjoyed full command of a brand new clipper and who was racing her southwards towards the Horn with every prospect of winning this so-called 'race' against *Sapphire*. Would that I were such a poor man, lamented Emma. Or any man at all, for that matter.

And yet, rather than Emma finding herself at a loose end because of her uncle's continued absence, there had appeared a welcome alternative in the form of one of *Achilles'* passengers; the well-to-do French lady who was traveling with her three maids. When, on the second afternoon out from New York, she had rapped softly on Emma's door and inquired of her in polite and near-perfect English as to whether the young mademoiselle would like to take afternoon tea, Emma had immediately discovered an agreeable alternative to her uncle's undivided company.

Emma now set aside the sheaf of papers she had been studying: the *Achilles'* design and rigging specifications as furnished by her builders, and she rose from her bunk to stretch, lifting her arms high and almost touching the ornate beams overhead. Taking in her surroundings again she smiled and shook her head, doubting that she would ever get used to this level of comfort. Not that she was about to complain about it. Putting on her woolen shawl, she stepped out into the main saloon and turned left, towards the captain's stateroom which was located directly opposite the small cubbyhole chartroom and which was separated from it by the companionway stairs leading up to the quarterdeck.

The captain's quarters measured a spacious twelve feet by eight. Spacious yet unbelievably messy, and Emma smiled again at the manner in which her uncle had acclimated himself to a standard of luxury that could only be viewed as unseemly, even downright decadent by any self-respecting whaler. His stateroom was even more ornately decorated than the passengers', although to see it now might cause one to doubt it. Tattered clothing, salt-encrusted oilskins, worn boots, paperwork and manuals were scattered all about, much of the clothing draped over the bulkheads to conceal the fancy wainscoting and on the deck there was little sign remaining of the carpeting beneath the numerous scraps of old sailcloth and burlap that had been lain down to create a more comfortable and familiar living space.

The French lady, Madame Fontaine, about whose life Emma was slowly coming to learn, although not yet having heard the better half of it, was already there waiting for her. She was chattering animatedly in her own language to Pepin, who was busily setting up the crockery on the large marble-topped walnut table that dominated the captain's stateroom, and she broke off to greet Emma with the most affable of smiles.

"Ah, there you are, my dear! Punctual, as always. Now there is a quality to be admired."

Emma seated herself, feeling as always that she must present the most ghastly of spectacles, adorned as she was in her dowdy old rust-colored wash dress, the best she owned, sadly. Madame Fontaine, in contrast, was clad in the finest blue cotton and silk-trimmed dress and appeared to Emma the very picture of elegance; with locks of blonde hair immaculately curled about her brow and with a complexion so flawless as to surely be the envy of any woman half her age. Madame Fontaine had clearly once been a lady of remarkable beauty, yet by no means was this diminished by the trials of time and she was now, in her fortieth year, a woman of singularly attractive proportions. There was a certain quality about her, one that Emma perceived as being that ambiguous attribute that defines beauty itself and one that, having its origins deep within, remained impervious to time itself. In short, Madame Fontaine appeared to Emma to be the very type of older woman that she herself had always aspired to be.

Emma thanked Pepin and took over the duties of pouring the tea herself and the steward reached up again to fiddle with the tight collar of his monkey jacket as he nodded and turned to take his leave. As Pepin departed, closing the door softly behind him, Madame Fontaine, who had thus far managed to stifle herself, burst into a musical peal of laughter.

"What a fellow, that one is!" she declared happily. "Wherever did you find him?"

Emma, bemused now, smiled uncertainly.

"It was actually my uncle who found him. Quite literally, in fact, almost ten years ago now. He was picked up half-starved in an open boat off French Guiana after being shipwrecked a month or so earlier. The captain of his fishing dory, Pepin's owner, had drowned along with the rest of his crew, so my uncle thought it only proper to adopt him. He managed to arrange the paperwork and to somehow obtain Pepin a Seaman's Protection Certificate, which makes him as good as a free man, but only for as long as he stays clear of the southern ports, where they'll often arrest negro sailors and detain them without question. Pepin has always been on board ship with me. I think of him as much family as I do my uncle."

"But why is he only the ship's steward? He seems to be a strong and able man, certainly not too old for other duties. He looks so uncomfortable serving tea! Why does he not work on the deck?"

"Oh, he is very able! The best sailor I have seen about his tasks, and an unparalleled harpooner. But for this voyage my uncle has ordered him to take the rank of steward. It is for our protection, madam, that he does this."

"Collette. Please, you must call me Collette. Madam is so..., well, perhaps not so appropriate, and a little too formal between friends, n'est-ce pas?"

"D'accord," replied Emma, smiling. "As I say, my uncle has his reasons for appointing Pepin as our steward. It is, as he puts it, an added assurance against any and all dissension as might arise from such an unruly crew as we have on board. Pepin has been posted here inside the trunk cabin to look after us, or more particularly, if I know my uncle, to look after me."

"Ah! Then I approve! For I have decided that he is a good man, and a clever one, too, although I am beginning to think that he does not quite approve of either myself or my girls."

Emma frowned.

"Why ever not? Goodness me, I could scarcely imagine Pepin to be disapproving of anyone without having a good reason for it. It's one of the qualities I've always admired about him; his sound sense when it comes to judging people."

Madame Fontaine replaced both her teacup and saucer onto the table and, detaching a thin slice of cake, she maneuvered it deftly onto her plate.

"I think perhaps now is the time for me to confess to what your steward seems to have already worked out."

She passed a plate across to Emma and then, in more subdued tones, she began to fill in some of the missing details of her life story.

Harry Jenkins was returning aft to the quarterdeck when he spied Sarah Doyle standing on the main deck beneath the mainmast shrouds. She was dressed in her summer finery, sporting a lace-adorned parasol to protect her from the fierce tropical sun overhead and, although appearing to gaze idly outwards at the distant horizon, was at the same time talking surreptitiously with William Scragg, who stood only ten feet or so away near the fife rail and was making a show of coiling and tidying some lines. With their backs turned to one another and with the occasional glance around to ensure they were not being seen, they were conversing in quiet tones, and in such a casual and familiar manner, it seemed to Harry, that immediately it raised his suspicions, as well as an unexpected twinge of jealousy.

Harry immediately ducked himself out of sight behind the corner of the deckhouse, then began sidling his way aft, hoping to catch a word or two of their conversation.

"Then I believe we understand one another, Mister Scragg?"

"I believe we do, yer ladyship."

Harry watched Sarah stroll away aft and he immediately joined Scragg at the fife rail. The packet-rat was grinning broadly as he watched Sarah twirling her parasol as she headed towards the door leading into the trunk cabin.

"Where did you find that one, Harry?" Scragg asked, still grinning and shaking his head. "She's bloody priceless."

"I'm starting to think it was her who found me," replied Harry, morosely.

"Aye. I believe it."

Scragg was absently coiling the line in his hand as he continued watching Sarah, with what appeared to Harry to be a disproportionate degree of admiration. As Sarah reached the trunk cabin door she turned, lowered her parasol and gave both men a cheery wave before disappearing inside.

"So, did you talk with her?"

"Aye. We talked."

Harry waited.

"So, what did you talk about?" he prompted.

"Oh, you know. This 'n that."

Scragg began chuckling.

"She stitched you up good an' proper, though, didn't she Harry? You poor daft sod."

"Ah. Then she told you everything?"

"Oh, I doubt that. She ain't the type to tell a man everything. Just enough to get what she needs."

"What she needs? I don't understand."

Scragg looked at Harry.

"Well, if *you* don't understand, there's no point me telling you, is there? I'll tell you this, but, Harry. If yer able to handle a woman like that, then yer twice the man I'll ever be."

Scragg then shoved the uncoiled line into Harry's hand.

"'Ere you go then, Mister Jenkins. Make yerself useful. Still a long ways to Frisco."

And Scragg wandered away forward, still chuckling to himself and shaking his head, leaving a rather bemused Harry to glance alternately between his departing back and the closed door of the trunk cabin.

In the forward alleyway of the trunk cabin Pepin was being confronted by an angry Robert Biggs.

Both the chief mate's and second mate's staterooms stood on the starboard side of the alleyway, the steward's cabin and officer's pantry on the larboard and within the latter Pepin was presently busying himself with cleaning up some of the tea crockery.

"A small warmer, by God! That's all I'm asking!"

"Sorry, Mista Chief. Cap'n's orders."

Pepin was remaining adamant, as was his right. For he

was *Achilles'* steward and as such he alone held charge over the officer's pantry. Only Robert Biggs was not about to accept it.

"By God, you are testing me!" Biggs, now fully exasperated, was standing in the doorway and glaring daggers at the steward's back, wishing heartily that he could strike the insolent bastard down here and now and be able to get away with it. But he knew full well that Pepin was the captain's own pet and his fingers now twitched of their own accord, grasping at thin air but, also realizing full well his powerlessness in this situation, was already set on trying another tack.

"Look, it's nothing really. Just a small flask of whiskey to shake out the night chills. To hell with this damned grog; grog's only fit for women and boys! Where's the harm in it?"

Pepin, being in no ways impressed by any such argument, did nevertheless understand that, although he might be lord and master of this small pantry, it was the chief mate who ruled the entire deck when all hands were called for and the steward was obliged to work the deck on such occasions. So he knew that a compromise was called for here, yet he had no desire to make it too easy for the chief mate, for in Pepin's experience men like Robert Biggs would only be encouraged to seek even more favors from it. So finally Pepin relented.

"I'll ask the cook. Maybe he got some extra in his stores."

Biggs, having finally gained his victory, felt it nonetheless a rather hollow one, in that he might have gotten his own way this time but he certainly had not made much of an impression on this steward. So he sought to gain something more and, looking around the pantry, his eyes finally alighted on the pile of dirty crockery.

"That shouldn't be your duty," he proclaimed. "That French woman, she's got three servant girls, hasn't she?

What the hell are they doing?"

"They's no servants, Mista Chief." Pepin frowned, wondering how it was that Biggs could be so dull-witted.

"They's whores," Pepin added, continuing to rinse his dishes and taking some pleasure now at the chief mate's suddenly bewildered expression.

"An' that lady? Why, she ain't nothin' but a whorehouse madam."

Chapter Ten
The Atlantic Doldrums

October 20, now sixteen days out from New York, saw *Achilles* crossing the twelfth degree of northern latitude and beginning to encounter the first indications of the approaching doldrums. It was not unexpected for the doldrums to extend this far north so late in the season but it was in no way welcomed, as *Achilles* had been making good progress so far. She had, in fact, been performing exceedingly well, as it was generally acknowledged that any ship that could reach the equator within five and twenty days of departing Sandy Hook was well in the running to make San Francisco within one hundred days.

To achieve this, *Achilles* would only need to cover seven hundred and twenty miles in the next nine days. Three and a half knots of average speed was all that was required. With the Trade Winds broad on her quarter she had been logging a steady nine to ten knots, oftentimes twelve and more when the seas did not run too high. On three consecutive days this past week alone she had made runs of more than two hundred and fifty miles from noon to noon. But here now were the doldrums, where the northeast and southeast Trade Winds collided under the searing heat of an equatorial sun and were each compelled by their opposing forces upwards and high into the atmosphere, leaving behind a wide band of low pressure filled with light, baffling airs interspersed with squalls and thunderstorms: one that encompassed the entire globe and which had, for centuries now, caused many a captain of Samuel Jacobs' temperament to attend a slow and oftentimes agonizing lesson in the virtues of both patience and humility.

By sunset of that day the wind had turned from a steady east-northeaster at twenty knots to a gusting, erratic blow arriving from almost due south. Now with skysails brailed in and royals clewed up, *Achilles* began hauling laboriously to windward on a taut bowline to make what little southerly progress she could before the winds failed her altogether. By dawn the following day her crew found themselves continually bracing yards in and up in response to a succession of confused squalls until, at the sounding of the noonday bell, she found herself all but stopped dead in the water, on a sea that still undulated with the residual swell of a wind that was now left far behind to the north.

Yet still, even in these light and paltry airs, Captain Jacobs drove his crew onwards and they did manage to make another twenty miles before sunset. But each mile cost them dearly in both effort and endurance, for what little air there was to be found would spill from the sails each time *Achilles* rolled to leeward and it was all the helmsman could do to keep her within four points of a south-southeasterly heading. The deck-wash pump was now manned and pails of water hoisted continually aloft to wet down the sails to lend weight to the canvas so that as little air as possible would be spilled and lost. And when finally the wind did die off altogether, reduced to only an occasional swirl created by the reflected heat of a glass-like ocean and all canvas above hung slack and nothing more could be done about it, Captain Jacobs posted lookouts aloft with orders to continually scan all quarters for any signs whatsoever of the wind's imminent return.

For five days and five nights the captain drove his crew in this manner, the former pacing the quarterdeck and becoming evermore frustrated while the duty watch either squinted outwards from high aloft or bent to the chief mate's orders, as Robert Biggs cared little for any man's comfort and the mere sight of any hand stood idle was a gross offense to his eye. As aboard any ship, there existed a ready list of chores that could be undertaken on short notice in any type of weather, whenever a spare moment or an idle hand presented itself for the devil's taking. Such as the picking apart of old rope-ends and rolling them into oakum to use as chafing gear aloft and for filling in the seams between the deck and hull planking as a binder for the hot pitch caulking. Or that perennial favorite of chief mates the world over: the task of 'holystoning' the decks, by using large bible-sized blocks of sandstone which, combined with seawater, a scoop of sand and a goodly measure of elbow grease, could scour any pinewood deck clean of all residual traces of tar, paint, oil and even blood.

So they worked on in that slow, methodical fashion that sailors so readily adopt for any and all such mundane tasks. They huddled together or sat alone in what little shade could be found and they worked in silence, not a word being allowed out of them, and they continued to swelter in the motionless equatorial airs and found relief only in taking their turn in going to the carpenter's shop to request the ladle, thence to the mainmast to dip into the scuttlebutt for another gulp of hot drinking water.

Atop the mastheads the lookouts would occasionally report the sighting of a cat's-paw dancing across the surface nearby, heralding another breath of air, at which all hands were immediately summoned to their stations and yards promptly braced about to catch every gust, which oftentimes would last scarcely more than a few minutes, and whenever the sails did fill they would draw *Achilles* ahead a length or two before she slowed to a stop again, at which they would either return to their mundane duties or to their sleep, all the while becoming evermore exhausted and evermore impatient with the weather and with one another.

The heat and stillness below decks, being stirred only by the occasional puff of breeze that was redirected below by canvas wind-scoops rigged over the opened scuttles and skylights, had become near to unbearable. To the extent that very few elected to take their refuge down in the forecastle, for it now resembled a steamship boiler room within which the entire crew's laundry might be dried within minutes and a barrel or two of fermented galley slops and rotting pig carcasses scattered around to positively freshen up the place. Because, quite frankly, it now stank to high heaven down there, with a mess of discarded food scraps laying about and with the combined odors of tar, grease, foul sleep and a score of unwashed bodies. So the off-duty watch milled around in whatever shady area could be found up on deck and tried to catch a few winks of sleep, in silence, for the slightest sound would alert the ever-prowling chief mate to his presence and he would be woken by the heavier end of a belaying pin and asked if he was presently on watch, and God help him if he was.

Not quite so rancid was the aft trunk cabin, wherein the

ship's officers and passengers resided, but certainly it was equally as hot and stifling. So much so that very few of the passengers were able to sleep in any comfort whatsoever, even at night. Nor did they have that dubious luxury, as had the crew, of sleeping up on deck without being continually mistaken for a shirking crewmember in the darkness and being rudely prodded awake for it. And so it was that, throughout these doldrum days, many a shadowy and sleepless figure might be seen loitering inside the trunk cabin during the darker hours without any undue suspicions arising from it.

Nate Cooper, having the middle watch on this particular night, descended the trunk cabin's aft companion ladder from the quarterdeck and headed directly forward through the saloon towards the officer's pantry to replenish his water flask. On passing a recessed alcove to his left he happened to notice a pair of indistinct shapes lurking within and he thought little of it other than it was doubtless a couple of sleepless passengers conversing on the settee, as he had seen time enough before throughout this past week. Only on returning aft and passing the alcove again did a noise cause him to glance in that direction and immediately, through the gloom, he saw enough to arrest him on the spot.

There was mischief in the making here; this was immediately apparent. The sound of a woman's muffled and protesting tones combined with the sight of a bulky figure that appeared to be restraining and pinning her down bodily against the settee. Through the darkness Nate could make out the paleness of the man's naked lower half as it rose and fell with a heavy and determined stroke, against which by contrast the woman's smaller figure was writhing in what could not by any means be misconstrued as willingness.

Without any thought to the contrary Nate strode directly

in, landing a heavy grip on the man's shoulder and hauling him roughly back with a reprimand ready on his lips but one that was never uttered; for as soon as he gained even a partial view of the assailant's face he could see precisely who it was.

"What the devil?" Robert Biggs snarled out of the darkness. The smell of whiskey was thick on the chief mate's breath as he irritably shook Nate's grip from his shoulder. As he did so the smaller figure, one that Nate now recognized as being one of the young French girls, darted rapidly from the recess and, babbling something in her own language, ran directly into a nearby stateroom and slammed and bolted the door firmly behind her.

"You should be on watch! Get back on fucking deck!"

Biggs, now glaring most dangerously at his second mate, began hauling his pants back up and Nate immediately sought to make his own escape, heading quickly back aft towards the quarterdeck and wishing fervently now that he had not been party to such a spectacle and cursing the fact that it was already far too late for that.

By the end of that fifth day spent languishing in the doldrums tempers on board had become noticeably frayed, not least that of Robert Biggs himself. Several times now he had flown into an unprovoked rage on some imagined slight or other and he had lashed out freely with both fist and belaying pin, for now he was as short on sleep as anyone else on board. In addition to which, as Nate was now reluctantly aware, there were certain other urges pressing on the chief mate, the specifics of which he sincerely wished he himself had never been made privy to.

Biggs now appeared to no longer trust his second mate to keep the crew occupied while he rested, nor to badger them continually in his absence, and therefore he took upon himself the full burden of such responsibility along with his readiness to blame Nate directly for it. But it was beyond any doubt now as to the primary cause of his displeasure towards his second mate, and Nate's incompetence as an officer had, if anything whatsoever, very little to do with it.

During the first bell of the second dog watch, while all remained unusually quiet up on deck and as the exhausted crew gathered around the fore scuttle to eat their supper and to enjoy a brief respite, Nate stood on the quarterdeck, alone apart from his helmsman, who for this two-hour 'trick' was the young Moroccan, Mahmood. This dark-complexioned and bright-eyed youngster had, after the initial shock of being crimped, recovered remarkably quickly from it and was now finding himself quite drawn to this new way of life. He was only eighteen years old and had arrived in New York three months earlier, where he had been obliged to work as a virtual slave on the docksides of Brooklyn as a fish gutter. So perhaps it was not so surprising, after all, that in contrast this life might actually appeal to him.

Mahmood stood at the helm humming quietly to himself in those strange and undulating tones so commonly associated with a Muslim in prayer, but he was not praying, rather reciting some tune or other from his homeland as he often did. The young Moroccan had already proven himself a natural helmsman but on this day there was presently not even a breath of wind to steer by. All sails aloft were hanging slack and *Achilles* was going nowhere for the present. So Nate was free to stroll around a little and this he did, pacing fore and aft along the quarterdeck and absently picking the day's accumulation of tar from beneath his fingernails with his jackknife. As he passed by the opened skylight of the trunk cabin he could not help but catch a word or two as it drifted up and out onto an otherwise silent deck.

"The man belongs in the fo'c'sle, not back here," Robert Biggs was saying gruffly. His mouth sounded full, and there was a pause while he swallowed.

"I don't question his competence as an able hand. He can reef and steer with the best of 'em. But as second mate? Well, let me say, cap'n, there are other men besides who would be more suited to the position."

Then Captain Jacobs' voice was heard, in a conciliatory tone that sounded to Nate's ear in no ways encouraging.

"Dost think? Well, 'tis true our Mister Cooper is new to his office. It may be that he has not yet found his proper stroke. Belike a little more time is needed."

"But we do not have the luxury of time, cap'n! This is a clipper, and one with an undisciplined crew. These men need driving, and driving hard, else we'll not even round the Horn, let alone reach Frisco! I say again, there are others on board who are more fitting for the office."

Samuel Jacobs grunted as if he himself was now well on the way towards agreement and Nate, standing unseen directly above them, felt quite certain that with the captain's next utterance his own fate would be sealed and back down into the forecastle he would go.

But instead it was with the surprised gratitude of a drowning man being tossed a line from seemingly nowhere that he heard the voice of the captain's niece rising unexpectedly through the skylight.

"And precisely whom would you have replace him, Mister Biggs?"

Her tone sounded sharp to Nate's ear. Almost scathing, in fact. She sounded, indeed, quite unafraid of Robert Biggs and this in itself made an immediate and striking impression on Nate.

"That Weeks fellow, I presume, who is always trailing at your heel like the most faithful of dogs?"

There was a long pause and Nate, smiling now, could see in his mind's eye Biggs gagging on his plum duff.

"That would be one option, ma'am," the chief mate responded, stiffly. "The man is at least an *experienced* second mate."

"Ah, yes, of course," Emma replied, and somewhat sarcastically. "And we all have Mister Weeks' word of honor on that, do we not?"

Then Captain Jacobs, who obviously regarded such matters as being relatively inconsequential, cut in,

"Let us at least give the fellow a chance! I shall observe our Mister Cooper more closely from now on and will arrive at a decision in due time. Now let us belay such talk. We would do better to spend our time in prayer, in beseech of our Good Lord to see fit to deliver us from these accursed windless latitudes!"

Following Emma's earlier discovery as to the true profession of Madame Fontaine and her girls she had found herself, much to her own surprise, spending more and more time engaged in conversation with the French lady and less time in reading and studying those subjects that she had until now never imagined she would ever tire of.

It was an ongoing effort to quell her own curiosity, now that she had discovered what Madame Fontaine and her ladies truly were. But perhaps not ladies. Yet still, in Emma's view they were, to all outward appearances, precisely this. Because each one of them, even the youngest of these girls, continued to behave and to appear as nothing less, displaying such irreproachable manners along with such immaculate sense of fashion that to even waft the term 'prostitute', much less 'whore', in their direction seemed downright offensive.

Yet in reality this was precisely what they were. Whores and harlots. Filles de joie. Even Madame Fontaine; particularly Madame Fontaine who had in her chosen profession risen by the equivalent path as from the forecastle to the aft cabin, having worked her way up through the ranks to become the proprietor of one of the most successful bordellos in Marseilles which, for such a notorious seaport, must surely be no minor feat.

It was not particularly surprising that, whilst dallying upon the subject of men, Robert Biggs' name would crop up again this evening; especially in light of the chief mate's most recent abominable actions here inside the trunk cabin only a few nights earlier. Inside Madame Fontaine's stateroom she, Emma and two of her girls, one of them, Yvette, having been the object of Biggs' unwelcome advances, sat sweltering and listless, alternately mopping their brows and drawing in gasps of warm, stagnant air. The four of them expended more energy in fanning themselves than they did in conversation and there were long periods, sometimes of several minutes, spent in silence between discourses.

"Such a beast!" declared Madame Fontaine again. And with good reason, for here inside her stateroom there was scarcely a breath of air stirring through the small opened casement directly above the door.

"Now we cannot even relax in the saloon, where there is at least some draft of air from the windows above. What is the matter with that wretched man that he cannot keep it inside his trousers? In this heat, too! However does he get it up in the first place I should very much like to know!"

If not for the heat Emma might have blushed at such an outburst, but as it was she lacked the energy and could do little more than frown in agreement. She was also sitting slumped in the lower bunk alongside Madame Fontaine, while the two girls occupied the upper bunk, each of them being so scantily clad in such delicate lace finery that the very notion of having Robert Biggs see them was forbidding enough to ensure that the stateroom door remained firmly bolted.

"What a devil that one is! An officer he may be, but he is certainly not a gentleman!"

Emma glanced at Madame Fontaine, for she had just been thinking the very same thing. She had also been thinking of what a shock it had been earlier that day to have faced the very real possibility of Frederick Weeks becoming *Achilles'* second mate. Perish the thought! To have another man like Biggs running the deck would, to her mind, create absolute mayhem. Emma was not blind; she had noticed the cuts and bruises on those men who came aft and even from the quarterdeck she had seen enough to know that Biggs ruled *Achilles'* deck with an iron fist. Frederick Weeks was clearly a man of similar character and would behave equally as brutally if given half a chance.

Then, as if reading Emma's thoughts, Madame Fontaine added,

"But at least our second officer appears to be of a more civilized disposition. There is a fellow, I think, who has more the qualities of a gentleman, n'est-ce pas?"

Emma shrugged, truly not knowing. Mister Cooper, although appearing bright and able enough, was still wholly inexperienced as a second mate. She very much doubted Weeks' abilities too, but to counteract such demands as Biggs was now making, Nate Cooper would need to firmly cement his position. This would require not only an impressive display of seamanship but so too a likewise array of navigational skills. But he appeared to have little grasp, if any, of the latter subject. It all seemed rather hopeless, and more than a little disturbing to envisage both Robert Biggs and Frederick Weeks living and dining here inside the trunk cabin alongside herself and *Achilles'* passengers.

"I fear it would take so little to send Mister Cooper back into the fo'c'sle," Emma admitted. "In truth he is little more than an able hand."

One of the girls, Gabrielle, turned to her young companion and said something that set both girls off into a fit of giggling. Madame Fontaine, with an indulgent half-smile, replied,

"Oui. Able hands." She then smiled mischievously at Emma. "You can tell a lot about a man from his hands."

This time Emma did blush and Madame Fontaine joined the girls in their laughter. Emma, in spite of herself, also joined in before protesting,

"But I am being serious here! Honestly, it may become a very real problem, if somebody with a lesser sense of decency than our Mister Cooper joins us here in the aft cabin. Was it not, after all, he alone who rescued Yvette the other night?"

This quickly sobered them into silence again and, after a moment's serious contemplation, Madame Fontaine declared,

"Perhaps it would be the clever thing to strengthen Monsieur Cooper's position as second officer. Perhaps he should be taught as much as can possibly be taught. And quickly."

Emma, considering this for a moment, found herself in agreement and was about to say so when Madame Fontaine, with a return of that mischievous look, smiled and added,

"And besides, I am beginning to suspect a possible affaire in the making here..." She regarded Emma with a sly smile.

"Non?"

Emma scoffed, smiling still, but as Madame Fontaine continued to regard her closely she felt herself reddening again and quickly sought to divert the conversation.

"I shall begin tutoring him immediately," she said. "And then we shall see how he progresses."

During the pre-dawn hours of the following morning, October 27, and to the profound relief of everyone on board, the wind finally returned.

It began with the occasional luffing of the skysail leeches high above in the darkness, then gradually proceeded to fill out the lower canvas, drawing each sail taut against its sheets until, by the time the sun was fully above the horizon, *Achilles* was once again moving ahead, albeit at a walking pace.

By mid-morning the wind had steadied out at a dozen knots from the east-northeast and now, for the first time in several days, those who lived below in the forecastle and in the aft trunk cabin were able to enjoy a cleansing breeze that washed away much of the foulness below decks, and no longer were they continually awakened by the hourly call of *'All hands ahoy!'* which had plagued them now for what had seemed an eternity.

As the sun was nearing its highest altitude, which in these latitudes was close to directly overhead, Nate Cooper was approached on the quarterdeck by the captain's niece, who was carrying a sextant.

Nate doffed his cap respectfully, still being grateful to Miss Jacobs for having come to his rescue the day before, but before he could even begin to express such thanks she asked, in a very business-like tone,

"How is your navigation, Mister Cooper?"

"My navigation, ma'am?" He was not quite certain how to answer this. His navigation was, as a first-trip second mate, still confined pretty much to conning the helm and monitoring wind against sail.

"I daresay your skills could use a little brushing up," Emma ventured, holding forth the instrument, which Nate was at least able to recognize as being a sextant. "Here. Let's get you started."

When it became apparent that he did not have the first clue as to how to hold a sextant properly, being all fingers and thumbs, Emma's fixed expression of severity gave way to a brief smile and this surprised Nate as well as eased his nervousness considerably. There was, he noticed now and for the first time, an attractive woman hiding under all the plain clothing and indifferent demeanor; one who had until now remained well concealed. And she also had the type of smile that was neither squandered nor made less by its habitual projection for the sake of mere politeness; rather it was one given in full sincerity whenever it was given and Nate's first and most natural response, being a man, after all, was to seek a way in which to make it reappear.

Yet fast in the wake of such inappropriate musings came the realization of where he was and to whom he was addressing and his earlier discomfort returned in full force. He stammered and hesitated and he almost dropped the fragile instrument altogether and he silently berated himself for behaving like such a damned foremasthand. Because he believed that he understood Miss Jacobs' intention here, and so he immediately sought to clear his mind and to make every effort to focus on the challenge she was offering him and to divert his energies to where they more properly belonged: inside his head.

A few minutes later he was peering through the sextant's

telescopic eyepiece towards the southern horizon and at the reflected image of the sun. By adjusting the instrument's mirrors and by a careful turning of its increment screw, it could be made to appear to sit directly atop the horizon. Emma, speaking now in a quiet voice that could only be heard by Nate, stood aloof and a fathom's distance from him as she guided him with words alone on how to operate the instrument. There were no more smiles or pleasantries from this point on as she continued to instruct him patiently until he finally got it right. Nate watched in fascination as the sun continued to climb steadily towards its zenith and he followed it by adjusting the increment screw to keep its image balanced atop the horizon until, at the very moment of apparent noon as the sun crossed *Achilles'* own meridian of longitude, it gradually slowed to a halt and hovered there for a full minute and more before finally beginning its lazy descent again into the afternoon.

On Emma's signal the helmsman reached for the bell's lanyard and sounded four sets of double rings to signal noon, shipboard time, the turning of the watch and the beginning of another sea-day. From forward came an echoing response from the bell situated over the windlass and the faint cry of *'All's well!'*, drifted back as Emma, opening up her books, began showing Nate how to calculate the noon sight.

At apparent noon the sun reaches its highest point as it crosses the observer's own meridian of longitude, and its bearing is always either due north or south, depending on which hemisphere the observer is in. So the angle measured between the horizon and the sun's geographical position will always translate directly into a true distance along this meridian and can be plotted directly onto any nautical chart. If the sun's geographical latitude, or declination, is applied to this measurement, then a simple addition or subtraction is all that is required to determine the ship's latitude position.

As Nate was still marveling at the simplicity of this method and was again peering through the sextant's shaded eyepiece toward the southern horizon, he noticed the small, nearly indefinable irregularity on its otherwise flat surface at the very instant that a cry rang out from high aloft.

"Sa-a-a-il ho-o-o!"

Such an announcement, coming as it did out here in mid-ocean, immediately roused all who heard it. Every man presently on deck, plus several who subsequently emerged from below, scrambled up onto the bulwarks and into the lower shrouds to gain a better view. Captain Jacobs himself emerged from the trunk cabin, glanced briefly and with some surprise at his second mate holding the sextant, then squinted aloft.

"Where away?"

"Bearing close on the starboard bow, sir! She's hull down!" Then there was a pause while the lookout aloft, the boy, John Palmer, seemed undecided. *"She looks like a clipper!"*

"Sapphire!" was Captain Jacobs' immediate response and he ordered his second mate to immediately lay himself aloft with the spyglass. Nate handed the sextant back to Emma with a brief smile of thanks at which he received a curt nod in response, then he was on his way forward, tucking the captain's spyglass safely into his jacket and jumping nimbly up into the mainmast ratlines and he began climbing, negotiating the futtock shrouds below the main top with scarcely any slowing of pace as he proceeded up into the topmast shrouds, thence the topgallant, the shrouds of which were now reduced to only a pair with a ladder of thin ratlines between them, then finally to the level of the hoisted royal yard, where the lookout sat perched atop the yard itself, peering forward and under the foot of the main skysail.

"Where away, lad?" Nate was gasping from the sudden exertion and he had to wrap one arm tightly around the tapered royal mast to steady himself while his vision momentarily blurred and spun.

John Palmer pointed and Nate squinted against the sun's reflected glare from the ocean ahead as he balanced the spyglass atop the yard and began scanning the horizon.

"Aye, she's a clipper sure enough." This much could be seen clearly, even from this distance. She was perhaps fifteen miles away with her hull still partially concealed below the horizon even when viewed from this height, which was almost one hundred and seventy-five feet above the waterline. But she was on such an aspect as to clearly display all three of her raked masts and her full dress of square sails. Her image shimmered and drifted in and out of clarity as the heat from the ocean's surface distorted everything on it and she appeared to hover suspended above the horizon; a ship with only half a hull and with patches of whiteness above that alternately melted and dissolved before returning to focus again.

Nate turned and called down to the quarterdeck,

"She's a clipper, captain! And she's heading south! She must be Sapphire!"

This caused an immediate commotion below. Looking down from high aloft, Nate had a clear view of the entire ship, as if *Achilles* were reduced to a toy-sized miniature. He watched as the tiny figure that was Captain Jacobs strode forward the full length of the quarterdeck to call for his chief mate, who in turn strode immediately to the mainmast to call for the duty watch and together they began to trim braces and adjust sail to maximize the effect of wind against canvas.

By the time Nate had returned to his station on the

quarterdeck all lines had already been coiled and stowed again and Captain Jacobs, being the whaler that he was, had positioned himself by the weather taffrail and was now alternately peering aloft then ahead towards his quarry.

"She does indeed work to weather like a pilot boat," he later overheard the captain state to his niece, who stood alongside him. "I'll warrant there's not a ship afloat can place *Achilles* in her wake when close-hauled in such light airs."

This bold proclamation only gained validation as the afternoon wore on. Working towards the southeast with all squares braced hard up, *Achilles* drew ahead at a respectable rate. She kept the breeze six points off her larboard bow and, when the log line was streamed at the turning-to of the dog watch, a full five knots disappeared over the transom before the sandglass emptied itself. By nightfall she stood barely five miles astern of the other ship and was now close enough, with the aid of a spyglass, to view her directly.

Gideon stood alone on *Achilles'* foredeck, peering ahead into the evening gloom. Even in this failing light he knew *Sapphire* well enough to recognize her distinctive markings. Such as the narrow tar stain running down her starboard counter, where that idiot boy had spilled the bucket homeward-bound from Frisco and had earned himself a taste of Gideon's knuckles as a reward for his clumsiness. And the manner in which her main topgallant leech continually fluttered when hauling on the larboard tack, due to the sailmaker's over-cutting it after that storm off Valparaiso.

There was no doubt it was *Sapphire*.

Gideon ought to be aboard her right now, brushing up on his navigational skills and preparing to take over from that po-faced Fergis as chief mate. Old Man Thaddeus had promised him as much. And, if not for a degree of rashness on his mentor's part, he would surely be doing so. Which was ironic. For was it not Gideon himself who was supposed to be the impetuous one? At least that was what Old Man Thaddeus had always been telling him, since as far back as he could remember.

But he was not angry about it, because he owed so much to the old man. He owed his very life to him. And where would he be now if not for the patronage and support that Thaddeus Oglesby had afforded both he and his mother? Admittedly, it had not been much: a modest stipend, but it had been enough to live on and, as Thaddeus himself had explained it to Gideon shortly before sending him away to school, it had certainly not hurt him to do without; it had not spoiled him as it had his own son, Thomas, and this had been the old man's intention all along. For now Gideon was more equipped to confront this world and all its challenges than any one of those Harvard milksops, Thomas included. Under Thaddeus Oglesby's patronage, Gideon had grown into a tough and capable man, as well an extensively educated one.

Now, as Gideon viewed his former ship and watched *Achilles* gradually and inexplicably gain on her, he realized again the wisdom of Old Man Thaddeus who rarely, if ever, left anything to chance. In these light airs the untested *Achilles* was indeed showing herself more capable than *Sapphire* and at this rate she would soon overhaul her.

Perhaps, Gideon now reflected, he would be needed here after all.

Chapter Eleven
Crossing the Line

The morning of Sunday October 28 found *Achilles* hard up on the stern of her quarry, by barely half a mile's distance and Captain Jacobs, being all the more spurred on by the sight of *Sapphire* standing so close ahead, now pushed all the harder to remedy that situation.

"She will be viewing *our* stern by sundown. All hands ahoy, Mister Biggs! Let's snug her up tight to weather and there'll be a Cape Horn measure when we spy her hawseholes!"

Again the entire crew was summoned to deck; not for their usual Sunday morning routine but instead to work lines and to tend sails in response to each and every variation in the already-faltering breeze, and to grumble quietly under their breaths as they did so. At Captain Jacob's urging and with Robert Biggs' active encouragement, every available trick in the book was employed, even down to the rigging of running cat-harping tackles to pinch the upper portions of all lower shrouds inboard and the rigging of jumper lines from the weather course yardarms. This, combined with a hauling in of all leeward lifts and the easing of yard trusses, allowed the yards to ride up and inwards an extra few feet against their lee shrouds and thus enabled them to be braced up another half a point into the wind. All weather topsail and topgallant sheets were hardened down and their lifts slackened away to create a likewise advantage and the result was that, with a skillful helmsman, in this instance Bacas, *Achilles* was able to successfully pinch another five degrees into the weather and remain there without luffing into stays or losing excessive headway.

Then, as noontime approached and it was determined by the sun's observation that they had now finally reached the equator, the wind, as if unwilling to trespass so much as a fathom beyond its own hemisphere, deserted them altogether and *Achilles* once again drifted to a stop on a smooth and utterly calm sea.

Yet they had achieved their most overriding objective, for now *Sapphire* stood most assuredly astern of *Achilles* by a full three cables, and both her hawse plugs could be clearly seen. It was a somewhat ambivalent Samuel Jacobs, vexed once again by the sudden abandonment of the wind but cheered in turn to see the other ship so decisively overhauled, who held his usual Sunday afternoon service from the break of the quarterdeck. It included both a prayer of thanks along with a further plea for the return of a fair wind. Then, against his own better judgment, for this being the Sabbath, but with him being also a man of his word, he stood his crew down and issued the promised Cape Horn measure at the beginning of the dog watches, and by the end of the first bell there was already much noisy and drunken skylarking going on up forward.

Robert Biggs, in his ongoing state of testiness, was finding himself in no ways comforted by the sight of his crew enjoying themselves so heartily; in fact it properly insulted him on a personal level to bear witness to it. Because he knew that, somewhere in the midst of it, they were talking about him, and that they were talking ill of him, and all the more so with their tongues loosened by a brimmer of whiskey as they now had to whet their damned whistles with.

It was consequently with no measure of joy whatsoever that Biggs noticed the approach of *Sapphire's* two longboats across the flat reach of ocean that divided the two ships, nor to see the closest one loaded to the gunwales with what was clearly recognizable as being ever more revelry in the making.

"Ahoy Achilles! Prepare to be boarded!"

As *Achilles'* crew went to her bulwarks to peer over there came several cheers from below, of cordial greeting from *Sapphire's* crew towards these, their fellow clipper-men. In the bows of the first of *Sapphire's* boats stood a tall sailor who was bedecked most oddly, or at least so to any landsman's inexperienced eye. The man stood upright with a whaler's harpoon in one hand, the tip of which had a makeshift wooden attachment that converted it into a trident, and atop his head was heaped a loose and untidy pile of yellow seaweed, the type of which floats freely in the Gulf Stream far to the north and which now cascaded about his shoulders like the healthiest of golden locks. He was almost naked apart from a strip of tattered green sailcloth wrapped around his waist, and the remainder of his body was stained and painted with various shades of green and blue. Behind him, working the oars, sat several men dressed in similar fashion, though none so elaborately as their bowman.

"None shall pass but ye true sons of Neptune! Ready thy swabs for initiation!"

The man with the trident was grinning up at *Achilles* as

the boat drifted in alongside and Captain Jacobs, seemingly not too surprised about any of this, promptly gave the order to lower the accommodation ladder. The captain's face now displayed a most unusual expression: one of mock seriousness as he stood by the head of the ladder and greeted this strangely dressed sailor, who was followed closely by his fellows, all of whom brandished tin cups and other metal objects which they were banging together to create a most deafening racket. Captain Jacobs wore the expression of an otherwise strict father who, against his own better judgment but with the full realization that tradition was tradition and naught could be done about it, felt it his obligation to indulge in this time-honored ritual.

"Welcome aboard, Your Majesty," he huffed, maintaining his deadpan expression. "Prithee afford us thy services."

King Neptune and his entourage made their way noisily forward to greet *Achilles'* crew and then they began, one by one, to initiate the newcomers among them. There were twenty-three in all, including all ten packet-rats, the nine Swedes and, appearing most reluctant of all, the Albanian carpenter, Darijo, who even after five years at sea had not yet crossed the equator.

Yet it was doubtful that, if not for William Scragg's approval, anything would have been allowed to occur at all other than an all-out bout of fisticuffs with these oddly dressed jokesters. But they had brought their own whisky supply with them, and a good deal of it, and it was Scragg himself who insisted on being the first one initiated, along with his packet-rat chums. Then together they helped out with the initiation of the remainder of their shipmates, and with a rougher measure of drunken gusto than even those hardened men of the *Sapphire* would have deemed appropriate.

Each man in his turn was baptized with a face-full of Stockholm tar that was applied liberally with a large paintbrush, then roughly shaven with a rusted iron hoop until his face glowed a fiery red. After which he was forcefully leaned backwards over a water-filled tub and made to drink a hefty gulp of seawater through the captain's brass speaking trumpet before being fully dunked. Even the sour-tempered carpenter could not escape it, and was made to endure this along with the reluctant Swedes, but at least each man was rewarded with a sizable measure of whiskey afterwards.

"Thou art now proclaimed a shellback proper, and a true Son of Neptune!" declared the king to each one in his turn. "And henceforth shall be afforded free passage betwixt north and south! More whiskey for this man!"

Tyrone Pete, having already removed most of the tar from his face by the liberal application of slush, which was made from animal grease, struck up a lively tune on his fiddle and the two crews began to exchange news and gossip. They compared the one ship to the other, sought out mutual acquaintances from their hometowns or from voyages past and then, just as Robert Biggs knew was the way of it, in quieter tones and with many a furtive glance aft, they began discussing the various qualities of their captains and mates.

In the meantime the second longboat from *Sapphire* had pulled up alongside and a no less odd assortment of personages had disembarked from it. Firstly her captain, Jonas Blunt, lumbered heavily up the ladder to exchange formal pleasantries with Captain Jacobs, while close behind him came Thomas Oglesby, sporting an air of arrogant nonchalance, while in contrast the man directly behind him seemed to make up for this by being extra attentive to everything around him as he peered keenly about, both aloft into *Achilles'* rigging as well as around her main deck, as if searching for something. Or perhaps someone.

All three men were ushered by Captain Jacobs aft towards *Achilles'* quarterdeck, but before they had even reached the ladder the third man, speaking in a somewhat Irish-sounding accent, proclaimed,

"I need to see one of your passengers, captain! It is a matter of the utmost urgency!"

Captain Jacobs paused and turned to view this man more closely. Seeing from his style of dress that this was no sailor and must therefore be one of *Sapphire's* passengers, he reluctantly pointed to the nearby forward door of the trunk cabin.

"You will find my steward inside, sir. He will assist you."

The Irish gentleman nodded. Then he waited for the three men to begin mounting the ladder to *Achilles'* quarterdeck and he surreptitiously reached into his jacket pocket to check again that the heavy object within was readily accessible. Then, with a determined expression now bent to his scowling features, he stepped purposefully through the doorway and into the trunk cabin.

Gideon had been alarmed to witness the approach of *Sapphire's* longboats, in particular the leading one that contained several of his former shipmates. If any one of them were to even catch a glimpse of Gideon, they would surely recognize him on the instant. All it would take, he realized, was for just one of them to call forth his real name and the game would be up.

Thinking fast, Gideon had hurried aft and mounted the ladder to the quarterdeck barely in time as the first of *Sapphire's* longboats drew alongside. Nodding respectfully to Nate Cooper, who presently stood the watch, and noticing with relief that one of the packet-rats, Billy Grimes, was at the helm, he had gone directly up to the second mate and said,

"I'm here to relieve the helmsman. I've crossed the line before."

Nate, standing to larboard of the trunk cabin and trying to catch a partial view of the festivities going on up forward, glanced only briefly towards him before nodding his assent and Gideon immediately relieved Grimes at the helm. Now, from where he stood, Gideon could remain unseen by anyone unless they actually came up and onto the quarterdeck itself and rounded the raised portion of the aft trunk cabin.

Which was precisely what Captain Jacobs, Jonas Blunt and Thomas Oglesby did only a few minutes later and it was with the utmost effort that Gideon kept his gaze averted from the latter two because he did not presently trust himself, in his fast-mounting rage, to maintain his neutral expression.

It was only when Captain Jacobs invited his counterpart below for refreshments and young Thomas, politely declining with the excuse that he would rather make use of this opportunity to admire *Achilles'* deck and rigging that Gideon, after making sure that they were out of the nearby second mate's earshot, hissed,

"What the hell do you think you're playing at?"

Thomas, now standing only a fathom's distance from the helm and gazing idly aloft with a casual smile, replied quietly,

"I decided we ought to drop by and see how you're getting along here."

"Do you have any idea of the risk you're taking?"

"*I'm* taking?" Thomas smiled in genuine amusement now, keeping his gaze fixed aloft. "You're the one being paid to take the risks, my friend, not I."

At which Gideon immediately bristled and, glaring openly

at Thomas now, responded,

"What do you think would happen if I'm discovered? What do you think your father would say about that?"

"He would probably think you a damned fool for getting yourself caught."

"And you a damned fool for provoking it!"

Thomas smirked, appearing to be enjoying himself now.

"Ah, but then he's *my* father, not yours. Or had you forgotten? Honestly, sometimes I do wonder, the way you carry on. You might be his favorite lackey, my friend, but I am his flesh and blood and perhaps you would do well to remember that. You are expendable; I am not."

Gideon, now sorely tempted to spit forth the truth, if only to witness the effect of it on Thomas' face, yet somehow managed to bite his tongue.

"Besides," continued Thomas, "there's no need to wet your pants about it. They've all been warned about you, and instructed to stay well out of your way."

"They'd damned well better, for your sake."

Thomas glanced at Gideon, frowning now.

"Was that a threat? I do hope not."

"No, that was a fucking promise," snarled Gideon, now making every effort to keep his voice low. He glanced again towards Nate to ensure that the second mate's attention was still directed elsewhere before adding,

"And here's another for you. If you *ever* interfere again with *any* task your father entrusts to me, I shall hunt you down and I shall kill you, and I don't give a damn whose son you are."

He glanced briefly at Thomas and at the expression now on the young man's face.

"Aye, and you know I'll do it, don't you? Now fuck off and

let me do my job!"

Sarah Doyle was awoken by a light tapping on her stateroom door.

It drew her slowly out of a dream state wherein she and Harry Jenkins had somehow and inexplicably become the closest of friends. So close, in fact, that there had barely existed sufficient clothing between them to maintain any degree of modesty whatsoever and, on opening her eyes, she retained just the vaguest recollection of a delicious confusion of warm flesh and thrashing limbs just as it faded into nothingness and she realized then that she was panting heavily and perspiring along with it.

"Bloody hell," she murmured as the tapping on her door continued.

Gathering her dazed thoughts together, Sarah tried to force the dream, nay, nightmare, from her head and with her conscious mind now causing her to feel somewhat nauseated about it, she staggering blearily across to the door and opened it.

Pepin was standing there with a troubled expression on his face. Next to him stood another man, one whom Sarah had never seen before and nor, she decided on that instant, did she particularly care to. Because he was scowling at her in a most menacing fashion and his right hand, which was immersed deeply into his jacket pocket, appeared to be twitching uncontrollably.

"Harry Jenkins! Where is he?" the man demanded, and most rudely at that. His entire arm was now twitching and Sarah, in her confused state, was about to blurt out that Harry wasn't actually here; it had all been a dream, you idiot, when thankfully Pepin intervened.

"Like I tell you! There's no *Mister* Harry Jenkins on

board! Only *Missus* Jenkins!"

The man did not appear very willing to accept this. Instead, he pushed roughly past Sarah, despite both her and Pepin's protestations, and began rummaging through her possessions. He opened the wardrobe, peered underneath the lower bunk, stared long and hard at the unused upper bunk; he even picked up Harry's carpet bag, though fortunately did not think to open it, before dropping it to the deck again. Then, at last appearing to accept that there was no evidence of male habitation here, he swore loudly.

"Damn and blast it! Give me that manifest!"

Pepin reluctantly did so and the man scanned the sheet closely. Sure enough, and just as Pepin had assured him, there was only a *Missus* Harry Jenkins listed on it.

"How can this be? Why, that bastard isn't even married!"

The man, who sounded a bit Irish to Sarah, glared furiously at her with his mouth repeatedly opening and closing, searching for something more to say but apparently was rendered speechless. This seemed a good enough moment for Sarah to interject, with her best display of righteous indignation,

"How dare you presume, sir! My husband, if you must know, was obliged to remain in New York on business. Perhaps if you would care to leave me your card…?"

The man stared blankly at her. Then with a loud reiteration of his earlier curse he stormed away forward and back out onto *Achilles'* main deck.

Pepin stood there looking helplessly at Sarah and he shrugged. She in turn stood there gaping after the man with her mind reeling. She was fully awake now, and she realized what she needed to do.

She had to get out there and warn Harry.

It was one of those odd little quirks of good fortune that saw Harry Jenkins, for the very first time in his life, standing there with his face smeared with such an abundance of Stockholm tar that even his own mother would not have recognized him. Indeed, he was at this moment heartily enjoying himself, what with all the whiskey, the initiation ritual and the good-natured crazy fun of it all. He was now a shellback, apparently, and jolly good for him. He was all but patting himself on the back about it as he stood there happily by the fore scuttle and cheered his shipmates on. As a consequence he entirely failed to notice the angry-looking Irish gentleman emerging from the trunk cabin and in turn the angry-looking Irish gentleman entirely failed to notice Harry. Instead, and with only a cursory glance forward and seeing nothing but a rabble of drunken sailors, most of whom had likewise blackened faces, he steered himself directly to the gangway, descended the ladder and sat himself down upon the longboat's thwart in a manner that could only be described as outright huffiness.

Meanwhile, inside *Achilles'* spacious passenger saloon, the two captains and Emma Jacobs were exchanging small talk.

"Lieutenant Mathew Maury? Ay, miss, I have indeed heard of the fellow."

Captain Jonas Blunt was taking stock of his surroundings as he spoke. He was comparing *Achilles'* aft saloon with his own and seemingly, to judge from the expression on his flushed face, was coming up short. The saloon was, on every modern clipper, a model of ornate craftsmanship: a joiner's competition and an owner's showpiece. Harding and Ives, holding true to such form, had spared little expense here. All bulkheads were wainscoted to their full height in carved mahogany and dressed with satinwood trim that was shaped into Roman arches and decorated with gilded moldings. Even the doors leading into the captain's and passengers' staterooms were ornately carved about their frames in polished black walnut and the overhead beams and skylight frames were painted a pearl-white, with their lower corners edged in gilt. From the center beam a gimbaled housing was suspended which contained a compass and a barometer, these indeed being the only indications that they were actually aboard a ship at all. The entire twenty-four foot by nine saloon was richly carpeted, velvet-draped and generously mirrored to enhance the illusion of spaciousness and in its center was a large oak dining table that was bolted to the deck, around which the two captains and Emma Jacobs were now seated.

Jonas Blunt's expression turned into a disapproving frown as he eagerly accepted another refill of Madeira.

"And I have also studied Lieutenant Maury's publications, or as much of them as any reasonably-minded man might deem tolerable. Barely half a dozen years spent at sea, and the man presumes to know all there is to know about winds and oceans and currents and tides. Poppycock, I say! He is nothing more than a charlatan in my opinion, and I would gladly tell him so to his face and let him put that in his pipe and smoke it!"

Emma was quite taken aback. She found herself hesitating with her charts unfurled on the table, reluctant now to take this subject any further. She had been hoping to cultivate a little support here, but instead it seemed to be working against her.

"My niece is quite affixed to the opinion," intervened her uncle, and with that particular manner that men seem to reserve solely for the apparent whims of their womenfolk, "that Lieutenant Maury be the answer to any swift passage by Cape Roque. Inshore, she quoteth, ever and eternal. Hold her close inshore, uncle dearest, and you shall yet find a good westerly breeze to speed you southwards to the Trades."

What was it, Emma pondered, about men that made them do this? It was simply infuriating, that whenever two or more were gathered together there seemed to lurk some unspoken agreement between them to belittle any notion whatsoever containing even the slightest hint of female origin. Her uncle would never have behaved this way if only the two of them were here together, not with such respect as he had always shown for her navigational skills. For mercy's sakes, it was enough to make one scream out loud.

"Inshore indeed!" responded Captain Blunt with an amused smirk at his counterpart. "Aye, and inshore forever! Why, tis common wisdom to any seafaring man that the prevailing current sets hard northwest onto that same cape! To sail close inshore is to invite calamity! No-o, miss, with all respect, for my own part I choose to keep a wide berth, and stay well out in the offing."

"As you will," conceded Emma, quietly, and she began rolling up her charts. There was no use, she knew this now, in pursuing the matter any further. At least not until she had her uncle all to herself again.

As it turned out there was little time available anyway for further discussion. Through the opened skylight above came the sounds of flapping canvas and then of raised voices, signaling the wind's return and *Achilles* was felt to heel slightly to her starboard. Both captains immediately rose from the table and neither squandered a moment further on pleasantries.

"A safe voyage, captain, and may the better ship win! I shall, therefore, be there to welcome you into Frisco! A pleasure indeed, miss."

Jonas Blunt turned and headed forward along the narrow passageway which led past the two mates' cabins, then out through the weather door and directly onto the main deck, while Samuel Jacobs steered himself in the opposite direction toward the companionway ladder leading up to *Achilles'* quarterdeck.

The crewmembers from *Sapphire* were already scrambling back to their boat, not a man among them appearing overly affected, despite the volume of whiskey they had brought on board, whereas in contrast the crew of *Achilles*, each one now inebriated to the point of being almost legless, were proving a challenge for their chief mate, who had the air about him of a man who had been waiting all week for just this opportunity.

"Hands to braces! Look alive, damn you! Ready tacks and sheets! Bear a hand there! If I have to repeat myself you'll pay for it, by God!"

The last man to descend the accommodation ladder was Thomas Oglesby who followed closely behind *Sapphire's* captain and, as the longboats began to pull away from *Achilles'* side, he seated himself on the adjacent thwart opposite an irritated and very disappointed-looking Irish gentleman. Jonas Blunt turned to the owner's son and he asked, softly,

"Well? Did you speak to Gideon?"

Thomas Oglesby glowered at *Sapphire's* captain.

"I did," he grunted, and said no more.

Harry Jenkins, despite his exceedingly drunken condition, yet retained a sufficient measure of innate vanity to pause briefly at the slush bucket before heading aloft so as to wipe his face clear of tar. Then, along with his equally-as-drunken shipmates, he began negotiating the foremast shrouds at the same time that Sarah Doyle emerged onto the quarterdeck and began looking anxiously around her.

Sarah quickly took in the scene: of *Sapphire's* two longboats now several yards off *Achilles'* side and moving swiftly away, then of Harry Jenkins who was just now reaching the lower futtock shrouds and stepping clumsily onto the foot rope of the foreyard. She watched Harry begin working his way unsteadily out along the yard with his shipmates and, with a sigh of relief, Sarah relaxed a little, for now it seemed that, whatever the Irish fellow's intention had been, Harry had safely escaped the man's wrath.

Then she saw the Irishman suddenly rise and stand upright in the nearest longboat and peer aloft with mouth agape. Barely an instant later a pistol appeared in the man's right hand and he raised it high to aim into *Achilles'* rigging and directly towards Harry and he called out,

"Jenkins!"

Sarah, without even pausing to think, also called out,

"Harry! Look out!"

In his bleary state it took a moment for Harry's mind to register his name being called from all quarters at once and he turned his head only an instant before a bullet whizzed so close to his ear that it ruffled his hair. A moment later another slammed into the yard directly in front of him and the wood exploded into a shower of splinters, one of which cut into Harry's face just below his eye and he yelped in surprise, along with those two men directly adjacent to him, Tyrone Pete and Billy Grimes, both of whom reacted likewise with alarmed cries and diverse blasphemies.

Down in the longboat the Irishman was already being subdued, with two of *Sapphire's* burly sailors now fully on top of him and pinning him against the boat's floorboards as they wrestled to retrieve the gun. When finally they had it, Captain Blunt himself made a show of tossing the gun in a high arc overboard and then, readjusting himself back onto his thwart, he, along with Thomas Oglesby, merely sat there with their combined gazes fixed resolutely on the longboat's coxswain, as if this were the most interesting of all views around and nothing whatsoever out of the ordinary was occurring here.

Aboard *Achilles*, the initial shock of what had just happened faded remarkably quickly, with those on the quarterdeck unable to do anything but gape down at the departing longboat and with Robert Biggs, being equally as taken aback but at the same time immediately assuming that one of his own crew was fully to blame for it, becoming even more righteously angered and in turn screaming up at them ever more loudly from where he stood on the foredeck.

Within minutes *Achilles* was hauling wind and turning herself toward the south-southwest, now beating a direct course toward Cape Sao Roque.

Chapter Twelve
Cape Sao Roque

The two ships kept company until sunset, each one bracing her yards and trimming canvas in response to every variation of this rising wind until finally it settled in from the south; a precursor to the southeasterly Trade Winds that lay beyond, yet remaining somewhat erratic for its being held in check by the nearby doldrums. It brought with it a heavy dark layer of overcast which contained numerous squalls within and, as darkness fell, so too did the rain, arriving now in torrential sheets, whipping in at times near to horizontal as it stung the eyes and drummed like fowling shot against the taut canvas, veering unexpectedly through several points of the compass then hauling back again just as suddenly, causing the sea all around to turn to a confused boil and the crews of both vessels to become rapidly drenched as they confronted each squall in its turn.

Captain Jacobs ordered reduced sail and *Achilles* luffed up into the lesser squalls, turned and ran with the heavier ones until, with the approaching of midnight, she found a steadier breeze that allowed her to carry all royals and skysails and to leave them set, hopefully for the remainder of the night. *Achilles* was now in the southern hemisphere, yet by no means was she free from the grip of the doldrums. This wide band of confused winds and squalls extended a good way south of the line and would likely hamper them for another two or three hundred miles, without any way to avoid it. Or so stood the conventional wisdom.

Aboard *Achilles* and *Sapphire* combined there existed only one person who had thus far paid any serious attention to Lieutenant Mathew Maury. Based upon his meticulous observation of several hundred United States Navy vessels' logbooks stored in the government archives at Washington, Lieutenant Maury's findings had been published only the previous year and Emma Jacobs had studied these with great interest. Now, having crossed the equator at the most favorable point between the meridians of thirty and thirty-five degrees west of Greenwich, Emma was determined to convince her uncle before they reached Cape Sao Roque of what they needed to do to ensure a swift passage southwards. And it was with an equal measure of determination that she set about reinforcing Mister Cooper's position as *Achilles'* second mate, to which end she continued to tutor him relentlessly.

The calculation of the ship's latitude position by observing the meridian altitude of the sun, moon or Polaris had been a common enough practice for centuries now, since ancient astronomers had been able to predict these bodies' declinations for any given day with a fair degree of accuracy. But without having any means of determining the precise time, to the very second, at which these observations are taken, the body's hour angle, or longitude, could not be found without the most complex of lunar observations which involved three or four hours of the most grueling calculations. So these theories had remained mostly confined to only the most mathematically adept, until the development of a reliable timepiece that could be taken to sea.

Accurate chronometers had now been available for several decades, and since their inception the techniques of ocean voyaging had changed dramatically. Whereas for centuries navigators had been obliged to first sail to the required latitude, thence steer either due east or due west along it using deduced, or de'd, reckoning to estimate their ship's progress, nowadays any navigator could daily determine, by the observance of any one of a number of celestial bodies, their true position to within a mile or two, depending on the accuracy of their chronometer.

Yet still the mathematics of it all, particularly to someone who was not accustomed to it, would more often than not prove sufficiently befuddling as to prohibit all further aspirations towards becoming a ship's officer. Nate Cooper was indeed fortunate to have the captain's niece by his side as he struggled with these elusive principles and not, as it would otherwise have been, the less-than-benevolent guidance of Robert Biggs who, Nate also suspected, did not himself fully grasp these theories but instead relied more upon the parrot-like recitation of applied formulas which were barely sufficient to get the job done. Under Miss Jacobs' guidance Nate was learning quickly and he was also beginning to comprehend the principals behind these calculations. From the 'shooting of the sun' in the morning or afternoon to the 'running up' or 'running back' of his noonday latitude observation, he was already enjoying the challenge of it and each time he passed his calculations on to Emma she would glance at them only briefly before nodding in agreement and heading below to plot them onto the chart.

The most important part was to estimate *Achilles'* position during these sightings as accurately as possible and this was done by keeping meticulous hourly accounts throughout the day between observations. The ship's speed through the water was measured by the hourly 'streaming' of the log: a triangular chip of wood with a line attached that was run out over the aft taffrail and timed with a thirty-second sandglass. The number of knots in the line that passed over the transom during this time corresponded precisely to the ship's speed in nautical miles per hour. Ocean currents and the effects of windage also had to be taken into account and this was applied as 'set and drift'. All these factors combined provided the most accurate estimate of the ship's position.

William Scragg, standing at the helm, reached into his pocket to retrieve his block of tobacco. Letting go of the ship's wheel altogether he withdrew his knife and deftly sliced a small quid off the corner and stuffed it into his mouth. Then with only a brief glance aloft he casually re-stowed both knife and tobacco and returned his hands to the wheel, recovering those spokes that had been drawn to weather and adding a couple more to leeward to steady her out, all but ignoring the compass that was jerking around inside its binnacle in front of him and trusting instead on the luff and fill of the skysails aloft as *Achilles* continued to pitch steadily into the oncoming seas. With his right hand gripping the wheel's topmost spoke and his left at the nine o'clock position, Scragg adjusted his bulk a little to larboard against the heeling of the deck until once again he attained a comfortable balance. Then, back on course again, he turned to Nate with a broad grin.

"Hex-traodinary!"

Both Nate and Emma paused momentarily, Nate with the sextant raised to his eye and Emma with timepiece ready in hand, and they looked to their helmsman in surprise. But, with Scragg now gazing wistfully aloft and seemingly immersed once again in his own thoughts, Emma turned back to her timepiece as Nate merely nodded, although in reality having no idea what was supposed to be so extraordinary. Scragg was still grinning happily, his cheek swollen with the quid.

"Modern technology," explained Scragg. "Why, bless me if it don't boggle the mind of any thinkin' man."

Nate grunted and nodded, still peering through the sextant's eyepiece.

"Ready..." he announced, rotating his wrist slightly, which caused the sun's reflected image to trace an arc that dipped a little below the horizon. With a small adjustment of the increment screw he raised the sun's image until the lowest point of its arc barely touched upon the horizon, then called, "Time!"

Emma noted the time to the very second and jotted this down on her slate while Nate took note of the reading on the sextant. She noticed that Scragg was appearing suitably impressed with Nate's handling of the sextant and this pleased her, though she dared not show it. Instead she retrieved the instrument from Nate and stated, casually,

"I'd like to check that index error again. I think we might be able to reduce it a little more."

She raised the sextant and looked through its eyepiece towards the horizon, on the pretense of aligning the index mirror by adjusting a tiny screw that was set into its frame and, as she lowered it again, neither Nate nor Scragg noticed her surreptitiously glancing at her timepiece.

"I meantersay, Mister Cooper," Scragg continued, now with the scholarly air of one who has himself spent a good deal of time pondering these very mysteries of the universe, "Consider this here, our present situation. Here we are, middle of habsolutely nowhere on the wide blue yonder wiv no land to be seen to any quarter. An' yet all we needs do is take our hobservations, apply our mathematicals, an' lo an' behold, here we are!"

Scragg peered aloft again and shook his head in silent wonderment and with the self-satisfied air of one who regarded himself, as a bona fide member of the selfsame species, properly entitled to his fair share of credit for this and indeed for all mankind's more impressive achievements.

"Hex-traordinary. That's the only word for it."

Nate continued working through his calculations and Scragg lapsed back into a reflective silence, neither man noticing as Emma slipped quietly away, her own mind now continually reciting both the sextant's reading along with the time, to go below to the chartroom and work out a more accurate position that would be entered, in lieu of Mister Cooper's, into the ship's logbook.

Robert Biggs, since their recent encounter with *Sapphire*, had been taking measures of his own to ensure that *Achilles'* crew were reminded in no uncertain terms as to who was in charge of her deck. And, under the concealment of both darkness and weather he was being particularly brutal about it. Notwithstanding the continued presence of his captain on the quarterdeck, there still remained many an area of the main deck that was hidden from view and he took full advantage of these by freely wielding his belaying pin whenever such opportunity allowed. Heads were struck and blood was spilled; before they had even properly settled onto the larboard tack one man, the oldest Swede, lay beaten and semi-conscious near the mainmast. And as the second night progressed so too, it seemed, did the chief mate's foulness of temper until, with the setting of the watches shortly after midnight, there was scarce a man or boy remaining on deck or retreating below to his bunk who did not bear some bruises or open wounds to show for it.

The old Swede, Karl Angstrom, was sixty-three years old and so it was natural for his younger countrymen to regard him as something of a father figure. It was therefore not surprising that such a brutal attack on their respected elder would upset each one of them considerably, and it was with much open grumbling that they carried the old man below to stow him gently on his bunk. Then they sent their spokesman, Anders Fersen, who was the only Swede who could speak any passable English, to the second mate, a man in whom they hoped to find a modicum of reason.

"He vill kill the old fellow," Anders complained to Nate. He was a fresh-faced man of thirty-two years, the second oldest of the Swedes and he was already proving himself the ablest hand amongst them, if only due to his ability to comprehend most given commands, the converse of which was fast becoming old Karl Angstrom's ongoing bane.

"Vy, he is haf-dead already, the poor man. Vy dosh not the mate haff any patience? Ve try to learn, but it ish not easy, vis all the shouting und the beating..."

Nate was mostly in agreement, at least insofar as the beatings were concerned. As for the chief mate's patience, well, he himself, with each league they now progressed towards the Horn, was finding his own tolerance shortening by the day. There was little room here for patience. But there was, to Nate's mind, room enough for some leeway here on the chief mate's part.

"I will speak to the chief mate," was as much as he could, or would, promise. "Now return to your duties."

To approach Robert Biggs directly on such a matter was, to Nate's mind, akin to grasping a sleeping tiger by its tail, yet he did not balk at it. He had witnessed for himself the old man being beaten, and for nothing more than his responding too slowly and for not understanding Biggs' own colorful vocabulary and he had already been of half a mind to approach the chief mate about it. Yet still he waited until daylight, until the turning-to of the forenoon watch at eight when Biggs arrived on the quarterdeck to relieve him for breakfast.

"Mister Biggs," began Nate, just as soon as he had made certain they were well beyond earshot of the helmsman and any other crewmember. "I feel duty-bound to inform you that some of the Swedes are becoming angered by all these unwarranted beatings, and..."

"Unwarranted?" Biggs was now regarding Nate with the air of a man who has just discovered a nest of weevils inhabiting his salt-pork.

"By God, that is enough out of you! Mister Weeks!"

On hearing the term 'Mister' spoken in association with Frederick Weeks, Nate clearly saw what was in the offing and his heart sank. And sure enough, at Weeks' prompt arrival on the quarterdeck, cap in hand and as deferent as ever, Biggs steered him directly down the companionway and into the captain's stateroom, to where the captain and his niece were busying themselves over their charts. Nate noticed the opened skylight at the aftmost section of the trunk cabin and he was unable to resist the temptation to eavesdrop. He made his way casually around to the cabin's lee side and caught most of the ensuing conversation.

"Dost speak for the crew?" Samuel Jacobs' voice rose

clearly, as did Weeks' response.

"Aye, sir. They are in sore need of a second mate they can respect."

"Be that so? And what say thee, Mister Biggs?"

"It is no more than I have professed from the beginning, cap'n. The man has no spine and little stomach for the job. He should be replaced."

"Indeed, if such be the truth."

"Then it's settled?" asked Biggs.

But once again, and to Nate's eternal gratitude and relief, this quiet savior of his, this woman who for reasons known only unto herself had taken to championing *Achilles'* stumbling second mate, spoke forth and when she did there was sufficient venom in her tone to encompass both chief mate and foremasthand, with plenty to spare.

"Is it not the custom in such circumstances," she began, with all the polite innocence as might be associated with true ignorance on the subject, "for the crew to be allowed to vote on the issue?"

There was a long pause following this and Nate could clearly envisage the varied expressions upon each of the unseen faces below. He did not realize it, but he was smiling to himself at the very audacity of this spirited woman, and for the moment any concerns for his own future became quite secondary as he waited with interest to hear what would come next.

"My dear," Captain Jacobs finally pleaded, "These are shipboard matters and..."

"And this ship, uncle dearest, is regarded by international law and to all intents and purposes as being United States territory, wheresoever she may be in the world. And on board a United States vessel I do believe it is our solemn duty to maintain our hard-won democratic principles and to allow each man to cast his vote."

There was another, longer pause this time before Captain Jacobs, clearing his throat loudly, spoke out.

"We shall take a vote on it. Gather all hands on deck, Mister Biggs."

With the entire crew summoned to the aft main deck under the break of the quarterdeck they were ordered by their captain, who stood looking grimly down upon them, to step to either one bulwark or the other; to starboard if they wished Mister Cooper to remain as their second mate, to larboard for Frederick Weeks to replace him.

Notwithstanding the odd remark that arose in muffled tones from the assemblage below such as, "What difference does it make, anyway?" and "My vote's for Jacko's monkey!" each man did as he was told and, with Robert Biggs and Frederick Weeks looking on in rising irritation and dejection respectively, only six of them stepped over to the larboard, including both the younger boys who only did so, it appeared, out of fear of their chief mate, along with both the cook and the carpenter. The remainder, including all ten packet-rats, the eight remaining Swedes, the sailmaker and the steward, opted for Nate to remain as their second mate and thus, with thanks due once again to Emma Jacobs who stood silently observing, the crew's democratic will was expressed.

As the crew was being dismissed by a clearly furious Robert Biggs, Nate happened to notice several of the packet-rats and even a few of the Swedes receiving a curt nod from William Scragg and he realized then the true scope of influence wielded by this man. And he decided then that from now on he would need to tread very carefully with Scragg. For it was now becoming clear that this man held a good deal more influence with *Achilles'* crew than did even her chief mate.

Cape Sao Roque was met with the dawn of October 31, its sheer gray headland standing some twenty miles distant and bearing fine on the leeward bow, precisely where it was expected to be and it was the first sighting of land in twenty-seven days. But it stirred little response from *Achilles'* crew other than on her quarterdeck, where the captain and his niece remained at loggerheads over the best means by which to pass it.

Samuel Jacobs was much in accord with Jonas Blunt in his opinion, in that to approach too close to this cape was to risk being caught and driven inshore by the prevailing current that was commonly known to set north and west towards it. But Emma, following her meticulous studies of Lieutenant Maury's findings, remained firmly convinced to the contrary. She had already proven, by urging her uncle to follow Lieutenant Maury's advice to the letter since they had crossed the equator, that there was more to these findings than mere poppycock, as Captain Blunt had so scornfully declared. By hauling *Achilles* close against these light southeasterly airs and by bracing her yards up fully they had managed to maintain a course of south-southwest towards the cape itself, leaving little room available to maneuver offshore and to windward should they find themselves drifting in too close. But, in the words of Lieutenant Maury, 'the chances are more than a hundred to one that the wind will hang steadily at southeast all the way from the line to St. Roque. When it hauls to east-southeast you can lay up and clear.' And so, by taking advantage of all such easterly slants in the wind, however momentary, to press her up even closer, and by maintaining a course that did not stray inshore of a line drawn from the equator to the cape, they had not yet found any cause to put *Achilles* about to regain any lost eastings and now were finding themselves in a most favorable position to pass the cape.

"There is a current," Emma conceded to her uncle, "that sets to the northwest. But it moves no faster than two knots, and for a fat merchantman of twenty years ago this would have been a serious problem. But for a clipper it would require at least three or four knots of set to be of any consequence. So think not of currents; they will not affect us."

"And what then of the wind?" her uncle asked again. "These southeasterlies will set us onto a lee shore yet if we maintain this heading, and yet thee'd venture even closer?"

"This southeasterly wind will surely dissipate," Emma insisted, "as we approach the cape. Because there is a stronger, more reliable land breeze that blows westerly from atop those cliffs, and once gained it will drive us southwards on a beam reach. But there is indeed a danger in approaching closer still, for then we risk falling into the lee of the headland itself, where those weaker southeasterly winds will return and, as you say, set us onto a lee shore. So we must stand boldly on until those westerlies are found and then immediately turn southwards and follow the coast along the forty-fathom line. Then we should pick up the beginnings of the Brazil Current north of Rio and it will speed us southwards even faster. It could save us three or four days of working through these lighter airs."

"Three or four days." Captain Jacobs peered aft to where *Sapphire*, having done well to keep up with *Achilles* throughout these past three days and perhaps now with a captain whose curiosity was stirred and who wished to observe more closely another ship following Lieutenant

Maury's advice, stood only a mile astern yet well out to seaward.

"Very well," he finally conceded. "We shall approach closer. But with caution."

With such little breeze as they had it took them fully until noon to reach the cape itself. As they proceeded Nate, who stood the forenoon watch, monitored their position carefully, with Emma's guidance, by means of a series of compass bearings taken of the cape itself and of its neighboring headlands. By streaming the log astern every half an hour they were able to calculate their set and drift and it was discovered that there was indeed a current setting them northwestwards at almost two knots but, as Emma had reassured her uncle, this was rendered all but negligible by *Achilles'* own speed and would not prove a hindrance.

A sounding was taken every ten minutes using the deep-water lead line which was dropped overboard from the weather foredeck and, as *Achilles* made headway, men positioned at intervals along the chainwales allowed coiled bights of the one-hundred-fathom line to snake from their hands until the lead struck bottom, whereupon all slack was promptly taken up and the fathom marker nearest the waterline was noted. The eighteen-pound lead weight had a hollowed out base which was 'armed' with tallow that could pick up traces of silt, mud, shells or sand from the seabed and, as the depth began to shelve up toward fifty fathoms, there was a noticeable change from mud to coarse sand and this corresponded closely to the notations that were printed on Emma's charts.

As they neared the forty fathom contour, with the sheer gray cliffs to starboard now visibly topped with greenery towering high and only a league's distance, the uncertain southeasterly breeze against which they had been hauling finally died away and in its place came the first breaths of a steady warm westerly wind, one that brought with it the thick taste of vegetation as well as the mourning cries of a host of seabirds nesting within the crags of the nearby rocky cliffs. Yards were braced about promptly and *Achilles*, now provided with a breeze she could finally work with, took off like a greyhound. Running south by east now on a beam reach, with the wind almost perpendicular to her heading and the weather clew of her mainsail hauled up to allow her fore course to fill and to lift her bows, she heeled over comfortably under all three skysails and was soon making a full ten knots of speed; the cape already passing swiftly astern and the shoreline to starboard held at an equal distance as they ran parallel to it with the breeze it had spawned remaining constant well into the afternoon.

Midway through the afternoon watch there came a hail from aloft and through his spyglass Captain Jacobs focused astern to where *Sapphire*, now lagging more than two miles behind, had also begun working herself to westwards in the hopes of catching this very same breeze. Captain Blunt, after watching *Achilles* steer inshore and fill out her canvas, had obviously changed his tune and he now sought to match this maneuver with one of his own. But, as *Sapphire* stood in closer to the cape, she did not bear away towards the south as soon as the land breeze filled her sails, but rather it appeared that Jonas Blunt, encouraged beyond prudence, sought an even stronger breeze further inshore and this was his undoing. Through his spyglass Captain Jacobs watched as *Sapphire's* sails began to spill, from her lower courses upwards until all canvas was cast fully aback even as Blunt, realizing too late his mistake, sought to turn his ship to seaward again. But already *Sapphire* was caught by the return of the same light southeasterly breeze which, now working in opposition to the offshore wind, created a confused and significantly weakened airflow, one against which he could scarcely make any headway whatsoever. *Sapphire* now lay trapped under the lee of the cape, with an onshore current and with too little breeze to effect any prompt return to eastward and it would be several hours before she was able to work herself free again.

Even at this distance those aboard *Achilles* could hear the shrill whistle of a boatswain's pipe, as well the corresponding yapping of a frantic-sounding dog which carried clearly across the ocean and this elicited a chorus of jeers from *Achilles'* crew as they gestured, for the most part very rudely, astern to their crippled rival. Samuel Jacobs, despite himself feeling humbled at this valuable lesson learned at another's expense, was significantly cheered nonetheless as he held *Achilles* close inshore and carefully followed the forty-fathom line southwards. They made good progress until the approaching of sunset, whereupon for safety's sake he bore away towards the fifty-fathom contour for the duration of the night, but still remained within that narrow band of blessed westerlies that hugged the Brazilian coastline.

The following day saw a continuation of the same offshore breeze and by mid-afternoon, having been detained and hampered for eleven full days by the Atlantic doldrums, the first signs of an opposing and more substantial southeasterly breeze began to paw at *Achilles'* skysails, causing them to luff with increased frequency until, by day's end, it took precedence altogether and they were able to brace all yards full about and haul weather tack lines forward to greet the welcome arrival of the southeast Trade Winds proper.

Aboard *Sapphire* a very irate Jonas Blunt stood watching

from his quarterdeck as, directly ahead of him, his crew continued to labor at the longboats' oars in an attempt to haul his ship back into the wind. They were standing two-hour shifts, achieving perhaps a quarter of a knot by Blunt's calculations and still had a long way to go before regaining those offshore westerlies that stood clearly visible up ahead almost two miles away. As he was turning to make his way below for another drop of reinforcement, Thomas Oglesby, as always selecting the most inconvenient of moments, arrived on the quarterdeck.

"Young Master Oglesby!" declared Blunt, loudly and at this juncture not giving a damn. "Have you come to witness the results of your impetuousness? See what you have achieved, sir! You have set us back by at least half a day!"

"I?" Thomas Oglesby sneered in response to Blunt's disrespectful outburst. "It is *you* who are captain of this vessel, sir, not I! That responsibility, I believe, is yours to bear and none other's."

"And you, sir, are the owner's son! When you tell, nay, *command* me under the authority of your father to cut closer inshore, then what am I supposed to do about it? Now you seek to absolve yourself of all blame? I do suspect, sir, that you have much yet to learn about honor, as well as decent gentlemanly conduct!"

At this young Thomas visibly bristled and, with his face reddening, he snapped,

"By God, I've a mind to call you out for that! How dare you speak to me so!"

This made Jonas Blunt laugh out loud, genuinely now, despite his residual anger.

"Call me out? Then what would be your pleasure, young sir? Belaying pins at five paces? Handspikes at ten?"

"Damn you! If you were not so drunk you would never

think to address me so!"

"Then I sincerely thank God that I am so drunk, sir! Now get off my fucking quarterdeck!"

"So, who was your friend, Harry?"

The unexpected voice from the darkness startled Harry out of his musings and he turned to see Sarah standing only a few feet behind him, all but invisible in the gloom of the aft main deck. Glancing around quickly and seeing that they were presently alone, he replied cagily,

"That's a long story."

"Let me guess. Something to do with gambling?"

"Certainly not."

"Women then. What was it, some dalliance with the man's wife? Not his daughter? Oh Harry, honestly, you are too much. Do you have no moral boundaries whatsoever?"

"Did you come down here just to torment me again? If so, I can tell you right now…"

"Oh, you're quite welcome," interrupted Sarah, haughtily. "Don't even mention it."

"Mention what?"

"The bit about saving your life."

"Oh, that. Well, thank-you. Much appreciated, I'm sure."

"Or the bit about talking to your chum, Scragg."

"All right. Thank-you for that, too. Not that he's my chum, but whatever it was you said to him it seems to have worked. What did you say to him?"

"Oh, you know. This and that. Honestly Harry, I'm beginning to wonder how on Earth you've managed to survive this long without my help. It really is rather lucky for you that I'm here, isn't it?"

At the sudden sound of footsteps approaching from

forward, Sarah turned and disappeared aft before Harry, his mouth now working like a beached trout, could even begin to respond to this.

Which is probably just as well.

Gideon had been furious to witness *Sapphire's* approach towards Sao Roque and her subsequent falling into the lee of the cape. Because he was certain that Jonas Blunt would never have acted so rashly of his own accord. It must have been that fool Thomas, who had always been in the habit of stepping in and playing captain whenever it suited him. He probably even went so far as to evoke the authority of his father in order to press her closer inshore and to consequently cause *Sapphire* to be hampered for hours, possibly as much as a full day. Now, if *Achilles* arrived in Frisco first, it would be entirely Thomas Oglesby's fault.

It was Gideon's task to delay *Achilles* and yet here was Thomas doing a better job of it himself with *Sapphire*! It was infuriating, because now Gideon was obliged to take action to correct the situation. He was going to have to start taking risks that he otherwise would not have had to, and all because of that damned fool Thomas Oglesby!

He now wished that he had spoken up earlier, while the two of them had been standing on *Achilles'* quarterdeck and Thomas had made the reference to his father.

Gideon would have very much enjoyed watching Thomas' reaction to being told that he was not, by a long shot, Old Man Thaddeus' one and only offspring.

Chapter Thirteen
A Dangerous Confrontation

The Trade Winds of the southern hemisphere are typically stronger than those in the north and, despite being close-hauled against them, *Achilles* was making good time once again. The wind had steadied out at twenty knots from the southeast and *Achilles* drew herself ahead at nine, creating an apparent wind on her larboard bow of almost thirty knots. This necessitated the handing of skysails, royals and outer jibs but, with inner jibs and lower staysails sheeted home snugly using luff tackles, this was mostly compensated for and she suffered little loss of speed from it. For the next three days she logged more than two hundred miles between noonday sightings: a very respectable rate for any clipper hauling to windward and she was fast proving both her owners and her captain correct in that her extreme sharpness allowed her to work to weather as well as any pilot boat.

On November 4, now thirty-one days out of New York, a sail was sighted bearing almost dead ahead: a small patch of brightness amid the scattered white-caps that remained unchanged in a manner that no white-cap ever did. By taking a series of compass bearings it was quickly determined that the distant ship was northbound and, having already crossed *Achilles'* hawse from starboard to larboard, was set to pass close within hailing distance along her weather side.

Captain Jacobs stood on the quarterdeck with brass speaking trumpet held at the ready and the crew began shuffling themselves towards the larboard bulwark, maneuvering their holystones in that direction as they knelt scouring the deck, or mysteriously opting to take their unpicked oakum or half-finished seizings over to the windward side to risk being doused by the bow-tossed spray which regularly made it up and over the high bulwarks, for all were now eager to hear any news that might be had.

She was an Italian ship, fully rigged on all three masts and she was running large with her topmast studdingsails set to burst. She approached rapidly, riding high on the swell and yawing freely before it, her tarnished copper sheathing reflecting pale green whenever the sea dipped away beneath her and she corkscrewed in such a fashion that it was difficult to conceive of the notion, to those lining *Achilles'* bulwarks, that they themselves must surely appear equally as weather-tossed. As she closed to within hailing distance it became apparent, judging from the two ships' opposing speeds, that there would be little time available here for niceties.

"Achilles! Thirty-one days from New York!" shouted Captain Jacobs, directly into the wind.

There was a momentary pause, yet long enough for both ships to close jib boom to jib boom and a mere hundred yards apart.

"Medina! Ninety-eight days from Frisco!"

The captain of the *Medina* would have required no

trumpet to speak through, as his voice carried clearly to them on the wind.

"What news from Frisco, captain?"

Achilles' sails luffed momentarily as she was caught in the other ship's lee as the two vessels drew abreast and then began passing astern of one another.

"Wood stoves! Dey ain't gotta no wood stoves! An' carpenter tools!"

There appeared the faintest suggestion of a smile on Captain Jacob's tired features at this news. *Achilles* had wood stoves aplenty down in her hold, as well as tools. He raised his speaking trumpet in salute to the other vessel and then, on a last-moment impulse, announced with uncharacteristic levity,

"Give my regards to Sapphire!"

The following day logged another two hundred miles and now *Achilles* was making up for lost time. Captain Jacobs, having still not fully recovered from the many sleepless nights spent on the quarterdeck as had been his wont throughout the doldrums, nevertheless remained diligently on deck throughout as he continued to urge his crew onwards without respite. But now his health was beginning to suffer for it, as was fast becoming evident in the marked redness of his eyes and in the occasional slurring of his speech and, more particularly, in the time it now took for him to make even the simplest of decisions.

There no longer existed any proper Sunday routine whereby the crew's duties were lessened and they were allowed to smoke and talk and mend their clothing during the slack afternoon hours, for there simply were no slack hours available to them. For as long as their captain stood the quarterdeck he retained command of the ship and, with

Cape Horn being their destination and with so few of his crew having experienced the transition from Atlantic to Pacific, it was now in Captain Jacobs' thoughts continually that they must be fully prepared for it. So he continued driving his mates and his crew relentlessly towards this end, with practice reefing, setting and furling of each individual sail and with preparations for lowering the topgallant masts, if needs be, and with the lashing down of all loose gear in readiness for what the more experienced mariner termed, and in no affectionate way whatsoever, Cape Stiff.

Three days following the encounter with the Italian ship the ladies were gathered together in Emma's stateroom for a light lunch consisting of tea, sandwiches and cake. On this occasion there was an addition to what until now had been the standard complement consisting of only Emma and the French lady. The erstwhile quiet and mysterious passenger, who until now had gone by the name of Mrs. Harry Jenkins, was joining them for the first time.

"Now then, ma chère," began Madam Fontaine, pouring some tea for Sarah. "Firstly, I must insist that we each one swear ourselves to confidence. We are all friends here, non? Not a word spoken here will leave this room." She turned to Emma. "Are we agreed?"

Emma nodded and turned directly to Sarah.

"You have my word of honor. As long as nothing you say affects this vessel or her immediate safety, then there is no need for this to go any further."

Sarah, now with a mildly amused expression, replied,

"I'm not sure that it would matter anyway. It would be Harry's word against mine, after all. And I'm the one holding the valid ticket."

Emma pondered this in seriousness for a while, then

nodded in agreement.

"That is correct. For the duration of this voyage there is nothing that the captain or anyone else can do about that. And if this Harry person still insists on prosecuting you, then he will have to take that up with the authorities in San Francisco. If any such authority exists, that is."

Sarah smiled.

"I think Harry has already worked that out for himself."

Madam Fontaine leaned forward and offered Sarah a slice of cake.

"Now then, Margaret, please tell us all about Harry."

With almost all of *Achilles'* crew obliged to remain on deck working throughout the day, it was relatively easy for Gideon to find the opportunity he now sought. All he had to do was wait for the turning of the watch at midday, when the entire crew was gathered aft to be assigned their afternoon chores and he himself stood forward, alone, next to the windlass.

At the distant sounding of eight bells from the quarterdeck, Gideon promptly reached for the windlass bell's rope and repeated the signal, following this up with a cry of "All's well!" Then, with only a brief glance around to ensure that he was indeed alone, he promptly ducked himself into the fore scuttle, drew the hatch cover closed above him and went down into the forecastle space.

The forecastle was empty, save for two inhabitants. As Gideon reached the foot of the ladder he saw the first one immediately: the old Swede, Karl, who was presently laying prone on his bunk, muttering incoherently. The other inhabitant was nowhere to be seen for the moment, but that was not important.

Gideon immediately moved to his starboard, around and

behind the nearest tier of bunks, to the hatch that was set into the deck close against the aft bulkhead. Pausing only to listen, and with the inward reassurance that he would have ample time to climb back out again unseen should anyone slide the scuttle cover open above him, he lifted the hatch, dropped the carpenter's auger into the space below, then followed it down.

Only a few minutes later he re-emerged, to find the old Swede still muttering in his bunk and the other inhabitant of the forecastle now sitting there alongside him staring at Gideon with what appeared to be an unparalleled degree of interest. But with only a brief glare in its direction the monkey visibly winced, screeched loudly and ducked itself behind the nearest bunk, out of sight, and stayed there.

Gideon paused only long enough to replace the hatch cover, brush the loose sawdust from his sleeves, then headed back up onto deck.

Madame Fontaine's laughter was both genuine and infectious and finally Emma herself succumbed to it, and to such an extent that she was obliged to put down her cup and saucer for fear of spilling her tea.

"Oh, the poor man!" she finally spluttered, lifting a napkin to her mouth lest she spray her companions with cake shrapnel.

"Poor man?" responded Sarah, smiling herself now. "Well, considering that he fully intended to rob me from the beginning, I would say it's no more or less than he deserves, surely."

"Well, yes, I agree. If that is indeed the case, then the punishment does fit the crime. But still. The poor man."

Emma's laughter finally died away and she regained her composure. But then she made the mistake of glancing at

Madame Fontaine and this set her off all over again. Finally, when she felt that she could safely manage it, she said,

"But what if you are mistaken? As you admitted yourself, he didn't *actually* manage to steal anything from you. What if he truly is innocent? Is there a possibility of him continuing to make this an issue? To stir up even more trouble below because of it?"

Sarah shook her head with confidence.

"Don't worry about Harry," she reassured Emma. "I'm not sure he even knows the definition of the word innocent." But I am sure that a few months of honest toil will do him no harm whatsoever. To the contrary, it might even help to keep him out of mischief for the duration. And besides, he might still prove himself useful, if the need arises."

"How so?"

"Well who else do you have down there inside the fo'c's'le? Harry could be a wealth of information if you ever have the need to gage the mood of this crew, wouldn't you think?"

Emma considered this seriously for a moment before nodding.

"That is a good point. Certainly something to keep in mind for the future."

The following morning, during the chill hours of dawn twilight as the morning watch and the idlers were beginning to gather on deck for the daily wash-down, it was Nate himself who first noticed the irregularity in *Achilles'* behavior.

He was standing the morning watch, which had always been his favorite, not only because there are so few sights in this world that can compare to the waxing beauty of a sunrise over an empty ocean but also, after being stood adeck since four of the morning and having worked the first watch of the evening before, it without fail afforded a man the heartiest of appetites for the best meal of the day, which was breakfast.

With such pleasing notions of hot flapjacks and salted bacon being cast adrift in a pint and more of thick, molasses-sweetened coffee, Nate was standing by the quarterdeck's weather taffrail from where he could monitor both sails aloft and the helmsman nearby without being obliged to shift anything more than his eyes. He was also keeping an authoritative watch on his own Starbowlines who, under his leading hand, George Evans' close supervision, were being kept busy with the morning wash-down. It was one of those rare moments of the day during which Nate was able to enjoy the deck all to himself, while the chief mate still slumbered below and the captain, who unexpectedly and for the first time in many a night had made no appearance whatsoever during his watch, remained as yet unseen.

As the growing twilight cast its varying hues against the clouds to the east, the view ahead from the quarterdeck along the main deck monkey rail and all the way to the raised foredeck appeared much the same as it ever did. It was a view that quickly became familiar to any captain or mate, as the weather quarterdeck was where they each spent the majority of their time while on watch. And so any variation whatsoever in the ship's aspect as viewed from this position, no matter how slight, was sufficient to bring about a nagging feeling that something was amiss.

Nate was experiencing just such a feeling this morning, and the more so for each minute that passed. He was looking ahead along the entire length of the ship, with her canvas now glowing a bright pink in the sun's early rays and contrasting sharply with the blackness of her lower masts and shrouds, and with her deck glistening wetly from the water from the wash-down hose, and he was trying to figure out just what it was he was seeing that was not right.

To his starboard the spanker boom, having been sheeted in to less than a fathom from amidships, strained to leeward and the redirected airflow from the sail above stirred and ruffled the carefully groomed and abundant locks of Bacas, his helmsman, who stood close beneath it. Directly aloft both mizzen topsail and topgallant yards were braced up sharply, their weather leeches shivering and luffing occasionally as the experienced Portuguese fisherman steered full and by, peering aloft to monitor these sails more often than he checked his compass.

Then, on returning his attention forward again, it suddenly occurred to Nate what it was he was seeing. It was *Achilles'* bowsprit and jib boom structure and their aspect in relation to the seas up ahead. She was no longer meeting the oncoming waves as easily as she had been earlier, slicing into and riding gracefully up and onto the crests of each one as she ought to with her outwardly flared bows. Rather she was beginning to plow into the larger of these waves, each time to the accompaniment of a near to imperceptible jarring of the deck underfoot and tall plumes of water were now rising each time from ahead and dissolving to leeward across her exposed foredeck in a rainbow of fine mist.

Achilles appeared to be down by the head. And this could mean only one thing: that she was beginning to take on water forward.

Being still not fully certain of this and not wishing to create any undue alarm, Nate promptly summoned the carpenter who was assisting with the wash-down. The Albanian, Darijo Durakovic, although being ten years Nate's elder was yet not half the seaman but as ship's carpenter this scarcely mattered. He still grumbled openly as he arrived on the quarterdeck, his pale and squared features twisted into a sour frown and his dark eyes continually shifting every which way except Nate's.

"What?" he asked rudely. "You wan' clean decks or you wanna stand here chit-chattin' all mornin'? Pump ain't gonna work itself."

"When did you last take soundings of the forepeak?" Nate demanded.

"What're you saying? I dunno me job? Every goddam mornin' I take soundings! After wash-down! Not before!"

With that the carpenter stormed off again, leaving Nate with the frustrating knowledge that there was nothing he could do or say that would make the man sound his spaces any sooner.

Yet it was only ten minutes later that Darijo appeared again, now in a state of high agitation.

"We got two fathom o' water in the forepeak! We're sinkin', by Christ! Where's the chief mate? We gotta start pumpin'!"

The chief mate was promptly summoned and, when his attention was directed forward to *Achilles'* bowsprit, he too immediately noticed the change in the ship's aspect. Without a word Robert Biggs set off forward along the main deck; his bright red jacket, which he had thrown on hurriedly, still unbuttoned and exposing the hairs of his broad chest and with a scowl on his face that struck alarm into all he passed along the way and they quickly redoubled their efforts at the handle of the seawater pump or leaned forward more acutely as they applied more weight to their holystones.

Achilles had been constructed with two 'tween decks below, each one having a little over six feet of headroom and which ran almost the entire length of the ship, and beneath them a lower hold space that was ten feet in height.

Separating these three cargo decks from both the crew's forecastle accommodation and the forepeak space directly below it was a watertight bulkhead that, in the event of a head-on collision or a shallow grounding, would help to protect the aft cargo spaces from becoming immediately flooded. Access to the forepeak could only be had by way of a small hatch that was set into the deck inside the forecastle space itself and it was to this that Robert Biggs now cut a direct wake.

When he returned some minutes later he was thoroughly soaked and gripping a tool in his hand: a large carpenter's auger with a one-and-a-half-inch bore.

"Sabotage!" he declared. "The entire forepeak's flooded to sea level!"

Then he turned angrily to the carpenter.

"Rig the pumps!" he snapped. "And then fetch me some plugs!"

The chief mate tossed the tool directly at him, where it struck the man's chest and clattered loudly to the deck.

"That's the size you'll be needing!" snarled the mate. He then squared angrily up to the carpenter who was now gaping stupidly at the tool lying on the deck.

"I want a full set of soundings for every compartment! And I'll have none of your bullshit excuses, you son of a bitch! There's two holes drilled through the outer hull and two more in the aft bulkhead, and if it weren't for a bunch of loose rope-ends and dunnage blocking 'em we'd be pumping our way into Rio right now! If I find as much as an inch of water covering the hold floor, you're going to feel the lash, I swear to God!"

Then the chief mate turned to Nate.

"All hands ahoy, mister! Get 'em mustered aft and we'll sort this business out!"

And with another parting shot at the carpenter for not keeping his tools under lock and key and properly accounted for, Robert Biggs, now with a truly alarming expression bent to his features, paused only to retrieve a belaying pin from the nearby rack rail and tuck it securely into his belt before descending the ladder again to the main deck.

With all hands except the carpenter and the helmsman gathered at the aft main deck the chief mate set about, as promised, with sorting this business out. He began with the old Swede, Karl Angstrom, whom he had forcefully dragged from his bunk in the forecastle space and he drew his English-speaking countryman, Anders Fersen, to the fore and ordered him to interpret.

"Ask him who it was! Ask him who went down into the forepeak!"

But the old man, being barely able to stand himself upright without the help of his younger fellows, had seen nothing apparently and this to his own misfortune as Robert Biggs was clearly not about to accept it.

"It was all of you bastards together, wasn't it?" the chief mate concluded. "You Souwegians! Every man jack of you!"

But, with his keen senses detecting no signs of guilt, let alone of comprehension, amongst this bunch, Biggs turned angrily instead to the packet-rats, in particular to their leader, William Scragg.

"I know what you sons of bitches are about! You're always on the lookout for mischief! What do you have to say for yourself?"

William Scragg merely smiled at the chief mate, which only served to infuriate Biggs all the more, and replied in the most reasonable of tones,

"Now, what would be the point on that, Mister Mate? I

meantersay, drillin' holes an' such inter the hull? Defies all common logic, if you don't mind me sayin' so, sir. Considerin' it's the gold fields we're out for, not some dago stinkpot like Rio."

Biggs nonetheless glared dubiously at each one of these packet-rats in his turn, none of whom dared to so much as shift his feet for fear of the attention this might draw, and with such a look of growing mistrust that it bordered on paranoid.

"Steward! Get you to the arms locker! Fetch a piece for the second mate and myself! We'll have none of this aboard my ship!"

As Pepin strode aft to the arms locker that stood adjacent to the captain's stateroom Robert Biggs, with belaying pin now gripped so tightly that his knuckles had turned white, continued to glare at his assembled crew, silently daring each one of them to lend him the first excuse, however slight, of wielding it proper.

And most unfortunately of all it was the old Swede, Karl, who without having any notion as to the seriousness of the situation, turned to Anders Fersen and began muttering something in his own language, which by its very tone suggested little beyond that of innocent inquiry but to Robert Biggs, in his ongoing fury, clearly suggested otherwise.

"What's this? More devilry? By God, I'll have that out of you here and now!"

And the mate swung his belaying pin in that direction and it connected solidly with the old man's head and the Swede, much like on that first day when he had stepped aboard *Achilles*, dropped like a sack of coal to the deck. One of his younger countrymen cried out in protest and made to stoop down to assist him and he too received the full force of the mate's belaying pin, which caused him to howl out in pain and stagger back into the throng of assembled hands. Now not a man or boy dared make any movement or sound whatsoever and Nate, seeing Pepin reappear on the quarterdeck not with the captain but instead with his niece, began to sidle his way cautiously aft, hoping to do so unnoticed as the chief mate focused his attention instead on his gathered crew.

Robert Biggs was now clearly worked up into the most dangerous of humors. Standing there with his legs braced fore and aft against the steady pitching of the ship underfoot and with his bared chest rising and falling from his most recent exertions, he stared down each man in his turn, still looking for his culprit. But so too were the crew themselves quickly rising towards such a mood and this could be seen clearly by Nate, who wondered why Biggs did not appear to realize it. The chief mate was, to Nate's mind, alike to a bear tamer who with belaying pin and reputation alone was managing for the time being to hold them at bay, yet such a situation was entirely off-balance and it would take but one misplaced word or gesture now to fulfill Biggs' own prediction, of the entire crew turning against him and thus in effect against all authority on board. But clearly he did not realize this and Nate, seeing only one chance remaining, made his way quickly up the ladder to the quarterdeck, to where Emma and the whaleman steward were both standing by the forward railing looking on anxiously.

"The captain is ill and taken to his bunk!" Emma hissed urgently to Nate. "We must not allow this foolishness to progress any farther! Does he not comprehend the danger?"

"I think not," replied Nate. He glanced at the steward, who had now armed himself with two revolvers, and saw that here, at least, he might find help.

"We dare not oppose him," said Emma. Then, with the

appearance of a most concerned-looking Madame Fontaine at the head of the trunk cabin's aft companionway, she quickly instructed both men,

"You must be seen to give him your full support. You must do whatever it takes to maintain control of the situation. That is of the utmost importance. Here, take this. I am about as practiced with these things, Mister Cooper, as you appear to be with a sextant."

And to Nate's surprise she actually made an effort to smile as she handed over the captain's revolver but this merely contorted her otherwise fair features into something rather alarming and it would have been a good deal more reassuring for Nate had she not bothered attempting it at all.

"The captain and I are relying on you to deal with this situation," Emma added, looking also to Pepin with emphasis and Nate was reassured to see that this steward's loyalties lay unquestioningly with the captain's niece. But before he could say anything in response Emma had already turned away to confront the French lady and her girls, all of whom had collected together on the aft quarterdeck and to whom she now sought to lend her most convincing reassurances before herding them safely below again.

Nate drew in a deep breath and steeled his nerves before descending to the main deck. With the steward following close behind and with both of them now brandishing their weapons, this very sight alone, it seemed, took much of the wind out of the crew's canvas, for now all eyes turned from Robert Biggs towards the revolvers and to the determined expressions now affixed to the faces of the two men who wielded them. The mood quickly altered: from the shifty-eyed gauging of predators seeking an opportunity to pounce to one of caution and a quiet rumble of angry mutterings began to arise from the gathered crew.

Two men in particular: the able hands Frederick Weeks and Silas Rigsby, were now standing together under the lee shrouds, whispering urgently to one another, their angry glares alternating between Nate and Robert Biggs. But the instant the chief mate noticed this he leaped upon it and, snatching a revolver from the steward's hand, he pushed his way into the crowd and began indiscriminately pistol-whipping both men, whose loud protests went unheeded as they sought to protect themselves. Then he grabbed the startled Rigsby by his collar and drew him out.

"It was the two of you, was it? You both want to go to Rio, do you? Well, by Christ, you can try swimming there!"

And Biggs in his fury would have thought nothing of heaving Silas Rigsby bodily over the side, and if it were not for the man's weight combined with *Achilles'* high bulwarks would most assuredly have done so. But instead he had to content himself with slamming the now dazed Rigsby up against the rack rail, to where he slumped helplessly to the deck, bleeding and stunned, and Robert Biggs, now quite beyond the limits of his own reason, grabbed Frederick Weeks roughly by his collar and propelled him bodily towards Nate.

"A dozen strokes for both these men, mister! Spare the lash and you'll get a dozen yourself!"

Amidst more angry mutterings Nate glanced aft in uncertainty, towards Emma who was still watching silently from the quarterdeck and, with lips pursed together tightly, she nodded quickly. Do whatever it takes, she had told him, to maintain control of the situation. Now, looking directly into Week's face, Nate saw that here stood the very tinder that would ignite this crew into outright revolt. This man was emboldened now, with all eyes of the crew upon him, and ready for a fight. Nate knew precisely what needed to be done here and yet it sickened him. But he had no choice. So he took a step towards Weeks.

"Don't you dare fucking touch me!" Weeks snarled and his hand reached immediately for his knife. But it never got there as Nate's fist connected solidly with Weeks' face and, with another thrown in for good measure and feeling rather surprised that it felt so good, Nate hauled the sailor upright by his collar and stared him fully in the face.

"Now, say that again," he challenged, feeling suitably angered himself now.

"You're a dead man Cooper," Weeks mumbled as he shook his head in an attempt to clear it and regain his balance.

But Nate gave him no time for this as he promptly set about his appointed task, pulling the dazed Weeks forward and lashing his thumbs tightly to the shrouds overhead. Meanwhile the steward remained looking on with pistol raised high and with a particularly dangerous expression directed at the assembled crew and watching closely for any further signs of a spark that might kindle them into outright mutiny. But with the sight of so many pistols now aimed in their direction the majority of them, even the clearly angered Swedes, now lapsed into a resentful silence.

Only Robert Biggs himself could have predicted to what degree his punishments would extend on this day and perhaps not even he, in his irrational state, could have foretold where they might have ended. Already he had two men selected for the cat: Weeks and Rigsby, and already he was busily singling out others from the crowd; those who displayed even the slightest suggestion of guilt, or those who did not appear sufficiently cowed and indeed the more he dwelt upon each one of these men and boys in their turn the more suspicious he was becoming. But it was unfortunate that, in his ongoing rage and in his diligent searching, he should momentarily forget himself and pick on one of the few persons among the entire ship's crew whom he ought never to have considered picking on.

When the young Elijah Johnson, himself a boy of only twelve and a particular favorite with many of the crew, not least the captain himself, glanced aft towards the quarterdeck and away from the man about to be flogged, Robert Biggs, without any thought, immediately rapped the butt of his pistol against the rear of the boy's head, causing him to cry out more in surprise than pain. But before the chief mate could even begin to admonish the boy for not witnessing punishment there came a furious shout from abaft.

"Hold fast!"

Captain Jacobs, who despite his weakened and exhausted state had nonetheless managed to make it up the aft companionway, was now standing at the quarterdeck's forward railing alongside his niece and was glaring down at the scene before him with a positively furious demeanor. The captain's glassy-eyed countenance was made all the more startling by the pallid tones of what until so recently had been the healthiest of bronzed complexions. His gray-tinged features were now deep etched and shadowed by the trials of his sickness and it seemed he could barely stand himself upright without the aid of his niece. Even his voice, which ought otherwise to have boomed forth loudly and with vigor, was reduced now to an uneven croak, in the wake of which came an alarming wheezing noise that seemed to teeter on the verge of an eruption into coughs.

"Hold fast, I say! Aft to me, mister! Smartly now!"

The captain was promptly disabled by a fit of coughing; a prolonged one that lasted near to a full minute and in the meantime Robert Biggs paused, clearly uncertain for the first time, and such was the volatility of mood all around him that, if not for the captain's immediate presence, the crew may well have descended upon him like hungry wolves at this, the very first sign of weakness, and torn him apart limb from limb.

"Mister Cooper," Captain Jacobs said, now in a more subdued tone. "Return these men to their watches. Duty hands to man the pumps. Let's have that forepeak dry."

The captain then turned to Robert Biggs.

"And precisely what manner of carnage dost thee intend to lay upon my ship, mister? I see a man fallen, a man tied in readiness for the lash and now thee'd strike at this young fellow who has done harm to no one! Where, precisely, sir, dost thee intend to finish it?"

As many words as these, spoken with such vehemence, were sufficient to weaken the captain again and he visibly slumped against the railing in the grips of another fit of coughing and had to be supported by his niece. Yet his eyes continued to blaze fiercely and in them could be seen that most dangerous of elements and one that, had he retained his proper wits about him, he would never have openly displayed. For it was mistrust, directed now at his own chief mate and it did not go unnoticed by the assembled crew, many of whom were still eyeing Robert Biggs closely and all but salivating at the prospect of applying their own two cents' worth.

Nate quickly roused the crew into action, shouting at them now to disperse either to their watches or to breakfast and with the help of the steward he began herding them forward and beyond earshot of their furious captain, leaving those in command of *Achilles* to their own problems on the quarterdeck.

For now a clear rift had been established between the captain and his chief mate. And, as with the element of trust itself, once broken could never be properly repaired. And all on board knew this, too, from the oldest salt to the greenest of hands, as well they knew that, for as long as it remained so, there would be nothing but misery gravitating in their direction from it.

Chapter Fourteen
Trouble on Deck

With this clashing of wills between the captain and his chief mate a perilous condition had now arisen aboard *Achilles*. All on board recognized this, too, for when at such odds a chief mate cannot rule with any force of conviction and a captain cannot likewise rely upon the other to adopt his own dictated principles and to promote his unspoken will.

It came to a head sooner than anyone had reason to expect, beginning with the emergence the following morning, November 8, of a dismayed Anders Fersen from the fore scuttle at the turning-to of the forenoon watch.

"Murder! Gott-dam murder!"

This cry was promptly taken up by several others as they too discovered the old Swede, Karl Angstrom, laying dead in his bunk, having never regained consciousness from the day before. It was a cry taken up in bold defiance of Robert Biggs, for there could be no doubting the cause of the old man's death any more than there could be of the absolute injustice of it. It was a cry that reverberated throughout the ship and within clear earshot of the captain and his two mates, yet never within their actual presence, for those who shouted it still feared a similar fate themselves. But now they at least held a modicum of hope in that their captain might possibly intervene.

But sadly this was not to be. Samuel Jacobs, still ailing poorly and thus with all the more reason to repair such ill-advised damage as he himself had created, now took measures to this effect. He called on his chief officer in full view of everyone on the quarterdeck and requested of him in polite terms to please take care of the unfortunate sailor and to make all suitable arrangements for his burial. Then, with a brief and noncommittal nod to each of his mates, and having to rely once again upon his niece to assist him down the companionway, he returned to his stateroom and was not seen again for the remainder of that day.

Robert Biggs was in a most unusual mood that morning. He appeared to Nate to be continually backing and filling, in a state of perpetual indecision as if unsure as to exactly how to proceed. On the one hand there was his usual testiness that appeared so firmly ingrained into his nature as to be quite inseparable from the man without, while on the other there was an underlying measure of caution to each of his actions, as if now and for the very first time he was actually experiencing within his own conscience an inkling of empathy towards the mood of his crew. Or perhaps, Nate guessed, this caution was directed more towards the very unpredictability of it.

It is a particular mood that affects all seamen with the loss of one of their own at sea; a mood by which each man experiences a drifting of his own thoughts towards such contemplations whereby all those petty and imperfect trimmings that surround his everyday life are momentarily peeled away and that which lies beneath is exposed to sky and element. It is a state of unusual clarity of awareness, in which he invariably calls into question the very purpose of his own existence in light of the countless perils that he and his shipmates must daily face. It would normally bring about a general softening of mood, and for a while it would force aside any such minor grievances and there would be a deal more tolerance and kindliness between shipmates, for a while at least. But in this instance, with the knowledge held by all on board that it was Robert Biggs himself who was the direct cause of this sailor's death, one could only guess as to what was going on inside any man's head on this particular day.

Biggs had, since the incident of the day before, surprised Nate considerably by way of a conversation undertaken later that evening, at the turning-to of the middle watch at midnight. Under cover of darkness and as the two mates had stood together on the quarterdeck, Nate had at first been unnerved when Biggs had gruffly summoned him to the leeward railing, from where any words spoken softly enough would be carried away into the surrounding blackness of the ocean. Nate had tensed in readiness for some reprimand or other for his perceived shortcomings but instead and to his surprise Biggs had stated, in a low voice,

"You performed well this forenoon, mister, in keeping those dogs at bay. You might yet have the makings of a second mate."

Nate, being entirely unaccustomed to any manner of praise whatsoever from this man, remained tensed in anticipation, waiting for whatever cruel punch line might be attached. But there had came none and Biggs, his eyes visible only as two pinpoints of reflected light from the binnacle's lantern, went on,

"There may be some changes in the offing." The chief mate's head had turned briefly towards the trunk cabin, then back to Nate. "The old man's pretty sick. And if you ask me his wits have already deserted him."

Nate suddenly felt pressed into a corner. He did not want to hear another word. If anything, Biggs' statement had more of a mutinous whiff about it than any that might have been extracted by flogging the entire crew, as had been the mate's intention that morning. He was, therefore, actually relieved when Biggs added,

"He may die of his illness."

Nate had remained silent, still unsure of what to say.

"Which means I shall be needing a chief mate, to rule over this rabble."

Nate had nodded earnestly, silently thanking his stars that both Weeks and Rigsby had now fallen out of favor with this man and that he himself would now be considered for the chief mate's post. But then fast in the wake of this notion came another, more alarming one: that of Robert Biggs taking over as captain of *Achilles* and just as quickly he felt the wind spill from his canvas and it was just as well that it was too dark for Biggs to read his expression.

"I will do everything I can to support you," Nate had declared lamely, for in all reason he could do little else.

Biggs' eyes had remained fixed upon Nate for a very long time; two pinpoints of light, unwavering against the blackness. Finally he had given a curt nod and walked away. Not another word had been spoken between them since.

Nate, not having gained a wink of sleep that night, now stood apart from the gathered hands on the main deck as he watched *Achilles'* chief mate conduct the burial service for the dead sailor.

Biggs stood next to the plank upon which the canvas-wrapped body lay, one end balanced on the monkey rail and the other on the shoulders of two of the younger Swedes, and he read the verses aloud from the captain's bible in a flat, monotonous tone. Now and again he would look up with a frown, to rapidly scan the expressions of his assembled crew, looking for what perhaps even he himself did not quite know. Yet his gaze did tend to linger upon those two men whose earlier floggings had not been so much cancelled as postponed. And both Frederick Weeks and Silas Rigsby knew this, too, for with their captain now ill and laid up below there were no remaining illusions on deck that this chief mate's authority was in any way diminished by it.

Biggs finished the verses and closed the book. Then on his command the plank was tipped and the old Swede, Karl Angstrom, who had still not properly learned his larboard from his starboard, was delivered in true sailor fashion to the deep.

Amidst much quiet grumbling and reluctant shuffling of feet, *Achilles'* crew was dismissed and each man returned to his duties.

The second dog watch, commencing at six in the evening with the serving of dinner, was met on this day with a heretofore unparalleled measure of silence and lack of enthusiasm. Not a soul elected to remain up on *Achilles'* forward main deck, as normally they would in such mild weather, to gather around the windlass to eat and talk and to laugh freely as they were permitted for the duration. They instead to a man retreated down into the forecastle, leaving only the duty helmsman and the lookouts at their stations, along with a rather bemused and increasingly concerned second mate on the quarterdeck with nothing to look at save an uncommonly empty stretch of main deck, a sea of surrounding whitecaps and the filtered yellow gloom of a sunset behind the heavy overcast that overhung the horizon to starboard, slightly north of west.

With the mess kid sitting all but forgotten atop Scragg's bunk the men inside the forecastle were busily engaged in their varied subdued conversations. Scragg was talking quietly with Jacko and Tyrone Pete, while Spuds, Billy Grimes, Jimmy the Bruiser and the remaining packet-rats listened in, occasionally turning their heads to glance at the other group who conversed at the far end of the space, equally as earnestly and equally as quietly.

This other group consisted of Frederick Weeks, Silas Rigsby and several of the Swedes, including Anders Fersen who was translating for his countrymen. It was Weeks and Rigsby, it seemed, who did most of the talking and Anders Fersen, along with the majority of his fellows, were repeatedly shaking their heads and appeared to be continually disputing the same point over and over, but did not seem to be getting very far with it.

Of the remaining diversity of the forecastle's inhabitants there came the occasional whispered comment from those individuals who sat or lay about on their bunks, but for the most part they remained silent and they watched and listened while these two larger groups discussed and, in effect, decided their futures for them.

Finally it was Frederick Weeks who stood up and made his way through the gloom to where the packet-rats were gathered and, squaring his shoulders and raising his chin toward Scragg, he announced boldly,

"It's decided. Tomorrow night. If chance permits, we'll do it tomorrow night."

Scragg, peering closely down at Weeks, pursed his lips and nodded slowly.

"We have to teach that son of a bitch a lesson!" Weeks declared, as if in need of justifying himself. "We have to show him that we stand together here. You understand that, don't you?"

Scragg, now with an amused grin, responded,

"No need to convince me, ol' chap. We shan't stand in yer way. Chief mate deserves a good spanking, I don't deny it." He nodded toward the other group of men. "All o' them Souwegians in on it, too?"

Weeks shuffled his feet uncomfortably. "Most of them," he assured.

"An' wot about the greaser?"

Weeks frowned at the reference to the second mate. He replied carefully.

"What about him?"

"You ain't got no beef with Mister Cooper. Understood?"

Weeks looked away as he replied.

"It's Biggs who's the problem here," he said. "With the captain down sick, he now gets full control of the ship. He'll stop at nothing. He'll flog us all to the bone, every last one of us. Including you."

Scragg, with a dismissive huff, did not appear overly impressed with that argument. He continued eyeing Weeks closely through the gloom.

"Then we have your support?" Weeks urged.

"Just a bashin'," Scragg reiterated. "Nothin' more."

"You have my word."

This caused Scragg to smile again, but without much humor.

"Wot, as a gentleman?"

"No. As a shipmate."

Scragg continued to stare closely at Weeks from atop his

bunk. As he did so the monkey, Smudger, suddenly appeared as if from nowhere brandishing a full bottle that he promptly deposited into Scragg's lap. Scragg glanced at the label, nodded approvingly and rewarded the monkey with a dried plum from his pocket, then returned his gaze to Weeks. Finally he nodded.

"We shan't stand in yer way," he repeated. "Providin' you leave the second mate out of it."

He uncorked the whiskey and offered Weeks the first chug with a calculated degree of civility, causing the other to stare dubiously at him, still unsure and not quite trusting Scragg. Scragg, in turn, continued smiling benignly.

"Hadn't yon boys better get back up on deck?" Scragg nodded towards the assembled Swedes. "Chief mate'll be stowin' away 'is puddin' about now. Wouldn't want 'im to start aspeculatin' on what's goin' on down here now, would we?"

Scragg watched as the Swedes, followed closely by Weeks and Rigsby, filed up the ladder and his smile faded away to nothing. He did not trust either man. Not a solitary inch. He was considering the upcoming situation, as well as he and his chums' prospects in relation to it. A little mischief here and there was one thing, he conceded, and normally he would be up to it in two shakes, if only for the mere distraction of it. But what these men were proposing here had all the makings of a situation that could all too easily get out of control.

Both Weeks and Rigsby seemed to share an uncommon grudge against *Achilles'* second mate and this was now creating some concern for Scragg. Because with he and his companions' only intention being to reach the gold fields, he was now finding himself playing host to an entirely novel set of internal values, not least of which and most alarmingly of all for him was that of a sense of loyalty: toward both this ship and to the one remaining officer, in the chief mate's and captain's absence, who might still be able to navigate her safely to Frisco.

"I'll be scuppered," he murmured to himself, shaking his head. Because he now realized that he, William Scragg, would have to look to Nate Cooper's back and, to all intents and purposes, regard this officer as he would his closest chum.

"Never thought I'd live ter see the day."

Emma placed a flat palm hesitantly across her uncle's pale brow and felt it to be somewhat cooler to the touch. Much cooler, if truth be told, than it ought to be and again she was unable to prevent the notion from re-entering her mind. What if he should pass away from his fever, out here in mid-ocean?

Whatever would she do without him?

They had only ever briefly spoken about such matters, and not nearly enough for Emma's satisfaction. Before boarding *Achilles* back in New York she and her uncle had touched upon certain subjects and he had expressed his own concerns regarding his niece's future, but his focus had always been directed toward the ending of this voyage rather than anything that might occur during it. When they arrived in San Francisco ahead of *Sapphire* there would be a ten thousand dollar captain's bonus which, Emma had since learned, her uncle intended to use to secure Emma's prospects and, when the time came, provide a dowry that was worthy of his niece.

It had dismayed Emma to learn this, and to conclude that the very driving force behind her uncle during this voyage, and indeed the very cause, she suspected, of his current illness, was towards this end: to finally have the means to secure his niece's future in marriage. Yet marriage to whom, she wondered. What kind of man had her uncle in mind? One who lived ashore and knew nothing of the sea, or one who had conversely mastered the skill in much the same fashion as she herself had? Probably the former, for she had long suspected that her uncle privately disapproved of any notions concerning women going to sea, as indeed did so many of his fellow captains. Most men, it seemed, shared this opinion.

It then occurred to Emma's tired and overworked mind that the very reason her uncle had accepted command of *Achilles* in the first place was likely to this end, to secure her future and this finally brought forth the tears she had done so well thus far to forestall and they began running freely down her cheeks.

There would be no bonus paid to a dead captain. It was just as simple and as final as that.

And yet, there would be. The chief mate, Robert Biggs, would automatically step up as *Achilles'* captain and he would without a doubt bedevil both this ship and her crew ruthlessly towards this same end and he would collect the ten thousand dollars for himself and it would not come cheaply; it would be paid for, every last cent of it, in the blood and suffering of this crew. And, while he was achieving this, Emma herself and the five passenger ladies would each one be at his mercy, subject to whatever whim, as captain, he might choose to indulge himself in.

Like a broaching wave these realizations swept over her and Emma, now resigned to the prospect that there would doubtless be plenty more tears where these came from before this voyage was over, was reduced to a series of painful sobs, now of the utmost despair.

The California Run

The following day saw *Achilles* thirty-six days out of New York and now beginning to experience a shift in the wind that heralded her approach into the Calms of Capricorn, a belt of variable winds interspersed with storms and squalls that encompassed the sub-tropical latitudes south of Rio. It signaled the waning of the southeasterly Trades and the gradual emergence of the prevailing westerlies that swept, unopposed by any significant land mass save that of nearby Patagonia to windward, around the entire globe south of the fortieth parallel and, because of such velocities as they were able to accumulate in these open waters, were termed the Roaring Forties. Here in the Atlantic lee of the tapering South American continent the transition was a fairly mild one in comparison to those raw westerlies that beset the Pacific side. It began with a discernible backing of the wind from southeast to an easterly, thence a northeasterly direction, all of which afforded a significant increase in *Achilles'* speed and, true to any clipper worthy of her title, she made full and good use of it while it lasted.

With Robert Biggs, in the captain's continued absence, now stepping in to take full command of the deck, it quickly became apparent that if this man were one day to become captain proper he would doubtless be of the type to carry on, as they say, 'New York fashion'. For he now pushed both *Achilles* and her troubled crew with all the urgency of Samuel Jacobs and with all the brutality of his own nature combined in equal measure. Nor was he content to remain on the quarterdeck, as was the usual captain's unspoken etiquette, but instead he freely roamed the decks with belaying pin held at the ready and now unchecked by either rule or conscience as he drove *Achilles* hands-on as if she were a postal carriage drawn by this crew of overworked horses.

Yards were braced almost to square and all canvas up to

skysails sheeted tightly home. Studdingsails were rigged to weather to catch this northerly airflow as it continued to haul steadily around the compass and, by nightfall, it was found on streaming the log that a full twelve knots ran off the reel and over the transom before the sandglass ran dry.

After a full day of all hands being worked to their physical limits in the face of these continually shifting winds, the breeze finally settled in from the northwest at a steady twenty knots and remained there, hopefully for the duration. The crew were returned to their night watches at eight o'clock and the off-duty watch, the Larbowlines, were sent below to sleep.

At midnight the Larbowlines were roused again to attend the middle watch and Robert Biggs arrived promptly on the quarterdeck, wiping the few hours of residual sleep from his face and, as was his habit, ignoring Nate completely as he strode to the binnacle to check on the course being steered. Then, with a brief glance aloft at the silhouetted outline of *Achilles'* towering rig against the clear starlit sky and the wind relative to her set of sail, he headed down the companionway and into the chartroom to study the logbook entries for the preceding four hours. When he emerged again five minutes later it was immediately apparent that all was not well.

"Where in hell is my watch?" he barked, peering through the gloom at Nate's helmsman, George Evans, who should have been relieved by one of his own men long before now.

Nate was equally as perplexed. He had sent one of his hands, Albert Tucker, down to call the Larbowlines ten minutes earlier yet scarcely a handful had yet reported to the aft main deck, where habitually they would gather to be counted before being assigned their duties. Within this small group were included all the Larbowline packet-rats, even

Jacko who was a Starbowline, all of whom seemed to be loitering unnecessarily by the foot of the ladder and who appeared to Nate not only to be making certain that they could be seen from the quarterdeck but, in Jacko's instance, to be in a state of some uneasiness about it too. This quickly stirred his own forebodings and he was about to turn to the chief mate when Albert Tucker finally reappeared on the quarterdeck.

"They's refusin' to turn-to, Mister Mate," he announced, clearly nervous and staring with a fixed expression down at his own bared feet.

"They're sayin' they got grievances, or sumever."

"Who says?"

"Them Souwegians on the Larbo'lin' watch, sir. They says they ain't turnin' to, simple as that."

"By God, I'll clap a stopper on that!" Biggs exploded, and without further thought he headed forward, swearing loudly as he stormed down the ladder and pushed his way roughly through the assembled hands and into the darkness of the main deck.

A minute later George Evans, who stood at the wheel, muttered quietly to Nate,

"Perhaps I should go forward too, Mister Cooper? He might need somebody to watch his back."

Nate turned immediately to Albert Tucker.

"Take the helm," he instructed, and for once the youngster appeared eager to do so and, rather than adopting his usual packet-rat pace, which was somehow neither too hurried nor unduly lacking all in the same instance, he strode directly to the wheel and, on being given the course steered by George Evans, repeated it with uncharacteristic volume and alacrity.

George Evans, the leading hand of his Starbowlines, was

a man in whom Nate, throughout the course of these past few weeks, had come to place an increasing level of trust in and had so far not been disappointed. Although he still knew very little about this quiet man, he yet knew enough to recognize a loyal seaman when he saw one and someone who could be relied upon to do as he was told.

"Follow him," he instructed Evans now. "And arm yourself with a pin. If there's any trouble at all come and report it immediately."

Gideon had timed it well.

Knowing precisely when and where the Swedes were planning to attack the chief mate with the intention of beating him up, it had not required too much effort on his part to coordinate his own actions accordingly. Because he knew that the remainder of the crew, to a man, would seek to place themselves aft and within sight of the quarterdeck during this event, for fear of being implicated along with the Swedes.

Concealed in the darkness forward of the deckhouse, Gideon sidled his way carefully to larboard and poked his head around the corner. There, in the gloom of the larboard main deck, the last two of the Swedes were finishing up. One of them was kneeling astride Biggs' prone body and was holding the chief mate's right arm firmly down against the deck while the other raised a heavy wooden mallet above his head and brought it down hard and, with the sickening crunching sound of several bones being broken, Robert Biggs, even in his unconscious state, groaned in agony. Then, with a final kick and the spitting forth of a curse both men promptly disappeared aft, leaving the mallet lying on the deck nearby.

Gideon did not hesitate. Drawing his knife as he

approached he reached down to grasp a handful of Robert Biggs' hair and he lifted the mate's head a few inches off the deck before slipping the knife underneath it. Then he withdrew it quickly with the blade facing upwards and, as the last jets of arterial blood were still staining the outer bulwarks, he was already rounding the forward end of the deckhouse again and striding aft down *Achilles'* starboard side, tossing the knife up and over the monkey rail as he went and pausing at the scuttlebutt only long enough to retrieve a scoop of water to rinse the blood from his hands.

As he continued walking aft he allowed himself a satisfied smile, silently congratulating himself on a job neatly done.

But this was only the beginning.

George Evans finally returned to the quarterdeck, wide-eyed and breathless.

"Trouble sir!" he hissed urgently into Nate's ear, beyond the earshot of the surrounding crew. "The chief mate's down! I believe he's dead!"

Nate drew Evans aside.

"This could be the start of something even more serious," he warned, in equally subdued tones. "Go rouse the captain's niece and the steward. Have them break open the arms locker and tell them what's going on. Then come forward immediately."

Then, with a rising sense of trepidation at what might so easily evolve into an uncontrollable situation, Nate descended the ladder into the darkness of the main deck, feeling along the rack rail as he went for a spare belaying pin of his own. As he passed those men who were gathered around the foot of the ladder, several voices arose.

"All's well, second mate, sir?"

"Need any help, Mister Cooper?"

None of which rang with any sincerity to Nate's keen ear for it sounded to him as if each man spoke up merely for the sake of having his voice heard and recognized and it served only to increase his forebodings and he barked to these men to hold fast and to remain where they were.

As he neared the larboard side of the deckhouse he could make out the figure of *Achilles'* chief mate laying on the deck, but nobody else nearby. Even under the dimness of starlight he could see that Robert Biggs had been severely beaten, his face swollen and lips bloodied as if several men had systematically taken their turn at him. His right hand, the one that habitually gripped a belaying pin, had also been smashed and broken. And then, only in the wake of such a beating, it appeared, had his throat been laid open from ear to ear, creating a wide pool of blood that flowed directly into the nearby scupper.

Nate was unable to find it within himself to feel much pity for the man. But he did feel anger, and plenty of it, at the cowardly manner in which it had been done. They had lain in wait for him, then hauled him into the darker shadows and set about beating him up and then murdering him. It angered him sufficiently to distract himself from his own fears, those concerning his own safety as well his misgivings about now having to take control of this situation.

Already several of the crew had followed Nate from aft and were arriving to either stand and watch or to mingle together with their chums by the fore scuttle and it was at this moment that Nate came to realize the full magnitude of what he might now be forced to confront. If what he now feared was true, if this was indeed the beginning of a mutiny, then these next few moments alone would determine the outcome of not only his own future but as well the ship's. He realized then that he could not be seen to hesitate, not even for an instant and so he called out,

"Everybody, move forward! Forward of the deckhouse! Silence on deck!"

The group of sailors now gathered about him were a combination of his own Starbowlines and the chief mate's Larbowlines and they now reluctantly began shuffling forward, remaining watchful, whether from uncertainty or expectation Nate was unable to tell. But his more immediate concern was the fact that he was presently surrounded and he now sought to correct this situation by placing the entire crew forward of him, so that he could at least see them all.

Then, just as he was turning his head to ensure that there was nobody remaining aft, a heavy blow struck the rear of his neck and the very surprise of it knocked him off balance and he stumbled clumsily against the fife rail, a bolt of sharp pain filling his entire head. As he dropped to his knees and tried to turn himself around to face his unseen assailant he saw the silhouette of the man who had struck him drop his belaying pin and reach instead for his knife, and the voice of Frederick Weeks hissed forth,

"Now you'll get what's coming, you son of a bitch!"

Amid startled exclamations from those all around, and despite the sudden cries of protest and the rush of several men in his direction, namely Scragg and some of his packet-rats, Weeks' knife had already begun its descent and Nate, kneeling stunned and helpless at the man's feet, realized with a chillness that despite their best efforts none of them would be able to reach Weeks before the knife reached him.

Then, inexplicably, the knife suddenly paused in mid-descent, at the very instant that Weeks himself, as if having been dealt an almighty blow by some huge and invisible hammer, was picked up bodily and cast back against the nearby foremast, where he struck against it with a loud, hollow thud and remained there, arms spread apart and still standing upright.

A chorus of shocked gasps and blasphemous exclamations arose as Weeks, with the knife now slipping from his hand and clattering to the deck, stared dumbly down at the shaft of the harpoon that now protruded from his chest and skewered him firmly against the foremast. Then his head dropped lifelessly.

The tall and unmistakable figure of *Achilles'* steward then stepped into view and, with only a brief glance at Weeks, Pepin commanded silence after his own fashion by discharging his pistol close above the crews' heads, which had the remarkable effect of causing every last one of them to drop to his knees and freeze on the spot. Pepin retrieved another pistol from the rear of his belt and handed this to Nate, just as George Evans also arrived on the scene, armed likewise.

Recovering quickly now and scrambling to his feet, Nate took the weapon from Pepin as the steward reported,

"I spoke wi' the cap'n, mister, but he's grievous sick. Can't get no sense from 'im."

With this there arose another unsettled whispering from the assembled hands, but Nate immediately cut it short. Turning to George Evans, he said,

"The next man who moves or speaks, shoot him!"

Evans nodded and raised his pistol in clear view, now eyeing each shadowy figure closely and giving every indication that he would have no qualms whatsoever in doing so.

Then Nate announced,

"All hands will remain on the main deck until sunrise! Not a word will be spoken by anyone unless in direct response to an order from either myself or Mister Evans!

Any man caught talking without permission will be shot for a mutineer and I will enter it into the logbook!"

Nate turned to Pepin.

"Get those Swedes from the Larbowline watch chained up and confined to the deckhouse. There's murder been done here and somebody's going to answer for it."

With relief Nate saw the steward nod his head promptly and, now wishing to cement further this perilous transition he now had to undertake, from second mate to acting chief mate, he strode amidships and stood there, trying to will his legs to stop trembling as he peered forward to where a trio of small nebulae, the Magellan Clouds, had been each night rising higher in the south and, from their aspect in relation to the silhouette of *Achilles'* jib boom against the starlit sky ahead, he rapidly estimated the helmsman's present course.

"Wind looks to have backed another half-point, Mister Evans." His voice quavered a little and he had to clench his teeth to prevent them from chattering. "No man goes aloft tonight. Rouse the carpenter and the cook and have them trim yards as necessary. Then rig a line athwartships aft of the deckhouse and stand guard."

"Aye, aye, Mister Mate," replied Evans promptly and for this Nate was profoundly grateful, and he may well have thanked the man if not for the lingering peril of the situation he now found himself cast lucklessly adrift in.

Chapter Fifteen
A Night of Decisions

When finally Nate returned to the aft cabin it was not to find the captain anxiously awaiting his report but the captain's niece. She sat alone at the large dining table: a small, solitary figure wrapped in a night shawl. Beneath the overhead lantern her pallid features, with every roll of the ship, underwent a continual alteration between stern inquiry and hollow-eyed dread. In front of her, on the table, lay her uncle's pistol and it was placed within arm's reach.

"Biggs is dead?" she asked quietly, as if fully expecting it.

When Nate nodded she slumped farther into her chair as though all the remaining wind had been knocked out of her and she sighed.

"As I feared," she whispered.

"Weeks, also," added Nate, at which Emma looked at him in surprise.

"The captain, ma'am. Is he...?"

"The captain is grievously sick, Mister Cooper. His wits are not about him, and so I am sorry to say that it is left to you and I together to resolve this crisis."

She was eyeing Nate closely now and he could understand why. She was wondering if he had within him what was now required. And in all truth Nate himself did not know the answer to that question. He could only hope that, whatever was now required of him, he would not make a complete hash of it.

"Tell me what happened, exactly." Emma's voice sounded tired. "And please, for the sake of us both as well as our ship's, spare me nothing."

Nate sat down opposite her and placed his revolver on the table. Its grip was damp and it glistened under the lamplight and his mind returned again to the chief mate's beaten corpse.

He related everything, or as much as he could recall, and when he was finished Emma sat in silence, now deep in thought and with a frown fixed to her face and she began to tap her fingers on the tabletop. Nate, his own wearied mind now reluctant to think too much about anything at all, watched them absently; so pale and slender and so unlike a sailor's calloused digits and he wondered what, precisely, there was to think about. For what option could there be now, other than to turn *Achilles* about and put her directly into Rio? What else could they possibly do without a chief mate or a coherent captain?

"So Scragg was there, yet none of his men attacked you?"

Nate hesitated before shaking his head.

"To the contrary. He seemed to make every effort to stop Weeks. I think that if Pepin had not arrived when he did, then Scragg would have taken Weeks down himself. But by then I would have been dead, without a doubt. I owe my life to Pepin."

"As I suspect we all do," Emma replied. "That is, those of us who live here in the aft cabin. If Weeks had managed to kill you, too, then the implication of guilt alone would probably have swayed the rest of them to finish off the job and dispose of all of us, if only to be on the safe side. At sea there can only be a limited number of witnesses, and none of them can run very far, can they?"

Nate inwardly shuddered at the notion. It had been done before. It was not so difficult for a crew to seize a ship and murder all officers and passengers, then take to the lifeboats and scuttle her, explaining to the first passing vessel that she went down in bad weather with all remaining hands. All it took was a reason.

With this disturbing fact to ponder Nate lapsed into silence as Emma considered further the plight they were now in. Finally she announced,

"Those Swedes. I'm finding it difficult to believe that their intention was to actually murder Biggs. Why would they have squandered the time and risked discovery by beating the man first? And why even bother to break his hand like that if they intended to kill him? I'm inclined to suspect that it was Weeks himself who stepped in afterwards and finished off the job. It would certainly explain his attacking you, too, immediately afterwards. As I said, killing both mates at once would have forced the remainder of them to seize the ship, and it was the only chance he had to escape punishment. Was by chance the English speaking Swede among the attackers?"

"Anders Fersen? No, ma'am. He's on my watch, and he was on the quarterdeck at the time."

"Good. Then I suggest we use him to translate for us. We cannot afford to lose so many men. If we can at least satisfy ourselves that these Swedes did not actually murder Biggs, I would prefer to put them back to work. I think we should question these men tonight. Sooner rather than later?"

Nate, who was still coming to terms with the realization of how close he had come to being murdered himself, finally picked up on Emma's tone and he realized then that this young woman, despite her modesty and slightness of frame, was displaying those very qualities that he himself was sorely in want of right now: those of strength and decisiveness, and without which he knew they would surely be lost. It was time, he decided, to begin playing the role of chief mate, even if he did not yet feel it properly belonged to him.

With this in mind he stood up and went forward, pistol in hand, and called out for Pepin who was standing guard by the forward trunk cabin doorway. In so doing, however, he managed to alert every last one of the passengers, whose startled faces began promptly emerging one by one from their staterooms and Emma was faced with the unenviable task of quietly placating each one and trying to persuade them to conceal themselves from sight, without even being offered the courtesy of an explanation. But both the French lady and Lady Margaret, to Emma's relief, both appeared trusting enough, for the present, and a couple of minutes later the four Larbowline Swedes, with wrists and ankles bound in chains, shuffled with much difficulty and noisy clanking into the aft saloon to stand nervously before the table alongside their compatriot, Anders Fersen.

Nate stood with his pistol held in plain sight while he studied the faces of these Swedes. The solitary lantern that was suspended over the table was on a level with their faces and it etched deep and alarming shades into each one of their frightened aspects, yet to Nate not one of these men had the look of a murderer about him. If anything, these Swedes had always appeared to him as being each day more fearful of being murdered themselves.

"Have them hold out their hands, palms down," Nate told

Anders, who translated. Each one of the Swedes, with his attention directed exclusively to the pistol in Nate's hand, did so immediately. Under the lantern light it could be seen that each of these men's knuckles were scuffed and bloodied.

"What weapons did they use?"

There was a tone of indignation to their replied mumblings and Anders announced,

"No veapons sir! They fight like men, vith the fists! Except for the hammer. That vas Veeks' idea."

Emma and Nate exchanged a glance and she asked,

"How was Weeks involved? Did he join in with the beating?"

"No ma'am! He veren't nowhere near. He keeps pushing these boys to kill both mates und take the bluddy ship! But they says no! Just a bashing for the chief mate, that's all they do! It vas justice they vanted, Mister Mate, for killing the old fellow! And to send a message, that ve all stand together now, like the packet-rats! You fight one, you fight us all!"

"Then who actually murdered the chief mate?"

After another round of whispered and animated converse, Anders replied,

"Not these boys, ma'am! Ven thcy stop vis the bashing, the mate's still alive, for sure! Rolling on the floor und moaning, he vas! That's how they left 'im!"

"And what of Scragg and his gang? What did they have to do with it?"

The Swedes' combined expressions immediately veered toward caution, as if the very mention of the packet-rats alone was enough to invite some manner of retribution, and Anders was quick to reassure Emma.

"Nothing, ma'am! Nothing vatsoever, und that's the Gott's-honest truth! They veren't nowhere near. But now they think it vas our plan all along to murder both mates und take over the ship. Now they're threatening to kill us in our bunks!"

Nate could at least verify some of this for himself.

"That is true. I saw Scragg, Jacko and most of the other packet-rats on the aft main deck while Biggs was being attacked."

Emma, after mulling this over for a while, finally turned to Nate.

"So, what do you intend doing with these men, Mister Cooper?"

Nate was unprepared for this, but did his best to recover.

"I'm inclined to keep them in chains for the remainder of the voyage," he replied flatly. Then, with a glance at Emma's frowning expression, he added, "But I might still be prepared to give them one last chance to prove their worth. If they each keep their noses clean and show themselves willing, I might yet pay them off as free men."

Before Anders had even finished translating this he was met with loud opposition from his countrymen and, after a full minute of animated conversation, he turned back to Nate.

"Sure, they keep noshes clean, und work hard, if treated right. Vith respect. Like men. No problem. But villing? No sir. You ain't never gonna make 'em villing. Ve're all prisoners on this ship! None of us vanted to leave New York! Is not fair to expect villing!"

This happened to coincide closely with Nate's own sentiments, but he dared not give even a hint of it as he responded sternly,

"Then at the very least they need to learn their business quickly, to become proper seamen and to practice their English a sight better. Otherwise they'll go straight back into chains. Those are my terms, and the only terms you'll get."

To this Anders Fersen and his four companions reluctantly acceded and, with the subsequent reassurance from Nate that, for as long as efforts towards this end were seen to be made, their irons would no longer be required, he stooped down with his key to begin unlocking their shackles.

"Where are these men's shoes?" he asked Anders, noticing for the first time the terrible condition of their feet. Notwithstanding the increased coldness that was daily making itself felt in these southerly latitudes, these Swedes were unaccustomed to life on board ship and their feet were as soft as any landsman's. Anders, who was himself shoeless and clearly suffering likewise, simply shrugged with an apologetic smile.

"Dunno, Mister Mate, sir. Must've lost 'em somevere."

"All of you? Along with your jumpers, too, I suppose, and the rest of your cold weather gear?"

Each of the Swedes, none of whom was clad in anything warmer than duck canvas trousers and a thin cotton shirt, shrugged evasively and looked uncomfortable and when Nate dismissed them they all filed out, muttering in Swedish as they went.

Scragg, Nate was thinking as he watched them go. What was he going to do about Scragg?

Meanwhile Emma was shaking her head in disbelief.

"Then it must have been Weeks all along. Five years' imprisonment and a five thousand dollar fine, and that's just for attempting to scuttle the ship. With the added charges of murder he would have been lucky to escape the gallows. What on Earth was the man thinking?"

Nate shrugged, pondering this very question as well as wondering at the manner in which even the smallest of issues at sea could so quickly become compounded in ways that no landsman could ever hope to fathom.

"Well at least it's not too far to Rio. Perhaps only a week?"

"Rio? Why, whatever are you talking about? We are not going to Rio."

"But to run all the way back to New York might take several weeks, ma'am."

"We are California bound, Mister Cooper," Emma stated coldly. "And to California we shall proceed. That is, if you still value your safety after tonight."

Nate did not understand and so Emma, with the same controlled patience she had used often enough in tutoring him in navigation, explained,

"These packetarians are for once compelled here by a motive beyond simple mischief. Reaching the gold fields is the only reason they have for keeping this ship going. Or for keeping you alive, for that matter, as they believe that you are the only remaining person on board, apart from their ailing captain, who is able to navigate them there. So do you really think that they will continue to support and protect you if you choose to do anything other than to continue on to Frisco?"

"Do you mean to say that they would turn on us yet, if we brought the ship about?"

"I mean to say," responded Emma, "that those Swedes are not the only prisoners aboard this ship, Mister Cooper. Because although you may now ostensibly be in charge of her deck, it is those men out there, or more in particular William Scragg himself, who will decide on this ship's ultimate destination."

Achilles' crew was summoned to the break of the quarterdeck at sunrise following a long and wordless night spent on deck, working through winds that continued to veer steadily around the compass and which now arrived from the northwest, still affording *Achilles* a large reach but now placing her on the opposing tack. But she had made scant use of it; since the events of the night before not a single man had been sent aloft to tend canvas or to shake out her topsail reefs, nor to rig studdingsails to her new weather side and as a consequence *Achilles* was now proceeding at a comparative snail's pace, sacrificing at least four knots of speed and consequently four miles of ocean for every hour that her crew stood idle on deck. At this rate *Sapphire* would certainly overhaul her again before she reached the Horn. Throughout the night both Pepin and the trusted George Evans had stood vigil from either side of the quarterdeck, each man armed with a revolver. Now these weapons were tucked out of sight but remained within easy reach as the crew gathered themselves aft to hear what Mister Cooper had to say.

Most of the crew were now weary enough to care little beyond returning to the comfort of their bunks or of quelling their nightlong famine with the opening of the galley's door at seven bells. A few still held a look of discontentment about them, most particularly the cook and the carpenter, both of whom had been roused from their bunks on Nate's order and made to stand the deck all night, for which they had already found much cause for resentment.

Nate now stood at the forward railing of the weather quarterdeck with as authoritative a pose as he was able to muster as he eyed the remnants of *Achilles'* crew. Close behind him stood George Evans who, at twenty-seven years of age, appeared the very image of any landsman's conception of the hale and hearty foremasthand. Bright-eyed and tanned with calloused palms, bared feet and a trim dark beard framing a weathered face that seldom displayed anything but an alert, capable demeanor. The very sight and bearing of this fellow alone, reasoned Nate, must surely go halfway towards persuading his shipmates to accept him now as an officer.

And what a scurvy bunch, Nate found himself thinking again, all the more so for seeing them now through a chief mate's eyes. He must now regard each man as an essential tool for this ship's use, taken together as a body of souls with a collective mind and spirit; an entity all to its own and one that must now, in the wake of last night's events, be kept in check either by brute force or, as was Nate's intention, by a much tougher yet far more beneficial combination of guile and cunning.

He therefore felt little compunction about opening his speech with a barefaced lie.

"The captain has authorized me to assume the duties of chief mate!" he announced, carefully gauging the upturned faces below. "We shall continue to crack on for Frisco, and there will be no more trouble on this voyage unless you wish to find yourselves chained up and handed over to the authorities when we arrive and put on trial for mutiny! Behave like proper seamen and you'll have the easier time of it! Mister Evans here is now your second mate!"

There were a few subdued mumbles and grumbles from the assemblage below at this announcement, particularly from the able hand, Silas Rigsby, who loudly and immediately vocalized his disapproval.

"Now wait just a God-damned minute!" Rigsby was glaring up at Nate. "What gives you the right to stand there telling us this? It should be the captain himself addressing his crew, not some damned first-tripper second mate!"

Rigsby looked around, seeking support but instead was regarded with as much stoicism as amusement by his shipmates and, with the realization that the support he was looking for here simply did not exist, he instead scowled fiercely at Nate and lapsed into a resentful silence.

Then came the announcement that both Nate and Emma had spent many hours agonizing over. An announcement that might very well, they both realized, make or break this entire voyage.

"The captain has also authorized Mister Scragg's appointment to the rank of ship's bosun!"

To this there was no more surprised an expression evident than there was on the countenance of William Scragg himself. Immediately on hearing this proclamation he emitted a short bark of laughter, in much the same way as he might have habitually responded to any such improbable suggestion. But, as he looked around at his chums and saw not his own humor reflected in their faces but instead a more sober demeanor and a general nodding of heads, it seemed that his own comportment rapidly corrected itself in accordance and his laughter promptly evaporated. He looked slyly up at Nate, his eyes narrowing into suspicious slits and he rubbed thoughtfully at his hair-strewn face for a moment.

"I'll be needin' a bosun's mate," he said, by way of testing the waters and Nate, in his profound relief, responded immediately,

"Choose your man."

Scragg looked thoughtfully around him, still rubbing at his beard and making something of a show of his apparent indecision. But it came as no surprise to anyone when his eye finally alighted on his closest chum.

"Jacko! You up to it, boy?"

Jacko clearly was and he nodded readily. Now, with a boatswain and a boatswain's mate officially appointed Nate, still unsure as to the wisdom of this decision and knowing that only time itself would tell, prepared to have the crew mustered forward to begin the unpleasant task of committing the two men's remains to the deep.

But once again it was Silas Rigsby who forestalled Nate by piping forth loudly from below.

"Where's the captain? I want to hear this from the captain himself!"

"The captain is in need of rest," said Nate. "He cannot be disturbed for anything but the most urgent of matters."

"And this isn't urgent?!" responded Rigsby with something close to outrage. "I demand that you..."

But he got no further as William Scragg's open hand connected solidly with the back of Rigsby's head, and this now being in a boatswain-like manner that was only slightly distinguishable from this man's former occupation as general all-round bully.

"Mind yer manners, Rigsby! You ought to know better'n to back-talk yer officers! I shan't be standin' for that kind o' behavior, so best you know it up front!"

Rigsby, now furious beyond all reason, turned immediately to Scragg and without thinking reached for the knife at his belt, but it took only one glance at the faces of those packet-rats who stood close around to forestall any further action. He froze on the spot, hand on knife and glaring dangerously at Scragg, who in turn gazed nonchalantly back as if taunting him until finally Rigsby regained his senses and, replacing his knife, growled,

"Just watch your back, Scragg."

"I'd sooner watch yours, old chap," Scragg responded readily, meeting Rigsby's poisonous glare and holding it. "An' I will be from now on. You can count on that."

Rigsby, uttering another curse, stormed away forward and out of sight, leaving Scragg to frown most disapprovingly after the departing seaman before turning back to the quarterdeck.

"Muster 'em for service now, Mister Mate?" he called up to Nate, in a gruff tone that was very much in keeping with the style of any ship's boatswain. Nate, already encouraged by the transition he had so much been hoping to see in Scragg, nodded readily and his boatswain began leading his men forward to prepare for the burial service.

It was a subdued event, especially in contrast to the sending off of the old Swede, Karl Angstrom, just a few days earlier. Subdued in the sense of more indifference than outward hostility being evident from those gathered about. Certainly no tears were shed for either man as Nate finished reciting the verses from the captain's bible and the planks upon which Robert Biggs' and Frederick Weeks' canvas-draped bodies lay were unceremoniously tipped, and away they went, over the side.

Indeed, the only comment Nate did catch as it drifted to him on the breeze was "Good bloody riddance," and this came pretty close to echoing his own sentiments to the letter.

When the crew were finally dismissed and returned to their watches, he drew his new boatswain aside.

"Some of these Swedes," observed Nate, quietly, "appear rather ill-equipped for the coming cold weather, wouldn't you say?"

Scragg, eyeing Nate suspiciously now, nodded carefully.

"Aye, well I suppose they do, now yer come to mention it. It do seem rather daft, don't it, wiv 'em coming from such a cold country. You'd think they'd dress 'emselves more sensible."

"Normally I'd break open the slop chest," Nate went on, "and let them buy whatever clothing they might need. But I thought I'd give the crew an opportunity first, in case they had a mind to it, to share and share alike as shipmates do.

Good shipmates, that is. The type who have nothing to fear from a chief mate who might get the notion to turn out their gear once in a while, just to see if there's anything worth finding."

Scragg nodded wholeheartedly as if fully in agreement, yet at the same time he absently fingered the collar of his own jersey and avoided looking his chief mate in the eye.

"Tell you wot I could do, sir," he offered, grandly. "I could get the boys to 'ave a whip-round to see what they can come up wiv. Conversely, I can 'ave 'em all roundly whipped 'til they comes up wiv somethin' worth the havin'."

Scragg laughed aloud at his own drollness and, with the tapping of a knuckle to his forehead, he hurried away, on far more pressing matters, it appeared, which involved the distribution of tools to the duty forenoon watch who were now gathered by the fore scuttle awaiting orders.

"I'm not going to spy on them!" repeated Harry Jenkins later that evening, for the third time.

"Why not?" asked Sarah. In the dimness of the aft main deck she could barely make out Harry's form against the mainmast's lower shrouds, let alone his expression. Nonetheless, the reluctance in Harry's tone was clear.

"Because they're my shipmates. We've bonded."

"Bonded?"

"Well, I talk to some of them. Occasionally. Look, have you seen the size of some of those fellows down in the fo'c's'le? If they catch me spying on them..."

"It's not spying, Harry. It's merely a safeguard, for all of us. Yourself included."

Harry did not appear too convinced, so Sarah pressed on.

"Listen, Harry. We, I mean they, Miss Jacobs and Mister Cooper, are offering each man two hundred dollars out of the captain's bonus money if we reach Frisco ahead of *Sapphire*. They just want to know if this is going to be enough incentive for this crew. To keep them going."

"Works for me," stated Harry. "That effectively doubles my wealth."

"Yes, but you're not the only one living down there in the fo'c'sle, are you?"

"Do you have to keep reminding me of that?"

"We just need to know what the mood is down there. Especially after all this recent trouble. Surely you can understand that?"

"Yes, of course."

"So? How *is* the mood down there in the fo'c's'le?"

"Well, it's a little tense, actually, now that you ask. Half of them still appear to be on the verge of revolt, while the other half are just waiting for their chance to revolt against the revolt. So, all in all, you might just say it's all rather bloody revolting down there."

Sarah sighed. She almost went as far as to reach out to touch Harry's arm reassuringly. But she did not.

"I know it's difficult for you down there, Harry, with all that's going on. Believe me, I understand. It's all very... regretful."

Harry turned to face Sarah in the darkness. There was a trace of amusement in his tone as he asked,

"Do I sense an apology in the offing?"

"Certainly not. I'm simply acknowledging that we are both presently in a position that is the result of a series of rather unfortunate events, and that I understand fully how you must feel about it. That's all."

Harry pondered this for a while, then shook his head wearily. He chose to say nothing.

"Well at least the chief mate's murderer was found and taken care of," Sarah tried reassuring him.

"The hell he was," responded Harry. "Weeks didn't murder anybody, I can tell you that for a start."

"How do you know?"

"Because I was watching him while it was all happening. He was lurking there in the shadows by the mainmast, looking all fretful and glancing forward a lot, around the corner of the deckhouse. It looked like he was waiting for something. He stayed there until the second mate went forward, then followed right behind him, so there's no chance he could have attacked Biggs as well."

"Shouldn't we tell someone?"

"What, that there's still a murderer on the loose and we have no idea who it is? How do you think that's going to help anyone? Especially now, when so many of them are looking for the slightest excuse to turn this ship around."

"Well, can you at least try to find out?"

"I could. But just remember, whoever it is, I'm the one who has to live and sleep down there in the fo'c's'le right alongside him, not you. Or do you keep forgetting that rather insignificant fact?"

It was Sarah's turn to act all put out now.

"Really, Harry. Must you keep flogging that old horse? Didn't we just discuss this?"

"Discuss what?"

"Well, fine. If that's the way you want it. I was rather hoping that we might be able to leave all that nonsense behind us and move on. You know, forgive and forget? Let bygones be bygones? But apparently you have other ideas. So fine."

And she stormed off into the darkness, leaving Harry to wonder why, exactly, he chose to come here every single night in the hopes of meeting this impossible, infuriating woman.

Gideon was still angry at Weeks.

It had taken him some time to finally persuade Weeks to go ahead with it: to incite the Swedes into attacking Biggs and at the same time to strike down the second mate himself, leaving this ship without a coherent captain or any competent officer remaining on board. Then they would have been forced by necessity to seize the ship, to dispose of her passengers and scuttle her, if only to save themselves from being tried collectively as murderers and mutineers. Gideon himself would then have stepped in to take charge and safely navigated the ship's longboats to nearby Rio, leaving *Achilles* to founder and that would have been the end of her.

But even with a plan as simple as this, Weeks had still managed to fuck it up. His only task had been to dispose of the second mate, and he had utterly failed.

But it was not all Weeks' fault; Gideon realized this. Not only had it been the unexpected appearance of *Achilles'* steward on the scene, but more significantly it was the packet-rats and their desire to press on for Frisco that had prevented the tide from turning last night. There were too many of them, and they dominated the forecastle. There was nothing that Gideon could do about that, but still plenty that could be achieved in other quarters.

Weeks had merely been a pawn, and Gideon had sacrificed him in exchange for *Achilles'* chief mate. It was still a good trade, and the game was still far from over.

He now needed to focus on *Achilles'* captain and her newly promoted chief mate, Nate Cooper. If Gideon was able to dispose of either one of these men before they reached the Horn, then hopefully this would be enough to tip the balance, to force *Achilles* to finally turn around and to head back north.

Chapter Sixteen
Murder and Mayhem

Inside his galley space Nikos the cook was busily engaged in the preparation of his specialty dish. And by the term 'specialty,' in the vocabulary of this food doctor, as well as in so many other cooks at sea, was meant any exception whatsoever to the everyday standard fare of lobscouse, sea-pie, salt-horse and duff, the daily issuance of which was generally adhered to with all the relentless inflexibility of a barnacle.

It was the usual thing aboard any ship that was set to round Cape Horn that all remaining supplies of livestock stowed in the topgallant forecastle would do well to be consumed beforehand lest either sea or weather claim them for Father Neptune instead. So every effort was made to ensure that the last hog was butchered and the last chicken plucked well before the Horn was reached. Nikos was presently engaged in just such an effort, with the intent of transforming *Achilles'* solitary remaining pig, who had thus far survived thanks to, or perhaps in spite of, Jerome Stiles' continued care, into this evening's roast pork dinner. Yet, despite his salt-encrusted and seafaring-like demeanor, Nikos nonetheless found himself hampered in no small way by an affliction that was, much to his own embarrassment, quite beyond his control.

It may seem rather strange at first that someone who made their living out of being a cook would find themselves so adversely affected by the sight of blood. Indeed, it might seem even stranger still that any such cook should willingly place himself in a position whereby, as a matter of course, it was expected of him to maintain a fresh supply of meat and thus to regularly perform any and all slaughtering of livestock himself.

At best he would vomit copiously. At worst he would pass out cold, and thus arose the obvious question of how Nikos had been able to survive in his chosen profession for so long.

The answer was, simply put, luck. For there always existed at sea a certain number of that element who positively reveled in such activities as the shedding of another creature's blood, and if they were, by constraint of law, hampered in the performing of such barbaric rituals upon their fellow man, then they would gladly settle for the next best thing. So it was that Nikos had, in all his years at sea, never once found any shortage of volunteers when it came to the butchering of his livestock.

As in this instance it was William Scragg himself who was always happy to oblige. Or at least he had been until now. With the new and exalted rank of boatswain having been placed so snugly and agreeably atop Mister Scragg's broad shoulders, he now deemed it somewhat beneath his station to indulge any further in such brutality merely for its own sake. Nor, indeed, for the sake of the unopened bottle of whiskey that was the agreed upon price from this cook. But, as Scragg now reasoned, and rightly so, that considering the fact that he had always willingly shared these alcoholic proceeds with his packet-rat chums, it was perhaps time now for one or two of them to reciprocate the favor.

"Wot do I know about killin' pigs?" responded Jacko when it was put to him as he stood there looking into the pigpen; its solitary remaining resident snuffling happily around inside the topgallant forecastle and quite oblivious to its approaching doom. "Bugger all, that's wot! I knows how to cook 'em, an' I knows how to eat 'em. But blowed I'll be, Scraggsy, if I knows the first bloody thing about killin' 'em!"

"But you've been to the countryside, haven't yer?"

"I robbed a farmhouse when I was ten. That don't hardly count."

"Why, there ain't nothin' to it," Scragg argued, looking around for another likely volunteer. "Spuds!" He held forth his own knife, as if this were the richest of all enticements. "C'mon, my son, show 'em how it's done."

But the Irishman backed away, eyeing both the pig and Scragg alternately and seeming undecided as to which he should fear the more.

"Oi never done such a thing before, Scraggsy! Beloike Oi'd feck it up good an' royally!" Spuds' desperate eye then alighted upon young Jerome Stiles, who stood watching from a distance with an expression of the most abject misery.

"Jimmy Ducks! Now dere's yer man! Sure an' it's only roight dat Jimmy himself should do the deed."

Jimmy Ducks' face immediately underwent a fearful change, clearly appalled at the very notion.

"Nah, he won't do nuffink," sneered young Albert Tucker. "That's 'is own little pet porker." Albert grinned unkindly at the unhappy Jerome. "He's even got a name for it, ain't yer, swab? Horace, 'e calls it."

"Horatio!" retorted Jerome with uncharacteristic

defiance. This earned him a dangerous glare from young Albert, but before he could respond Scragg cut in.

"Bertie, me lucky lad!" Scragg's beefy hand clapped down on Albert's bony shoulders, almost knocking the boy headlong into the scuppers. "The very fellow, I would say, to get the job done!" Scragg smiled in a most becoming manner as he opened the gate of the pen, forced his knife into Albert's reluctant hand and shoved him inside.

"The three of yer together ought to prove equal to the task. C'mon Spuds, Jacko, in yer go! Now, first things first; grab 'is head. No, the other end, you daft hayp'th, it's his bloody neck what needs slicing, not his goolies! Yer trying to kill the bugger, not castrate him! Lor' bless my soul, wot a sorry spectacle you make, the lot o' yer!"

Inside Madame Fontaine's stateroom she and two of her girls were busily arranging and packing an assortment of articles and luggage that would not be required for the time being and which consequently might be stowed safely for the upcoming passage around Cape Horn. Emma was assisting, albeit in a purely supervisory capacity as she reclined in one of the lounge chairs which itself had been lashed firmly by Pepin to the nearby bulkhead. The steward was presently busying himself likewise in the adjoining stateroom and at first Emma's exhausted mind supposed that the odd assortment of noises that she was now hearing from somewhere beyond the closed door were coming from that quarter. A distant thump, as of a door being flung open, the clatter of something loose falling to the deck, then a couple of hoarse, agitated whispers that Emma knew for a certainty were not Pepin's.

Emma hauled herself upright in her chair, now alert and with all her senses strained outwards. With recent events still fresh in her mind, she was now busily sifting through all possible explanations as to what it might be.

Yet were she to spend the remainder of the voyage in such an attitude, sat upright and listening intently to the strange noises coming from without, it was unlikely that she would ever have come even close to guessing the truth. And it was unfortunate that, as Emma hesitated so, one of Madame Fontaine's girls, the young Yvette, with her arms filled with superfluous clothing, should choose to open the door at that very moment and step outside.

Yvette's piercing scream tore the air apart and caused all those inside the small stateroom to visibly jump. Emma turned to see a most terrifying sight: that of Jacko Jackson stood there squarely in the doorframe with a long blood-stained knife gripped tightly in his hand and with a mass of gore splattered across his face and bared chest. Emma herself might have screamed also had not Jacko, sporting a likewise wide-eyed and startled expression, jumped back and emitted a panicked yelp of his own before disappearing quickly behind the doorframe.

"There 'e goes! Get 'im, Jacko! Don't jus' stand there like a lemon!"

Their voices could be heard clearly now by Emma, along with the anguished and hysterical sobs of both Yvette and her young friend Dominique, as well as Madame Fontaine's alarmed protestations, but instead of closing the stateroom door again, Emma made so bold as to look out into the aft cabin.

A loud and desperate squealing sound was coming from forward, inside the officer's pantry, and gathered close outside were two of the packet-rats, Spuds and Albert Tucker, both of them also gripping knives and equally as smeared as Jacko with blood. Jacko was nowhere to be seen, but William Scragg was just now entering the trunk cabin from forward, his bared feet squelching on the carpet that was now stained with dark pools that led directly into the pantry.

"God's Holy bollocks! Just kill the bugger an' have done, will yer?"

"Jaysus feckin' Christ, Scraggsy! Loike dat's what we're tryin'!"

"Keep 'im still! He won't stop fidgeting!"

Emma's first thought was of brutal murder and she called urgently for Pepin. But she need not have, as the steward hove into view at that very moment, armed with a broad kitchen knife and with a most fierce expression bent to his features as he strode boldly forward and directly into the thick of the fray. But to Emma's initial surprise he did not steer himself towards the murderers standing outside the pantry; rather to the unseen victim within and he pushed his way forcefully between Spuds and Albert and began plunging his knife into the space repeatedly until the squealing was abruptly cut off.

It was by pure chance that Gideon was at that very moment descending the aft companionway ladder into the trunk cabin, on his way to the chartroom to fetch a writing tablet and a pencil.

On reaching the foot of the ladder it took him only a moment to size up the entire situation; another to realize that there might be an opportunity in the making here.

Directly opposite the chartroom stood the captain's stateroom. Its door stood slightly ajar and Gideon could see inside to where the recumbent form of Captain Jacobs lay atop his bunk in what appeared to be a deep sleep. Forward, beyond the saloon and in the passageway outside the officer's pantry, several people, including Mister Cooper and Pepin, milled around, each with their attention being directed solely toward that quarter and aft, up the ladder to the quarterdeck, could only be seen a square of clear blue sky, with no persons visible.

It was incredibly risky. Foolhardy, even. But the potential benefits were huge.   This act alone would surely tip the balance. And the icing on the cake was that it would not even look like murder.

On this impulse Gideon stepped boldly into Captain Jacobs' stateroom, closed the door quietly behind him and walked directly to his bunk. He kept a close weather eye on the door as he grabbed a pillow and placed it over the captain's face and pressed down hard. If anyone should enter and see him he might still be able to bluff his way out of it, by saying that he felt obliged to check on his captain's condition during all this commotion and to ensure his comfort. At least for the next two minutes, until his captain was dead.

Then came the truly risky part. Replacing the pillow beneath the dead man's head and now, with his heart pounding almost painfully inside his chest, not from fear but from the pure exhilaration of the moment, Gideon returned to the door and slowly pushed it open. Now, indeed, he was taking his own life into his hands and, with a thrill of perverse pleasure, he stepped boldly out into the main saloon and across to the chartroom, glancing only briefly fore and aft as he went and noting with satisfaction that no eyes were presently directed his way.

Then, with writing tablet in hand and feeling more alive than he had for a long time, Gideon ascended the ladder again to the quarterdeck.

By now the forward passageway of the trunk cabin was

filled, not only with people but, most horribly, with blood, which had spilled, gushed and splattered to just about every quarter imaginable, as well as many that were not. It adorned the feet and arms of the packet-rats, particularly Jacko who was as good as drenched from head to toe, and it had somehow found its way into the saloon itself, now splattered across the white linen cloth of the main dining table and even up as far as the gilded ceiling beams and the skylight. It was, in short, a scene of utmost carnage and while Emma remained busy with distracting the passenger ladies and seeking to herd them all back into their staterooms lest their rising hysterics reach whatever breaking point might be reached in such a situation, it was left to Nate to deal with William Scragg and company.

"B'your leave, Mister Mate," Scragg tapped a knuckle to his forehead as he busied himself otherwise with having the pig's carcass hauled out from underneath the small pantry table. It was just Scragg's style to play such an event down, to act as though it were no cause whatsoever for fuss. "We'll 'ave this chap out o' here in a couple of shakes, then we'll be out of yer way."

Scragg even managed to sport a hearty grin, while at the same time urging Jacko, Spuds and young Albert on with a combination of furtive shoves and kicks.

"Roast porker for dinner, then, is it? Good for you, sir! Cheerly now, boys! Two-six, up an' over!"

As they hefted the pig aloft between the four of them, each man struggling to maintain a grip on its wet, slippery legs, Nate caught full sight of it and exclaimed,

"Good God, man! You were supposed to butcher the damned thing, not murder it!"

Scragg paused, seeming rather surprised at the mate's response.

"Well, aye sir," he said. "An' that's just wot we done. Wot I meanstersay is, that's how Spudsy done it. It's the Paddy method o' butchering, ain't that right, Spuds?"

The Irishman nodded wholeheartedly, without having the first clue as to what Scragg was on about. But, with the sharp application of an elbow from the boatswain, he picked up on it readily enough.

"Oh, aye, to be sure it is, sorr! Best to let 'em bleed a bit first, see, cos that way it softens up the meat. Cooks a sov'rin treat then, so it does. Sure an' we always do it this way back home."

Nate, still appalled at the carnage, looked skeptically at the pig, then to Pepin, who shook his head wearily as he eyed the mess all around him. The forward passageway now resembled a slaughterhouse and it would be a horrendous task to clean up.

"You can drop that off in the galley," stated Nate peevishly, "then draw yourselves some fresh water and plenty of it. Supper's in three hours, and when I come down to eat the only pieces of pig I want to see are the roasted variety sitting squarely on my plate!"

And with this Nate departed, leaving Scragg to grin happily after him and, with an approving nod, he cheerfully set about doing just this.

It was another half an hour before Emma finally found the time to return to her uncle's stateroom and check on his condition.

It was immediately apparent on entering the space that all was not well and, after only a cursory examination, she realized with some surprise the full extent of it and it caused her to stop in her tracks, suddenly overwhelmed by uncertainty and, for the very first time since she had begun sailing with her uncle, truly not knowing what to do.

Finally she turned around and quietly closed the cabin's door, drew up a chair alongside her uncle's bunk and, taking one of his cold hands gently in hers, she recited a prayer. Then, with a wearied sigh and with the full knowledge that there was scant opportunity here for any such self-indulgence, she nevertheless began the slow and painful process of mourning.

Captain Jacobs was delivered to the sea that afternoon, with as much somber and befitting dignity as the weather allowed, for the wind was beginning to freshen now with a sizable swell building up from ahead and to larboard. Each man fought continually to maintain his balance on the main deck as the verses were read aloud by Nate, his voice raised high above the wind, and it required four men to safely balance the plank on the monkey rail for the duration of the service.

Then the plank was tipped, the service concluded and the crew returned quietly to their duties.

It was only a few hours later, at the approaching of twilight, that the cry of "*Sail ho!*" reverberated once again throughout the ship.

Nate, who had been busy down in the chartroom, arrived on the quarterdeck just as the call came down from the masthead.

"*Bearing dead ahead, sir, an' steering north! She's schooner rigged, with tops'ls!*"

Through his spyglass Nate could see the approaching ship's topsails, a brace of them located high on her foremast and visible just above the horizon as they billowed ahead of her as she ran freely on the wind. She was set to pass down

Achilles' larboard side, running a little east of due north on a reciprocal course. She was approaching quickly and, with the captain's speaking trumpet held at the ready, Nate had little time to think about what information he might wish to acquire of her, if any at all.

But he did not need to think too much, because the news that this ship bore did not need to be asked for.

"Ahoy Achilles!" announced the schooner's captain through his trumpet, without preamble and without even bothering to exchange his own ship's details. As the schooner glided by barely a cable's length to leeward her captain waved cheerfully and raised his speaking trumpet again.

"I have a message from Sapphire! She'll begin rounding the Horn tomorrow! Captain Blunt sends his warmest regards!"

Chapter Seventeen
A Lapse in Confidence

As the wind continued to haul steadily towards the west and forward along her starboard side, so too did *Achilles* continue on her course of south-southwest, steering a direct run now for Cape Horn. These prevailing westerlies, however, remained disrupted by the tapering continent beyond the horizon to windward and so their full strength, which might reach as much as a hurricane's when augmented by even a moderate gale, would not be realized until the latitude of the Cape itself was reached.

The breeze from that direction now born a chill dampness to it and *Achilles'* crew, for the first time since crossing the equator, began dressing themselves in extra layers for the night watches. Trousers made of heavy duck canvas and monkey jackets were now the fashion on deck and, as the hands began to assemble in the twilight for the morning wash-down, Nate noticed with satisfaction that the Swedes were now dressed more appropriately; that is, in their own clothing once again.

There had been a noticeable lapse into both uncertainty

and discontentment on the crew's part since their encounter with the schooner the day before. Coming so close on the heels of their captain's demise, with such news as the other vessel had imparted there had settled an even more despondent mood upon *Achilles'* crew. Until now there had at least remained some hope of beating *Sapphire* to Frisco and thus for them to earn the two hundred-dollar bonus that had recently been offered to each man. But now, with *Sapphire* already beginning to round Cape Horn, it suddenly appeared beyond even the remotest of possibilities. Thus another reason to despair of their lot, and another reason to turn back rather than needlessly risk the perils of the Horn.

It was the very worst of luck for such news to have come at so sensitive a time, for within only a few more days *Achilles* herself would have reached the Cape and, by rounding it, would have been well beyond that point of reasonable return, either to Rio or New York. But for as long as they stood here on the Atlantic side there would always remain that same question, voiced within the forecastle, of whether they ought to continue onwards or to turn back.

It was a decision that was ultimately the captain's to make, but there was no longer a captain on board, merely a second mate whom many deemed neither qualified nor able enough to effectively assume command of this ship. No law required any crew to remain dutiful to their second mate, nor to their captain's relatives, for that matter. In the strictest sense of the law they could no longer even be held accountable for mutiny should they choose to turn the ship around in the absence of both a captain and a properly appointed chief mate. Physical assault and murder, yes, but not mutiny. And they knew this, too.

As *Achilles* labored southwards these undecided sentiments continued to fester below, in particular with the disgruntled able hand, Silas Rigsby, along with the entire Swedish contingent who remained reluctant to continue onward. Indeed, it was work enough for Nate, with William Scragg's assistance, to keep her steered on a southerly heading and not, as many would have it, to heave-to altogether and to drift aimlessly until a decision was subsequently made. It was fortunate that *Achilles'* new boatswain was of the opinion to press onwards, for his burly influence alone, it seemed, was the main driving force that was at least permitting them to pay out seven knots over the transom each hour, as opposed to none at all, while such a decision was being arrived at.

"Apparently," announced Sarah to both Nate and Emma as they sat alone together in the captain's stateroom, "there's still a lot of talking going on inside the fo'c's'le. Obviously, the bonus money is no longer much of an incentive. No one expects us to beat *Sapphire* into Frisco now."

"Can we not offer them a sum of money anyway?" asked Nate. "Win or lose?"

Emma, now dressed in mourning and with an aspect befitting it, wearily shook her head. "We cannot offer them what we do not have. There will be no commission for any of us from selling this cargo. If we don't beat *Sapphire* into Frisco, there will be no money at all, except for whatever captain's salary my uncle earned up until now."

"That's true," agreed Nate. "Even combined with my salary, that will still amount to next to nothing."

"Every one of the Swedes wants to turn back," continued Sarah. "Rigsby keeps telling them how dangerous it will be to even try rounding Cape Horn now, saying that we will surely run afoul without any experienced captain or chief mate on board."

"Rigsby," repeated Emma with distaste. "Why do we always hear that name? Is he not an experienced seaman? Why can he not do as he is told?"

Sarah turned to Nate.

"He's certainly not helping with all that poisoned talk. He's clearly envious of Mister Evans' promotion to second mate and he's also trying to undermine the crew's confidence in your abilities as captain."

"If I thought I could get away with it," said Nate, "I'd put Rigsby under the lash to quiet him down, but there's no telling what would happen if I did that. It might end up making him a martyr in some of their eyes. The way things stand right now, we are utterly dependent upon the goodwill of this crew. Or the lack thereof."

"Scragg is trying his best, apparently," reassured Sarah. "He keeps telling them that things will get easier after we round the Cape. But now, without any guarantees of a bonus, he's having a difficult time getting the Swedes to see it that way."

"Our best hope, then," Emma concluded reluctantly, "remains with Mister Scragg. Lord help us all."

The following day Emma went below to the chartroom after shooting the noonday sun. She had been remiss, as had Mister Cooper, these past several days in that neither of them had taken a proper sun sighting; partly due to the overcast weather but mostly because, being out here in deep water now and with all manner of other business to attend to, it had not been of the highest priority to plot their position every day. Now, as she set about her calculations inside the cubby-hole chartroom, a part of her mind lingered on the sad inevitability that even the hope of beating *Sapphire* to Frisco could no longer inspire this crew and, if this present mood prevailed, even the packet-rats would eventually come to realize the necessity of turning around and heading into Rio, where they might find another captain, another mate and probably another crew.

That part of her mind that lingered on these thoughts was clearly the larger part, for when she arrived at the bottom line of her calculations she concluded that somewhere down her neatly drawn column of figures she had made an error. So she reworked the problem, and to her surprise arrived at the very same answer.

Two minutes later Emma was standing breathlessly on the quarterdeck, talking earnestly to Nate.

"I'm not saying that it *will* be done," she reiterated, "only that it *can* be!"

"Look here," she said, collecting up her paperwork and pointing with earnestness at the scrawled calculations. One glance at Nate's pained expression, however, caused her to immediately change tack and instead she unfurled her Southern Atlantic chart on top of the steering box, at which the helmsman, young Albert Tucker, who was easily distracted at the best of times, turned to view it also.

"I had not realized that we had come this far south!" Emma exclaimed. "Look, here we are as of noon today. See how far we have come! We are not even two days behind *Sapphire*! And with Lieutenant Maury's help we ought to be able to reach fifty degrees south on the Pacific side in only ten days from now, which is two days less than most ships would normally require!"

Nate, equally as impressed, looked around to find Scragg and he beckoned to his boatswain.

"I think our crew needs to hear this," he said and Emma, nodding in agreement, quickly drew him aside, beyond young Albert's earshot.

"Then it is important that you do all the talking," she whispered, "not I."

Nate nodded in agreement and, as Emma replaced the chart onto the steering box, he turned to his boatswain. Albert Tucker, now grinning broadly, seemed more intent on Emma's slim figure as she struggled to hold the chart down against the breeze as he did on the chart itself, and much less so on his steering of the ship.

"We're only two days from the Horn ourselves!" declared Nate. "And with the information Miss Jacobs has, I have every confidence that we will be able to catch up with *Sapphire* on the Pacific side."

Scragg nodded soberly, rubbing at his beard and nodding sagaciously as he peered down at the chart, yet maintaining his doubtful expression, while Albert continued grinning inanely. Finally he turned to Nate.

"It might still take a fortnight an' more to get properly around it, but. What then, Mister Mate? Don't reckon them Souwegians'll have the patience for it if it took us that long. Aye, we could probably beat the work out of 'em, but as you say we wants 'em willing. Tricky."

"Ten days!" Nate responded quickly. "That's all we'll need to properly reach the Pacific side, and by then it will be too late to turn back. We just need to keep them distracted for ten more days, and to prevent them from rebelling against us in the meantime. What do you say, Mister Scragg?"

The boatswain continued rubbing thoughtfully at his tangle of beard while frowning down at the chart. Without even looking up he growled at Albert Tucker, "Watch yer 'eading, son," as he continued his perusal. Until finally,

"Aye. Belike I might be able to persuade 'em. I'll give it me best shot, at any rate. Ten days from now, yer say? Aye, I might be able to keep 'em optomistical for a few more days at least, until we get into the thick of it. Then they'll have other things to think about, won't they?"

Scragg then looked at Nate.

"So it's your opinion we still got a sportin' chance with *Sapphire*?"

Nate, making every effort to resist glancing towards Emma, nodded confidently.

"We certainly do. And this is what I need you to convince them of, Mister Scragg. That we still have, as you say, a sporting chance. As long as they all bend-to willingly, and even then it might still take a deal of luck, but yes, it can be done."

Scragg appeared content enough with this reassurance.

"It still won't be easy," he sighed, making a show of his misgivings. "But I'll see what I can do."

Scragg headed off forward, leaving Nate to stare after him and to wonder how, exactly, he was going to achieve this.

"We really ought to consider ourselves fortunate," stated Emma, "that Scragg and his company are so intent on proceeding to Frisco."

"They're the only ones. Everyone else seems reluctant as hell."

"Then we need to change that. We need to make them all willing."

"And how will Scragg manage that? How will *we* manage that?"

Emma contemplated this for a while. Finally she turned to Nate with a reassuring smile.

"I may have an idea or two..."

"I have absolutely no idea!" declared Emma to Madame Fontaine only ten minutes later as she poured the tea and handed a cup to Sarah. The three of them sat alone in the captain's stateroom with the door firmly closed.

"How can we possibly encourage these men?"

The French lady merely shrugged, in the way that only the French are able to, and remained silent. All three of them remained this way for several minutes, each immersed in her own thoughts.

"Pardon me," interjected Sarah finally, replacing her cup carefully onto the table in front of her. Both Emma and Madame Fontaine looked up at her.

"I just want to be sure that I understand all this correctly," she stated. "So, we are looking to find some way of encouraging these men to continue on to San Francisco, instead of turning back. Are we not?"

Both of her companions nodded.

"So we need to raise their spirits, somehow," Sarah continued, "to take their minds off their present predicament. Give them something to look forward to."

Her companions both nodded again.

"These men," repeated Sarah. "These sailors."

Sarah paused, but no response came. So she pressed on, her gaze now fixed solely upon Madame Fontaine.

"Who have now been at sea for, what, six weeks?"

"Mon Dieu!" The French lady almost spilled her tea with the sudden raising of a hand to her forehead. "How did I not think of it?"

Emma, bemused, glanced alternately between the two passengers until finally she caught on.

"Good Lord, no!"

But, as she continued glancing between her companions she saw that they were indeed serious.

"Absolutely not! It's out of the question!"

"But, ma chère, this happens to also correspond quite perfectly with an idea I have already been considering."

"Sorry, but I have said no, and there is an end to it!"

Madame Fontaine was eyeing Emma closely now.

"Very well," the French lady conceded, and in a very matter-of-fact way. "Perhaps I am indeed missing something here. So please, explain to us exactly why this is not an idea that is even worthy of some consideration."

"Well, for a start..." began Emma.

Later that evening William Scragg was awoken by the sound of knuckles rapping quietly against his cabin door.

Since being promoted to the rank of boatswain Scragg had been enjoying the comparative luxury of berthing inside one of the four small two-bunk cabins that were situated inside the deckhouse. Of all the visitors he might have expected at this time of night, be it one of his chums who had received another full flask of rum or whiskey from the ever-roving Smudger, or the chief mate perhaps with a task that could not wait until morning, his very last guess would have been the French passenger lady, Madame Fontaine.

She was standing there in the narrow dimly-lit passageway just inside the doorway of the deckhouse, the hood of her traveling cloak draped fully over her head and her pale, almost luminescent features protruding from beneath. She was clearly uncomfortable about being here, Scragg noticed, and perhaps with good cause, having made the fifteen-yard dash across the open main deck from the forward door of the trunk cabin in the dead of night to stand here now before him, a man whom she barely knew and who might just as easily take advantage. Her eyes shone brightly under the light of the solitary lantern that swung close overhead and it was clear to Scragg that she wished to speak to him in confidence and so, with a brief glance to either side to check that they were indeed alone, he promptly ushered her inside.

"Monsieur bosun," Madame Fontaine began and Scragg, with an amused grin, raised a tar-stained hand to forestall her.

"Plain ol' bosun'll do jus' fine, mum. Or Scraggsy, if yer wants to be more convivial." He was eyeing the madam closely now and, although he liked well enough what he was seeing, he was yet astute enough to realize that to adopt anything other than a respectful demeanor here would not work to his advantage.

"Monsieur Scraggsy," said Madame Fontaine, now with a slight smile. Both of the French lady's hands, Scragg noticed, remained concealed beneath her long cloak. "I have a proposition to make to you."

Scragg nodded, remaining silent.

"Firstly, I would like you to know that I have been observing you very closely these past weeks, and I am now decided that you are a most able and, what to say, commanding man? I would therefore like to invite you to come ashore in San Francisco and to work for me."

"Work for you? As what, mum?"

"As head caretaker. As doorkeeper, bouncer, whatever you would like to call yourself. But you would be in control, as you are here, of as many men as would be necessary for the safety of my girls and myself."

Scragg leaned against the boards of the upper bunk and he thought about this for a while. Then he squinted down at the French lady and asked, slyly,

"Pays good, do it? That kind o' work?"

Madame Fontaine gave a casual, almost nonchalant and very French-like shrug.

"If you consider one hundred dollars a week to be good. With full room and board."

"Bless my soul! There are some ripe pickings to be 'ad in that hoccupation o' yourn, ain't there, mum?"

"Perhaps more, if the gold digging is still good."

"Blind my eyes," muttered Scragg, thoughtfully. "Now that would be a sore temptation and I shan't deny it. I would, o' course, need to give it my most partickler consideration, but."

"There is plenty of time to decide," assured the madam. "Until the end of the voyage, shall we say?"

Scragg inwardly grinned at the prospect of earning so much money, as well as at the notion of having all his chums, Jacko, Pete, Spuds and company, together with him and in effect running a Frisco whorehouse. What larks. This was a marked improvement on their original plan, of heading blindly into the hills in the hopes of muscling in on some lucky digger's claim.

"The second thing," Madame Fontaine went on, "is to ask for your assistance in a particular matter. If you will agree to allow my girls access to this cabin, I believe I can ensure that your fellow crewmen will be willing to sail this ship to San Francisco. Perhaps twice a week for each man?"

Scragg grinned, admiring the way in which this woman's mind worked.

"Sounds as fine a plan as ever I heard, mum. Though I'm thinkin' twice a day'll be more likely to seal the bargain."

She smiled again, warmly, and Scragg found himself smiling back without thought for she was, to his manly eye, a particularly handsome piece and no mistaking it.

"Bon," she said. "Twice a week it is. And I will rely upon you to organize this as well as to ensure that my girls remain safe. This, I think, will also be good practice for your new job, non?" Then, studying Scragg a little more closely, she added,

"I will, of course, be quite happy to pay you a commission. Of a more personal nature, entre nous, and under the same conditions. If this is agreeable to you?"

Scragg nodded, now with ill-concealed enthusiasm.

"Then we have an agreement. I shall bid you bonne nuit."

Madame Fontaine closed the door on a most bewildered William Scragg. He remained standing there for a good long while, scratching his head and grinning inanely.

As the French lady made her way aft again across the open deck, returning to the doorway of the trunk cabin from which she had emerged, she carefully un-cocked the derringer pistol that had been gripped tightly, concealed and at the ready, beneath her cloak.

Early the following morning, while Nate and Emma were busily calculating the sun's azimuth to obtain a compass error, Scragg arrived on the quarterdeck.

"All sorted, Mister Mate sir!" he announced grandly.

"Finally got them scurvy swabs ter see common sense. Won't hear another peep out of 'em, you can take my word on it. Every man's more than happy to sail wiv us to Frisco."

As Scragg departed Nate stared after him, not quite knowing what to say. He turned to Emma, his eyebrows raised. She merely shrugged, appearing a little uncomfortable, it appeared to Nate, before returning to her calculations.

"Common sense?" he repeated. "More than happy?"

Emma avoided looking Nate in the eye.

"It might be better not to ask. As long as they are willing. That's the important thing."

She could not prevent herself from glancing briefly up at

Nate.

"Is it not?"

Emma returned to busying herself with her sums, leaving Nate to glance alternately between her and his departing boatswain and wondering if perhaps he was missing something here.

Chapter Eighteen
Cape Stiff

At the southernmost extremity of the South American continent, two hundred miles beyond the narrow entrance to the Straits of Magellan and southwards farther to the Isles of Tierra Del Fuego, there lies a small, gray and wholly inconsequential rock of an island. It is quite unremarkable in as far as either rocks or islands go, being of a dull, mostly lifeless and windswept nature and home only to the most determined of seabirds and the occasional migrating seal and, if not for the incidental nature of its location, its very name would have passed by all but unnoticed along with so many other small and inconsequential rocks scattered throughout the world's oceans. But with its southernmost promontory being located as it was as a natural beacon for the navigator as well a grim, mute witness to so many a hardship and tragedy throughout the ages, its very name has become synonymous with peril itself and with the unceasing toil and recurring disappointment that has been its unwitting lot to behold.

Cape Horn is not so much a location as it is a concept. It

epitomizes in the mind of the deep water sailor all the hardships and inherent fears as might, in the measure of a lifetime spent at sea, become his accumulated burden and it compresses them all into a single, sharply-focused and terrifying point, to deliver it to him head-on in a barrage of tormented ocean and screeching gale, of relentless thunderstorm and ice-laden blizzard, of sleet, snow, hail and, for good measure between times, a varying mixture of low overcast and thick heavy fog interspersed with drifting bergs and scattered packs of razor-sharp ice. And throughout all this the prevailing and ever-persistent Pacific groundswell from the south and west, driven relentlessly by wind and ocean current, affords no respite whatsoever and conspires even on the calmest of days to raise a ship towards the vertical from stem to stern and to strain her masts and rigging to their utmost, and by so doing shake loose anything and everything that is not expertly lashed down both above and below decks.

Cape Horn, to any who have previously rounded it, and more especially to those who have done so from east to west, is not for the faint of heart. For those who have not yet had the pleasure, it surely could not be *that* terrible, could it? Such was the concept that defines the Cape, in all its unspeakable simplicity. You had either been around it before or you had not.

To those aboard *Achilles* who had rounded the Cape before, numbering only five in total, there could be little doubt as to the seriousness with which precautions must be taken. In addition to Emma Jacobs and Pepin, both of whom had together passed between Atlantic and Pacific several times now, George Evans had also done the return trip once. The able hand Silas Rigsby had also done the California run before, or so he claimed, and the last of these five was Caleb Clarke, a fact that proved much to Nate's advantage, as this wily old sailmaker had known from the very beginning of this voyage what his duties and obligations would be, and he had been quietly and diligently undertaking them ever since.

When Nate arrived with George Evans at the topgallant forecastle beneath which the sail locker was situated he found old Caleb there, perched comfortably atop the drum of the windlass and puffing at the long stem of his clay pipe, chatting idly with the fisherman Bacas and the Swede Anders Fersen as he surreptitiously eyed the two men's approach with the air of one who had watched this particular act unfold before and so was able to anticipate each line before it was spoken. On Nate's inquiring as to the status of *Achilles'* heavy-weather canvas, old Caleb grinned from beneath his beard and announced, casually,

"Why, I do believe thar's a full dress o' Cape Harn sails in yon locker, Mister Mate."

"A full dress? Surely you mean just the regular storm sails, don't you? Lower stays'ls, jibs and the like?"

"A full dress I sayed, sir, an' a full dress I meaned to say. All fifteen o' the buggers."

The old sailmaker did not possess that measure of guile that might otherwise have allowed him to maintain a stoic expression, so his grin merely spread all the wider across his face until it extended so far that Nate could not help but pick up some of the excess for himself and he smiled back.

"We gots all th' reg'lar starms'ls, nacherally, Mister Mate," explained Caleb, "But I also been warkin' our spare canvas. I been doublin' up on th' bolt ropes an' beefin' up th' clews."

"You did all this! However did you find the time?"

Caleb chuckled and took a long draw on his pipe.

"Now, what d'ye imagine I been a doin' thar inside me warkshop arl this voyage? Knittin' wooly jumpers, p'raps? Or winter booties fer me shipmates?"

Bacas took particular delight in this and he fell to laughing out loud and slapping his knee in merriment, while Anders looked on in uncertainty, smiling tentatively. But it surprised Nate that George Evans seemed to find their laughter such an immediate cause for offense.

"On your feet!" Evans barked angrily to both the Portuguese and the Swede. "You think this is a joke, do you? Well, you won't be laughing so damned hard with a rope-end across your back! Bear a hand, the pair of you! Break out these sails and get 'em aloft!"

As Evans roughly bullied the two sailors into the topgallant forecastle Nate, whose smile had faded to nothing, was now wondering what manner of dog he might have unleashed here. In turn old Caleb looked at Nate and raised an eyebrow, in a casual manner yet one that clearly bespoke that he, Caleb, was not even in the least bit surprised at it.

"Best I give 'em a hand, Mister Mate," he said. "Lest they bends th' wrang darn sail ter th' wrang darn yard, or gets 'em wrang sides up, or fronts ter back, or some such darn thing."

Nate nodded as the old sailmaker shuffled away and he continued eyeing his second mate. He was beginning to wonder if George Evans, for all his erstwhile quiet efficiency and calmness of manner, was yet a man whose own hard-gained experiences at sea had imbued him with that belief that authority carried with it an obligation to haze and bully all those beneath him. He was also beginning to suspect that he might be witnessing another Robert Biggs in the making here, and such a realization, given their present situation, was by no manner of means either a comforting or a pleasing one.

Mark. A. Rimmer

Close-hauling against a freshening southwesterly breeze and adhering to the sage advice of Lieutenant Maury, *Achilles* cut a wake between the Falkland Islands and the Argentine mainland, sacrificing the chances of a fairer breeze to the east of the Falklands for the advantages of gaining as much westerly progress as she could before the Horn was reached. Still sheltered by the lee of the mainland, they would remain protected from the combined Southern Ocean current and prevailing westerly wind until the last possible moment. It would not be until they passed through the narrow gap between Cape San Diego and Staten Island that they would begin to encounter the full force of such opposition and until then they were able to proceed under full sail and still achieve a good rate of seven knots over the ground.

For a smaller vessel the Straits of Magellan, with its entrance some two hundred miles north of the Cape, might have offered a shortcut into the Pacific. But this crooked, narrow passage with its variable currents and extreme tides would have proven hazardous for a vessel the size of *Achilles* and would also have required extensive work with both lead line and ground tackle. And besides, *Achilles* was a clipper, a ship of the ocean and she belonged in deep water and this alone dispelled any such notion from even a cursory consideration.

With a full dress of reinforced canvas now bent to her yards and with only reefed topsails, double-reefed spanker and lower storm staysails set and with life-lines rigged fore and aft along both sides of her open decks, *Achilles* hauled southward through the narrow passage between Cape San Diego and Staten Island. A host of seabirds, mostly storm petrels fearing the disruption of their nesting grounds, now reeled and screeched overhead, while ahead and to the south, where the winds blew stronger and were less disturbed by the intervening land mass, soared the albatross, as many as a dozen of them with wings fully splayed as they soared gracefully aloft before dipping down between crest and trough; the very length of their disappearance into the latter attesting to the depth of the swell they were soon to encounter. To the southwest the land began to fall away and, against the grayness of the weather-beaten coastline, distant plumes of surf could now be seen rising to the very heights of the cliffs themselves. On the increasingly frequent gusts from that direction could now be heard the dull hollow sound of waves crashing against rock and with this also came the first traces of a windswept spray that arrived in a chill mist of droplets so fine that each individual fiber of rope on deck became visibly highlighted as well as each strand of hair upon those heads that remained uncovered.

When the first of the swells arrived it was immediately noticeable, not only by a general shuffling of feet and the reaching out for life-lines by everyone on deck but equally by the sounds heard from below decks from all those loose items that had been overlooked or forgotten. A crashing plate here, a sliding chair there, a loose spar breaking free from under the bulwarks; already too late now to secure what might have so easily been lashed down only minutes before, as *Achilles'* forefoot dropped with a stomach-wrenching plunge to drive her bows hard into the oncoming slope of water, slicing obliquely into a cascade of roaring foam and almost immediately her bows began lifting again to meet the next oncoming wave and once again the process was repeated, as it would continue to for as long as this heading was maintained.

And maintain it they must; for with such a steep

southwesterly swell placed so close against her bows and with the wind now settling in from the west-southwest, *Achilles* could not afford to stray as much as a point in either direction. To allow her head to drift too close into to the swell would immerse her bows fully, swamping her entire foredeck with several tons of water and would bring her to a shuddering halt, allowing the wind to turn her stern away and so cast her in irons and at the full mercy of the weather, while to bear away too much would cause this same wind, which now lay a risky six points off her starboard bow, to catch her beam-on instead and cause her to heel over steeply and possibly to remain there with the full force of it in her sails. So only the most reliable of helmsmen, in this instance the Portuguese Bacas and the steward, Pepin, together stood the first trick at the helm; standing to either side of the steering box with one eye to the sea and the other aloft, for so useless now was the floating compass card that whirled around inside its binnacle that it was altogether disregarded. The wind itself, still disrupted by the nearby landmass, had not yet reached gale force but it soon would and, as *Achilles* hauled southward into the unprotected waters off the Cape, she began to feel its increased force and she began to corkscrew, violently at times, putting so much strain on her topsails and spanker as she rolled to weather that any notion of setting topgallants, skysails or royals were quickly dismissed. To the contrary, it very quickly became necessary, in order to reduce her top-heaviness and thus her tendency toward excessive rolling, to lower all royal and skysail yards to the deck and to prepare to do likewise with the topgallant masts on a moment's notice should the need arise.

Pressing onwards in such a fashion and now fully exposed to the force of an unimpeded west-southwesterly wind, *Achilles* maintained much of her former speed and, despite the steep swell that she continued to shoulder into, was still making five knots on average. At the lowest point of the deepest troughs, when to all quarters could only be seen steep walls of green, foam-streaked water reaching almost to the caps of her topmasts, her sails would fall slack and she would drift almost to a dead stop until the next wave lifted her bows high onto the oncoming crest, upon which all sails would suddenly fill out again in a deafening volley of wind-blown canvas and she would haul herself forward, now surfing downwards into the next trough, gathering speed as she went and with a loud churning of wake vibrating beneath her counter, until her bows slammed into the steep seas up ahead and she began to slowly rise again, and so it went on.

It soon became apparent, however, by looking astern at the Cape from the crest of each swell, that she was experiencing a considerable set towards the east, but with such a combination of wind and groundswell they could do nothing to prevent this. She could not pinch up any closer than six points to the wind, on a heading of due south and, with a one knot current setting her back toward the north and east, her course made good was almost a full point east of this heading. At this rate it might take a full week to crawl southwards far enough to wear her safely around onto a northwesterly heading so as to clear the Cape, and then perhaps another full week to regain such latitude as they had subsequently lost.

For the next two days the prevailing groundswell remained unchanged in its height and direction, and for two full days the wind remained from the west-southwest and steadily increased in velocity until it reached a gale force of thirty-five knots, creating its own rising swell which conspired with the one already present to assault *Achilles* from that direction also. On the quarterdeck both Nate and Emma remained affixed to the weather railing, monitoring the progress and the condition of their ship. For Nate it was nothing short of nerve-wracking to watch this continual plunging of *Achilles'* bows into the oncoming seas, oftentimes with the ominous accompaniment of the ship's bell sounding from forward with each jarring shudder, and then to see her bowsprit immersed fully with every sixth or seventh wave as the two swells combined in unison and her foredeck was consequently swamped to the height of the capstan top, then to feel the accompanying vibrations in the deck underfoot as her forward frames and timbers groaned audibly in protest as they fought against the weight of several tons of water as she tried to lift her bows clear again. And each time her bows lifted, a cascade of water poured from her wash ports and scuppers back into the deep trough that divided the green mountains of ocean she now labored through.

Nate ordered soundings to be taken every bell and was surprised to find her bilges remaining relatively dry, and he wondered how much longer they might reasonably be expected to stay that way. Yet Emma, who stood for the most part silently alongside him and who likewise held on like a drowning person to the nearby life-line, seemed not to share any such misgivings, even in the slightest. She seemed, to the contrary, to be having the time of her life and whenever Nate ventured to seek some reassurance as to either the weatherliness of their ship or the length of time they might reasonably be expected to endure this, he received the same cryptic response each time. She would merely smile at him in a pleasant and disarming fashion and, with a certain mysterious air as though she were in possession of some secret that was not his to comprehend, look to him and reply,

The California Run

"She was made for this weather, mister! Let her enjoy it!"

As the second day dissolved into a pale gray twilight and the night descended once again on everything except the ship herself, continually weather-tossed and relentlessly assaulted for hour upon increasingly miserable hour, the attention of all the senses was compelled inwards, rebuffed by the darkening void that closed in beyond the bulwarks until *Achilles* became the center of everything: the heart of this small universe and the only tangible reality there was.

Above decks was a continual chaos of wind and spray, of breaking wave and rumbling surf, of loudly flapping canvas and of low, undulating howls reverberating through the rigging aloft. There was absolute blackness all around, except for the faint circular looms from the trunk cabin's ports and the eerie visage of two ghostly apparitions stood to either side of the lurching helm, their pale forms cast aglow in the binnacle's yellow lantern light as they fought to maintain control of the wheel against the erratic pitching of the deck underfoot. Sore hands, numbed by the ever growing coldness, grasped with difficulty onto life-lines when making the passage between fore and aft, and rivulets of icy spray found its way down the backs of necks, up the sleeves of oilskins and streamed like tears down the cheeks, bringing the sting of salt to lips already parched and cracked from alternating days and nights of constant exposure to wind and sea.

Below decks a chaos of illumination from wildly-swinging lanterns cast a restless light upon those equally as restless forms clinging to their bunks in whichsoever method might prevent their tumbling promptly from them, with knees and elbows braced hard up against the bunk-boards to either side as they lay on their stomachs without appetite and immersed in the stenches of foul sleep, unwashed bodies and the retchings of themselves and their fellows, and with the continued relentless pounding of the ship's bows as she drove forcefully into the seas ahead, and with the creak and protest of overworked timbers, the loud clunking of heavy sheet blocks, the windswept cries of those who stood watch on deck all mixed and resounding together in a wild cacophony of noise from directly overhead.

Then, with an unearthly squeal accompanied by a deafening slam, the scuttle was flung open and the boatswain's voice called down to them,

"All hands ahoooy! Tumble up, ye idle buggers, an' chuck another reef inter the main tops'l!"

At which each man roused himself without thought in a numb continuation of his ongoing stupor, dazed and wearied and with little concept of which direction was up and which was down, to either fall directly back into his bunk again or find himself helplessly cast against the bunk opposite and with a chorus of curses, pained oaths and silent prayers for eventual peace they reached out for whatever clothing seemed the least saturated and, pulling it on blindly as they went, they filed one by one up the companionway and out onto the open deck. Still half-dazed and pausing only to ascertain which side was the windward they staggered to the monkey rail and began ascending the ratlines, in fits and starts, clinging on with tired muscles as *Achilles* rolled to weather and making what little progress they could as she rolled back to leeward, with extra care being taken at the futtock shrouds, until they reached the main top and divided themselves into equal teams, larboard and starboard, before climbing the shorter distance up to the topsail yard.

Yet still half asleep, but with this maneuver so well ingrained by now as to require only semi-wakefulness, each man set about his appointed task: reef tackles were promptly hauled taut, weather braces rounded in, studdingsail booms triced up to allow access onto the yard and, with the second mate leading the way onto the weather yardarm they each laid themselves out, one by one, onto the topsail yard, feeling with numbed feet for the narrow foot rope and taking care to lean their upper bodies forward by pushing aft with their feet so as to never allow the foot rope to go directly underneath and forward of the yard, for that would spell certain death for all. With arms flung over the top of the yard to maintain their balance they lined themselves shoulder to shoulder and set about hauling the sail to windward, to bring the weather clew to the yardarm. George Evans, taking his place of honor as second mate, sat fully astride the yardarm with his feet braced against the Flemish horse, the outermost short length of foot rope at the yard's extremity, and with all hands to assist him he fought with an equal combination of blasphemy and brawn to haul the reef cringle towards him, leaning well back into the wind as he cursed and strained until finally it came home and he secured it. Then the same was done with the lee cringle, by Bacas, who also yelled aloud into the wind an indecipherable litany of Portuguese interspersed with crazed, manic laughter as he perched himself likewise on the opposite yardarm, until his cringle was secured too. Then those men who lined the yard itself let go of their reef lines and worked in unison to furl the short length of canvas by which the main topsail had been reduced. They beat down on the ice-encrusted sail and fought for a purchase with numbed fingers and they each swore and cursed as seldom they had before as the wind, which remained broad on *Achilles'* bow, continued to fill the hollow tube of canvas and balloon it atop the yard, flapping against their arms and faces and all but knocking them senseless until they finally managed to spill the air along its entire length and then to pass their reef-bands around and secure it to the top of the yard.

"Get down, yer motherless feckin hoor!"

"Son of a God-damned bitch!"

"Who'd sell the farm an' go to sea for this shite?"

When George Evans, maintaining a steadfast gruffness of manner, called testily for silence aloft he was rewarded with a chorus of spontaneous jeers, mostly from the packet-rats who, although working diligently enough at their task, seemed altogether dismissive of having anybody tell them how they ought to go about doing it. Indeed, they worked especially well by themselves, beating down against the slatting canvas and hauling on their reef lines and bending the tails together to secure the reefed portion of the sail into a tight, secure bundle. But this, apparently, was not good enough for Mister Evans.

"You wouldn't be half so glib if you were real damned seamen! This is a proper blow we're in here!"

This was met with several loud scoffs, again from the packet-rats, who seemed to fairly revel in this type of business and Tyrone Pete called out cheerfully to his mates,

"Beloike dis feller never sailed the Oirish Sea in winter, boys! Now dat's what Oi'd call a blow!"

"Too right, Pete!"

"This ain't nothin'!"

"I seen worse!"

And with such noisy and disrespectful chatter they began laying themselves below again, descending into the blackness, fully awake now, to begin the task of re-hoisting the main topsail yard then perchance to retreat again to their bunks for what was fast becoming the uncommon luxury of a fitful hour's rest before being called out again.

The California Run

It finally fell to Nate, as dawn broke again on a chilled, storm-tossed and miserable wetness that blended both sea and sky into the same amorphous shade of gray, to inquire of Emma precisely when, in her judgment, the optimum moment might occur for them to finally wear ship and come about onto a northwesterly heading. For surely, he reasoned, it would be preferable for them to try regaining some northings, even if this did mean pinching up close and making minimal headway, than to continue southwards as they were. From studying the charts he estimated that with this west-southwesterly wind remaining constant they should be able to get away with only one more tack towards the south again before being able to safely come about and clear the leeward western shore of Chile by at least twenty miles.

He broached the subject tentatively at first, being well aware of the disparity of their skills when it came to navigation. But now they stood a good three hundred miles to the south of the Cape, approaching the latitude of sixty-one degrees and closing rapidly with the Antarctic Ocean. For the past day and more now they had been sighting several small chunks of freely floating ice, as well as a marked drop in air temperature with an alternating chillness to it that suggested larger floes might also lurking in the vicinity.

In response to his question Emma detached herself from the weather railing and made her way unsteadily across to the compass binnacle and she peered down into it before returning just as unsteadily to the rail. She was still clad in her black mourning dress with her hair belayed stiffly aback, except now she also wore a heavy pea jacket and a woolen shawl that she used as a scarf. She gave Nate a wearied smile, her eyes red-lined and glassy and her breath emerged in thick white puffs that dispersed immediately to leeward as she said,

"It's beginning to back! Look, now it's closer to southwesterly!"

Sure enough, when Nate himself peered into the binnacle's tiny salt-encrusted window he saw that *Achilles* was now heading on a course of south-southeast; still close-hauled with the wind held six points off the starboard bow but now with the potential of wearing directly onto a west-northwesterly heading that should clear the Cape with room to spare. He was about to ask her if she had been expecting this to happen all along, but she seemed to anticipate this and, with a tired nod and a smile, she added,

"Lieutenant Maury predicted this! By this time tomorrow, if all goes well, we should be enjoying an even fairer wind, and considerably less of it!"

Throughout that night, as if adhering to the very letter to Lieutenant Maury's affirmations, the wind continued to back until, by dawn, it was arriving from due south. It had also slackened off by a good ten knots, which allowed the shaking out of a reef from each of *Achilles'* topsails and even a tentative setting of the reinforced fore and main courses. This augmented her speed by almost two knots and, when finally she did wear about at first light and onto a heading of west-northwest with the wind now placed close abaft her larboard beam, she heeled over steeply yet at the same time not so steeply as to risk broaching, and she began to swallow up her erstwhile sacrificed westings in a very satisfactory manner. The heavy swell that she had been beating her head into for so many days now was still present, but was much reduced, standing a good six points off her bow and now the waves broke ineffectually against her inclined weather planking, as loudly and with as much spray rising as ever before but without those accompanying painful shudders that had been threatening her forward timbers.

The next four and twenty hours saw a continuation of this same favorable wind, which maintained its southerly direction and eased evermore in strength until finally it settled in at around fifteen knots and remained there. Nate promptly ordered all upper yards hoisted back into place and, with all canvas set up to her topgallants, he took full advantage of this opportunity by setting her lower weather studdingsails also and *Achilles*, now heeled even farther to expose another two strakes of her hull planking, took off readily on this most favorable wind, cutting a bold, foaming wake as she sped northwestwards and into the Pacific Ocean.

On the afternoon of November 27, precisely ten days following Nate's pronouncement to his boatswain that he could make it so, *Achilles* crossed the parallel of fifty degrees south on the Pacific side of the South American continent and thus, officially, had rounded Cape Horn.

It was now the fifty-fourth day of the voyage and, although nobody on board was aware of the fact, *Achilles* now stood only six hours behind *Sapphire*.

Chapter Nineteen
Day of the Dead Horse

Now properly into the Pacific Ocean and leaving the cyclic rotation of low pressure residing south of the Horn well behind, the wind gradually returned from the west in full force and again *Achilles* was obliged to brace up close into it and reduce sail, making good a course of north by west and returning to that monotonous pounding created by a heavy groundswell held broad on her bow.

It was fully expected for the wind to turn even more foul as she proceeded north and away from the fiftieth parallel and over the next couple of days it did just this; maintaining its velocity of almost twenty knots and veering steadily around until it reached northwest. It would more than likely remain this way until the southeast Trades were finally met somewhere around the thirtieth parallel, and until then *Achilles* was obliged to make the best of it, now steering a little east of north but, having gained sufficient westings since rounding the Horn, at least being in no imminent danger of closing with the Chilean shore.

"So what do you plan on doing when you reach Frisco, Harry?"

Harry visibly jumped, once again, at the unexpected voice coming suddenly from the darkness close behind him. But in the same instant he felt rather pleased about it, as it had been several days now and he was beginning to wonder if somehow, during their last conversation, he had offended Sarah. But of course he should have known better. She was not the thin-skinned type. It was just another of the several qualities that, despite himself, he was reluctantly coming to admire about this woman. He now turned to face Sarah's indistinct form and, although he might have otherwise been tempted to respond in a more civilized fashion, he instead replied cagily,

"Oh, I have some ideas."

Sarah smiled. "I'm sure you do. But you'll only have a few hundred dollars. How far do you think that will get you?"

"Me? Don't worry about me. I've gotten along just fine with less than that before."

Sarah was eyeing Harry closely through the darkness. It was no use, she realized. She was unable to get the idea out of her head. But at the same time she could not just blurt it out. That was unthinkable. So instead she responded,

"But this is San Francisco we're talking about."

"As long as there are card games to be found, I'll get along just fine, thank-you very much."

"Ah, yes, that reminds me."

Sarah delved into her purse and held forth a pack of playing cards.

"You're going to need some practice with these. Your bottom-dealing is still rather sloppy, and as for your cuff-draw, well, suffice to say it could do with a little brushing-up."

"Oh, this is too much! Just who in the hell do you think you are to tell me how to..."

"Listen Harry," Sarah interrupted, softly yet forcefully. "We are in America now, where men like to carry guns. Especially the type of men who also like to play card games with strangers. In a town like San Francisco I would not imagine that you'll find too many exceptions to that rule. We're talking about life and death here, Harry. If you get caught cheating out there it won't be fisticuffs at dawn. It'll be a proper gun fight!"

This was a sober realization for Harry and it caused him to pause reflectively. It was one thing to endure the social embarrassment of being caught cheating at a London gentleman's club. But in a gold rush saloon? He nodded and conceded,

"I suppose you're right. There won't be too much room for mistakes, will there?"

Sarah hesitated, with the words right there on her lips but with the full knowledge that she would never, ever utter them. For how could she? How could she simply blurt out, "So, have you rogered any French whores lately, Harry?" So instead, as she turned to leave, she responded in a rather testily manner,

"There certainly will not. So you'd better start practicing, for your own sake."

Captain Jonas Blunt emerged, and somewhat unsteadily at that, from the aft scuttle and onto *Sapphire's* quarterdeck, where he stood and peered aloft into his ship's rigging. It took only a moment, or so it seemed to him, for his mind to register that something was amiss here, and another couple of moments to decipher what, precisely, this was.

"We *did* replace our spare dress of sails in New York,

Mister Fergis, did we not?"

It was a fair question. Because, at present, all that Blunt was seeing up there was the remnants of his old top hamper. The Cape had delivered *Sapphire* a sound beating this time around, and it showed. His storm sails had fared well enough but his conventional canvas, particularly his royals and skysails, were now literally hanging in tatters. It would take several days to repair each of them, one by one, and until then *Sapphire* would be a lame duck, with only her lower canvas to haul her northwards and at a greatly reduced speed. Which was why she carried a spare set of sails.

"The requisition was sent in the day after we arrived, sir."

"Yes, I remember."

"But they gave us the wrong receipt, cap'n. It should have been the yellow copy, but those fools in the counting house gave us the blue copy by mistake. I left it on your desk that same evening, if you recall."

Blunt did not. What he did recall, however, and vaguely at that, was being obliged to employ the nearest flimsy of paper, which also happened to be of a distinctive bluish tinge, to mop up a spillage on his desk that very same evening.

"Did you follow up on it, Mister Fergis? As it was your duty to do?"

"I did, captain. When they didn't arrive by the end of that week, I went myself to the counting house to see what the problem was. I re-submitted the requisition and this time they gave me the proper receipt."

"And so what happened?"

"Well, this was late on the Friday, so Requisitions didn't have a chance to send it on to Purchasing until the following Monday morning, and by then we had entered a new fiscal quarter, which meant that the requisition was now invalid, because it should have been a pink paper, not a yellow one, and could no longer be filled, at least not for general ship's supplies, but it still allowed us to purchase the sails as cargo."

"Cargo?"

"Aye, cargo. Which also meant that we were obliged to stow them on board as cargo, down in the hold, at least for the time being, for the purposes of insurance."

"Where are my spare sails, Mister Fergis?"

"They were sent ashore again in New York, captain. To make room for the chinaware."

Jonas Blunt paused as he digested this news and allowed his mildly befuddled mind to catch up. When it finally did, only one question arose.

"And on whose instruction?"

Fergis looked away, to the far side of the quarterdeck where young Thomas Oglesby presently stood gazing idly aloft at the men working in *Sapphire's* rigging. Blunt returned his gaze to his chief mate, who now stood there regarding him stoically and with eyebrows raised, as if daring him to go any further down that road.

"Lord have mercy on us," declared Blunt quietly. He took an unsteady step towards the scuttle, then paused.

"I find myself hard pressed, Mister Fergis. Hard pressed indeed. You must protect me now. This is your new commission."

"Protect you, cap'n?"

"From the gallows, sir! From the gallows! As I am now afflicted by the most serious of misgivings. I am in true doubt as to my own ability to conclude this voyage without first committing cold bloody murder."

It came as a welcome distraction, as well a temporary relief, to witness *Achilles'* crew greeting the morning of December 4 with something more than their usual deadpan expressions. Now that they had been at sea for a full two months, each one of those men who had handed over his two months' note to the New York crimps was now cleared of his debt, and the money he would earn from this day onward would be his own.

There was, indeed, a palpable feeling of optimism throughout the ship on this day and it seemed as though those tasks that had appeared so grievously unpleasant and taxing up until now came just a little easier, for some reason, and the quiet grumblings and mutterings which invariably accompanied all such tasks held a touch less conviction to them, for now each man worked as much for himself as for his ship and no longer was he working to 'pay off the dead horse'.

And if this were not cause enough for celebration, then what was?

It began with the noisy emergence from the fore scuttle, before even the last of eight bells had been struck to signal the turning-to of the first dog watch, of the packet-rats Billy Grimes and Danny Devlin. They hauled between them a wide cumbersome burden consisting of a large bundle of canvas with several loose attachments affixed, the bulk of which was stuffed with straw. Only when they emerged fully onto the main deck could their burden be properly recognized, and only then with a considerable stretch of the imagination, as a crude effigy of a horse, and this primarily because its limb attachments numbered the required four and its 'head' was daubed with patches of tar that vaguely resembled two eyes and a leering mouth. A hearty chorus of cheers greeted its arrival nonetheless and, with much eager jostling and loud shouts of encouragement, the horse was tethered by its neck using a hangman's noose and, to the accompaniment of a chantey led by Tyrone Pete, was ceremoniously hoisted aloft, out over the monkey rail and up toward the lee main yardarm. They heaved slowly, in time with Pete's chantey, and the horse gradually ascended, spinning as it went and swaying uncontrollably with the movement of the ship, knocking against the shrouds then dipping low enough to almost touch the water as *Achilles* continued to corkscrew into the seas ahead.

When finally it was hoisted into place the line was belayed and William Scragg, brandishing his knife and sporting a wide grin, stood ready by the rack rail. He sliced through the line and the horse plummeted into the ocean, accompanied by a loud cheer from all hands. It bobbed and began floating away aft until finally it drifted astern and beyond sight, whereupon the crew, now symbolically relieved of their burden to the New York crimp, turned inboard again while their boatswain cut a direct wake for the galley doorway and thrust his head inside.

"I never 'eard such nonsense!" Nikos declared, nervously backing away into his galley as he did so, for Scragg was the type of fellow that only a man with a deal more mettle than this cook possessed would ever dare oppose without the utmost degree of caution.

"It's only tradish'nal, yer daft begger!" countered Scragg genially and with his grin still bent firmly in place. But this seemed to have a contrary effect, in that it made the cook ever more fearful. "C'mon now, Doc, give it up! A damper apiece, that's all we're askin'."

Nikos, now backed up perilously close to his stove upon which a duff pudding was immersed in a pan of simmering water and which, with every lurch of *Achilles'* deck, slopped over the rim and hissed loudly on the hotplate, did a rapid mental calculation, multiplying a brimmer of whiskey times a score and more of thirsty crew members and arriving at a figure that failed to encourage him in the least. In a rather unconvincing act of defiance he made a theatrical show of ripping off his apron, wiping his hands on it, tossing it to the deck, then ducked quickly out of the galley's opposite doorway, scurrying fretfully aft towards the quarterdeck and to where he might find some support from Mister Cooper.

Nate was standing by the weather railing close alongside Emma and they were engaged in quiet conversation. The cook, appearing neither aware nor in any way considerate of this, barged directly in with his own share of problems.

To Nate this seemed at once the most trivial of matters, yet at the same time one that did require his immediate attention. He had been watching the crew skylarking and having their fun up forward and had enjoyed seeing it, almost to the point of wishing himself back in the forecastle again. But he now felt instead a sense of remoteness from these men that spanned far beyond that short distance between forecastle and aft cabin. And with this came a sense of immeasurable responsibility, toward both these men and the ship herself.

"One brimmer apiece," Nate declared, and much to the cook's dismay. Before Nikos could even begin to argue he added, "And Mister Evans himself will supervise the ration."

Nate then turned away from the cook, who remained standing by the quarterdeck railing as if ready to argue further. But finally he shrugged, cursed under his breath and relented.

"Aye cap'n," the cook grumbled, then staggered away forward in the most surly of huffs, leaving Nate and Emma alone again. Emma was watching Nate closely, appraisingly.

Yes, she decided. She too could see the difference in Nate's demeanor, just as the cook had done. And this was the first time she had heard Nate referred to as 'captain' by any of the crew. Hopefully not the last. This was good.

"They need to enjoy themselves," he told her. "After the Cape, I'd say they've earned it."

Emma nodded, noticing also that for the first time he had addressed his opinion in the form of a statement rather than a question. This was also good.

"Perhaps you should go below and rest a while," he added. "I have the deck."

Indeed, now wearied and drained beyond measure, she was willing enough to comply. He'll do just fine, she reassured herself. So she gratefully headed below, in the hopes of getting some much-needed sleep.

Left alone on the quarterdeck with only his helmsman in attendance and with *Achilles* laid out in all her splendor before him, her taut dress of shivering canvas towering high aloft and with her bows slicing easily into the seas ahead, Nate drew in a long deep breath of sea air, held it in for a time, then released it in a prolonged sigh.

Such ambivalence was there inhabiting his soul at this moment that he truly did not know whether he ought to smile or to frown; to laugh out loud or to weep privately with dread; to revel in this, his first command or to focus instead on all those unseen perils that must surely still lay ahead.

Jimmy Ducks was not much of a boxer. This much was obvious; as plain as day to anyone who stood around the fore scuttle looking on as the two youngsters toed the chalk line that had been drawn on deck and traded punches, one for one, with each other. But he was, they were beginning to notice, a surprisingly hardheaded son of a bitch.

The California Run

Jerome Stiles was really not much of anything, if truth be told, which is the reason he had ended up on board *Achilles* in the first place. When his disappointed father had shipped him off to sea under the pretense of toughening the boy up he had done so without fully comprehending what this might entail, except for having some vague notion that, with his being immersed in a real man's world, young Jerome would by necessity be compelled to either sink or swim accordingly, thus to determine once and for all the true mettle, if any, of his troublesome and wayward son.

If Jerome's father had been standing here watching his son trading equal punches with the young Albert Tucker, and to his credit going at it like there was no tomorrow, he might actually, and for the first time in his son's life, have experienced an unusual and heretofore unfamiliar sensation: that of fatherly pride.

But his father was not here today and Jimmy Ducks could not have cared less anyway. He had had enough. Enough of everything. Enough of the hazing and the taunting; enough of these packet-rats and enough, by all that was holy, of Albert Tucker himself, who was the biggest pain of them all. Jerome no longer gave much of a damn about anything, except getting Albert Tucker off his back once and for all.

Jerome raised his arms again to either side of his head in a defensive posture, just as Harry had taught him, and stood ready for Albert's next punch. It came sooner than he expected, as Albert's clenched fist suddenly appeared head-on and Jerome barely had time to dip his head into it to avoid having his nose smashed. Instead, Albert's right fist landed squarely against Jerome's forehead, to the accompanying jeer of many an onlooker, but there was little force behind it and Jerome was thrown only slightly off-balance for an instant before recovering quickly, his feet remaining firmly planted on the deck.

Now it was Jerome's turn and he eyed Albert carefully, watching the other boy's movements as he stood with arms raised to protect himself, knees slightly bent and with a confident grin on his face. And with good reason, for it was already becoming clear that Albert Tucker was no newcomer to boxing. Jerome was looking for a gap, a weakness in the other boy's defensive posture, just as Harry had told him to do. But he could not see it. At least, not yet. So once again he made a clumsy swing with his right fist and this was easily met and countered by Albert's left arm and once again several of the sailors gathered around jeered and hissed. They had obviously been hoping for a more evenly balanced match and were quickly becoming disappointed.

Readying himself for Albert's next punch, Jerome adopted the same posture as before, with both hands held close to either side of his head and once again Albert opted for the head-on approach, his punch lacking in force but connecting solidly, this time with Jerome's left cheek and for an instant he almost lost his balance and was lucky that *Achilles'* bows were at that moment on the upward pitch and this assisted in keeping him upright.

Jerome shook his head to clear it, becoming increasingly concerned at the prospect of being soundly beaten by Albert Tucker without even getting a single punch in. As he continued watching the other boy closely he could still see no opening in Albert's defenses. He could only hope that he would survive the next blow. Again he weakly swung his right fist, and it was easily deflected by Albert's left arm, again to a chorus of disappointed jeers.

Albert Tucker was grinning openly now. He knew he would win this challenge and consequently he would have Jimmy Ducks wrapped around his little finger for the remainder of this voyage. He was enjoying the prospect, and was in no great hurry to finish his opponent off. Let him suffer a bit first, learn him a lesson, put him in his proper place. So he once again opted for the short and direct jab at Jerome's face, and this time it was the other cheek he connected with. Now both Jerome's cheeks were bloodied and he staggered back a little, as if about to fall, but managed to recover in time and maintain his footing.

Albert then glanced briefly aside to his chums with a smirk, and by doing so utterly failed to notice that, instead of staggering, Jerome had slyly shifted his footing so that now his right foot was atop the line. A split-second later Jerome's left fist came around in a wide arc and smashed squarely into Albert's face. The young packet-rat dropped on the instant and landed heavily on the deck, face down, and remained there.

A sudden silence ensued as a score of shocked sailors stood looking down at the dazed Albert Tucker, then suddenly and with a loud cheer a dozen heavy hands began pounding on Jerome's back and it took him another few seconds to realize, with some amazement, that he had actually done it.

William Scragg was grinning happily and was the first to congratulate Jerome. He tousled the youngster's hair and declared,

"By God, I wouldn't 'ave thought you 'ad it in yer! Nice work, my son!"

Jerome, his face streaming blood, was grinning just as happily, and as he looked around his eyes met those of Harry Jenkins and his grin broadened all the more. Harry merely nodded and tipped his pupil a sly wink, smugly ruminating that if there was any one thing in particular that he prided himself on being especially good at....

Chapter Twenty
Flying Fish Weather

Now with *Achilles* safely around the Horn and with the dead horse paid off, her crew had become noticeably more willing to continue on to San Francisco with Nate Cooper as their captain. But, as with any ship's crew, and as earlier events had proven only too clearly, it was the chief mate who remained the primary concern for those men who inhabited the forecastle. And the only obvious candidate for this post, now that Nate had secured his own position as captain, was George Evans.

Evans remained something of a mystery to Nate and he assumed that to the crew he must appear doubly so. For Nate could at least comprehend those processes of thought which accompanied one's initial appointment to the rank of officer, as well as those combined pressures born of uncertainty and trepidation which might so easily cause any newly appointed mate to appear overly zealous, if not unduly cruel, at first. With George Evans there appeared to exist a rather chaotic mixture of each of these elements, as well as certain others which Nate could only suppose were the result of this man's own unique experiences throughout the four years he had spent inside the forecastle.

During the course of his most recent conversations with Evans, Nate had learned much about this man's history, not least of which concerned his education, which had led him as far as Yale College before becoming a seaman. It had become quite the fashion in recent years, as indeed it was in Nate's own case, for many a young American scholar to take a year or two away from his studies and to spend them at sea, working 'before the mast' with the intent of not only improving one's general health but also affording some outlet for those accumulated energies inherent to any youngster who was immersed in an otherwise studious lifestyle. But it had been George Evans' misfortune at the age of twenty to become stranded on the West African coast under a tyrannical captain who, being a particularly spiteful type, had doggedly refused to allow him to either step up to the second mate's position or to transfer to any homeward-bound vessel for a period of three long and difficult years. During this time both the opportunity to return to his studies at Yale had become steadily more remote and his transition into an able seaman steadily more affixed.

Now that he was able to finally spread his wings, so to speak, George Evans appeared to be all too aware of the time he had thus far squandered and was naturally keen on making up for as much of this as he could. Or at least such was Nate's guess. But whatever the truth of it, Nate also realized that it was too late now and there was very little he could do about it, except hope that he was not making a grave error in appointing this man as his chief mate.

But in truth there was nobody else. Certainly not Silas Rigsby, who would more than likely create as much hindrance as help if promoted to the post. Ironically it was

Bacas who had steadfastly shown himself to be as good a seaman as either Evans or Rigsby, but on being approached by Nate about this the Portuguese had remained adamant in the extreme that he would by far prefer to remain comfortably down inside the forecastle, as it was his right to do.

So a compromise had been reached, with Nate appointing Rigsby and Bacas as leading hands of their respective watches while George Evans and Nate himself commanded each of the watches and their boatswain, William Scragg, performed all the duties of a second mate aloft and on deck. Of course Rigsby had promptly flown into a rage at this news and had complained most vociferously, until bluntly ordered by Nate to either shut up and do as he was told or feel a half-dozen strokes of the lash.

Overall, however, and to Nate's relief as much as to his bewilderment, the majority of *Achilles'* crew, since rounding the Horn, were exhibiting such a degree of combined motivation and cheerfulness that it bordered on outright baffling. Nate could only wonder at the source of such motivation. Whatever methods his boatswain was employing here were clearly producing the desired results and, with Nate's ongoing suspicion that, in some way large or small, Miss Jacobs herself seemed to be a party to whatever scheme was underway, it caused him to remind himself once again that it was probably best to let sleeping dogs lie, at least for as long as things continued to run smoothly.

Because he both trusted and respected Miss Jacobs. And, for as long as this situation lasted, this was good enough for Nate.

Coincidentally, and scarcely more than a fathom's distance directly beneath where Nate stood on the quarterdeck pondering these mysteries, Emma Jacobs sat around the tea table with Sarah Doyle and Madame Fontaine discussing these very same issues.

"You would be surprised," observed the French lady as she poured the tea, "at the ways in which some men behave."

Sarah could not help smiling at this and remarked,

"Oh, I wouldn't be too sure. I've met some peculiar ones in my time, believe you me."

The French lady appeared unimpressed as she continued filling the teacups.

"I am talking about the ways in which they behave in private. With my girls."

Sarah had been wondering about that, also. Too much so, if truth be told. Almost to the extent that she now regretted having suggested the whole thing in the first place.

"I would imagine," observed Emma, "that between yourself and your girls, you are now able to paint a fairly accurate picture of the overall mood of our crew."

"Indeed," agreed the madam. "And thus I am happy to reassure you that, as things stand right now, the mood is good."

"Do they talk much?" asked Sarah. "To your girls, I mean."

"Oh yes," replied the madam, replacing the teapot on the table. "Sometimes that is all they do. Despite the fact that my girls can barely understand what many of them are saying. These are men, after all, and no man wishes to appear unwilling before his fellows when it comes to the subject of women. So they all feel obliged to visit my girls, but not all of them feel obliged to act. So they talk instead."

"What do they talk about?"

"Anything. Everything. Or nothing. Many of the Swedes are married men. Did you not know this? Oui, and some of them also have children, all of whom were left back in New York and not knowing to this day what has happened to their husbands and fathers. This is mostly what they talk about."

"Good Lord," declared Emma, truly shocked at this. "I must confess, I did not even consider that. It is no wonder that they have remained so reluctant throughout this voyage. Those poor men."

"I would not be so quick to feel sorry for them all," warned the French lady. "Even among the Swedes there are good ones and bad ones, as it is with men anywhere in this world."

"How do you mean?"

"I mean that there are still some who will not forgive. Whose one and only desire is to turn back for New York. But at least they are now in the minority, and not such a danger as before."

"And their overall behavior?" inquired Emma. "Are they conducting themselves in a civilized fashion when they are with your girls?"

"These are men, ma chère. Most do, some do not. There is always the occasional fellow who is unable to control himself. Men like Rigsby, for example. He has already been spoken to twice by Scraggsy."

"Scraggsy?" Sarah's amused smile was countered with a glower of uncharacteristic defiance from the French lady.

"I consider myself very fortunate to have such a man to look after my girls. As should we all, I think. He is, as you might say, a natural at his job."

"Oh, I don't doubt it," agreed Sarah, her smile remaining fixed in place. She was envisioning, or at least attempting to envision, Madame Fontaine and William Scragg together, but somehow was entirely unable to.

"As I say," continued the French lady, gazing pointedly

now at Sarah, "every man is different, and so will interact in his own particular way with my girls. Consider your Harry, for example…"

"Oh, please, not *my* Harry!" Sarah scoffed, without even thinking.

Madame Fontaine paused, then reached for the teapot.

"Then pardon me," she stated politely, and said no more. She began refilling the teacups, now with an affectation of nonchalance and seemingly quite oblivious to Sarah's continued staring at her.

"Sugar?" offered the madam politely, proffering the bowl along with a smile that was somehow even sweeter than its contents.

Oh, that wicked French cow, Sarah was thinking. She's just waiting for me to ask.

"Thank-you," accepted Sarah, with a smile of her own that was downright treacly.

Well I bloody well shan't, decided Sarah. Let's see how she likes that.

But, to Sarah's disappointment, it appeared that the French lady did not mind in the slightest.

On December 6, as *Achilles* was passing several leagues to the west of the Juan Fernandez Islands, its forested peaks laying barely visible above the horizon and which were made famous by the marooning of Alexander Selkirk, who in turn gave rise to the fictional character Robinson Crusoe, the wind from the northwest began to falter. Throughout the following two days, by shifts and hesitant starts, it progressively backed around into the south until, approaching the latitude of thirty-two degrees south, it finally gave way to the full force of the southeast Trade Winds.

With all studdingsails set and with every available scrap of square canvas except for the mainsail sheeted home, but without using tackles so as to allow each sail to balloon forward and collect the maximum breeze possible, *Achilles* began racing northward at an unprecedented speed. With a steady twenty knots of wind held broad on her larboard quarter she took off towards the west-northwest at such a clip that to some on board it seemed that she might actually take to the air instead and leave the confines of the sea behind. Indeed, the more superstitious hands, of which there inevitably existed a sizable number aboard any ship at sea, began to fear that this would indeed be the case if they did not shorten sail soon. The Swedes, in particular, became convinced of it, even to the point of stowing their dunnage up on deck and sleeping atop it, ready to leap to the bulwarks the moment she began to take to the air. And if not that, they argued, then surely at such speeds her timbers would work themselves loose and begin to fail her, or she would end up plowing her head into the ocean one too many times, along with themselves to their mutual destruction.

Despite such clear nonsense as any person with even the most rudimentary of educations might offhandedly declare while stood upon dry land and with these observations regarded from a pleasantly remote distance, had they instead been standing there on *Achilles'* quarterdeck and been fully immersed within this extraordinary experience of a clipper running free under full canvas with an optimum wind held on her optimum quarter, they might well have succumbed themselves, and quite understandably, to these very same superstitions as now beleaguered several of her crew.

Nate, for one, was awestruck by the magnificence of this vessel as she now performed without fault the very business she had been intended for as she raced northwards toward the equator. She was now clipping along in the style of a true thoroughbred: lean and swift and with the bit clamped firmly between her foaming jaws, her billowing canvas spilling nary a waft of breeze and her streamlined hull creating so little friction with her clean copper sheathing and concave run that she barely left a stirring of water in her wake. On her present aspect *Achilles* was showing herself worthy of the title, 'Greyhound of the Seas': an expression Nate had heard spoken often enough in association with the extreme clipper yet until this very day had not fully appreciated.

Emma Jacobs, for another, could not have described it better herself. And thus she did not, even when Nate did put these thoughts into words as they stood together watching from the quarterdeck. She merely smiled, nodded, and left it at that.

The streaming of the log at the end of the forenoon watch on December 8 was not the usual mundane and lackluster event that it had been at the turn of each successive watch throughout the past sixty-five days. On this occasion it was regarded more in the way of a spectator sport; a main event for which every member of the crew, the idlers and even the passenger complement, assembled eagerly aft to bear witness to. For this noon-to-noon period had been one of singular achievement, or at least such was the prediction, as the wind had remained strong and consistent throughout, filling her sails to capacity day and night and she had also been enjoying the benefits of a well-proportioned groundswell rising beneath her counter; one that had assisted her progress without being so high as to impede the set of her lower studdingsail booms, nor her hull's forward progress through the water. So it was fully anticipated by all on board that this day in particular might well prove to be one, as they say, for the books.

William Scragg held the singular honor of tipping the sandglass on this day. He stood aft at the quarterdeck's leeward railing and he made sure that the two men who held the pole upon which the log line reel was mounted were positioned just so, and at such an angle facing aft that the least possibility of snagging might occur as the reel began to rotate. The pole had been smeared with tallow for this occasion, as too had the taffrail over which the line would run and the boatswain made a show of checking both before carefully eyeing the following swell, licking at his palm and holding it aloft, looking upwards to gage the aspect of wind against sail, then barking out gruffly to Taffy Owens, one of his reel men, to stand fast, damn his slack trousers, and stop shuffling his bloody feet. Then, with a grand gesture that involved the raising of the sandglass high aloft so that even those who, being barred from the quarterdeck and who stood huddled together instead on the lower ratlines of the main shrouds, could see clearly, he raised the log chip in a likewise fashion and, with a glance to his captain who promptly gave him the nod, he tossed the chip over the taffrail.

The triangular chip bobbed and churned about in the wake beneath *Achilles'* counter for a moment before drifting aft, drawing the ten fathoms of stray line with it. As the wood chip cleared the turbulence and dug properly into the water astern the stray line began snaking out over the taffrail at a steady rate, causing the reel to begin rotating on its pole and, to those who were observing it closely, the speed of this initial rotation did, in itself, already appear promising. The end of the stray line was marked with a strip of white cloth that signaled the beginning of the log line proper and, at the very instant it passed over the taffrail, Scragg flipped the sandglass over and positioned it upright alongside the now fast-snaking line.

Each knot was positioned fifty feet apart and as the reel continued to turn Scragg counted them off aloud. The sandglass was timed for thirty seconds and each knot was spaced at a one-hundred-and-twentieth part of a mile. Short lengths of knotted twine woven into the log line denoted its numerical measurement and as each disappeared over the taffrail Scragg called it out and, judging by the brief periods of silence between each number, it quickly became apparent that they were proceeding at a rate thus far unseen on this voyage. As the eighth knot was called it seemed that the sandglass had barely half-emptied itself and now several voices joined in with Scragg's as he counted, along with several calls of encouragement as if *Achilles* were now held in their collective minds as a racehorse to be urged to the finish line.

"Ten...eleven...twelve..." So fast now was the log line snaking out over the taffrail, and so heavy was the length of line being dragged astern that, despite the tallow lubrication, tiny wisps of smoke could be seen arising from the charred paintwork and several voices attested loudly to this, which only increased the overall excitement of it all.

"C'mon, ol' gal! Gi' us fifteen!"

"Fifteen be blowed! She'll give us sixteen!"

"Fourteen...fifteen...sixteen..."

A loud cheer went up, but only a brief one as all eyes remained fixed on *Achilles'* boatswain, who was looking intently into the sandglass, surely about to call time with his next breath, and many of those who looked on now held theirs in anticipation.

"Seventeen!"

Another cheer, and surely the last one as Scragg positioned his hand to raise it, with only a few more grains now left in the sandglass, yet still another half a second elapsed, interminably slowly, until...

Suddenly the two men holding the pole lurched aft, thrown unexpectedly off balance as the log line came up short against its reel and, with the full weight of nearly a thousand feet of line pulling at them, they tumbled precariously aft and against the waist-high railing. But William Scragg, with the sandglass still held firmly in his right hand and watching it closely, casually extended a brawny left arm without even looking up and this checked the two men's progress and quite possibly saved both from tumbling overboard.

"Time!" he shouted, then turned with a broad grin.

"Bugger me if that warn't eighteen!" he declared. "We ran her off the bloody reel, boys!"

A feverish cry of jubilation arose at this and when Nate, retreating quickly down into the chartroom, applied this number to his daily workings, he said to Emma,

"Three hundred and seventy-one miles, noon to noon! That makes...fifteen and one half knots on average. It must be a record!"

Emma, with a shared smile, responded,

"Close to it, I should warrant."

She picked up her dividers and measured the increased distances between noonday positions over the past few days.

"I declare, we must be hard up against *Sapphire* by now. We still have every chance of bettering her."

This seemed to cheer her up further and then, as if some notion were only just now occurring to her, she paused with a thoughtful half-smile and looked out of the chartroom's small porthole set high into the bulkhead, through which the bared feet of several of the forecastle hands who still stood about congratulating themselves heartily could be seen.

"I have an idea," she announced, then mysteriously disappeared into her stateroom.

A few minutes later several of those men who still lingered in the vicinity of the aft main deck were somewhat surprised to see the former captain's niece emerging from the forward door of the trunk cabin.

They were even more surprised to see what the former captain's niece was holding in her outstretched hand and this, combined with the very sight of this young woman clad so somberly from truck to keel in her black mourning dress, as well the slow, deliberate pacing of each step as she trod her way carefully forward, had the immediate effect of causing several of the more superstitious among them to cross themselves and several elbows to connect harshly with several ribs, creating a universal cessation of all talk and laughter, as well a unanimous and rather nervous doffing of caps.

Emma, maintaining a neutral expression yet inwardly smiling at the obvious effect she was having, continued to pace slowly forward. She held her right hand steadily out in front of her, the tallow candle remaining lit, incredibly, even out here in the middle of the exposed main deck. She had to shelter the flame with her left hand, as the eddies and swirls of air being deflected from the canvas aloft were many, but her point was being well made in that *Achilles* was now close to matching the speed of the wind itself and, as the news spread swiftly ahead of her, one after another the crew arrived to watch this odd ceremony, several of them falling into pace behind her with eyes wide and with jaws, for the most part, hanging low and forgotten in their amazement.

It was risky, Emma realized this, given the superstitious nature of the sailor and yet at the same time she felt quite confident that it would, overall, be taken as a good omen and nothing contrary in the way of witchcraft or devilry. When finally she reached the foremost part of the main deck she placed the candle carefully atop the windlass and it remained there, lit and flickering but unextinguished, and to the continuing astonishment of all.

She had heard of this being performed once aboard another clipper that had been running free with these very same Trades, but until now had doubted that rumor's veracity, knowing only too well the extent to which any seaman's yarn might be stretched beyond all credibility by time and repetition. But now she had proven that it was possible, and what finer a way to promote *Achilles'* future reputation than this, with a forecastle now filled with first-hand accounts which over time would travel with each man's future career at sea and would quite possibly, in time, come to acquaint a sizable portion of the seagoing community with the extreme clipper *Achilles.*

This being achieved, Emma returned happily aft, leaving the crew to gape with much head scratching and open-mouthed wonderment, alternately to her and then to the flickering candle and the only blemish on this whole episode was that her poor dear uncle, bless his departed soul, had not been here to witness it for himself.

The southeasterly Trades persisted for another four days, throughout which *Achilles* maintained her heading of north-by-west, keeping the reliable breeze only three points from dead astern and now propelled onwards at speeds that were continually in excess of fourteen knots and which each day saw another three hundred and fifty miles of smooth wake laid out astern of her.

Once again referring to Lieutenant Maury's inestimable

publications, Emma proposed that they seek to cross the equator between the longitudes of one hundred and one hundred and twenty degrees west of Greenwich, so that the northeast Trades, once gained, might be stood on with 'a good rap-full' and would drive them northwestwards on a comfortable beam reach without taking them too far out into the Pacific. Then, on reaching the latitude of San Francisco, they would be able to tack around to due east and haul straight into port. Nate, as grateful as ever for any advice from Miss Jacobs, complied willingly. His own plate was piled high enough anyway these days, with the sifting through of all the ship's documents and with his ongoing efforts to comprehend precisely what it was that was expected of him now that he served as *Achilles'* captain.

Atop Captain Jacobs' desk lay a teetering mountain of official paperwork, much of which remained incomprehensible to Nate despite his best ongoing efforts. There were several copies of *Achilles'* Certificates of Registry and Enrollment that provided a detailed description of the vessel's particulars, her owners and her port of registry, all of which seemed pretty straightforward. A number of Sea Letters which had something to do with the ship's cargo but were printed in no less than four different languages, three of which Nate did not comprehend, and the fourth, being English, proving equally as unintelligible no matter how many times he read it. The Crew List and the Passenger Manifest gave detailed particulars of all persons aboard, with names, dates and places of birth. The Bill of Health that was attached to these documents seemed self-evident enough if its title was anything to judge by; that is, until one actually attempted to read the damned thing, whereupon it promptly boggled the mind into an inescapable quagmire of legal gobbledygook. Likewise with the General Clearance

Manifest, the Invoice and the Bill of Lading, all of which pertained somehow to *Achilles'* cargo but, after several hours of giving it his best shot, Nate finally had had enough and with a despairing sweep of his arm he cleared the entire desk into a draw for later reading, reverting instead to the one and only document that he was actually familiar with: *Achilles'* logbook.

In a careful hand he copied down the most recent pages from the ship's working log, which was kept in the chartroom, into the captain's official logbook. It included all the details of Captain Jacobs' demise and of the varying promotions arising from it. As he reached the part concerning George Evans he paused, again hoping that he had made the right decision in allowing this man control over *Achilles'* deck. Because he realized now that with all the duties of a ship's captain now incumbent upon him, and without his knowing the first thing about most of it, he was going to be too busy for the remainder of this voyage to keep more than a cursory eye on either his crew or his chief mate.

It appeared to Nate that, just as he had feared, Evans was steadily becoming another version of Robert Biggs. Oftentimes the only difference seemed to be in Evans' choice of instrument, this being his rope 'starter' instead of a belaying pin, which he wielded with equal readiness upon those who were slowest coming down from aloft, too lethargic about their duties or simply not cowed enough for his own level of satisfaction. Yet interesting it was for Nate to observe that, similar to Robert Biggs, Evans' more extreme punishments would invariably stop short when it came to the packet-rats, and so too now with the Swedes, who had also organized themselves into a likewise collective of mutual protection. A shove and a curse or the raising of a fist and they would bend-to willingly enough, despite the affected scowls and the muttered oaths, much of which was done for the sake of appearance only, and they would usually delay just long enough to make their point before setting diligently about their work.

Nate knew that it was his boatswain, William Scragg, who in reality maintained overall control of *Achilles'* deck, for without his approval or say-so nothing would get done at all, despite George Evans' attempts to the contrary. He wondered if Evans himself fully realized this, and if not would he be foolish enough to openly challenge Scragg, thus to enter a power struggle that he had little hope of winning.

Nate found himself sincerely hoping that George Evans was indeed as intelligent as he appeared, for all their sakes.

It was another couple of days before Sarah finally arrived at that point beyond which she was unable to contain her curiosity any longer. On spying Madame Fontaine taking the afternoon air on the quarterdeck she approached the French lady directly and, without preamble, stated,

"All right. You win. So tell me, what does Harry do?"

In response the madam smiled cordially at Sarah, then replied,

"Well, at first he did nothing at all."

"Nothing?"

"My girls did not even see him until, oh, perhaps a fortnight ago."

Sarah's heart sank. That would have been around the time of her last conversation with Harry. What had she said to him? Had she gone too far? Had she been overly mean? Had she somehow driven him to it?

"So he's been...taking advantage of your offer for a fortnight now?"

"Well, I would not say taking advantage, exactly. At least

not in the way you might think."

"What do you mean?"

The madam's smile was benign. It was, in fact, as if the French lady was able to read Sarah's thoughts as clearly as if they were tattooed on her forehead.

"I mean, ma chère, that he plays cards."

"Cards?"

"Oui. Cards."

Sarah scoffed. "Yes, and a lot more besides, I'll warrant."

"Non. Only cards. Mostly poker."

Sarah found herself rather speechless at that. Speechless and unaccountably relieved, if truth be told, her surprise at which left her even more speechless.

"Apparently, he is quite good at it," added the madam with a cheerful smile. Then she sauntered casually away.

Sarah watched her departure, her mind now spinning. She did not even realize that she herself was now smiling, and even more broadly than was the French lady.

Chapter Twenty-One
Doldrum Days

On December 12, now sixty-nine days out of New York, the Trades began to falter as *Achilles* approached the latitude of five degrees south and now Nate Cooper, much as Samuel Jacobs had upon approaching the Atlantic doldrums, was faced with a likewise torment of rising frustration and mounting impatience.

Once again they found themselves so near yet so far. Being only three hundred miles from the equator it was made all the more galling now to have the wind fail them so completely and the sea settle again into that tiresome, monotonous doldrum state. Without a breeze worth harnessing to fill her canvas and to check her movement, *Achilles* returned again to that slow steep rolling on the remnants of a southeasterly swell while the tropical sun, once again passing directly overhead at noon, conspired likewise to melt the tar and tallow aloft into a hot molten state that dripped like rain to the deck and soaked into the teak so thoroughly that the continued application of water, sand and holystone now sounded its familiar chorus throughout the ship from dawn to dusk.

But in marked contrast to that languid and dissatisfied state as had been the lot of *Achilles'* crew throughout the Atlantic doldrums, there existed now an underlying resolve towards a more cheerful state, evinced on occasion by the spontaneous and boisterous eruption of laughter from aloft or from forward, as well as a general tendency toward good-natured ribbing as had been noticeably lacking throughout the first half of this voyage. Despite the increased frustrations now being wrought upon them by George Evans, who was fast proving himself a dab hand with his rope-end starter, and despite the closely paralleled frustrations created by this light, baffling and generally fickle series of undecided airs through which they now were obliged to work, the crew remained for the most part an uncommonly cheerful bunch. Even the sufferings imposed on them by this relentless heat and toil seemed unable to dampen their spirits and, now that each man had proven to himself and to his fellows that he was deserving enough to be considered a valued member of this ship's complement, there was no longer any real conviction behind the mockery or the hazing that had occurred so naturally in the earlier stages of the voyage.

But, as the next week wore on in much the same manner, with *Achilles* clawing her way fitfully northwards through alternating calms, violent squalls and generally light and baffling airs, any residual liveliness and enthusiasm amongst the crew gradually began to wane and to give way to a rising frustration as they came to realize, once again, that their hopes of beating *Sapphire* into Frisco were each day drifting further away beyond the flat horizon up ahead.

December 18 saw *Achilles* seventy-five days into her voyage, and still with no signs yet of any reliable wind that might haul her with any expediency across the remaining twenty miles that now separated her from the equator. In the still and torrid heat of the exposed upper decks the crew sweltered about their various tasks, with the continued hoisting of water aloft to wet down sails and with the increasing discomfort of those intolerable stenches within the forecastle space keeping them, by choice of the lesser of evils, up on deck, there always seemed to be some ready cause to growl and so growl they readily did. But not in any serious fashion; not yet. This would depend on how long they were made to endure this most disappointing turn of events.

With such idleness as these tedious days now imposed upon her, Emma once again found herself spending more and more time below in the company of Madame Fontaine. It was something of a relief to her that, despite all the varied troubles and upsets that had beset them throughout this voyage, she had such company as the French lady to turn to.

It was the easiest thing in the world for Emma to reassure these passenger ladies that the worst of it was now over, and that their only remaining concern might be that of a rather insipid conclusion to an otherwise impressively swift voyage. Not so easy, perhaps, to assure them that, as more than two years had now elapsed since the actual discovery of gold in California, the matter of a few days, or even weeks, ought to be of little concern to any of them. Emma considered herself fortunate that she was not of the type to be so easily dazzled by such prospects, despite the fact that she herself was presently intent on reaching these very same gold fields. But on reflection, now that she finally had the time to begin considering her own prospects beyond the conclusion of this voyage, she realized that perhaps this was not so fortunate after all.

"I honestly haven't thought very much about it yet," she

confided as the two of them sat alone in the French lady's stateroom. "Since my uncle passed away I've been too concerned with seeing this voyage through, mostly for his sake. I would very much like to have been able to claim a record passage in his name, or at least one of less than a hundred days, but that possibility is becoming steadily more remote with each passing day. But still we have every chance of beating *Sapphire,* especially if she is also laboring through these same light airs."

"Did I not hear something," Madame Fontaine asked, adopting a suitably delicate tone, "about a reward? A sum of money if you are able to arrive in Frisco before *Sapphire*?"

"Yes. A captain's bonus. Ten thousand dollars."

Madame Fontaine pursed her lips. "That is a considerable sum."

"Indeed." Emma sighed. "Poor man. My uncle so much wanted that prize. It was to secure my future, or so I discovered only a short while ago. Poor, foolish man, bless him. A dowry, of all things." She then smiled wryly. "Poor me, perhaps I ought to be saying."

"But surely there is other money? An inheritance of some sort? Your uncle was a successful captain aboard the whaling ships, was he not?"

"Yes. But unfortunately he was not such a successful businessman. After the last voyage he was unfairly swindled out of almost everything he owned by the ship's underwriters, a bunch of scheming Nantucketeers, damn them. Pardon me, but that is simply how I feel. There is next to nothing left, after all is said and done, which is the very reason he agreed to accept this command in the first place."

"But surely you, as his heir, must be deserving of some portion of the prize?" Madame Fontaine replaced her cup noisily onto its saucer, clearly becoming quite upset at this unexpected revelation.

"Sadly not. It is, after all, a *captain's* bonus, and payable only to the man who actually commands the ship to her final destination. Whether deserving or not, it will all belong to Mister Cooper. That is the way of it, I'm afraid."

Madame Fontaine, in that most singular French fashion, gave a combined frown, huff and a shrug all at once, clearly expressing her contempt for any such rule. But before she could say anything more Emma reassured her,

"There will be a couple of months' captain's salary, however, so I shall not be altogether destitute. It should be enough to pay my passage back to Boston, so please do not concern yourself on my account. I shall do just fine."

"But what then?!" Madame Fontaine was now almost beside herself at this most unjust situation. "What prospects will you have on returning to Boston?"

Emma understood that the madam was exhibiting genuine concern here, yet still this made it no less difficult to openly admit that in actuality she had no prospects whatsoever that she could foresee. So, by way of forestalling any further discomfort arising from this conversation, she began busying herself with tidying up the cups on the tray and making ready to leave.

"I ought to check on Mister Cooper. I promised him I would be on the quarterdeck for the turn of the watch."

Madame Fontaine was indeed outraged, but she said nothing more about it. As she watched Emma depart she realized that discussing this further would achieve very little, much in the way that she knew that a little planning on her part might possibly achieve a great deal. Because she believed that she might be able to help Emma, and considerably, in this particular regard.

Up on the quarterdeck the mid-afternoon sun was beating down forcefully and with an oppressive heat that could be felt on Emma's neck and shoulders even through the thick material of her wash dress, one that was now exhibiting all the varied salt and tar-stained symptoms of long-term shipboard wear and tear. Emma paused at the head of the companionway, unthinkingly brushing some loose strands of her hair aside as she saw Nate standing alone and gazing moodily ahead across a flat calm ocean. He was stooping low to peer beneath the canvas that hung all but slack from her main and fore course yards, hardly a breath of air filling either of them. She joined him by the railing, which in these calms could be defined as neither weather nor leeward, and Nate immediately appeared to brighten on seeing her, though just as quickly he made a belated attempt, or so it appeared to Emma, to cover this apparent lapse. She was surprised at this, and a little disconcerted. She looked away also, out across the vast emptiness of the open sea.

"I was just thinking," stated Nate, "or rather hoping, that *Sapphire* herself is sitting becalmed somewhere nearby."

Emma smiled at this reflection of her own thoughts.

"We can only hope. If that is the case, then we still have every chance of beating her." Then, with a glance up at Nate, she added, "Perhaps this crew will get their bonus, after all."

"Aye, they might," Nate replied. He returned to his musing, once again feeling that he could use a little leeway here in regards to his ongoing relationship with Miss Jacobs. Because he believed wholeheartedly that they might get along very well together, if only they could get beyond this stiff formality and professionalism that had become so habitual between them now, and that they might actually become friends. But in light of the fact that he himself had, in effect, usurped her beloved uncle's position as captain of *Achilles*, he felt that the best he could reasonably hope for here was to be tolerated by her, if such a thing was even possible.

"Even as little as two hundred dollars apiece will be the equivalent of several months' wages to these men," Emma was saying. "And that would still leave you with, what, almost four thousand? That's still a sizable sum."

Nate was genuinely surprised.

"Me? Why, that money, should we be fortunate enough to earn it, will belong every cent to you, and my blessings with it."

It was Emma's turn to be surprised. She looked Nate fully in the eye now and it was entirely to his misfortune that he was at that moment smiling so benignly down at her that she at once misread his intention altogether. Her eyes suddenly blazed and with such fierceness that it took him aback.

"Meaning what? Am I now to be regarded as a charity case? As some poor, pitiful creature whose gratitude is now up for sale? It is a *captain's* bonus, mister, and you are the captain, not I! Honestly, I am surprised you have the nerve!"

At which she turned abruptly and made to leave, but Nate himself was now quickly becoming angered; that he would be thought of so poorly by her! He was not going to stand for it. With one long and purposeful stride he cut Emma off before she reached the companionway scuttle and he stood there blocking her way.

"Do you really believe that I would stoop so low as to lay any claim to that money?" His voice was a low hiss but it could be heard quite clearly by Bacas, who now stared intently into the compass binnacle as if his eyes were bound to it with glue.

"I would not even be standing here if it were not for you!

All that you have done for me; why, that alone makes you so much more deserving! And that's not even the half of it!"

Emma was quite appalled at this most unexpected outburst. She was suddenly fearful, too, for her own safety and her wide eyes scanned Nate's with all the intensity of a cornered prey until she finally reassured herself that there was a good deal more upset there within Nate's expression than there was pending violence. She looked down then, feeling suddenly guilty at having leapt to such a hasty judgment. Perhaps, she realized, he truly did believe that she was more deserving. But she was not about to relent so easily, nor to humiliate herself into the bargain.

"Then what is the other half of it?" she demanded, loath now to even meet his eye and so she instead looked past him and into the companionway.

"Out of respect for your uncle," Nate went on, a little calmer now yet still visibly fuming, "whom I regarded a most capable seaman. I would be honored to pass on any such prize to his surviving heirs! That you yourself happen to be that heir is entirely coincidental, madam, and therefore as far as I am concerned the acceptance of it is for your conscience to deal with, not mine!"

Emma remained staring intently past Nate towards the entrance to the companionway. She was feeling increasingly stupid, rather grateful and absolutely humiliated all in the same instance and it was a combination that she was not relishing in the least part. It did not help, either, that she could still feel Nate's eyes boring down into her and finally, with the greatest of efforts, she raised hers and almost choked out the words,

"In that case, I shall consider your offer. On my uncle's behalf."

Then she returned to staring intently past him and at the

companionway, willing him to move out of the way, blast his eyes, and to allow her to escape with at least some shred of dignity remaining intact. But it took another, now desperate glance up at him before he finally twigged to it and stepped immediately aside to allow her to slip past him and down the steps, back into the shadows below, with her face now growing a full shade redder with every passing second.

"I've been thinking, Harry."

"Oh no."

"About what to do when we get to Frisco. It seems to me that we might both benefit from some kind of mutual business arrangement."

Harry turned to face Sarah in the gloominess of the aft main deck.

"What are you talking about?"

"Eggs and bacon!" declared Sarah.

"What?"

"And coffee. Flapjacks too, probably, and whatever else gold miners like to eat."

"Perhaps you'd care to elaborate?"

"I'm talking about opening up a restaurant, Harry! You see it occurred to me, judging from all I've read and heard about the gold fields, that it's almost exclusively men out there and hardly any women at all. And when you think about what, exactly, women can do for men, only three things come to mind. The first, obviously, is out of the question and the second would be mending clothes, which quite frankly I've had my bloody fill of, but the third would be cooking, which happens to be something I do rather pride myself on being especially good at."

"So you want to open a restaurant."

"I want *us* to open a restaurant. Because the truth is that I can't do it by myself, not without any starting capital. And that's where you come in. If we were to spend just a few weeks in Frisco to begin with, I'm sure you'll be able to win enough money to get us started. Then we'll head out to the gold fields and set up shop, with me doing all the cooking and you, as an investor, sharing in half the profits."

Harry considered this for a moment.

"I'd rather stick to playing cards," he admitted.

"And so you can! Just imagine, Harry, how much gold you could win by playing nightly card games with miners who are living in isolation with nothing else to occupy themselves with!"

"So you feed 'em while I fleece 'em."

"Well, that would be a rather crude way of putting it but I think you're getting the gist."

Harry peered closely at Sarah's shadowy form and he found himself unwittingly smiling in admiration. Here, he realized, stood a woman to be reckoned with. How could he possibly refuse?

"Let me think about it," was all he said, then walked away into the darkness.

Sarah stood there watching as Harry disappeared forward. She was smiling broadly now, and nodding to herself in a most satisfied manner.

The equator was finally reached the following forenoon, on December 19, but without any ceremony nor with much more than a hatful of wind to accompany them across the line and into the northern hemisphere. The doldrums remained doggedly upon *Achilles*, thwarting her every effort to break free of them and denying her even a breath of useful air and by now even the squalls and thunderstorms had waned to nothing and she was left to drift alone upon a flat, calm and silent ocean.

Throughout this the crew continued about their daily routine, of wetting sails, cleaning decks and rolling oakum, now with about as much joyful optimism as that of a condemned man facing the gallows steps. They were becoming increasingly disappointed and they were also becoming increasingly bored, to the limits of restlessness, despite the chief mate's, and now even William Scragg's, heartiest efforts to keep them busy and to keep their minds suitably occupied with other things. It was tough going, as even Scragg himself was forced to admit, on board a ship that was less than three months off the blocks. Even her shrouds and backstays required nary a brushstroke of tar to maintain their glisten, nor the masts more than a dab of slush to keep their yard slings well-greased and frictionless. Perhaps Robert Biggs had had the right idea after all, Nate pondered, in that bullying the crew into continual wakefulness during such idle times kept them also too weary to become overly restless about anything at all. George Evans was still putting forth his best efforts toward this end and he was continuing in his steady evolution into another Robert Biggs. He now shared Biggs' absolute lack of any sense of fair play or justice as he kept *Achilles'* crew on their toes and continually guessing. And, as it had been with Biggs, this was also beginning to serve as a detriment to the overall respect he was earning as chief mate.

Nate also had Miss Jacobs to deal with. Not that she actually required 'dealing with', in any particular sense, but the situation as it stood between them was certainly uncomfortable and he now sought ways in which to repair any ill feeling between them. There was little enough room aboard any ship for animosity to be allowed to run free and unchecked, and if left unresolved it would more often than not increase tenfold rather than simply disappear all of itself. Suffice to say that some manner of repair work was required between the two of them. She could not go on avoiding him as she had been since their recent heated converse, nor could he continue in his resentment towards her for having entirely misconstrued his own motives. Perhaps this evening, he decided, he might tentatively approach her on the pretense of discussing Christmas and what might be done to distract the crew for at least one day of this disappointing week. Then, perhaps, he might find some way to make amends for what she seemed to perceive as a gross insult to her own sensibilities.

"I am such a dolt!" declared Emma, at about the same time as Nate stood directly above her on the quarterdeck pacing fitfully fore and aft and thinking likewise of himself.

"I should have realized what he was thinking! Of course he is not the type to take advantage of a lady's misfortune!"

Madame Fontaine sat opposite, eyeing Emma with a sympathetic smile as her girls busied themselves around her with airing out their clothing and stowing it into trunks in preparation for their eventual arrival in San Francisco.

"I simply did not think," continued Emma. "I suppose I am just so accustomed to men, particularly seafaring ones, being so single-minded, that I did not for a moment consider it to be otherwise. I also took it as a most cruel slur on my uncle for him to try using that money, of all things, to try buying himself into my favors."

"And yet his true intentions were quite the opposite," pointed out the Frenchwoman. "He sought to honor your uncle, instead."

"Dash it!" Emma rose from her chair. "Well, it can't be

helped now, can it?"

She sought to distract herself by sifting through some of the particularly fine items of clothing that were hanging up to air, and by doing so found much to occupy her interest.

"I suppose there's no fixing it, is there? Now he thinks me a pompous fool and there's an end to it."

Emma selected a fine lavender floor-length skirt with a trailing chiffon shawl to compliment it and she held the ensemble up against herself, smiling now despite her otherwise gloomy mood. Madame Fontaine smiled back and, with an elegant wave of her hand, indicated to Emma that she should try it on, which she set about doing without needing to be invited twice.

"And the worst of it is that I don't think I even have the courage to apologize to him, although it is sorely required of me. It would just be so humiliating!"

"But do you not value this man's good opinion of you?"

"Mister Cooper?" Emma paused to think. She frowned, then glanced sideways at the madam before answering, rather evasively,

"I respect him as a good seaman. And I would hope that it is reciprocated. Well, yes, all right, I do admit that his opinion of me in certain other regards is not altogether a matter of indifference."

Emma made some final adjustments to the dress with the help of Dominique and then turned towards the mirror and loosened her dark hair, releasing it in a rich cascade that tumbled loosely about her pale shoulders. The effect was most satisfactory and she could not help but smile to herself, which increased the overall effect, Madame Fontaine noticed with surreptitious approval, by at least threefold.

"But there is nothing to be inferred from that, if that is what you are thinking." Emma turned to the Frenchwoman with a forbidding frown.

"The man despises me! That much is obvious! Especially now! And I am not about to humiliate myself further by having anything more to do with him, at least not on any subject that is not of a purely professional nature. So there!"

Emma took a turn in her dress, to the general approval of all, then sought to lighten her own mood by declaring,

"A hundred dollars a day? La! Perhaps I *do* have prospects after all."

They all laughed and Madame Fontaine, who had always prided herself on recognizing an opportunity when she saw one, suddenly found herself staring one directly in the face.

"A ribbon!" she declared, her eyes flickering involuntarily toward the sound of pacing footfalls on the quarterdeck overhead. "That would be the perfect touch! And I think I know the very one! It is in your stateroom, I think. The white one, with the lace trim?"

Emma smiled happily in agreement.

"Yes!" She reached for the door handle then paused to regard herself in the mirror. She considered for a moment, then shrugged at her own silly prudishness and, holding a bare arm across her rather immodestly-exposed cleavage, she opened the door and made a bold and barefooted dash across the full width of the aft cabin towards her own stateroom.

Madame Fontaine immediately turned to Yvette and whispered in her ear, at which the girl, with a smile of understanding dawning on her pretty face, nodded eagerly and set off through the door and up the companionway to the quarterdeck. The madam hushed her two remaining girls, who had immediately begun chattering to one another and when Yvette promptly returned to the cabin nodding her head excitedly they all stood there in expectant silence, with the door left slightly ajar so that they might peek out.

Moments later Nate came down the aft scuttle, a bewildered expression on his face and, to the absolute delight of all four French ladies who were secretly watching, the madam's little deception could not have been timed better.

Emma emerged from her stateroom at the very moment Nate stepped from the foot of the ladder and the two immediately collided headlong into one another. Nate found himself, to his astonishment, gripping Emma's bare shoulders and looking down into her wide and startled eyes which, being framed as they were by her loosened hair and offset by the finery of her dress, caused such an unexpected thrill within him that he was literally struck dumb. He was looking at a stranger, yet not. Here, suddenly, was a strikingly beautiful woman, one whom he did not even know and yet, so oddly, he did. And Emma, being all too suddenly aware of Nate's strong hands remaining for the moment forgotten on her shoulders, and he with such an intensity of expression with which he now regarded her, found herself experiencing a similar and equally as unexpected thrill; albeit one of alarm yet still mixed with a certain measure of confused and indefinable excitement.

It was a moment that lasted scarcely a couple of seconds yet within that brief span volumes might have been spoken for all that passed in silence between them. And then, an instant later, it was entirely gone as propriety reasserted itself with Nate's realization that he was still gripping Emma's cool bare shoulders and with Emma's likewise realization coupled with the observation that his large hands felt pleasingly warm and that she was standing here in the aft cabin barefooted and with her cleavage exposed and consequently behaving like a shameless hussy.

Emma was the first to regain something approximating composure and she coughed, loudly, as a pretense of allowing the raising of an arm to cover her chest, and she kept it there, affecting such a pose of endearing modesty that, to Nate, it only seemed to confound the knot that his stricken tongue was now bent into.

"I...er," Emma explained, glancing with helplessness toward the half-opened door of Madame Fontaine's stateroom, but it stood more than fifteen feet away and so was impossible to make a respectable dash for. She looked back at Nate. "I was, er, just helping with some dress alterations."

"Oh," was about as much as Nate could think to utter. He did not quite know where to direct his eyes, except back to Emma's, but on doing so he immediately regretted it and it only seemed to confound the situation. "Yes, well..."

It was at this moment that Madame Fontaine, with her exceptional sense of timing, chose to emerge from her stateroom and save the day.

"Ah, captain!" she greeted Nate happily and this allowed Emma to escape and, with a brief nod to Nate and with her eyes now safely averted, she ducked quickly back into the madam's cabin. "I merely wished to discuss with you our plans for a Christmas Day celebration..."

But Nate was only half listening. He kept glancing towards the door that had now closed in Emma's wake and his mind was reeling. He made an effort to nod and to smile pleasantly, all the while seeking to extract himself from the madam's attentions and escape back up the companionway. For suddenly it seemed to him a whole deal safer up there on deck; at least up there he knew where he stood, and who he was. He suddenly felt the need to reassure himself of this and, as he made his excuses and finally managed to make his way back up the ladder again, he was thinking once again of that old axiom: of ships and women and how never the twain should be brought together, for the sake of all concerned.

Chapter Twenty-Two
The Trades Recovered

It took another two days for the northeast Trade Winds to properly settle in and this finally occurred on the morning of Christmas Day as *Achilles* was crossing the eighth parallel of northern latitude. The Pacific doldrums had hampered them now for a full fortnight and with this return of a decent spell of weather the crew bent-to willingly with the setting and trimming of all sails. Studdingsails were set alow and aloft on her weather side to harness this most reliable of breezes, and by keeping it held squarely on her starboard beam *Achilles* heeled comfortably over to leeward, exposing her uppermost strake of copper sheathing to the approaching white-caps and she began cutting a smooth and direct wake towards the northwest at a very respectable twelve knots.

Emma remained convinced that they were still very much in the running when it came to overhauling *Sapphire*. These Trades were expected to hold fair until they approached the Californian coast, whereupon they would give way to those predominant northerlies which had a nasty way of bedeviling any ship approaching San Francisco from due south. But for every day this northeasterly wind remained constant they would gain more valuable westings of longitude, and when the time came to bid the Trades farewell and come about onto the larboard tack, they should, with a little luck, find themselves hauling directly in on a fair breeze towards the Golden Gate.

Now with *Achilles'* speed picking up again there came also a palpable feeling throughout the ship of an ending in sight, as well a rekindled hope of earning a healthy monetary bonus into the bargain. With the cooling Trade Winds now tempering their approach into the sub-tropical latitudes, the weather was just as clement as one could wish for and, with it being Christmas Day, Nate allowed the crew the afternoon off with a double ration of whiskey to both help them celebrate as well as to lift their spirits in readiness for the final leg of the voyage.

Around noontime Madame Fontaine approached Nate on the quarterdeck as he was busily calculating his sun sighting and cordially invited him to dinner that evening. It would, she explained, be a most opportune occasion that only the most boorish and indecent of palates would even think to squander. A particularly succulent menu, she assured him, was to be presented for the occasion, including several French delicacies such as pate, truffles, chocolates and an especially fine vintage of Chablis from her own dwindling supplies. Such a gracious offer was beyond either Nate's ability or inclination to reasonably decline and so a time was agreed upon, at the ending of the second dog watch at eight of the clock, down in the aft saloon.

Eight bells heralded the ending of the second dog watch and the beginning of the first watch and was accompanied by diverse cries of *"All's well!"* from various quarters as *Achilles* settled in for the ninetieth evening of her voyage.

When Nate arrived in the aft saloon he found that the large dining table had been set for seven places and was decorated most elegantly, with polished silver candelabras and centerpieces woven from various rope-stuffs, all of which held a distinctly nautical flavor. He thus deemed it prudent, in light of such finery, to perhaps take a little time to dress himself for the occasion and so he headed directly to his stateroom to take care of just that.

The captain's stateroom was in much the same state of disarray as Captain Jacobs had left it, as Nate himself was also a seaman who shared his former captain's unease with any such fanciful trimmings. Besides, Nate possessed only the one sea-bag, the entire contents of which could easily be accommodated either in an untidy heap at the foot of his bunk or inside the small narrow wardrobe that stood adjacent to it. From this wardrobe he now selected his cleanest white shirt, a fairly respectable, if not particularly clean, pair of blue duck trousers, his best shore-going shoes and his pea coat, to which a double row of brass buttons had recently, in accordance with his rank, been sewn. He took a while to apply some polish to these and then, feeling suitably prepared despite his growing nervousness at formally dining as the solitary male amongst six ladies, he stepped out into the aft cabin feeling very much uncertain as to whether he ought to feel confident or terrified at the prospect.

The candles on the table had been lit and the oil lamps on the bulkheads and those suspended from the beams overhead had all been extinguished, transforming the ambience of the aft saloon to one of soft, warm coziness. The richly-polished dark mahogany wall paneling and the numerous mirrors to either side enhanced this effect and, if not for the gentle rolling of the deck underfoot and the occasional lurching as *Achilles* nudged herself into the oncoming swell, he may well have believed himself to have somehow stepped directly into some affluent family's front parlor.

Emma sat alone at the foot of the table. She was dressed for the occasion also, now wearing a light blue dress that was not cut excessively low yet still lingered well below her shoulders. Her hair had been carefully and expertly dressed so that the bulk of it now lay in rich dark cascades to either side of her face and, this being combined with the way in which she suddenly glanced up with wide eyes and in a rather self-conscious manner at Nate's arrival, made such an impression on him as to rekindle that very same thrill as he had felt before. She herself also seemed a little put out, he noticed, by the fact that not a single one of *Achilles'* passengers had yet made an appearance and that she and Nate were now obliged to sit here together, for the time being, all alone.

Nate nodded to her stiffly, not having the courage to fully meet her eye and wondering where exactly he stood, at present, in Miss Jacob's most unpredictable graces. And she, as if in a similar state of unease, called out anxiously to Pepin, who was busying himself in his pantry, to ask him once again to check on Madame Fontaine to see if she was ready to join them. Nate seated himself awkwardly at the captain's place at the head of the table and there the two of them sat, in a growing state of mutual discomfort, while the steward knocked politely on the Frenchwoman's door and disappeared within.

Emma coughed quietly, which caused Nate to glance up at her with an uncertain smile, one that faded quickly when he saw that she was looking instead at the madam's closed stateroom door. She in turn glanced in his direction just as he himself looked toward the closed door. And this rather comical routine might have continued so, tit for tat, for who knew how long, if not for Pepin's prompt reappearance. The steward closed the door softly behind him and, stepping directly up to Emma, spoke quietly into her ear.

"Seasick?!" Emma exclaimed. "What, all of them?"

Nate could see Pepin nodding and in the dimness of candlelight could not be sure if indeed there was the trace of a smile there behind the steward's impassive expression as he whispered again into Emma's ear.

"At least another hour? And they asked us to begin without them. I see."

She nodded, now with a small frown and an air of vexation; one that Nate was by now quite familiar with, and she asked Pepin to serve the wine.

"It would appear that we are dining alone together this evening, Mister Cooper," she announced to Nate, but not before downing half the contents of her glass and in a way that precluded the suggestion of any quarter whatsoever being given. Pepin, seeming to have anticipated this, stood by to promptly refill it. The steward also topped up Nate's glass then set the bottle judicially at the midpoint between them, where neither could properly reach it, and headed back into his pantry.

Emma looked directly at Nate and she surprised him then by smiling.

"In case you have not twigged to it yet, mister," she said, lightly, "We have both of us been rather wickedly deceived."

"I was beginning to suspect it," Nate admitted. Then he too smiled, and this at once helped break the tension between them.

"That woman!" Emma looked towards Madame Fontaine's closed door. "She is far too devious for us. Too much for her own good, I suspect. She believes that she sees a match here."

Emma, without realizing she was doing so, glanced furtively at Nate as she said this, as if his reaction to this statement was of an importance beyond which she would ever have openly admitted to. And when he failed to smile back in the same dismissive manner she felt an inexplicable mixture of relief combined with her anxiety. At once taken aback by such a contradiction of feelings, and rather than to experience any further discomfort by dwelling upon the significance of any part of it, she instead drained her glass again and set it deliberately back down onto the table.

"Well, if nothing else, we shall at least have ourselves a decent dinner out of it!" she announced, and with a somewhat affected joviality.

Nate tried to conceal the sudden moroseness he was now feeling. Was it really so unthinkable to her, the possibility that they might actually make a fairly tolerable match? Clearly it was. So he too resigned himself to a likewise affectation of nonchalance and scorn for any such ridiculous notion.

"We might as well make the most of it," he agreed. "We might also call this an end-of-voyage celebration dinner into the bargain."

At this Emma's expression adopted a more serious demeanor and in the soft candlelight her frown appeared to Nate to accurately reflect his own uncertainties regarding the future. Yet at the same time he understood how much more difficult it must be for her, which prompted him to ask, albeit hesitantly,

"Have you given any thought to my, er, suggestion, as regards this captain's bonus?"

To which she nodded heartily and in a way that implied

that any and all acrimony concerning this particular subject had now been fully dispelled from her mind.

"In all fairness," she said, "I would have to insist that it be divided equally between the two of us, but only after the crew receives their share. If you are agreeable to such a compromise then, on behalf of my late uncle and myself, I gratefully accept."

She raised her empty glass to Nate in a silent toast and the sheepish expression he perceived through the dimness indicated clearly that, with this being said, the subject was best stowed away and forgotten about.

"You do realize, don't you," Emma said, "that with an extra two hundred dollars in each man's pocket the odds are pretty slim that any of our crew will choose to remain on board for the return voyage?"

Nate nodded. "We shall certainly be needing the crimps again in Frisco."

"But what about yourself?"

Emma looked at him with more intensity than she realized as she asked this and Nate, now beginning to feel the soothing effect of the wine, got up to refill both their glasses and, seating himself again, replied quite frankly,

"Oh, I'll certainly choose to remain on board, but I've no idea what as. Probably as second mate again. Perhaps as chief mate? That's up to the ship's agent in Frisco, I guess. But I still don't know exactly how I'm going to feel about that. I mean, only three months ago I was down in the fo'c'sle. Now here I am as captain, of a clipper of all things! It's a rum position to be in, because now I feel that I would be downright miserable if I had to go back to working even as chief mate. Now that I've had a taste of command I feel as if there's no going back."

"Like a door that's been opened and which cannot be

closed again?”

“Exactly! Only now I find myself with aspirations that extend far beyond my own abilities. I realize that I am still hardly proficient enough to even serve as second mate.”

“It would certainly require more learning and more hands-on experience on your part, but you are without a doubt intelligent enough for it. A fast learner, too, and so far you’ve proven yourself well up to the task in all respects.”

Nate smiled in thanks.

“But still it scares the life out of me! On the one hand it’s the most incredible feeling in the world to be up there on deck with full control over every line and scrap of canvas and with the entire ship under your command. And such a ship! *Achilles* is the finest vessel I’ve ever stepped aboard and she’s a joy to sail. But as captain? Why, the captain answers to no one and yet holds absolute control over the lives and destinies of all on board. That responsibility alone is daunting enough, let alone all the additional learning that would be required.”

Emma was studying Nate closely as he spoke and through her mind now flowed a succession of thoughts that, although she was unaware of it, was a familiar enough occurrence in such a situation. For she was just now beginning to perceive the true possibility in Nate. She was now viewing him no longer as a stumbling, inexperienced foremasthand, one who for the sake of the ship must be judged with perpetual skepticism so that all his shortcomings might be anticipated and circumvented before they occurred. She no longer regarded Nate as a collection of mistakes, but now as an assemblage of potentials.

Emma smiled without even realizing she was doing so, and she said,

“I think all you need is a little more practice and a touch

more confidence."

"Oh, I don't deny it! But still it's a terrifying prospect. There is so much more to be learned!"

"It's only terrifying when you don't know what you're about. And the quickest way to learn is through trial and error. Why, in only these past two months alone you have learned more than any other first-tripper mate would have in as many years! Do not be so eager to sell yourself short. Would that I were in such a position as you."

Nate could well imagine. He smiled at the notion and said,

"I do appreciate all that you have done to help me, ma'am."

"Do you think we might drop all this ma'am business? At least for these times that we are alone together. My name, in case you are not aware of it, is Emma. And, as it appears that we are to be shipmates for probably another three or four months at least, then surely we can dispense with all the ma'ams and misters?"

"Shipmates?"

"Yes, shipmates. Why, did you think I would choose to remain in Frisco all by myself? No, I shall be booking a stateroom aboard *Achilles* just as soon as we dock, for the return voyage to New York."

"As a passenger?"

"Of course. What else? And, if all that I have heard about the difficulties of finding good seamen in Frisco are true, then who knows? Perhaps you will retain your present rank. And if that is the case then I shall be more than happy to assist you whenever you may require it."

Nate smiled broadly at the prospect. Emma smiled back, now equally as openly.

"Then perhaps the notion of me remaining as captain is

not so far-fetched after all."

He raised his glass in a toast, feeling inexplicably pleased now with the knowledge that there would, for the time being, be no pending good-byes between himself and Miss Jacobs.

On January 6, Nate's observation of the noonday sun found *Achilles* to be crossing the twenty-eighth parallel of northern latitude and, when this was correlated with Emma's afternoon sightings from which a position line was obtained, they found that *Achilles* now stood only four hundred nautical miles from the harbor of San Francisco. But by now the northeasterly Trade Winds had begun to back towards the north and so *Achilles* was obliged to bear away in accordance and even though she maintained a good speed for being close-hauled, she yet barely managed to trim a handful of leagues from that distance over the course of the next couple of days.

When finally, on January 9, it being now the ninety-seventh day of her voyage, *Achilles'* noonday latitude placed her at thirty-four degrees north, it was agreed between Nate and Emma that they might now come safely about and run directly in on a 'soldier's wind', or beam reach, toward San Francisco. At the turning-to of the first dog watch all hands were called to deck and ordered to make ready for tacking ship.

On this occasion it afforded Nate an unusual degree of pleasure to witness his crew now working together as a willing and cohesive body of men to perform this most complex and demanding of tasks. As *Achilles* began the maneuver he observed closely and with a critical eye as his chief mate positioned himself on the foredeck to manage the headsails, the boatswain to the waist to oversee the yard braces and the idlers took their places by the fore and mainsail tacks and sheets. No longer did any man need to be told where to go or what to do and an unusual quietness now pervaded the entire deck, which trembled beneath two score and more of bared, running feet as each man and boy hastened to his designated post.

Ordering the helm down to swing *Achilles'* head into the wind, Nate watched closely as head sheets were eased away, tack lines let go and all yards braced to square as the wind approached dead ahead, whereupon all main and mizzen yards were braced promptly about while her foremast squares remained cast aback to assist the turn, until the wind crossed her bows fully onto the larboard side, upon which all yards on the foremast were braced fully around and all jib and fore staysail sheets hauled tightly in and belayed as the wind filled her main and mizzen squares and she began rapidly gathering speed on the new tack.

Only then came the noisier aspect of the entire maneuver, one that entailed a final trimming of all yards as the chief mate stood beneath the foremast, the boatswain the main and Nate himself the mizzen, each of them calling out to those men at the braces.

"Main t'gallant's well! Main royal too much!"

"Well the fore tops'l! Fore skys'l haul to weather!"

"Small pull on the mizzen t'gallant! Well on the mizzen! Heave tight and belay!"

Lines were secured to their pins and cleats and promptly coiled down, then both watches were sent below for their dinner, leaving only Nate and Emma alone with the helmsman up on the quarterdeck. Nate could not help but remark,

"Finally, we have a crew to be proud of. And on the very eve of landfall."

"That's the law of the Irish," replied Emma. She smiled

up at Nate. "It's always the way. No matter how long of a voyage it is, it's always the very last maneuver and none other they actually manage to get right."

Nate nodded, smiling himself now and feeling pretty good about everything. Only a few hundred miles beyond the twilit horizon ahead lay their destination. If this breeze remained on their larboard beam they would arrive at the Bar the day after tomorrow, with any luck before sunset and in time to pick up a pilot.

That night *Achilles* did herself proud by covering a full one hundred miles of ocean before the sun appeared again, leaving in her wake a broad trail of green phosphorescence which could be seen as an unbroken line extending more than a mile astern. To either side of her sharpened cutwater the crests she forced aside with every pitch sparkled and tumbled into foamy peaks, and just beneath the surface the ghostly green outlines of several dolphin could be seen darting playfully about, as ever unconcerned and unimpeded by the fast-moving ship's hull. The sky above was clear and moonless; the broad band of the Milky Way arcing directly overhead and filling the void with countless shimmering stars that illumined the sails aloft, and the overall effect was both a sublime and a ghostly one as *Achilles* glided ahead smoothly and quietly into the long winter's night towards her destination.

Under any other circumstance it might have been considered romantic for Harry and Sarah to be standing there side by side at the bulwark gazing out at this wondrous scene. But such was the ongoing situation, of his being a common deckhand and she a passenger, and with *Achilles'* chief mate George Evans showing himself no more tolerant than had been Robert Biggs concerning any interactions between the two, that for the sake of prudence as well as Harry's own safety they continued to meet only under the cover of darkness and during those early hours of the middle watch when the ship was at its quietest.

"Well?" whispered Sarah. "Have you thought about my proposal?"

"It does have certain merits, I'll give you that," replied Harry offhandedly, despite his inward agreeability at the idea. "In fact, I might even be tempted to give it a try."

Sarah's brief smile went unseen by Harry.

"There would be conditions, of course," she said.

"Conditions? Now wait a minute. Shouldn't I be the one making conditions?"

"No Harry. You're the man. You don't get to make conditions."

"I might have known. All right, what are they?"

"There has to be absolute honesty between us at all times. No lies, no deception. None. Do you understand?"

Harry regarded her with amusement before replying, "Well, that works both ways, doesn't it? If you play fair by me, I'll play fair by you."

"I said," repeated Sarah, "do you understand?"

"Yes, yes."

"Secondly, no monkey business."

"I'm sure I don't know what you mean."

"You know perfectly well what I mean Harry Jenkins so don't you even try pretending otherwise."

Harry snorted derisively and responded, "Please, don't flatter yourself. You're perfectly safe in that department, you have my word on it. Anything else?"

"So, do we have an agreement?"

Sarah held out her hand. Harry shook it. She was secretly

delighted, but she was no more ready than Harry to openly show it, let alone admit to it.

"Now then," Sarah continued, in a lighter tone. "Who shall we be when we arrive in Frisco? I think that if you want to get into the best card games, then we ought to go the full course and give ourselves a proper title. I mean, who's going to know? I doubt that we'll meet too many English gentry out there who'll challenge us on it. What do you think of Sir Robert and Lady Fairfield? Doesn't that have a rather prestigious ring to it?"

"You've already thought all this through, haven't you?"

"I certainly have not."

"Sounds like you have."

"I just happen to possess the ability to think quickly on my feet. As I assumed you did too. Don't make me doubt you, Harry, I shall be most disappointed. Now, what do you think of this idea...?"

The following day saw a continuation of this same northerly breeze and by midday, when the log was streamed, it was found that another fifty miles had gone by the stern since dawn. The mood on board now began to shift, with the knowledge that they should be arriving in port within the next two days. The crew remained busy at their tasks, all of which were now directed towards the enhancement of *Achilles'* outward appearance. Paint was daubed and tar was applied in liberal quantities to respective topsides and standing rigging, while on deck the crew busied themselves with rags and holystones, scouring the deck and cleaning up any and all spillages.

Into the early hours of the eleventh of January, this being now the ninety-ninth day of her voyage, *Achilles* herself continued to display as much eagerness, or so it seemed, as did her crew in making this her final burst of effort towards the finishing line. It was another clear night, once again illumined brightly to all quarters between the open heavens and the glistening phosphorescent ocean, and with little danger as they rapidly approached the coast of any unexpected landfall or unseen ship to impede their passage in these busier waters. For whereas normally it might have been the more prudent course of action to heave-to for the darker hours, on this night the visibility was near to as good as daylight, and if any other ship had been in the vicinity they would surely have seen her clearly from at least five miles away.

But as dawn approached it became evident that such rare visibility as they had enjoyed these past two nights was now beginning to wane, and gradually it faded to such an extent that no longer could any but the brightest of stars be viewed overhead, nor could *Achilles'* illuminated wake be seen stretching aft towards the horizon, for now it disappeared within only a couple of ship's lengths astern and there was no longer any horizon to be properly seen.

And before even the rising sun had cast its diffused light upon the engulfing grayness the wind had already begun to fail them, and now it died away to a mere whisper as *Achilles* found herself completely and inescapably bound by fog.

Chapter Twenty-Three
Fogbound

It was as dense as the proverbial pea soup; a heavy blanket of chill dampness that clung to everything it touched and dripped like rain from the shrouds and rigging aloft. From the quarterdeck not even the foremast could be seen, which was unsettling after three months of being accustomed to the same view from aft. What little breeze remained continued to propel *Achilles* eastwards at a rate of four knots, thereby proving once again her seaworthiness when it came to hauling into light and near-to-absent airs. But she proceeded blindly now, towards a Californian coastline that now lay less than one hundred miles ahead and, without the ability to shoot the sun and gain a position line, her progress could no longer be accurately measured.

As the morning wore on the perils of such a condition became evermore acute, as both Nate and Emma began to envision, as all navigators are wont to under such circumstances, the pending calamity of either an unexpected grounding or running into one of the many fishing vessels that always frequent any busy harbor. But at least for the time being there was no possibility of *Achilles* reaching the coast until well into the night. But if no accurate fix could be obtained by nightfall they would be obliged, for the sake of prudence, to heave-to for the darker hours and thus impede their chances of reaching San Francisco the following day, which would be the one-hundredth day of the voyage and one that both Nate and Emma now fervently aspired to achieve.

From forward the ship's bell was sounded vigorously every two minutes and a keen listening watch maintained throughout, by one man posted aloft and another who sat astride of and far out towards the end of the jib boom. It was seven bells into the forenoon watch when another vessel was heard, as a faint and distant tolling of a bell on their starboard side. It was the first contact they had had of any other ship for several weeks now, and under these conditions it was far from welcomed. But this turned out to be a fortunate occurrence because only now did it occur to Nate that perhaps he should send his masthead lookout, who was presently perched atop the main topmast crosstrees, farther aloft and as high up as he could possibly climb, on the off-chance that perhaps the fog might be thin enough up there to allow some glimpse of the other ship. One of the younger Swedes by the name of Jons, who had by now become as valued a hand as any of his countryman, disappeared quickly up into the fog on his captain's order, then called down immediately on reaching the head of the topgallant shrouds.

"By Gott I shee 'im! I shee 'is royals! The sky ish blue up here!"

Down on the quarterdeck it was a close call as to who, between Nate and Emma, responded more readily to this unexpected announcement. Nate immediately moved to fetch his spyglass with the intent of making his own way aloft while Emma, quickly glancing at her timepiece, muttered quietly to herself as she calculated, then proclaimed,

"I believe we can still get a noonday sighting!"

Nate, stopping short on his way to the main shrouds, paused to regard her skeptically. Then, realizing that she was indeed serious, he frowned and looked aloft.

"Masthead! Do you see any horizon to the south?"

There was a considerable pause before the reply.

"Yesh! I mean no! It comes, then it goesh! I dunno!"

"I'll take the sextant aloft and maybe..." Nate began, but Emma had already disappeared down the companionway, clearly intent on fetching the instrument herself. Only a couple of minutes later she reappeared, not only with her sextant but now dressed in a most peculiar rig: one consisting of a pair of her late uncle's loose baggy trousers, an old canvas shirt and an unbuttoned pea coat. She was also wearing a pair of well-worn soft leather moccasins and her expression, on meeting Nate's, was of such defiant stubbornness as to completely forestall any further argument on his part. She was clearly ready to go aloft, and aloft she was determined to go.

"It won't be as simple as taking just one sight," she muttered as she handed Nate the sextant, the lanyard of which he promptly looped around his neck. "There will be some other calculations involved." Then she looked to *Achilles'* chief mate, who had arrived on the quarterdeck.

"Mister Evans. I would be considerably obliged if you were to send a man aloft as quickly as possible with paper, pencils and an almanac. And I will also need to know the exact height above the waterline of, let us say, the main royal yard. And I mean *exact*."

George Evans nodded respectfully and, only after Emma had turned away and was striding towards the mainmast shrouds, did he raise a quizzical eyebrow at Nate, who merely nodded his assent before hurrying to catch her up.

The very sight of a woman, any woman, ascending the ratlines dressed as a seafaring man could not help but cause something of a stir aboard any ship at sea. On board *Achilles* there was no exception to this rule and accordingly something of a stir did arise from it. Even the least superstitious of those foremasthands who stood adeck staring with mouth agape at this most unusual sight could scarce do so without at least some sense of disquiet worming its way into his very soul, and for those who were of a more superstitious bent it was as if, in keeping with the very nature of this thick and heavy fog, the sky itself had indeed fallen in on them. They watched Emma nimbly ascending the mainmast shrouds, as agile and as able as any man jack of them, and they also watched their captain following closely behind, which in itself was also cause for concern, for a captain's place was on the quarterdeck and nowhere else. But all eyes in this instance remained fixed upon Emma and, the farther aloft she proceeded, the more pressing the unspoken question shared by them all became until finally it was given voice by young Albert Tucker who, like everyone else, looked on with something approaching awestruck amazement.

"She'll use the lubber's hole. Won't she?"

"No chance o' the futtocks, boyo," agreed Taffy Owens quietly, also keeping his eyes glued aloft. "Women don't 'ave the arm strength for it, see, an' she'd be a particularly daft, if not a particularly wet and dead article, look you now, if she was to even think about it."

There was a good deal of sage nodding in response to this, until William Scragg offered his tuppence worth.

"I wouldn't be too sure about nothin' with that there

lady," he said, grinning aloft at the sight. "I reckon she'll do it."

"Then put your money where your mouth is, bosun," challenged Taffy, who did not like being gainsaid, even by Scragg. "My dollar says she'll use the lubber's hole."

"Then mine says she won't."

And a flurry of hasty wagering ensued, which lasted the full ten seconds it took for Emma to reach the iron bars of the lower futtock shrouds and, as she did, a hush fell upon those below who, with all notions of superstition and bad omens now superseded by their greater interest in the speculation of it, held their breaths to a man. Emma now faced a choice, of either continuing up the lower main shrouds and through the small lubber's hole in the base of the main top platform, or taking the more difficult course up the backward incline of the futtock shrouds, those six extra ratlines that led sharply outwards to the edges of the top and which any sailor who took any pride whatsoever in calling himself such was obliged to use else risk being labeled a landlubber himself.

Emma knew these things, as well she knew that the eyes of the ship were presently upon her. And she also knew that if an accurate sighting could be taken and a position line obtained, *Achilles* would be able to steer landwards and into the foggy night with absolute confidence. But, above all else, she knew that it would be this ship's crew that would have the final say on that, so she felt it of paramount importance that they also have full confidence in both their captain's and her own abilities. And to this end she barely hesitated, despite her sudden misgivings, in grasping the aftmost futtock shroud as she reached it and proceeding up and outwards toward the main top.

She was surprised at first by the very steepness of the

incline, as the bulk of her own weight was transferred immediately to her arms and she found herself having to rely solely upon her upper body strength. She had never experienced this before; now she understood why the futtocks were considered to be the greater challenge as well the greater danger in climbing aloft. She paused for a moment, gripping on tightly with whitening knuckles against the increased gravity and she willfully gathered every last ounce of resolve and strength before continuing doggedly upwards with increasing concern now and with doubts that perhaps, after all, she was not up to this.

It was consequently with a huge amount of relief that Emma finally reached the outer deadeyes of the main topmast shrouds and, whereas she might otherwise have tumbled safely into the top, and in a most unladylike manner, to regain her breath along with her strength, with the eyes of so many looking up at her from below she could do little else but continue onwards and up the topmast shrouds, now with Nate following closely behind, which in itself was encouragement enough for she was not about to be seen to impede the progress of their captain. Looking down as she approached the next set of futtocks that led up to the main topgallant shrouds she could see the outline of *Achilles'* deck, now more than one hundred and twenty feet below, as a dim gray shape that was barely discernible through the mist. Then finally, as she continued steadily upwards, the ship beneath her disappeared altogether and moments later she emerged from the fog into brilliant sunlight.

Directly overhead was a sky of deepest blue, while below and all around lay an irregular-shaped mass of thick white cloud that drifted slowly downwind and, most significantly, through which she was able to catch an occasional glimpse of distant horizon to the south, against which she might now measure the sun as it approached its meridian passage.

"I can work up our noon latitude from here," she announced breathlessly to Nate as he arrived close beneath where she now stood, balanced on the narrow ratlines that formed the ladder between the two main topgallant mast shrouds. She gripped onto the aftmost shroud with one hand and looped her other arm over the main royal yard, working her fingers beneath the tight robands at the head of the sail so as to gain a more secure purchase. She could feel her arms and legs trembling from the climb and, as Nate stepped nimbly across the four-foot span that separated the shrouds as they narrowed towards the head of the topgallant mast and climbed up to her level to hand her the sextant, she looked toward the other ship which stood barely a mile away and which remained, much as *Achilles* herself did, almost wholly engulfed by the fog. Only her royals and skysails could be seen with any clarity, and even then only in brief glimpses.

"Another clipper, for certain. Inbound. She *has* to be *Sapphire!*"

Nate retrieved his spyglass and wedged himself in securely against the shrouds with one foot resting on the foot rope beneath the royal yard, then focused on the distant vessel.

"That is *Sapphire's* rig!" he confirmed, "but I wonder if they've even seen us yet. I see no lookout posted."

Emma then smiled at Nate and, in the manner of someone who has just discovered they are party to a valuable secret, and despite such unnatural silence as there existed here above the clouds, her voice dropped to a whisper.

"Keep a weather eye on her, will you? If you see anyone climb aloft, I'll tuck this thing out of sight. I wouldn't want to give them any ideas."

She held the sextant to her eye and Nate smiled, at the same time retrieving one of the loose gaskets from the royal yard. Stepping back across to the starboard shrouds, with nothing beneath save a one-hundred-and-fifty-foot drop to the deck below, he came up close behind where Emma stood and, much to her alarm, gripped onto the shrouds close to either side of her waist. For a moment Emma was flustered and was about to ask what, exactly, did he think he was doing, until she realized that he was merely ensuring her safety. As Nate hauled on the tail end of the line it cinched Emma securely in against the shrouds and she found that she could now ease her grip and even lean back a little against the line, all of which considerably aided her stance and her ability to hold the sextant.

"Captain's orders," Nate told her. She could feel his breath close against her neck as he worked to secure the line. It felt warm; indeed, it felt pleasing and it caused her to promptly tense up and she remained standing there, rigidly, thinking at the same time how ridiculous this was, in such a situation, to be even thinking about such things.

"You're far too valuable," Nate added, then he promptly returned to his own side of the topgallant mast, from where he resumed peering through his spyglass at the other ship.

Emma's heart was still beating rapidly from the climb aloft and it was an effort to clear her mind and to return to the task in hand: that of determining where, exactly, they presently were. A brief glimpse of sunlight combined with a patch of horizon suddenly appeared to the south and she immediately raised the sextant.

"Our dead reckoning puts us well into the western half of this time zone," she murmured as she adjusted the sextant's increment screw. But, as she peered through the eyepiece, the horizon dissolved again into the flat whiteness of fog. She lowered the instrument and carefully retrieved the pocket watch on its lanyard from around her neck. She passed this, with the greatest of care and not without some inner misgivings, across the four-foot space to Nate and was somewhat reassured to see the care with which he accepted it.

"We are fortunate," she went on, "that it hasn't yet approached apparent noon. At this longitude the sun should cross our meridian closer to one o'clock than twelve. That should give us time enough to begin plotting a graph."

"Why would we need to plot a graph?"

"Because I have little hope of being able to shoot the sun at the precise moment of apparent noon, nor do I have a good enough approximation of our longitude. A simple ex-meridian sight won't be enough. I'll need to gain a series of sightings, both before and after the meridian transit, so that we can run each one either forward or back using the antithesis of the ship's own speed and heading. As we're presently on a heading of due east, and therefore with our latitude remaining more or less a constant, it should be pretty simple to work out."

"Ah. I see," was about as much as Nate deemed it wise to utter. It was at this moment that William Scragg appeared, laden with pencils and tablets and, with the shrouds swaying alarmingly underfoot as he mounted the final few ratlines to stand directly beneath Nate, he breathlessly announced,

"Chief mate reckons it to be one 'undred an' sixty-seven foot to the main deck from the main royal yard. An' that'll be good to the nearest foot."

"The nearest foot?" Emma frowned and looked to Nate. "That's not nearly good enough. A difference of one foot will translate into at least two miles of latitude. That could make all the difference between clearing the Farallons or not!"

"The Farallons?" asked Nate.

"That group of islands which stand due west of the Golden Gate. The Southeast Farallon is the tallest; it's a huge, conical rock. It's generally used as a landfall and you can't miss it on a clear day."

"Then we'd best get the most accurate measurement we can."

Emma was still looking to the south in search of a clearing through the fog, of which there appeared several but not yet one through which she might gain a sighting of both sun and horizon together. She was leaning into the narrowing shrouds with her left arm wrapped fully around one of the thick hempen stays and using that hand to balance the sextant while the fingers of her other rested on the increment screw. As she stood waiting thus, she quietly reminded Nate,

"I shall be needing the most reliable measurement that can be made, of my height of eye. To within inches, if possible."

"Then Jacko's yer man, miss," announced Scragg. The boatswain looked to Nate and explained,

"Unnat'ral it is, sir, an' I don't doubt you'll question it, but that Jacko's a reg'lar Imperial Standard. Why, 'e can break out a cable's worth of any size of line and 'ave it down to the nearest inch. Bless my trousers if I know how 'e does it, but 'e does it all the same."

"I'm sure he's pretty accurate," agreed Nate, doubtfully. "But I still think we should use a heaving line and a carpenter's rule, just to be sure."

Scragg nodded and, with a shrug, he began his descent.

"I'll have Jacko double-check yer figures. Just in case."

Several heaving lines soon arrived aloft, each one measuring ten fathoms apiece, and Nate began bending these together end to end, securing the tail of the first to the royal halyard tye which was on a precise level with Emma's eye. When finally the line reached the main deck it was pulled taut and marked by Scragg with a strip of cloth which he tucked under one of its strands and Nate, after likewise marking his end of the line at the base of the knot, untied it and allowed the entire length to fall to the main deck. No sooner had he done this than Emma called out,

"Ready..."

Nate quickly retrieved the timepiece from around his neck as she called, "Time!" and he checked its reading.

"Twelve forty-two and thirty-eight seconds." He jotted this down, along with Emma's sextant reading.

"Twenty forty-two, Greenwich Mean Time," she reminded him as she returned to peering through the eyepiece. She remained this way for a full three minutes, until once again she caught a brief glimpse of both sun and horizon together.

"Ready... time!"

With this second reading it was seen that the sun was still ascending and this reassured Emma and she relaxed a little, resting the sextant atop the royal yard for a moment to ease her tired arms.

"Any activity aboard *Sapphire* yet?"

Nate focused his spyglass on the nearby ship and shook his head.

"I doubt they've realized yet just how low this fog bank is."

Emma smiled and said,

"I'd estimate they have about five more minutes to figure it out. After that they will have no idea of their latitude until perhaps this evening, when they might possibly gain a Polaris sighting at twilight, or even of the moon later on, after it's risen high enough. Either way, they won't have any reliable estimate of their longitude before nightfall, and that should stop them dead."

Nate was still watching *Sapphire,* with her topgallant sails now partially visible through the fog and this, he thought, must surely now alert her crew as to the true thinness of the cloud aloft. And sure enough, as he continued to peer through his spyglass, a lone tiny figure scrambled aloft to the level of her main royal yard.

"I think they've finally figured it out," he said. A moment later Emma called "Time," and, studying the reading on her sextant, she smiled.

"Too late, I'm sorry to say. The sun's already descending. That's a shame."

Now Nate could spy a second figure, one clad in a pea coat and with what appeared to be a sextant secured about his neck, arriving at *Sapphire's* main topgallant yard, and he smiled also. Then, at Emma's urging, they began making their way down to deck again.

"I'll work these figures up just as soon as you give me my height of eye," Emma promised as they arrived at the main deck and she steered herself directly to the chartroom. Nate headed forward to see about the measuring of the heaving lines.

"One hundred an' sixty-five foot, eight an' three quarter inches, sir!" Jacko proudly announced as he reached the final fathom's length and studied the excess closely to be sure of his estimate. He had just finished measuring the line in six-foot lengths, by stretching it as far apart as his arms would allow, as Jacko himself was precisely six feet tall and most men's heights were closely in accord with the full span of their arms. Despite such a seemingly haphazard method, Jacko now appeared quite confident in his findings as the line was taken to the carpenter's shop, to where it might now be measured properly.

Many of the crew, in particular the packet-rats, now gathered about the carpenter's doorway as Darijo, with about as much enthusiasm as he ever displayed about anything whatsoever, used his three-foot rule to mark off segments of the line. When finally he reached the last increment and took careful measurement of the final few inches, a satisfied cheer went up.

"One hundred an' sixty-five foot, six an' one quarter inches," Scragg reported to Nate. "Two 'nalf inch difference, sir." The boatswain glanced at the carpenter before adding, "An' I'd take Jacko's word on that, if I was you, sir, afore I'd take that rum chippy's. Like I said, a reg'lar Imperial Standard."

"Then we'll split the difference," Nate said. "Let's call it seven and one half inches. And our freeboard?"

"Ten foot, two an' one half inches, sir. An' that's good no matter how you measure it."

With these two figures added together Emma was able to calculate the sun's meridian passage, and subsequently the ship's latitude position at twelve o'clock. It was, in her opinion, a good result, accurate to within a mile. Nate agreed to return aloft later that afternoon, at around three or four o'clock when the sun had traveled far enough into the west to allow a good angle for the two position lines to cross. With an afternoon sighting that could be run back to their noon latitude position they would gain a reliable longitude that would set them in good stead for the coming night.

"Whichever way you work it," stated Emma, later that afternoon, "we'll be able to continue making at least four knots throughout the night. But we'll have to steer a little south of due east so as to ensure that we do miss the

Farallons. But, even allowing for the most extreme of tides and currents and the maximum possible leeway, we should remain safe on this speed and heading until sunrise. At which time, if I've worked this out properly, we should find ourselves pretty close to the Bar."

"And if you *haven't* worked it out properly?" Nate ventured. But he immediately wished he had not, for the intensity of Emma's frown alone caused him to retreat promptly from the chartroom, to avoid both the embarrassment and discomfort that would surely have resulted from his remaining there.

Chapter Twenty-Four
Landfall

The fog remained with them until sunset: a damp white blanket that thinned only slightly during the afternoon as the winter sun descended into the west, it being too low and without sufficient heat to burn it off altogether. *Sapphire* was sighted again from *Achilles'* masthead shortly before sunset and, with the knowledge that her captain had gained no reliable latitude position to enter into his logbook, Nate wondered aloud if he might possibly now be able to use *Achilles* as a guide, in that having spotted Emma shooting the noonday sun from aloft, their captain might well suppose that *Achilles'* present course and speed was now set precisely to gain good landfall by sunrise. With the aid of a lead line, Nate suggested, *Sapphire's* captain should be able to safely match *Achilles'* course and speed into the night with the belief that for as long as he monitored his depth closely and did not exceed *Achilles'* present rate of four knots, he should find himself faring equally as favorably.

Emma looked closely at Nate as he voiced these thoughts and, appearing rather abashed that she herself had not considered this, replied,

"Then perhaps we ought to give him cause to believe otherwise." She peered aloft into the failing light and saw that the fog was already thickening considerably again with the approach of darkness. Another half an hour would see both ships blind once more, to the night as well as to each other.

"If we strike our royals and skies, and perhaps bear away a point..." Emma began, but she did not need to go any further as Nate was already calling for his chief mate.

"Brail 'em up cheerly now," he instructed Evans. "And drop the yards, but only as far as the lower tops, before it gets too dark. And no more sounding of the ship's bell, nor any noises whatsoever on deck. I want a silent ship tonight. Pass the word."

Evans hesitated, unexpectedly, and it seemed to Nate that he was ready to argue the point. Perhaps from some misplaced notion of honor or fair play, Nate supposed. But then his chief mate appeared to think better of it and without another word he headed promptly forward while Nate ordered the helmsman to bear away a full point; eleven and one quarter degrees by the compass. Now, on an aspect that would set them several miles to the south and downwind of San Francisco, and at a reduced speed that would hopefully be noticed by the other vessel, *Achilles* lay on this new heading until darkness fully descended, whereupon the masthead lookout returned to deck and reported that *Sapphire* had indeed fallen for the ruse and had herself reduced sail and altered course a point towards the south.

"Captain Blunt must think himself rather clever," Emma noted. Then, recalling the conversation she had had with Jonas Blunt two months earlier, added, "Serves him right, the pompous fool."

Achilles then came up again onto her former heading and reset her royals and skysails, now amidst much subdued and excited chatter and laughter, for all on board now knew of the ruse and all, it seemed, approved of it most wholeheartedly.

"*Sapphire* will be safe enough," Emma reassured Nate. "I've studied the charts carefully, and she'll encounter no hazards before dawn. But it's sure to teach her captain a valuable lesson."

With the sun's setting the residual fog cooled quickly and thickened even further until, even from high aloft, it blotted out all sight of stars and planets, and by the time the half-moon rose shortly before midnight it too was invisible. But no longer was this such a cause for concern, as Emma had gained two workable afternoon sightings and now, as they proceeded blindly into the night, she held every confidence that for as long as they maintained this heading and did not exceed four knots of speed, they would find themselves in a most favorable position to cross the Bar before noon the following day.

The wind remained from the northwest as a light breeze throughout the night and afforded *Achilles* her required four knots without the necessity of reducing her spread of sail. With lookouts posted at her main truck and far out on her jib boom, and with continual soundings being taken from her fore chainwales and relayed aft by whispers to the quarterdeck, she proceeded silently into the night.

By now Gideon was almost beside himself with frustration. *Sapphire* was going to lose this race through *Achilles'* trickery and he himself would be blamed for allowing it to happen. Jonas Blunt needed to be alerted, somehow, to the fact that he was presently steering an erroneous course toward the Gate and that at this rate he would end up several miles to the south and downwind of it come sunrise.

Sapphire needed to be made aware of this.

Somehow.

At the turn of the watch at midnight the majority of *Achilles'* crew milled about as they usually did at the aft end of the main deck beneath the break of the quarterdeck; the oncoming Larbowlines waiting to be assigned their duties and the Starbowlines, on being relieved at their various stations, returning aft to be counted, and as usual there was a period of a few minutes during which many a shadowy figure could be seen scurrying fore and aft in the darkness of the main deck, and thus a brief moment of general confusion.

Nate was standing on the quarterdeck waiting for his chief mate to oversee the assembling of his watch before coming up to take over from him. He could hear George Evans' voice clearly below, barking out orders to this man or that, and when the familiar sound of *Achilles'* bell sounded from forward to signal the turn of the watch he thought nothing of it at first. Then suddenly it struck him that they were keeping silent ship this night and he immediately marched forward to whisper urgently down to his chief mate.

"He's already headin' forward, sir!" responded the voice of Billy Grimes. "Now wot bloody twit's doin' that? Don't they know they'll give the game away?"

A general murmur arose from the darkness below as another set of double-rings sounded from forward, then a third, but no more. A minute later George Evans reappeared, bodily hauling the culprit with him and, in the dimness of light being shed through the forward windows of the trunk cabin they could clearly recognize the able hand, Silas Rigsby.

"Son of a bitch!" Evans declared. He was still gripping a belaying pin in his right hand and had clearly made good use of it, for when he unceremoniously let go of Rigsby the man dropped lifelessly, and with his head bleeding profusely, to the deck.

"He must have been trying to signal *Sapphire*!" declared Evans. "When I told him to stop he made to ring it again, so I had to use this."

Evans held the bloodied pin aloft and Nate went down to the main deck to take a closer look at the unconscious man.

"You all but killed him in the process!" Nate declared, now quite shocked at the wounds Evans had inflicted. He glared up at his chief mate, who in turn stared back with such uncharacteristic defiance that Nate's blood suddenly chilled at the realization that Evans truly did not give a damn.

"Well, you stopped him, at least," he conceded. "But probably not in time. *Sapphire* is sure to have heard it."

And, to confirm this, from *Achilles'* starboard quarter there now came the distant sound of a boatswain's whistle, followed by a dog's excited yapping.

"Damn!" Nate rose to his feet, now peering closely through the gloom at his chief mate. He was only now beginning to appreciate how dangerous a man George Evans was. He motioned to the prone figure by his feet.

"Put this man in irons and stow him in the livestock pen. It wouldn't surprise me if he was employed by *Sapphire's* owner or her captain to hinder us all along. But he'll do no more damage now."

Achilles pressed on silently into the night. With the first glimmerings of dawn looming faintly ahead to the southeast came also the first indications of imminent landfall. Midway through the morning watch, around six o'clock, the forward lookout came aft to report an increasing amount of flotsam by way of branches and weeds, as well as an abundance of seabirds sitting in the water all around. Two hours later, as all hands were busy about the morning wash-down and doing their best to remain silent about it, the varying hues of grayness all around began to slowly dissolve until suddenly *Achilles* emerged from the heavy blanket of fog that had engulfed her for more than a day now and found herself in the full brightness of a sunlit morning.

And directly ahead lay her destination.

The Golden Gate loomed dead ahead by about five miles; its narrowing approach still shrouded in mist and framed to either side by the gray-silhouetted Point Bonita to the north and Point Lobos to the south. Beyond and above the latter stood Telegraph Hill, the highest point overlooking both the town and its seaward approaches, with its makeshift wooden tower and solitary mast upon which could be seen a pennant requesting the arriving ship's number. Of the town itself nothing could yet be seen, as it still lay a short distance beyond the Gate on the northeastern slopes of the wide peninsula that reached up from the south to create this narrow, mile-wide entrance into one of the world's most impressive natural harbors.

When Emma arrived on the quarterdeck to witness this sight she smiled to herself in satisfaction, but said nothing. Because to gloat, she knew, would be unseemly.

As *Achilles* stood her course, now logging in excess of five knots with the freshening morning breeze, the gradual clearing of the residual mist aft and to seaward finally brought a hail from aloft, that of the sighting of another sail. Only a few minutes later *Sapphire* herself hove into view, now under full sail and hauling directly toward the Golden Gate. But she now stood well astern of *Achilles* to the southwest by almost two miles, caught to leeward of the harbor entrance and with her captain now obliged to work his way to weather for the approach. The sight of her was greeted by several contemptuous jeers from those on *Achilles'* deck and Emma turned to Nate and asked,

"Would you mind if I took the helm, at least until we reach the pilot station?"

"Certainly not." Nate looked to his helmsman, Bacas, and gave him a brief nod, one that the fisherman answered with a broad grin as he stood aside with a deferential bow as Emma took hold of the ship's wheel. She stepped in readily and with an air of casual familiarity, using both hands to grip the wheel's spokes at the twelve and three o'clock positions and maintaining a close reach against the northeasterly breeze, keeping her eyes for the most part fixed aloft and on the shivering luff of *Achilles'* skysails. Nate, by way of a series of surreptitious glances, kept an admiring eye on Emma and wondered as he did so if there were indeed any limits to this woman's abilities.

"Another four miles to the Bar, I would estimate," stated Emma, remaining unaware of Nate's attention and now enjoying herself immensely. "And it's only nine o'clock. We should still catch the end of this flood tide and, more importantly, finish this voyage within one hundred days, albeit barely. Have they responded to our signal yet?"

"For a pilot? Aye, they've acknowledged us."

Nate raised his spyglass. "Here he comes now."

The small sloop could be seen emerging from the harbor entrance and already it was crossing the Bar and heading directly for *Achilles* on a broad reach, heeling sharply with its large mainsail bowed out to leeward. It would only take a short while to reach them and Nate called for his boatswain to prepare the rope ladder up which the pilot would climb to get on board. As the sloop neared, Emma made preparations to hand the wheel back to Bacas, but Nate forestalled her.

"You appear to be enjoying yourself. Why not make the most of it?"

She smiled in response. "Why not, indeed?" Then, in a quieter tone, added, "Perhaps now might be a good time to begin taking some way off?"

"Main yards abox!"

On Nate's command the crew dashed to their stations and began hauling in on all five weather braces of the mainmast, until the wind filled each sail aback and *Achilles* slowed to a crawl, allowing easier access for the pilot as his sloop now wore about and came up under the lee of her starboard side. Of those half-dozen figures that could now be seen gathered on the sloop's foredeck, only one of them was even recognizable as being the pilot, and this solely because he was wearing a pilot's cap but even this remained doubtful, for the fellow seemed equally as interested in the contents of a bottle that was being passed around as he was in *Achilles*. Indeed, he appeared more than slightly inebriated and, as he stood there squinting aloft blearily from beneath the peak of his most grubby-looking cap of office, this short and rather unimpressive man seemed not so much intent upon the foot of the pilot ladder as he did on *Achilles'* quarterdeck. Nate, standing at the rail, politely doffed his captain's cap, assuming that he himself was the object of the pilot's attention, but instead the pilot called forth, in a slurred tone,

"What goes on here? A woman, b'God!"

Nate then realized that it was Emma who was being

referred to. She was still standing at *Achilles'* wheel, clad in her wash dress and pea coat and appearing equally as at home as any seaman. This, clearly, was being regarded by this pilot as something most offensive.

"Do you seek to make a mockery of my profession, sir?"

Emma, frowning now as she regarded this wretched article below, muttered,

"He appears to be managing that quite well on his own."

Nate called immediately for Bacas to take over the helm, then to his boatswain to stand by the ladder, but it was already too late. With a litany of curses and growls and with a gesturing of his arm toward where *Sapphire* still labored to windward some two miles in the offing, the sloop suddenly veered away from *Achilles* and sped southwards, with the voice of the pilot trailing in her wake.

"Anchor before the Bar at the twenty fathom sounding! I'll take you in on this evening's tide!"

Chapter Twenty-Five
End of Passage

"Son of a bitch!" Nate turned immediately to Emma, who was also staring in disbelief at the departing sloop, and she responded,

"We cannot anchor! We must cross the Bar now!"

Nate was shaking his head. There was nothing, to his mind, that they were able to do about it. At least, nothing that any officially appointed and legally recognized captain was able to do. Which led him to ask,

"Am I actually bound here by any particular rule of law?"

Emma, still glaring at the departing sloop, declared,

"I would not imagine that there *is* much rule of law in a town like this."

Scragg then arrived on the quarterdeck and, with a gesture towards the sloop, he asked,

"Anythin' amiss, sir?"

Nate looked at Emma. She met his eye and it was immediately clear to him that she was thinking the very same thing. She paused for a moment, frowning in thought as she alternately peered aloft, aft towards *Sapphire*, then ahead at the approaching harbor. Finally she looked directly at Nate again and gave him only the briefest of nods.

"I can do this," she whispered.

Nate turned to his boatswain.

"Nothing whatsoever. So long as the crew would not object to Miss Jacobs remaining at the helm as we take her in?"

Scragg grinned broadly, as too did Bacas who stood nearby.

"I'll be a blessed Dutchman if any man jack of 'em would, sir! A most agreeable notion, if I might say so."

"Then what are we waiting for?"

With Emma remaining at the helm and with Nate confident that there was none other on board who could come even close to matching this woman's piloting skills, he gave the command for *Achilles'* main yards to be braced fully about again and she began regaining headway.

Emma now steered directly toward the Bar, which lay across the approaches to the Golden Gate. As the soundings being called from the fore chains steadily decreased, the choppiness of the water all around increased in proportion as the slackening flood and the varying currents within and without the bay converged in these murky shallows. They watched as the Bar shelved to as little as eight fathoms, then fell away again and it was Nate's singular pleasure to go below and to enter this very occurrence into the ship's official logbook.

1746 GMT. Inbound San Francisco Bar. End of Passage; 99 Days 21 Hours 15 Minutes.

He returned to the quarterdeck to discover an overall cheerfulness now pervading the entire ship. They had beaten *Sapphire* into Frisco, and the sounds of boisterous laughter and banter drifted aft to the quarterdeck, as well as down from aloft as the crew celebrated their sudden increased richness of two hundred dollars apiece. It caused Nate to smile, and Emma to look away from her heading just long enough to display a likewise grin before returning to the more serious business of completing this voyage in the proper fashion. For they were still several miles short of their destination.

"We'll soon find ourselves in the lee of the north shore," she warned Nate, quietly, "and with these strong currents we might yet have our work cut out for us. Are both anchors readied for letting go?"

"Both are run out on their slip lines, ready to drop."

"We may need them on short notice. Without a pilot on board, we'll have no assistance from a steam tug either, so we're going to have to do this the hard way."

Emma continued making minor adjustments to her steering, glancing alternately now at the approaching hills to either side of *Achilles'* bows, trying to gauge her leeway as she felt her way in on the flood tide. It was now a month into the rainy season and the hillsides to either side of the Gate were carpeted with fresh grass and interspersed here and about with an assortment of red-tiled brick houses, many of them appearing as old as the former Spanish mission and as many again appearing to have been constructed only recently. These were clearly the homes of the wealthier inhabitants, just as clearly as were the dense concentrations of tents and wooden shacks that adorned the lower slopes the homes of the lesser fortunate. As *Achilles* proceeded onwards, the shorelines to either side gradually closed in until the northern hillside created a lee which caused her lower courses and topsails to begin luffing and spilling, yet the loftier sails maintained their fill and provided headway enough for Emma to maintain steerage. On the southern shore could now be seen several people, some of whom were waving heartily and, toward the peak of Telegraph Hill, several tiny figures could also be seen milling about, all of them, it seemed, with their attentions fixed upon these two arriving clippers.

Emma, squinting up at Telegraph Hill, smiled and looked at Nate.

"See that hoist?" She pointed to the telegraph station that now displayed a solitary flag on its mast.

"That means, anchor immediately and await instructions."

Nate was about to offer some sarcastic remark but his words were forestalled, as indeed was all other conversation on board, by the sight that suddenly loomed ahead as the southern slope fell away to expose a glimpse of the inner harbor itself, which included the waters closest to the town's northern shore.

"My God. Look at them all."

The view now ahead of them was a disquieting one, to say the very least, if not downright frightful. It was as if an entire forest of trees stood baring their way into the bay. Yet these were not trees; they were ships. Dead ships.

"There must be at least a hundred of them, and we're not even through the Gate yet!"

It was a sobering sight, and a sense of dread arose in Nate and Emma alike as they continued peering ahead as *Achilles* proceeded through the Golden Gate proper and into San Francisco Bay. For what they were seeing here was a graveyard; of abandoned vessels that had barely, it seemed, entered the Gate before being altogether discarded. Many had subsequently drifted ashore and now formed a most unusual if not surreal sight as they lay grounded and interspersed along the shoreline with their rigging in disarray. Many of them displayed gaudy signs that proclaimed these once-proud vessels to now be laundry houses, restaurants, hardware stores or rooms to rent, with both nightly and hourly rates posted.

Now fully inside the Bay, the northern quarter of San Francisco could be seen ascending all the way up to Telegraph Hill and down its slopes now proceeded a line of people following *Achilles* into harbor and to Nate's mind came the image of a pack of hungry wolves descending upon them. Even Scragg, down on the main deck with his packet-rat chums, was no longer smiling as he now warily eyed the fleet of small boats that were busily casting off from the town's northern shore, most of them laden to capacity.

"It's like the Sirens of Greek mythology, isn't it?" Emma wondered aloud. "Except here it's the promise of gold that lures the mariner to his doom."

Nate nodded and watched as many of these fully laden boats set a course that would soon intercept *Achilles*. He could already hear their cries: the merchants, chandlers, bum-boatmen and others who were calling out their various wares and services, but most importantly it was the crimps he was keeping a close eye on. He could see at least three crimp boats, these being all but impossible to mistake by the very nature of those men who occupied them; the burliest, most disagreeable-looking types, many of whom held aloft flagons of liquor and gold coins as an enticement for the crew to jump ship there and then. And, if this was not encouragement enough, there were the women, several of whom were also shamelessly displaying their wares as they approached.

"The harbormaster is obliged to have at least one dock reserved for the next arriving ship," Emma said. "And by all rights that dock belongs to us. See that island ahead, the one that looks like a belly-up whale? That's Alcatraz. If we cannot find a dock on the northern shore, then we'll have to try the eastern side of town, which means wearing around to the south after we pass the island." Emma then pointed to the approaching boats. "But it will mean keeping our crew with us."

Nate was looking down at the main deck and was watching his boatswain's and the other packet-rat's response to the hails of the crimps.

"I don't think that's going to be a problem," he reassured her, smiling now.

Scragg appeared on the quarterdeck and, with a brief knuckle to his forehead, he inquired,

"Permission ter pump bilges, sir! To save us the bother after we get alongside."

"As you wish, bosun."

Scragg promptly marched to the break of the quarterdeck and called down to Jacko, who now stood by the starboard bulwark with the deck-wash hose that unaccountably had been rigged directly to the bilge pump.

"Roll the temperance wheel, boys!" called Scragg and immediately Nate saw Jacko's expression light up, and in that very manner as he had become so familiar with regarding these packet-rats. It was an expression that invariably preceded mischief and on this occasion there was no exception.

"This round's on us, mateys!" shouted Jacko, and with a nod to the two men at the flywheel pump they gave it their utmost and a stream of black water shot forth from the hose's nozzle in a long wide arc that landed squarely inside the nearest crimp boat.

"Drink up boys! There's plenty more where that come

from!"

Loud guffaws and taunts from *Achilles'* crew accompanied this and even Emma, despite her growing concerns that they would need to begin shortening sail soon, chuckled at the sight. The view of these imposing-looking fellows manning the crimp boat now reduced to panic as they began frantically bailing out water at the same time as trying to backstroke and veer away from *Achilles'* side was indeed priceless. It had been made clear to all on board that their two hundred dollar bonuses would not be paid out until *Achilles* was properly secured to the dock, so this crew intended to see this voyage through to its conclusion.

Emma watched as Scragg returned to the quarterdeck and, as their eyes met, the boatswain, still grinning, gave her a casual nod. It was the simplest of all gestures; an acknowledgement given by one shipmate to another, yet for Emma the underlying implication was of a far greater significance. For two people who had scarcely exchanged as many sentences throughout the duration of this three-month voyage it spoke clearly Scragg's acceptance of her and for all she had accomplished and this was as satisfying to Emma as if Scragg had openly heralded her praises in front of the entire crew.

The boatswain reached the aft taffrail and stood there rubbing absently at his beard as he studied his surroundings. He drew in a deep breath of air.

"Do you smell it, miss?"

Emma, puzzled, frowned and shook her head.

"That's opportunity, that is."

Scragg grinned and tapped his forehead to the floundering crimps and the others who now drifted aft and astern and, as *Achilles* closed with the first of the several ships that were anchored up ahead of them, he turned to go down to the main deck again to prepare his crew for the upcoming maneuvers.

"My kind o' place, I reckon," he said as he departed and Emma, nodding and smiling after him, could not but agree wholeheartedly with that.

It took another full hour for *Achilles* to work her way along the North Beach, weaving first one way and then the other and making her way carefully eastwards, continually trimming sheets and adjusting yards as she went. Now fully inside the Bay, the northeasterly breeze picked up again, although it remained somewhat broken by the steep hills ahead to the east and, as they proceeded, Emma suggested to Nate that they begin clewing up the lower courses, as these were becoming increasingly spilled by the lee of those ships they passed close to. Of the small boats that had set out from the shore on *Achilles'* arrival only a few remained, doggedly tailing their progress despite the packet-rat's continued discouragements. Many had headed away to intercept *Sapphire* instead as she now approached the Gate, a full two miles behind. The boats would return, however, once *Achilles* was finally docked and it would be all but impossible to prevent their inhabitants from swarming aboard but, for as long as they managed to secure *Achilles* before this happened, it would matter a great deal less.

Passing close to the south of Alcatraz they continued eastward, Emma concentrating on her steering and trying to estimate the width of *Achilles'* turning circle when the time came to wear her around, while Nate remained busy with his spyglass, scanning the shoreline in search of an empty berth. Those anchored ships they passed along the way were in varying states of disrepair; some with nearly all their rigging laid bare, as well their deckhouses and other structures stripped of all planking and some were even missing their topmasts altogether, reducing them to little more than floating hulks. Others were in a more seaworthy condition and appeared ready enough to sail if not for the lack of a crew. Many appeared to have been sitting here for months, if not years, and Nate could only guess at what exorbitant prices the crimps were charging in this town. Those ships that were still inhabited appeared to contain only skeleton crews at best, and most likely these consisted mostly of captains and senior mates: those who held a personal interest in either their ship or its cargo. As they continued to pass these near-abandoned vessels Nate could not help but envision *Achilles* herself falling victim to this very same fate. In less than a week she too might be sitting here as just another obstacle to hinder the next arriving ship.

There was no end to this floating graveyard; they could see this now as *Achilles* rounded the northeastern shore and the view southwards along the eastern strand of the town came into sight. As far south as Rincon Point the channel was all but blocked by floating hulks and it quickly became apparent that they would not be able to make any farther progress in that direction.

"We must wear around now!" Emma was becoming increasingly agitated; with the breeze beginning to luff and spill from *Achilles'* royals and skysails she knew that within only minutes they would lose the required momentum. "We cannot proceed much farther south and I don't want to anchor, because then it will take us forever to unload! We must find that dock and take it, otherwise *Sapphire* will unload first and get the best prices!"

Nate was beginning to perspire. He was still searching the nearby shoreline through his spyglass. He could see no spaces whatsoever among the mass of shipping that was secured alongside the dozen and more piers and jetties that jutted out from the North Beach. Then suddenly a gap revealed itself, between two ships on a pier that extended more than a hundred yards out into the Bay. But through the spyglass the gap appeared small; perhaps too small for the two hundred and twenty feet that *Achilles* would be requiring.

"Over there! I see an empty dock! But it looks like a tight fit!"

He strode to the wheel and handed Emma the spyglass. She peered anxiously through it, hesitated for a moment, then nodded.

"It will have to do. Ready about, and quickly!"

Nate relayed the order and from forward the voices of his chief mate and boatswain responded immediately as each man went to his station for this final and most public maneuver. For now there stood several hundred people along the shoreline, all of them watching in anticipation of a good morning's entertainment as a fully-laden clipper attempted to berth under sail alone and without either steam tug or pilot to assist her. And, most incredibly of all, with a woman at the helm!

Emma began hauling down on the large spokes of the wheel until, at three and a half full turns, it came up short, then she called out to Nate,

"The helm is up!"

She returned to looking ahead at *Achilles'* jib boom, and her gaze remained fixed intently upon it as all around her she heard the trampling of feet and the barking of commands as the crew readied themselves at their sheets and braces. Directly overhead the spanker was brailed in tightly and both mizzen and main yards were braced towards square, until all of *Achilles'* aft canvas began to luff and spill. Then, as the deck settled into quietness again, she waited, still staring ahead, until finally she saw *Achilles'* bows beginning to turn to starboard, slowly at first then with gathering momentum.

"Lay the head yards square. Shift over the head sheets."

Emma spoke softly, as she was quite content to allow Nate to relay her instructions and for him to at least appear to be in command. It was enough for her to be given this opportunity and it would be challenging enough in itself without having to yell out commands in the process. She now shifted her eyes up to the mizzen topsail, watching closely as the wind came abeam and, with a shivering of its luff, filled and lifted the canvas slightly, whereupon she ordered,

"Keep those mizzensails spilled! Brace with the turn."

With the breeze now passing astern to *Achilles'* larboard quarter, Emma was finally able to judge her approach to the dock. The wind would be blowing almost directly onto the dock and, with such a tight space to fit into without use of either tug or pilot, it would indeed be a challenge.

"Fore tacks and sheets. Square the head yards. Haul down your jibs."

The aft yards were braced up sharply and several hands arrived on the quarterdeck to begin hauling the spanker out again, but Emma forestalled them.

"Reduce all sail to skies and royals. Stand ready by the main braces."

Nate continued relaying Emma's commands and, as *Achilles'* topsails and topgallants were hauled up on their bunts and clews into untidy heaps beneath their yards, and as the wind began working its way forward along her starboard side, he stated,

"We seem to have a welcoming committee. There's at least a dozen armed policemen waiting for us on the dock."

Emma shook her head, not even looking in the direction

Nate was pointing.

"Not police. Perhaps vigilantes; probably mercenaries. Hired guns. It's the responsibility of the ship owners, as well as the merchants and underwriters, to guarantee the safe unloading of cargo. There are no proper police in this town. You'll realize that soon enough."

The narrow berth alongside which Emma now sought to fit *Achilles* came into view off the larboard bow and she countered the ship's turn with another full spin of the wheel and steadied her out on that heading. With only royals and skysails remaining set, *Achilles* now slowed to a crawl, on a course that would lay her parallel to the dock and at a distance of only fifty feet. It was a tight angle of approach, but Emma had already decided that there was neither the sea room nor the turning space available here, and that the only possible way to get *Achilles* alongside was to squeeze her bodily in. And that was going to be the most challenging maneuver of all.

"I would be obliged if one of our men, perhaps that Jacko fellow, would call out distances from the jib boom," she said. "It looks like it might be a snug fit."

Nate was now wondering if it could even be done. The space between the two ships already berthed alongside the dock appeared incredibly small from this angle. But he was not about to argue with Emma and so he dutifully relayed the order forward.

Much noise and commotion could now be heard coming from ashore; shouts of encouragement from some, jeers of derision from others but above all came the endless call of the crimps, who were now vocally urging the sailors on *Achilles'* deck to drop everything now and to jump ship. They promised gold, women, drink and all manner of other temptations if the crew took to their boats and came ashore immediately, to leave the ship drifting helplessly as it was. No matter, they called out, as the law guaranteed that each seaman would still be entitled to draw his full pay from the shipping office. But *Achilles'* crew remained standing at their stations, awaiting instructions. They waited, yet none came. For Emma was now in full control and she had made certain that all of the more complex sail handling was completed before they approached the dock.

It was, according to those who related or retold the story throughout the months to come, the singular most impressive feat of seamanship they had ever born witness to, and the fact that it was performed by a woman made it all the richer for telling.

Using only royals and skysails, *Achilles* worked her way gradually into position alongside the dock, remaining a good fifty feet off and remaining clear of the extended lower yards of those ships that were already alongside. Then, when she stood barely half a ship's-length short of her intended position, she backed her main yards and lost all headway and drew to a complete stop. Keeping her main yards aback, she used the wind to set her in toward the dock and, by utilizing only the braces of her fore royal and skysail to alternately fill and spill the air, and this depending on the distance being called from the man stood out on the jib boom, she maintained a precise fore and aft position against both tide and current as she continued to drift sideways, into a space so tight that her iron jib boom cap actually scraped away the uppermost layer of paint from the counter of the ship ahead of her. And when all four of her mooring lines flew ashore into the waiting crowd there was not a man could be found, or so the telling went, that would admit to having expended a single ounce of strength beyond that of taking up the slack. Nor could a man be found, as *Achilles'* fifteen hundred tons finally touched up against the flimsy wooden dock, that would attest to having felt anything more than the slightest of tremors in the wooden planking beneath his feet.

Chapter Twenty-Six
San Francisco

Silas Rigsby finally regained consciousness toward mid-afternoon.

Nate had been kept busy throughout the day with an endless stream of official ship's business, but with Emma's assistance he had finally managed to clear his desk of paperwork, as well as *Achilles'* main deck of lingering officials, leaving now only the local stevedores on board, under the supervision of George Evans, to assist with the unloading of her cargo.

Already most of her crew had departed: paid-off in full and away to seek their fortunes in this captivating boomtown. Nate considered himself fortunate that all eight Swedes, along with his able hand Bacas and the young Jerome Stiles, had elected to remain on board for the return voyage to New York. Indeed, not a one of these men had any intention of even stepping ashore here in San Francisco for fear of being crimped again. Having this skeleton crew aboard would enable Nate to shift *Achilles* safely out to the anchorage after unloading and, with the profits gained from her cargo, which had already been estimated by Emma as exceeding one hundred thousand dollars, twice *Achilles'* construction costs, it should not be too difficult to purchase a sufficient number of crimped sailors to fill her forecastle again.

When Nate arrived forward and entered the topgallant forecastle space he found Rigsby sitting upright against the bulkhead, his feet bound in chains that were secured to a nearby ringbolt and carefully nursing his injured head. The front of his shirt was mottled with his own dried blood and, on entering the space, Nate demanded brusquely,

"Well, what do you have to say for yourself?"

Rigsby snarled back with equal rudeness.

"Me? What the hell are you talking about? It's that fucking chief mate of yours you need to be speaking to! Damned near killed me! What the hell is his problem?"

"It wasn't him who rang the bell," responded Nate.

"No, but it was him who told me to do it!"

"He what?"

Rigsby glared defiantly up at Nate, still rubbing his sore head.

"When I reported aft for my watch! He tells me to go forward and ring eight bells! I tells him it ain't allowed, 'cos we're silent ship! He tells me go do it or suffer the consequence! He's chief mate, so what can I do? Then when I go to do it, he comes up behind me and starts bashing me about the head!"

Nate stared down at Rigsby for a long while. Then he shook his head in disbelief and turned around to view the main deck. His chief mate, who had been standing by *Achilles'* main hatch only minutes earlier, was nowhere to be seen. Nate strode aft, calling out for him, then went below to search further.

But George Evans was nowhere to be found on board.

"Harry Jenkins! Look at you!"

Dressed in his best suit with his face clean-shaven and his mustache neatly groomed, Harry did indeed cut a dashing figure as he strode boldly down *Achilles'* gangplank to where Sarah stood waiting below. She was also dressed up, in one of Lady Margaret's finest outfits of dark blue with a green silk trim. As Harry paused at the foot of the gangplank, he twirled his mustache, tipped her a sly wink and replied,

"Sir Robert, if you please."

"But of course," murmured Sarah, adopting a classier tone of accent herself now and eyeing Harry up and down appreciatively.

"I must say, Sir Robert, you do clean up right proper."

"Why thank 'ee kindly, m'lady. One does one's best. After all, looking the part is half the job, don't you know?"

Sarah smiled. "Oh, I do indeed."

She placed her hand into the crook of Harry's arm and gave it a light squeeze.

"Now then. Shall we see what this fine town has to offer?"

Harry could not resist another glance out into the harbor, to where *Sapphire* lay anchored less than half a mile from the shore. She had let go her anchor only an hour after *Achilles* had docked, but it had likewise taken her another few hours to be cleared by the doctor who had gone on board to inspect her crew and passengers for cholera or any other contagious diseases. Now her quarantine flag was down and one of her longboats was pulling swiftly away and heading towards the shore. In its stern sheets sat two men dressed in dark suits, one of whom, Harry was willing to bet the farm on, was of Anglo-Irish descent.

"Let's do," he smiled at Sarah. After giving instructions

for her trunks to be taken ahead of them by carriage to Baldwin's Hotel, they set off into the town itself.

"Well, it's not New York," Sarah quickly decided, glancing uneasily at the diverse mixture of people around her. "In fact, some of these characters do appear downright unsavory."

"Not to worry. You have me to look after you now."

"Oh, and that's supposed to make me feel safe, is it?"

"Well, doesn't it?"

As they strolled along Market Street they continued scanning their surroundings with interest. Brick buildings were being constructed to either side and mixed in with these were the shabbiest-looking shanties one could ever imagine any person being able to live in. Such a marked contrast of rich and poor existing so closely together Sarah had never before seen and it served to reassure her that yes, having Harry here alongside her was indeed a great comfort. Not that she would have ever considered admitting to it.

"Listen," said Harry, at last. "About that business back in New York..."

"Let's not have that conversation again, Harry."

"But I only wanted to..."

"Let's just not."

George Evans no longer existed.

The moment his foot had stepped from *Achilles'* gangplank onto the dockside Gideon had cast aside that persona forever. Now he was himself again, and he was on his way back to *Sapphire*.

But first he had a certain matter to take care of.

He knew how upset and disappointed Old Man Thaddeus was going to be when he found out. Upset at losing the fifty thousand dollars wager with Henry Harding, and disappointed with Gideon himself for having failed him so utterly. It was humiliating. It was more than humiliating. It was damned near unbearable.

Walking briskly along the shoreline and glancing out across the harbor he could see *Sapphire's* longboat approaching. In its stern sheets sat two men dressed in dark suits, one of whom, Gideon was willing to bet his life on, was his half-brother, Thomas Oglesby.

As *Sapphire's* longboat neared the piers lining the shore Gideon's pace slowed and he pulled his cap farther down to cover his face and found a nearby doorway to duck into, where he might watch and wait as the boat's occupants disembarked. The other, unknown man in the suit stepped ashore first and headed directly towards him, along the road down which Gideon had just come. One of the man's hands was thrust deep into his jacket pocket and there was a fixed expression of grim resolve on his frowning features as he marched purposefully by, without even a glance in Gideon's direction.

The other man in the boat was indeed Thomas Oglesby: Old Man Thaddeus' only legitimate offspring and thus sole legitimate heir to his vast fortune. And therein lay the key word: legitimate.

He watched closely as Thomas disembarked the longboat and began strolling inshore at a relaxed pace, clearly taking in all the sights around him and seeming quite oblivious of the fact that, in a lawless town such as this, it was probably not too wise for any young gentleman to go strolling down any narrow alleyways, nor to be wandering too far from the beaten path without an armed escort. After all, anything might happen.

What will the old man do, Gideon wondered, when he

suddenly finds himself without a legitimate heir? Would he finally concede to publicly acknowledging Gideon as his own?

Or would he be so angered by Gideon's failure that he would disown him and bequeath it all instead to a pack of useless half-cousins, who would promptly tear his shipping empire apart in their haste to divide it among themselves?

Gideon was about to gamble his entire future on the former outcome. He did not believe that the old man would, in the end, have any other choice.

The knife's ivory handle slipped from his cuff and into Gideon's right hand as he fell into place close behind Thomas, with the intention of finding out the answer to this question, once and for all.

THE END

About The Author

Mark M. Rimmer

Mark was born in London and grew up on the south coast of England. Since as far back as he can remember there have been two passions in his life—tall ships and writing.

Not surprising, then, that he took full advantage of an opportunity to sail aboard a square-rigger in New Guinea when he was 16, then went on to join the British merchant navy as an apprentice navigation officer on cargo ships worldwide. After graduating with his Mate's license he moved to Hong Kong to teach sail training aboard a brigantine in the South China Sea, voyaging between Hong Kong, the Philippines and Japan.

Since then Mark has spent many years engaged in sail training in the Old School fashion aboard a variety of tall ships, teaching naval cadets and civilian trainees how to traverse the world's oceans using only wind, stars, a sextant and a compass. From the complete re-rigging of the replica galleon Golden Hinde to achieving four transatlantic crossings aboard a full-sized clipper, Mark is presently one of only a handful of captains worldwide who is qualified to command a fully-rigged ship the size of the clippers he writes about in THE CALIFORNIA RUN.

A lifelong fan of such authors as C. S. Forester and Patrick O'Brian, it occurred to Mark at an early age that a large proportion of the Nautical Fiction genre is occupied by fighting sail. As a merchant mariner, perhaps Mark might be forgiven for having subscribed to that inherent bias which prevails among his peers, that your average historic naval vessel is all but identical to any merchant ship of its time, except with more guns and bigger hats. Besides, as Mark's own experiences have shown him, and as events in THE CALIFORNIA RUN portray, life aboard a merchant ship and the interactions between those who sail them can be equally as exciting, if not as terrifying, as any full-on naval engagement.

Mark has also enjoyed his own share of adventures, having so far survived three hurricanes, one typhoon, been bombed, shot at, shipwrecked, assisted numerous yachtsmen in distress, helped rescue the crew of a burning oil tanker mid-ocean and has led one successful mutiny aboard a storm-tossed brigantine in the middle of an Atlantic hurricane.

He finally stranded upon the shores of America, quite literally, after being shipwrecked himself off Bermuda, rescued by a passing Greek tanker and landed ashore in Long Island in only the clothes he stood up in and a soggy 'tenner' in his pocket. His original US immigrant status of Shipwrecked Mariner is one that, as a proud seafarer, he displays on his wall to this day. He has been living in Oregon ever since.

If You Enjoyed This Book
Visit

PENMORE PRESS

www.penmorepress.com

All Penmore Press books are available directly through our website, amazon.com, Barnes and Noble and Nook, Sony Reader, Apple iTunes, Kobo books and via leading bookshops across the United States, Canada, the UK, Australia and Europe.

BREWER'S REVENGE
BY
JAMES KEFFER

Admiral Horatio Hornblower has given Commander William Brewer captaincy of the captured pirate sloop *El Dorado*. Now under sail as the HMS *Revenge,* its new name suits Brewer's frame of mind perfectly. He lost many of his best men in the engagement that seized the ship, and his new orders are to hunt down the pirates who have been ravaging the trade routes of the Caribbean sea.

But Brewer will face more than one challenge before he can confront the pirate known as El Diabolito. His best friend and ship's surgeon, Dr. Spinelli, is taking dangerous solace in alcohol as he wrestles with demons of his own. The new purser, Mr. Allen, may need a lesson in honest accounting. Worst of all, Hornblower has requested that Brewer take on a young ne'er-do-well, Noah Simmons, to remove him from a recent scandal at home. At twenty-three, Simmons is old to be a junior midshipman, and as a wealthy man's son he is unaccustomed to working, taking orders, or suffering privations.

William Brewer will need to muster all his resources to ready his crew for their confrontation with the Caribbean's most notorious pirate. In the process, he'll discover the true price of command.

PENMORE PRESS
www.penmorepress.com

The Captain's Nephew

by

Philip K.Allan

After a century of war, revolutions, and Imperial conquests, 1790s Europe is still embroiled in a battle for control of the sea and colonies. Tall ships navigate familiar and foreign waters, and ambitious young men without rank or status seek their futures in Naval commands. First Lieutenant Alexander Clay of HMS Agrius is self-made, clever, and ready for the new age. But the old world, dominated by patronage, retains a tight hold on advancement. Though Clay has proven himself many times over, Captain Percy Follett is determined to promote his own nephew.

Before Clay finds a way to receive due credit for his exploits, he'll first need to survive them. Ill-conceived expeditions ashore, hunts for privateers in treacherous fog, and a desperate chase across the Atlantic are only some of the challenges he faces. He must endeavor to bring his ship and crew through a series of adventures stretching from the bleak coast of Flanders to the warm waters of the Caribbean. Only then might high society recognize his achievements —and allow him to ask for the hand of Lydia Browning, the woman who loves him regardless of his station.

PENMORE PRESS
www.penmorepress.com

Fortune's Whelp
by
Benerson Little

Privateer, Swordsman, and Rake:

Set in the 17th century during the heyday of privateering and the decline of buccaneering, *Fortune's Whelp* is a brash, swords-out sea-going adventure. Scotsman Edward MacNaughton, a former privateer captain, twice accused and acquitted of piracy and currently seeking a commission, is ensnared in the intrigue associated with the attempt to assassinate King William III in 1696. Who plots to kill the king, who will rise in rebellion—and which of three women in his life, the dangerous smuggler, the wealthy widow with a dark past, or the former lover seeking independence—might kill to further political ends? Variously wooing and defying Fortune, Captain MacNaughton approaches life in the same way he wields a sword or commands a fighting ship: with the heart of a lion and the craft of a fox.

PENMORE PRESS
www.penmorepress.com

GREEK FIRE
BY
JAMES BOSCHERT

In the fourth book of Talon, James Boschert delivers fast-paced adventure, packed with violent confrontations and intrepid heroes up against hard odds.

Imprisoned for brawling in Acre, a coastal city in the Kingdom of Jerusalem, Talon and his longtime friend Max are freed by an old mentor from the Order of the Templars and offered a new mission in the fabled city of Constantinople. There Talon makes new friendships, but winning the Emperor's favor obligates him to follow Manuel to war in a willful expedition to free Byzantine lands from the Seljuk Turks. And beneath the pageantry of the great city, seditious plans are being fomented by disaffected aristocrats who have made a reckless deal to sell the one weapon the Byzantine Empire has to defend itself, *Greek fire*, to an implacable enemy bent upon the Empire's destruction.

Talon and Max find themselves sailing into perilous battles, and in the labyrinthine back streets of Constantinople Talon must outwit his own kind—assassins—in the pay of a treacherous alliance.

PENMORE PRESS
www.penmorepress.com

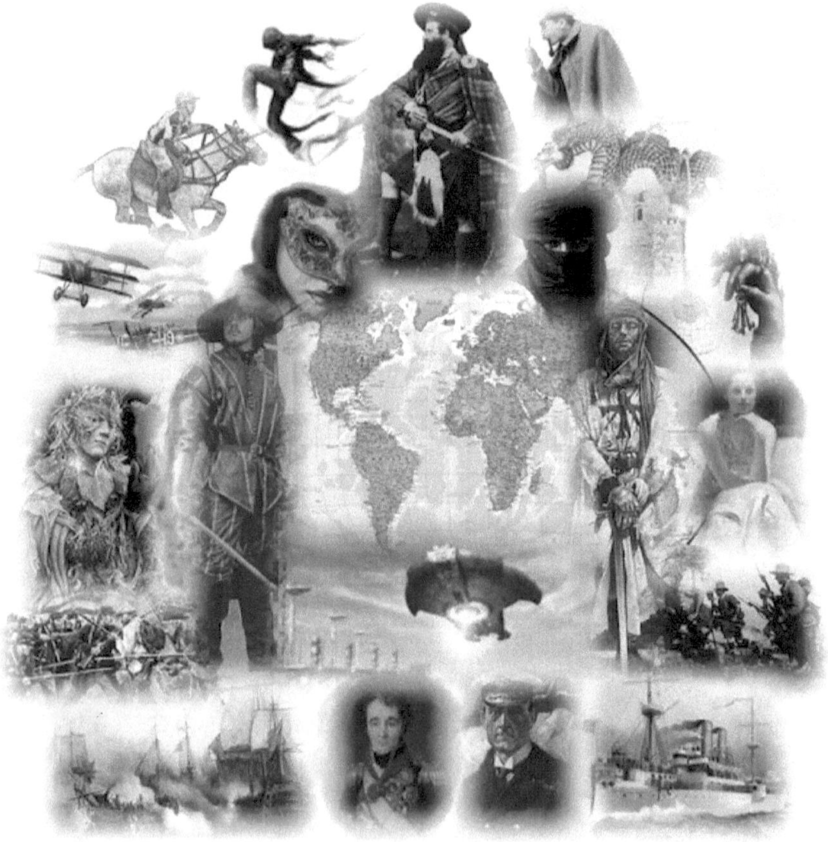

Penmore Press

Challenging, Intriguing, Adventurous, Historical and Imaginative

www.penmorepress.com